Y Coed Remembers Beibio

The Saga of the Early-Flowering Linden

Roger V Crawley

Whisper, thou Tree, thou lonely Tree,
One, where a thousand stood!
Well might proud tales be told of thee,
Last of the Solemn wood!

From The Last Tree of the Forest

By Felicia Dorothea Hemans, 1793-1835

Published by Blasted Zest
Cobbles Cottage
Port Isaac
Cornwall PL29 3SR

First Published 2018 Blasted Zest

ISBN 978-19164951-6-6

Printed and bound in Great Britain by:
TJ International, Padstow, Cornwall

Roger...

We have carried out your wishes.

Sally rationalised the paperwork;
Rob did the proof reading;
Andy did an amazing job of sorting out the
text, layout and tricky computer bits;
And I, as you know, have contributed the
illustrations.

A great many thanks to all who have brought
your Novel to life.

We hope you like it!

Your brother Trevor

CHAPTER 1

'There is a northern English shire
With eastern shores of sand,
A southern wall of Whin Sill Stone,
A western wedge of land,
Where wastes of moss and fells of mire,
Brown heaths and fibrous hags,
Consume the tales of dry stone walls below eroding
crags.'

Owen Forrest 1987

⸺⸻⸺

The reading of his poem about Northumberland was interrupted as the train came to another gentle halt in the Shropshire countryside. The peace of the almost empty carriage, married with the stillness of the train, brought another moment of calmness to the momentum of the journey. He reflected once again on why he had not written any more lines to the poem. Maybe there was no more to add? Poetry had never come easily to him. Perhaps, he thought, he should accept that it marked the end to his sojourn in the north. His mind returned to the next phase in his life. Would his sister's world in Herefordshire make the same impression on him as Northumberland? At least her absence would allow him to familiarise himself with the area in his own quiet way. He hoped that her friends would make his introduction a simple one. He looked up from his notebook and surveyed the countryside. He appreciated the opportunity afforded by the halt to observe the Shropshire landscape at its own pace of movement. But while focusing his eyes upon a forlorn row of bleached dead elms, and thinking about the tragedy of their decline, the trees began to move slowly to one side. The train was moving again as gently as it had stopped.

His daydreaming returned as the scenes slid by with gathering pace. An area of low-lying marshy ground came into view. His mind responded to the levelness of the scene and he was imbued with nostalgia. A solemn summer evening, sitting on the edge of English Strother Moss in the Cheviot Hills listening to the drone of a circling snipe, entered his thoughts. He recalled the dipping flight of the diminutive wader with the dagger-like beak, and the distinctive buzz it made as the air vibrated its tail feathers. For him, this noise of the dusk was the balm to soothe any spiritual turmoil. But, like any remedy for unhappiness or melancholy, it was seasonal, transient, and had to be searched for. Nevertheless, such a nostalgic cameo of levelness was always there to rest the mind, as the one outside was there to rest the eyes. He knew he was in need of rest.

During the previous summer, he had experienced a succession of marshy cameos. As the field assistant to a palynologist*, who was piecing together the vegetation history of a part of Northumberland, he had trudged through numerous mires and mosses. For him, the miniature wilderness quality, and the intimacy, of these marshy cameos gave them an atmosphere of naturalness that was heavenly. Penetrating their successive layers of pollen-dusted peat with a flange augur had been a messy way to appreciate this naturalness; indeed, it had been an infringement of it. The thought of puddled ooze terminated his reminiscence. He came back to the present and to ploughed fields sprouting cereal life.

It was a wrench to move from one place to another, even though he had lived in Northumberland for only eleven months. The landscape lying to the north of the River Coquet had made deep impressions upon him, as did all rural wastes, or what was left of them, especially the mires and mosses which had been his place of work during the summer of the previous year, and the broadleaved woods where he had walked. He had attempted to pull these impressions together in his poem, but had managed only one verse. Another verse about woodland had been in his mind but his close attachment to broadleaved woods, which he wanted to express, had become emotionally dislocated by the vast acreages of coniferous plantations that had over-awed him. It was a consoling thought that his destination in Herefordshire was part of another borderland, the Welsh Marches, which might echo some of the impressions still vivid in his mind, and where he knew that broadleaved woods and trees still held their ancient place.

The winter that had drawn to a close had been the coldest one of his life; physically and spiritually cold. Caravans were not winter homes, and certainly not comfortable accommodation for the horrendous gales of autumn 1987. He had found six months of temporary employment in a second-hand book shop an interesting experience, providing reading material for a lonely existence. Having graduated in biogeography, after working in a botanical garden for two years, he had decided to take a gap year to reflect on the future course of his life. Postgraduate study was a possibility; so, too, was a qualification in arboriculture. A return to landscape management in a botanical garden was at the forefront of his mind. Some opportunities in this direction were available to him. But for the moment, he had committed himself to being a caretaker. After a rather lonely winter, his hope was that the move from Northumberland to Herefordshire would provide the change he needed and perhaps lead towards a new phase in his life.

He was on his way to look after his sister's cottage while she joined a botanical expedition to study alpine flowers in the Pyrenees. She was an illustrator, who had secured a place in a party as its artist and one of its photographers. She had asked him to be the caretaker because her lodger, a close friend, had moved out to live with her boyfriend. She was also a little concerned about him. He had written more letters to her during the winter than was usual for him. She sensed that he needed a change. He had agreed to house-sit for her, but had not been looking forward to being there while she prepared to go abroad. Her ordinary chaos was trying enough. He knew how its bounds would be broken - indeed, shattered in the excitement of her preparations to go away. It was while preparing himself for this unlimited chaos that he received the letter he had beside him in his notebook, only a week before he was due to leave the caravan. As ever, her letter was simply headed "The Goggin", followed by an indecipherable date (actually the 1st April) and her usual opening endearment, all penned in huge, sweeping letters...

'Dearest Owen,

You'll never guess what's happened. I have to leave earlier than planned because I shall be travelling through France with someone else - a man! - whose departure date is different. So I won't be here when you arrive on the 7th. Sorry. I was going to welcome you with a dinner party and stir you up a bit. Now you will have to settle in without me around. Will you cope? He! He! He!

I've asked Alison to feed you when you arrive. Her food is not bad. On special occasions, it's usually adventurous. Just what you need to start you out on an adventure in Ewyas. Her boyfriend, Milo, will collect you from the railway station. And if you want adventure and excitement of the other sort, you can contact another close friend of mine, Catherine, a beautiful woman who has always wanted to meet you. (All my friends want to meet you!) She knows the sort of guy you are - I've told her everything!!! Ring her up - she'll be delighted.

I will now be away for at least three months, I think, from well before the Easter weekend. Other than my seeing you, everything seems to have fallen into place perfectly. I've got some gorgeous Pyrenean months ahead of me; some beautiful flowers to draw; some fine scenery to go mad over; the equivalent of paid leave; and a lovely man to look after my cottage for me. Am I rubbing salt into your winter wounds? Wash it off in the brook; no-one will see you. They never see me. Just relax and retire. There are countless places for you to

5

escape to, and your noisy sister won't be here when you get back. I'll leave a list of the places you can run away to in preparation for my return... and the telephone number of Catherine's arms...

And if you want something to do while you're here, you can build me a gazebo on the side of the house to replace the old one that blew down in the gales last autumn. I've already drawn a detailed plan of what I want - I'll pin it to one of the beams in the living room where it will be easy to find. And the garden needs some attention. You could resurrect the vegetable patch, nurture the soft fruit with your soft soul, and cherish my precious herbs - as well as mowing the grass (the mower is in need of some minor repairs!). You can have the back bedroom - the one that faces the hill. Alison used to have it. If you can stop the roof leaking, and repair the window, you'll be snug. The door doesn't close properly either, so you could fix that too.

Don't you dare change the place around or "tidy" it up. I want to return to my cottage as it is. The decorations in the back bedroom are Alison's doing, so you can do what you like there. I've asked someone to show you where all my artwork is so you can protect it and wile away the hours communing with your sister in the quietest way possible. Keep it all safe for me.

The postman leaves the mail in a box on this side of the footbridge. The refuse collection is on Monday at the ridiculous hour of 7.15am. You will have to dump the rubbish on the other side of the bridge. Don't you dare use my slippers to carry the bag across the garden!

Get ready for my return... and don't run away before I get back! I promise to let you know the date when you can welcome me with open arms!

Love, Suzy xxx

P.S. Telephone Milo on Darren 503 to let him know the time your train arrives. My transport will carry me away tomorrow. Bye,Bye.'

Her given name was actually Susan, but once her personality became known at school, her friends changed it to Suzy. Their parents eventually gave in to the change, although they used both names, depending on their mood. Suzy had seen his caravan but he had yet to see her cottage, except its front façade as the background to a photograph of her. She had made countless incidental references to it in her letters, asides usually which gave only fragmentary information. To anyone who did not know her, it would be surprising that someone who could encapsulate a plant in a sketch could not convey a picture in words of the place where she lived. Owen could have sorted through her letters, extracted all the references they contained to the cottage, and then pieced together an overall description, but reading one letter at a time was enough for him. Nevertheless, he did have some idea of what the place was like from the few allusions to it which had made an impression upon him. He had already found it, he thought, on the Ordnance Survey map of the area. If it was the right dwelling - and there was nothing else marked to qualify for the isolated privilege - it rested close to the base of a small, conical hill, from which it must have taken its name, beside a river with a Welsh name - the Dol Barcut Brook - which eventually found its way into the River Monnow in the south-western corner of Herefordshire. There was a footbridge over the brook close to the tiny black dot he was looking at. Fortunately, the cottage was on the south-eastern side of the hill with the promise of a sunny aspect, unlike the northern outlook of his caravan.

He put the letter back into its envelope. As he did so, the train reduced speed and slowed progressively to another halt in the countryside. He had another landscape of stillness to contemplate. Across the fields, a wood was being felled. Or rather, it had been felled and was now being erased, for a bulldozer was attacking the stumps, and knocking over what spindly trees were left standing, gathering the ruins together into untidy heaps. Did it have to be done in such a brutal manner, he asked himself. He presumed that the wood was being erased so that the land could be used for agriculture. The adjoining fields had been enlarged. On the edge of the enclosure that had, until recently, been wooded, there was a pile of large timber butts awaiting shipment. Nearby, stood a squat oak tree with a short but wide bole, carrying a multitude of heavy limbs - a pollard; perhaps an old boundary tree? Was that to go as well?

The site itself was a gentle slope, very uneven in the configuration of its ground, and bisected diagonally by a small stream. The whole place had the inevitable appearance of catastrophic change. Its starkness, and the methodical progress of the bulldozer, conveyed the impression of clearing up after the battle was over. He knew that when a wood or a forest has its best trees, and all its useful timber, removed, leaving behind only a vestige of the former cover, it is described by the forester as "devastated". Whoever first used this epithet for a wood shattered by felling was not only describing precisely what had actually happened - the laying waste of an area of trees - but also implying abuse and a lack of care for the life and resources once inherent in the wood. Surely, a forester or a woodman would not devastate a wood without some feelings of sadness?

He tried to imagine the site as a place before the tree cover had been taken apart. It would have had a number of layers, openings, seasonal colours, habitats and inhabitants. These would have given it a sense of place, an identity created by the passage of considerable time. Had the wood had a name, he asked himself? If it had, would the farm workers and other local people refer to the new field as the "something - wood field"? He recalled the place-name studies he had done at university, and how the countless assarts of history - the open land created from the original wildwood - often carried tell-tale names consisting of the old identity and the new. Of the Old English suffixes indicative of the advance into woodland, he could remember only two - the common one of "ley" or "leah", and "ridding".* Ridding was certainly appropriate in the present circumstances. He started to make a quick note of the sighting in his notebook, but he was interrupted.

The train began to move again. He returned to the book on The Southern Marches that his sister had sent him as an introduction to his forthcoming surroundings; a book by H.J. Massingham, one of Britain's foremost writers on rural life and conservation. He had lost his place again, even though he thought it was the best book his sister had ever recommended to him. She had also sent him Kilvert's Diary which, although he had read only a few passages, had already given him ideas of writing more comprehensively about the places he visited. He determined to start in this vein with his new surroundings. He was an avid reader: a thoughtful young man who was forever delving into writings about countryside and nature, and reading landscape poetry. One of his favourite poets was John Clare.

It took him a while to find the section he had been reading.

As before, he could not keep his mind on the book. Either the scenes passing by outside the window, or another reflection, would distract him from the text. Transitional states of mind are not conducive to concentration. And a transition was occurring outside. The train had reached the outskirts of a town. It was Hereford, a place he had never seen before. The appearance of the town in the dusk and the circuitous approach to it prompted thoughts of a frontier post in bygone days. His disjointed reading had made an impression after all. He began to gather his possessions together – a rucksack and a shoulder bag – and then he moved down the carriage to be close to where his bike was stored. It had taken quite an effort to manoeuvre his machine, with its loaded saddle-bags, and his luggage between the station changes on his journey. His bike was his only means of transport, other than his long legs.

CHAPTER 2

'Meanwhile the mind from pleasure less
Withdraws into its happiness:
The mind, that ocean where each kind
Does straight its own resemblance find;
Yet it creates, transcending these,
Far other worlds and other seas,
Annihilating all thats made
To a green thought in a green shade.'

From The Garden by Andrew Marvell (1621-1678)

Owen's preparations to leave the train delayed any thoughts of the rendezvous with his sister's friend. They had not arranged to meet beside or beneath any special architectural features - Hereford railway station has none of these - for Milo had said on the 'phone that he would recognise him easily enough. He would, for there were unlikely to be numerous passengers with ginger-coloured hair disembarking all at once. This was Owen's most distinctive feature. Other than his hair, which was pale and soft, his looks were unexceptional: average height; average build; unobtrusive, except for his locks and legs. Yet, his face, upon closer view, carried an element of intriguing quality; a far-awayness; a capacity for its owner to appear to be present and absent at the same time. It was, of course, an aspect of his eyes which imparted this quality. Their colour was not startling; not the blue or grey or green of special eyes; simply brown, but with an innocent brightness and appealing depth.

Upon leaving the train at Hereford, a nondescript two-platform halt, Owen's main concern was for his bike, which a member of the railway station staff disembarked for him. He had told Milo, who was meeting him, that it needed transporting, too, so that was another feature of recognition for Alison's friend. Fortunately, the bike did not have to be dismantled because the vehicle sent to collect him was a pick-up. Milo was surprised to see such a loaded bike, but he was more interested in the individual he was meeting.

"Suzy showed us a few photographs of you", he said as Owen's possessions were dumped into the back of the pick-up. "Then she said that I should ignore anyone coming out of the station with a smile, or a hint of a smile, on their face."

Even Owen relaxed his face at this comment.

"Did you make all your train connections on time?"

"Every one of them. I think I was lucky."

"What else has my loving sister told you about me?" asked Owen as he opened the door of the vehicle to get in, his question spoken in exaggerated tones of confidence.

"Do you really want to know?" replied Milo, teasingly, starting the engine and looking at Owen for an answer before driving off. Owen nodded his assent, somewhat self-consciously.

"Well, she said that despite your conspicuous hair you are usually a difficult person to find; that whenever you go off for a walk, you sometimes forget to come back. Is that true?" Milo smiled as he spoke, but beneath his amusement there was much curiosity.

"I often wonder what she tells her friends about her relationship with her brother. Yes, I suppose it is true, in a way, but is that all she said?"

"Well, it's the gist of what she said. She gave us a few examples of your disappearances when you last stayed with her near Bristol. Is she telling the truth?"

"More or less. But did she say that my disappearances only happen when we're staying in the same house together?"

Milo nodded negatively.

"She sometimes creates too much chaos for me, that's all. When we were living at home, the house often became unbearable because of the chaos she caused, especially when our parents were away. If they were at home, my father would hardly notice any change in the homely hubbub but my mother would become unsettled.

"But what about your actual disappearances?" Milo was obviously more than just curious.

"Well, the first time we were left alone for a weekend, I felt like a break by the Saturday afternoon so I said I was going for a long walk and told Suzy not to bother about me. I didn't return until the next day. I spent the day with a book in an old overgrown quarry which was a kind of retreat for me, and the night with a friend. Suzy didn't realise I hadn't come back until

I walked in the door with the paper the next morning. I got into the habit of dismissing myself whenever the chaos became too much for me. I've been doing it for peace and quiet ever since. Surely you must have noticed that my sister has boundless energy which can be exhausting to others? Or do you and Alison lead a chaotic life as well?"

"No more chaotic than the average. And I suppose I know what you mean because Suzy and I can rub each other up the wrong way. Alison has sometimes kept out of her way. At first, I just assumed that they had fallen out or got tired of each other for the time being."

"It's more than that. You have to live with her to appreciate the chaos she causes. It seems to be her way of de-fusing tension by exploiting it."

Owen was a thoughtful young man; perhaps too thoughtful. He had gained a reputation in his family for his disappearances, his day-dreaming, and his reflective nature. One of his aunts had tried, whenever she was about, to moderate his sister's calls upon his attention. But his parents had not protected him in any way. He had found his own ways of escaping the disturbances, whether real or imaginary, that she caused.

"Maybe you react more than most because of sibling undertones", observed Milo.

"Perhaps, but I won't be disappearing unless she posts me some chaos from the Pyrenees. Anyway, I'm at a disadvantage here. As yet, I don't know where you escape to - your habits are unknown to me."

Milo smiled - at least his eyes and his upper cheeks did, for he was heavily bearded - and then he proceeded to give Owen a potted history of himself. His full name was Milo Pychard.

For the last year, he had been working for the Nature Conservancy Council* carrying out a survey of lichens and mosses ('epiphytes' he called them)* in various woods in Mid-Wales. The last summer had been the first phase of the survey; the coming summer was to be the second and final phase, although there was the possibility of more work next year. The object of the exercise was to see which species of lichens and mosses were exclusive to ancient woods; that is to say, found only in woods which had existed as such from the time when the country was virtually covered with trees.

"What most people don't realise", he explained, "when they look at any landscape of fields and woods is that the woods have been gradually isolated by the cultivation and the husbandry of the land around them; that some have always occupied their sites - the ancient ones - while the rest have arisen upon cleared land as secondary cover, with intervals of anything from decades to centuries between successive woods. Today, woods are more or less islands in an intensively farmed landscape, connected to each other only by hedgerows..."

"Wordsworth's 'little lines of sportive wood run wild'?" interjected Owen.

"...their wildlife an indication of their ecological history and what they were like when their contact with the original wildwood was severed. What was that by Wordsworth?"

Owen repeated the quote.

"'wood run wild', that's a good description because some of them must be linear remains of the original woodland left in place as boundaries when fields were being created. Where did he write that?"

"In a poem called "Lines Written Near Tintern Abbey',

which is not far from here, is it?" replied Owen. "He also speaks of 'wreaths of smoke sent up in silence from among the trees'; smoke from the making of charcoal, apparently."*

Owen admitted to being fascinated by woodland history and by the work Milo was doing, so the conversation continued to be about trees and woods although it was now too dark for Milo to introduce his passenger to the arboreal places, passing by outside, which he knew so well. He merely gestured to shadowy features alongside the road and uttered a succession of names, most of them Welsh sounding, which only bemused Owen by their strangeness, until at last he turned off the road into a lay-by and skidded to a halt. They had arrived at The Goggin.

All Owen could see as he got out of the pick-up was a light, about one hundred metres away, shining through some trees at the end of a narrow track which connected with one end of the lay-by. He could hear the rippling noises of the stream which he knew lay between them and the house. They gathered up the baggage, Milo taking the bike and Owen his rucksack and shoulder-bag, and proceeded down the unmade track to the stream where some steps led on to the simple wooden footbridge that gave access to the dwelling. Once over the bridge, it was only a short walk across a large garden to the front door which opened as they reached it.

"Welcome to The Goggin" said Alison as the two men entered the cottage through an unusually wide doorway.

Immediately, Owen knew he had arrived, for his sister's personality jumped out at him from everywhere. In the living room, the decorations, the wall hangings, the posters, the notice board, the pictures, the books, the dried flowers, the plants - the cacophony of colour and objets d'art was overwhelming. And this was only the beginning. The old features of the room, the stone fire place, the wood panelling, the oak beams, had already been overwhelmed by the clutter. Between the beams, the strips of ceiling were decorated with three different wallpapers, the wallpapers which covered the three walls of the room. Only the walls of the kitchen, which was connected to the living room by two openings either side of a partition of wood panelling, itself covered with posters, displayed unison, being painted turquoise; but they, too, were overwhelmed with fixtures of all sorts. Even the doors and the windows were obscured, the former by various hangings and the latter by various plants standing on the stone window seats and by clusters of dried flowers dangling from the wooden lintels. The style and the colour of the furniture were equally as motley as the decorations.

Alison could see that Owen was outfaced. She offered him a glass of wine and said that the food was ready to eat, hoping that the meal would help him settle in to his new surroundings. As he sat down to the food they had prepared, he had to ask her how she had coped with living with his sister.

"How did you get on with these surroundings and living with Suzy?" he exclaimed quietly, unsettled by the activity of the room.

"Oh, the place freaked me out when I first saw it, but I gradually got used to its character by the time I moved in. When Suzy's around, the surroundings recede into the background. Living with her was an incredible experience - I needn't tell you that - and the excitement of it all hardly gave me time to reflect upon the decor. But it wasn't long before I needed a break. She's a great friend, and I love her, but I had to get away sometimes. I wonder if I would have fallen into Milo's arms so quickly if I hadn't needed to unwind." She looked across the table at Milo and smiled.

"This food is good" said Owen, "Thanks for welcoming me."

"Milo prepared the food" said Alison. "He thought he would be better at vegetarian food than me, something simple after such a long journey rather than an exotic dish. I made the yoghurt."

"And Suzy made the wine", said Milo, although Owen was expecting him to make some comment about Alison's exotic dishes after what his sister had said in her letter to him. "Her wines are fantastic - I'll say that for her. This one is made from elder flowers. Your quote from Wordsworth, Owen, about sportive woods running wild certainly echoes your sister's connection with hedgerows. In her hands, their wildness is given free rein."

"You've got a supply of hedgerow teas in the cupboard over there as well as wines", said Alison. "Don't forget that. Excuse me while I get the dessert."

After the meal, Alison gave Owen a disorganised introduction to a cluttered kitchen as the two of them did the washing up while Milo finished off the wine in an armchair. Owen tried to listen attentively but his attention was absorbed more by the person than by the guidance she was giving. She was quite a plainly dressed person; plain in the sense that there was nothing about her which stood out or immediately caught one's eye, except, perhaps, her absence of femininity. Her face was broad and somewhat angular, especially her jaw. It was only her gentle voice that held your attention. This characteristic was probably an asset to her in her work for she was a journalist on a local newspaper. She did not impose herself upon you, project her personality, or induce a reaction to her presence. Such plainness and unobtrusiveness exerted a calming influence upon Owen that was welcome after the ending to his train journey and the introduction to his sister's home.

"What prompted you to take up journalism?" enquired Owen when they rejoined Milo in the living room.

"I always wanted to be a journalist, right from the time I started reading newspapers. My father had a friend who was a journalist and he gave me a lot of encouragement when he knew I was bent on becoming one."

"What sort of articles do you write?" enquired Owen further.

"Everything. When you write for a local newspaper, you find yourself looking into and writing about every aspect of life from the droll and the mundane to the mundane and the droll. The drollest article I've ever written was a feature concerning the project Milo's been working on, and that was composed with inside information." She smiled sideways at Milo whose mind seemed to be elsewhere because he did not notice that he was being teased.

"She's being modest" he said. "It was a good article and an essential one because it explained simply what we were doing and why, and how we needed the co-operation of farmers and landowners to make the project a success. There is quite a lot of opposition, you know, towards wildlife buffs like me who spend their time peering at bark through a hand lens. The only one around here who is genuinely sympathetic to our cause is the owner of Llandyfrig Court."

"You're bound to bump into him sometime, Owen, if you go walking over by the Court", added Alison. "He owns the deer park and the eastern flanks of Rhibo Mountain. We should call it the Deer Haye, that's its proper name, but we've got so used to saying 'park', being outsiders."

"Why 'Haye'?" enquired Owen.

"You'll have to ask Humphrey de Bohun that; he's the best person to explain the name. It will be worth waiting for his answer. He's a bit nutty. Suzy is very friendly with him and his wife Matilda. I'm fascinated by the rumours that he talks to the trees in the deer park. You saw him once, didn't you Milo, talking to himself by a tree in the park?"

"Yes, I did, but whether he's nutty or not, he is well disposed to us lot surveying his trees and his woods. We could not get permission from his neighbour, Carling Medlar, the 'Meddling Baron' as we call him, who owns The Prospect, halfway between here and the deer park. He's a man you should avoid, Owen, if you go for a walk near his place. Suzy made the mistake of entering the dark life of The Prospect. It was Medlar's son who messed up her alliance with The Prospect. She had one of her explosive romances and it backfired. She should never have..."

"Okay, Milo. That affair is over now. I'm sure Owen doesn't want to hear about the nasty side of one of his sister's boyfriends."

She looked to Owen for confirmation.

"Not particularly", he said.

"Why don't we show Owen the layout of the area, and where all these places are?" she suggested, helpfully.

The rest of the evening was spent with the map on the table and with Alison and Milo giving Owen an introductory tour of the district. He was shown the locations of Llandyfrig Court, The Prospect, Milo's small place on the outskirts of Elchon, and was given an assessment of the local villages. He made notes of the footpaths he could follow to reach various places of interest, and Milo outlined the boundary of the 'Medling Baron's' land, including the dwellings and parcels of land he had acquired during his ten year domination of the area. The geography of the area, however, was eventually overtaken by Milo discoursing about the trees and the woods of the district, subjects which were clearly a consuming passion for him, and perhaps the bane of Alison's recreational life. His enthusiasm was encouraged by Owen marking the special sites he mentioned and making notes as to what was worth visiting.

The discussion of woods recalled to Owen the felling he had seen from the train, so he told them about it. Milo's reaction was to lament, angrily, the recent clearance of a small wood on the land of one of the Medlar's neighbours, a wood which disappeared before he could look at it. He had, that day, discovered its name from a large scale map. It had been called 'Masarnen Gwydd'. In English, it was the equivalent of 'Maple Wood', a translation which had only added to his annoyance, for field maple was one of his favourite trees. Alison attempted to moderate his annoyance by suggesting that the name might not guarantee that the modern wood had consisted of maple. Milo was not placated. He could remember seeing numerous dead elms in the wood, a tree often found growing with maple. His retort to Alison was that whatever had been its composition, the wood had once contained enough maple to give it a special identity. Gradually, Milo's mood subsided from agitation into quiet disappointment.

It was at this point that Alison dragged him away, leaving Owen to reflect upon the intensity of purpose of the conservationist. As they departed, Alison suddenly remembered something – "Oh, yes, and there's those two books which Suzy found for you in Hay-on-Wye just before she went abroad: The Book of the Tree by Georgina Mase and Spirit of the Trees by Ruth Cresswell. They're on the bedside table in my old bedroom." Once alone, Owen was left with a certain amount of sadness in the air, gazing at the chaotic surroundings and the all pervasive personality of his sister. Without the distraction of conversation, his new surroundings loomed large again. He went quickly to bed.

Notebook - 7th April, 1988.

> *'As I pass on with my one thought*
> *To find a quiet place with trees....'*

W.H. Davies, from 'Trees'

CHAPTER 3

'And this our life, exempt from public haunt,
Finds tongues in trees...'

From 'As You Like It' by William Shakespeare
(1564-1616)

Upon waking the next day, Owen experienced that brief state of consciousness commonly felt in the languor of early morning after a long journey of displacement. At first, he was still in the caravan feeling lethargic and yearning for a different routine. Seconds later, he was disoriented by the strange surroundings of the bedroom and did not know where he was. For a moment, he was confused. Then he became more or less awake and realised that he was in the back bedroom of his sister's cottage. He had slept well; perhaps too well. The back bedroom was more comfortable than the caravan.

Reluctant to emerge from beneath the covers, he attempted to recall the welcome of the evening before. It had been a long time since meeting some of Suzy's friends. Those he had previously met, he found relatively easy-going. Milo, though, gave a first impression of being rather head-strong; too much to take for long periods of time. Like Suzy. Perhaps this was why Alison had been able to cope with Suzy.

His memory of the evening was mixed. Milo cataloguing the campaigns of conservation he was leading - the habitats lost, those under threat, and the few saved. His hatred of Carling Medlar - 'the Meddling Baron' who, in his eyes, was the arch-enemy to conservation locally: Alison restraining him from becoming too intense: her job as a journalist with a local newspaper: the random introduction to a cluttered kitchen: Suzy's home-made wines and herb-teas - the only part of the kitchen he could remember: an equally random introduction to the local places and people of interest: and the all-pervasive personality of his sister. This was when his head had started to spin. The decor of the downstairs rooms came into his mind and he rolled deeper under the covers.

The most interesting recollection of what he had been told by his sister's friends was of the man who owned the local deer park - Humphrey de Bohun. Two things had stuck in his mind: the fact that there was a local deer park, and Milo's claim that its owner communicated with his trees. Owen, himself, had experienced many memorable moments standing beside venerable or otherwise remarkable trees feeling that he was being enveloped by strange sensations.

After stumbling down the stairs - they were too steep for the state of his mind - the loudness of the living room startled him again. His sister's personality jumped out at him from everywhere. The decorations, the wall hangings, the posters, the cluttered notice-board, the pictures, the books, the dried flowers, the house-plants - the cacophony of colour and objets d'art were too much. And this was only the first day.

He was reminded that the old features of the room - the stone fire place, the wood panelling, the oak beams - were hardly noticeable, and that, between the beams, the strips of ceiling were decorated with three different wallpapers, the wallpapers which covered the three walls of the room. The turquoise of the kitchen made an especially jarring impact on his early-morning eyes; so, too, did its fixtures of all sorts - coloured jars, and racks of home-made wine.

Ignoring Suzy's edict, he relieved the noisiness by taking down some of the posters and the hangings so that the structural parts of the room could be seen. He revealed the doors, the panelling and the beams, the reappearance of which did something to lessen the visual cacophony that unsettled him. Or was it the sibling connexion inherent in the decor which was unsettling? Until the arrival of Suzy's last letter, he had been trying to prepare his mind for the imminent presence of his sister's personality. At least one piece of clearance brought an old map to his attention, immaculately framed and carrying the inscription: 'To Suzy, with love Catherine'. It seemed to be of the local area.

Almost automatically, he thought of his bike which was in an undecorated backroom that Suzy used as a store for all her garden implements and other oddments. Fastidiously, he checked it for any damage caused by its transportation in the pickup. It was okay. He spent a lot of time tinkering with his bike to keep it in fine condition and in perfect working order. It had been a gift from a long-time friend who was a keen cyclist.

Having an orange frame, it was a very distinctive machine, and one that was to become a familiar sight in the area, padlocked to gate-posts, to railings and whatever was available to keep it secure. The wanderings of its owner were to arouse considerable local curiosity. In rural communities, it does not take long for the presence of a newcomer to be noticed and discussed. The fact that Owen's sister had preceded him, only made the intrigue and the gossip that more fanciful. Suzy was well known - Owen had expected that - and her personality must have been the subject of many local conversations. Gossip, however extravagant, did not bother Suzy; it was just another of the background forces which energized her. But Owen was different; he preferred to be and to feel anonymous, and to come out when he wanted to. He would rather his bike be the subject of the local stories – it had the character to be noticed.

Returning to the main part of the house, he entered the cluttered kitchen with thoughts of breakfast stirring in his head, but the paraphernalia of the place was too much for him. Being unfamiliar with its apparent lack of order and with the location of the sustenance it contained, the immediate task of finding his way around was daunting. It depressed the appetite which had started to rise. It also caused his head to spin a little, so he found the fridge and some fruit juice, grabbed a cup, and returned to the living room via the other opening. It was then that he saw his name written on an envelope pinned over other papers on the notice-board, an envelope bordered with zigzagging lines in the same florescent colour as his name. And above it, pinned to the nearest beam, the plans for the gazebo.

The envelope contained two simple lists in Suzy's sweeping scrawl.

The first was headed 'Retreats and Runaway Places', some of which Milo and Alison had mentioned the night before:-

'The Melglyn Dingle	An old lime tree - you will wilt!
The Deer Haye	Humphrey hooting.
Coed Tirion Glas	Your kind of wood - Ugh!
The Cwm	Naked abandonment...
Rhibo Mountain	Your kind of hill.
The Goggin	My hill - remember that!'

The second was headed 'Friendly Support and Sustenance'. It, too, included names which rang the bells of the evening before.

'Bodcut Farm	The Farr family - Catherine: ooh! 491
Llandyfrig Court	The de Bohun playhouse 498
Trescoyte	Ali and her serious man 503
Shop in Gulible	Emergency rations but no muesli.
Green Man pub	Keep the Forrest flag flying...
Goggin Cottage	Haunted, but ghastly ghost on holiday.'

He left the plans where they were. He did not feel ready to enter into the detailed thoughts of his sister. He never did. In fact, he had had enough of her personality for the moment. He quickly satisfied his thirst, returned the juice to the fridge, and then looked around the living room for something he knew to be there.

Grabbing his coat, which lay nearby covering up a colourful chair, he opened the wide panelled door and stepped outside. The brightness of the morning daylight completed his waking up. Daffodils were everywhere, and on either side of the path there were chalk-blue drifts of speedwell. He received an impression of having advanced in time - spring was there already.

Before him lay a lawn sloping gently down to the brook. Although only thirty metres away, this could not be seen from the porch for the cottage and its garden were set on a terrace about three metres or so above the water. He could see the footbridge to his right beyond the lawn. Beside it there stood a large oak tree which he had not noticed the night before. It was almost as wide as it was tall. Walking along the path towards the bridge to get a closer view, he saw that the tree was right on the edge of the brook. It was anchored in place by massive roots which disappeared into the exposed soil of the stream-bank and which merged into a lower bole that was a flat wall of wood almost two metres broad and flush with the line of the bank. The tree had been pollarded sometime in the distant past for it had several limbs radiating outwards and upwards from its massive butt. On one side a limb had been lost, leaving a long, narrow crevice which was becoming calloused over. Standing against it, he tried to spread his arms from one side of the trunk to the other and only just covered the span. He stepped away from this gnarled giant and contemplated its presence for a while. It felt familiar for some reason.

All around the bridge, on either side of the stream, there were trees. Some of them were breaking into leaf, and beneath them, numerous primroses were in flower. There was another large tree on the other bank, its trunk arching over the water so much that it looked close to the point of toppling. It was a wych elm, its pendant branches making a canopy over the stream and the edge of the garden, almost offering an alternative passage to the footbridge. The signs of Dutch-elm disease were evident in the die-back of some of its top-most shoots. Most of the other trees were alders, their bushy bases merging to form a hedge-like barrier.

Beyond the elm, at right angles to the water's edge, a threadbare box hedge separated the lawn from the other sector of the garden, the vegetable patch where there was another large tree. Owen walked alongside the streamside towards it, passing a wide break in the alders which gave easy access to the brook. Until he was beneath the tree's leafless crown he was unsure what it was, but he soon recognised it as a walnut, a specimen somewhat passed its best and looking rather ghostly in its decline, pock-marked with black bark blisters.

On the far side of the vegetable patch, in the corner of the garden which abutted the hummocky beginnings of the Goggin Hill itself, there stood, or rather stooped, a hoary crab apple, a tangled mass of branches and twisted twigs blotched in several places with mistletoe still carrying a few berries. Running away from it down to the stream there was a newly and neatly laid hedge, coming to life with the bright green of unfolding hawthorn leaves. The two structures contrasted starkly with one another. But it was the Goggin which now held his interest. The hill was as distinctive as the map presentation of it had suggested. Its concave lower slopes of pasture ascended steeply to meet even steeper convex slopes covered in bracken and broken by a line of rock outcrops. It had to be climbed - even though it was his sister's hill.

The view from the top was worth the stiff ascent on an empty stomach. On a really clear day, the vistas would be superb. He had an aerial view of his new dwelling and its environs. The layout of the plot was obscured by the trees around it, but the course of the stream was clearly visible as a sinuous line of vegetation curving around the garden. The overhanging elm merged anonymously into the waterside belt of trees, but the oak rose up above its companions. And locking into the sylvan brook there was a network of hedgerows, unusually well stocked with trees, connecting with an assortment of copses and rough places roundabout. Emerging leaves coalesced in places to give further hints of spring.

To the west, the edge of the Black Mountains appeared awesome. Away to the south-west there was a much larger and more pointed version of the hill upon which he was standing. The map of the district, which was still in his coat pocket, revealed it to be a National Trust property called Ysgyryd Fawr - however that was pronounced - an angular and isolated eminence of rock near Abergavenny. In the immediate foreground, to the north-west, there was another hill of less mountainous proportions, a whale of a hill called Mynydd y rhibo. His eyes gave it more attention than any part of the upland backdrop. There was something restful about its lines; something calm about its shape. It was more a part of the managed landscape than an outlier of upland or moorland, although there was a vestige of heathland on its top. Dominating its eastern side was a great area of broadleaved woodland, named on the map as Coed Tirion Glas, stretching from its middle reaches away to the north. Below the woodland, and visually a part of it, there was an expanse of parkland where bracken covered slopes, merging with pasture, could be seen beneath large and fulsome trees. The map showed it as the deer-park of Llandyfrig Court. The appearance of Mynydd y rhibo evoked a peculiar fascination for him which caused his eyes to return to it over and over again until he finally pulled himself away from the romanticism that was there for the taking. He may have made the right decision after all in agreeing to take care of his sister's cottage.

It was nearly lunchtime when he returned to the cottage. The foray of exploration had to give way to the needs of the stomach. He had descended the hill on the other side and found his way along a footpath to a three-way intersection of lanes where there were signposts to Gulible and Ewyas, Onen, and Elchon. His map told him that the road to Elchon, a road which clung to the base of the hill above a picturesque river valley, would take him back. Although Alison had brought some fresh food with her to last him a day or so, he needed to get provisions. So while attending to his stomach's immediate pangs, he compiled a shopping list and prepared for an exploratory visit to the nearest grocery store which, according to Suzy's list, was located in the village of Gulible four miles away. How many, if any, of his favourite foods would the store stock? He now knew which road to take.

On his bike - the only expensive possession he had - it did not take him long to reach the intersection he had come upon earlier in the day, and it was only a short distance beyond this junction that the village sign to Gulible appeared, almost lost in the rampant roadside growth of the previous year. He expected to see the village any moment, but he saw only a few scattered dwellings and a farm before arriving several minutes later, and rather suddenly, at a bridge and a public house.

He soon discovered that Gulible did not have a centre, in the usual sense, where everything congregated. The church was at one end on its own, set back from a lane by a small green; the pub, the Green Man, was at the other end between the bridge and a junction of lanes; and between the two there were a few houses, some enclosures and another farm. Upon asking a curiously diffident local inhabitant the whereabouts of the shop, he was directed to a cul de sac which led down to the church and the river. There, at the end of a terrace of three houses, was the store. A weathered board above an enlarged ground floor window carried the sign 'Gulible Village Stores' in very faded pre-war script. There was hardly any window display, a few very old stickers on the glass, and darkness inside.

The shop was one large room cluttered with shelving and eye level partitions. Dinginess prevailed. The only artificial light flickered from a dirty bulb in the centre of a ceiling consisting of tongued and grooved boarding of a reddish brown hue. Similar boarding covered the end wall, which had a chiller cabinet in front of it containing a few cheeses and a piece of ham whose appearance was not enhanced by the poor lighting. Despite the drab interior, the shop seemed to be well stocked with tinned food, although the selection of commodities was limited to staple and traditionally established brands.

He moved around the shop, squeezing himself between the aisles and trying not to knock items off shelves with his saddlebags as he turned one way, then another, to familiarise himself with the range of provisions. As he did so, he sensed that he was being watched. There had been no-one in the shop when he entered, but now, behind the cabinet of ham and cheeses there stood a tiny woman gazing intently at him. He smiled at her and said 'hello'. Her delayed reply was a squeaky 'good afternoon', followed by a frown as she peered even more intently at him. When he looked towards her again, she had been joined by a very round man, presumably her husband, who also scrutinised him while the two of them talked quietly together. It was obvious from their manner that his entry constituted more than the ordinary response of shopkeepers to an unknown customer. By the time he had collected all he needed, and approached the cabinet and the antiquated till beside it, the man had disappeared, but the woman was still there as quizzical as before.

"Where have you come from?" she enquired bluntly, in a voice that was distinctly Welsh.

"Oh, I've just moved into the area to stay at my sister's house by the Goggin", replied Owen in an exaggeratedly friendly voice.

"So that's it!" she exclaimed, as if the answer to some puzzling question had been revealed at last. "Edward!" she called with a lilt in her squeaky voice, "I was right."

Her husband came through to the shop again as she said to Owen, "I thought your face looked familiar. You resemble your sister very closely. My husband thought I was imagining it but I'm good at recognising faces. We haven't seen your sister for a while. Where is she?"

Owen explained where she had gone and his caretaker role while she was away. When he eventually left the shop, the woman continued to watch him through the dingy window as he attached his saddlebags to the bike. He was puzzled by her attitude towards him. Even when she had discovered who he was, she had not ceased to look at him in an overly curious manner, as if she expected something dramatic to happen.

On the return journey, he decided to cycle back to the cottage by an alternative route which would take him in a northerly circuit around the Goggin Hill, passed the southern tip of the deer park. The narrow lane made a gentle ascent along the side of a beautiful little valley wedged between the Goggin and Mynydd y rhibo, the course of its stream defined by a belt of trees seemingly squashed into the ground. Hedgerows and trees were so numerous, and the hills so close, and closing with the climb, that he felt he was going along a dead-end road into a wilderness.

At the head of this narrow valley some drops of rain touched his freckled face. Automatically, he went for his cape, but he had left it behind to make way for the food. With his bike propped against him, he found himself almost opposite the entrance to a very dilapidated farmstead, so overgrown as to be unobtrusive. Its hint of times past was exactly in keeping with the scene on the other side of the lane beyond the hedge - a scene of squat ancient trees strewn across a vast expanse of pasture. There were, however, signs that it was not abandoned, although it appeared to be virtually derelict, its buildings askew and badly in need of repair. At the side of the lane, amongst the spring grass and herbs, there was a very weathered wooden sign carrying the name, Gwenynog. He was looking towards a farmhouse across a muddy flag-stoned yard where missing and broken flags and pools of ugly slush continued to suggest abandonment. But there was a senile sheep dog lying across the front door. To one side of the house, between the lane and a barn which had its nearside gable-end leaning precariously outwards, there was a paddock, a quagmire of mud puddled with the hoof-holes of a solitary roan-coloured cow that laboured to move around. The scene could have come out of an eighteenth century print. He was prompted to write a description of the place in his notebook, which he always had with him, but a sudden downpour forced him to press on.

From the ridge connecting the two hills, a magnificent scene opened up to the north-west towards the broadleaved wood flanking Mynydd y rhibo and below it, the deer park, only a few fields away. The descent took him closer to the park but an overgrown hedgerow on his left prevented a clear view of its interior. He stopped beside a gap in the hedge to take in the view. Turning at another junction, he came upon a gentle climb that ended with a short and steep descent into a dingle. The lane became sunken, overhung by oak trees clinging to its steep banks. The primroses were phosphorescent in the gloom. By now, the wet conditions were affecting his brakes; he was travelling faster than he wanted to in the circumstances. Where the lane levelled off to cross the stream in the dingle, there was a sharp bend which he prepared to negotiate. But on approaching the bend, the lane narrowed and the primroses became profuse, so profuse that they captured his gaze and almost dazzled him.

He did not see the tractor, pulling a trailer across the lane from a farmyard on his left into a field opposite, until it was too late. He had no choice but to swerve into the yard, which was covered in mud and muck, missing the trailer by inches. Foolishly, he applied the brakes too fiercely and lost control. The back wheel slid sideways; he parted company with his precious machine and slid himself through the freshly moistened filth of the yard, ending almost face downwards near a pool of dark and foul-smelling liquid. Gritting his teeth in discomfort as he raised himself up onto his elbows, he spat out whatever might have entered his mouth and exclaimed irritatingly, "sshit", and then wiped his mouth on his coat. For a moment, he felt too filthy to move again, aware that to extricate himself he had to wallow first.

He was soon joined by the tractor driver, who turned out to be the farmer. The man helped him to his feet and, seeing that he was unhurt, started to smile.

"You might not agree, lad" he said, "but you're lucky you didn't pass by this way last year because the yard used to be cobbled until I concreted it. And if I'd not kept some heifers in the yard recently, there wouldn't 'ave been all this muck around to soften your landing. I haven't had time to hose it down. Anyway, the drain's blocked; that's why there's so much water about. Quickly come over here to this tap and swill your mouth out. I don't want you coming down with e-coli poisoning or something."

Owen merely stood still, saying nothing and holding his arms away from his sides. Both legs were sodden and he could feel his breeches sticking to his cold skin. He was wearing a light weight coat that was not water (or slurry) proof, so parts of this garment were drenched through as well. His face and his pale ginger hair were splashed with slurry and coated with pieces of muck; and although he had not swallowed any filth, he had to spit out saliva several times just to lessen the feeling of filthiness. His obvious discomfort and motionless state caused the farmer to help him to the tap, where Owen gave his mouth and his face a really good clean. Then the farmer asked if he was alright.

"Yes, I'm alright", he muttered dejectedly, in a rather sorry-for-himself tone.

"Now come into the house and get out of those clothes", urged the farmer, continuing to smile.

Following the man across the yard, he could feel cold liquid running down his neck and down the inside of one leg. He hunched his shoulders and halted, but this only wetted his neck more. By the time he reached the entrance to the farmhouse, the farmer had explained the incident to his wife. They were both concerned to revive him, but the farmer had to return to his tractor and trailer, so he left Owen in the care of his wife, who was nursing some ailing lambs in her kitchen. Owen's bleating was silent. She showed him where he could undress, ran a bath for him (to his surprise), and found some replacement clothes. When he eventually returned to the kitchen, clad in garments that were loose fitting, if not baggy, the farmer was having his tea. And the lambs were still there; two of them in hay-filled boxes set against the Rayburn, and a third tottering around on a paper-strewn corner of the room.

"Come and join us, lad", entreated the farmer. "How do you feel now? Better I 'ope."

"Much better, thanks. That was one of the best baths I've ever had. Your bath is nearly big enough to swim in. Thanks for the change of clothing; I'll return them as soon as I can."

"You were lucky to 'ave missed me. A fraction earlier and there wouldn't 'ave been the room to slip into the yard." He smiled as he realised the double meaning in his words. "By the way, I've put your bike to one side and hosed it down for you. It don't appear to be damaged, but those bags of yours are a bit messy, and 'eavy too. That's what made the bike go over so easy."

"Where were you going?" asked his wife.

"Back to the Goggin", replied Owen, and before he could explain any further she spoke again.

"I thought you must be Suzy's brother. Someone with your looks couldn't be related to anyone else. What a coincidence. She's a good friend of our daughter, Catherine. Before she left to go abroad, she told us to look out for a mad cyclist. She is funny. She's a marvellous girl; so full of life. Our W.I. has already booked her to give a talk on the Pyrenees when she gets back."

With that, they formerly introduced themselves as Lloyd and Martha Farr, and their holding as Bodcut Farm. They apologised for being in a mess. It was lambing time and the normal routines had to go by the board. They both wanted to talk to him at length, but the demands of the ewes and their offspring allowed only short breaks. He was told that he was welcome to visit the farm any time he liked. Suzy always dropped in uninvited. Just as he finished the tea before him, Lloyd Farr insisted on taking him and his bike back to the Goggin in his Landrover. Then, just as they were about to leave, Mrs Farr invited him to join the family for sunday lunch.

"That's a good idea, Martha, it'll make up for what he's tasted already", said her husband.

"We know you're a vegetarian, Owen", added Mrs Farr. "Catherine can sort something edible for you."

Owen could not refuse such friendly hospitality. Whether he was ready or not, the meeting with his sister's friend was to come sooner than he had intended.

Back at the Goggin, he spent the second evening as a caretaker finishing the book he had been reading on the train, and checking the passages he had noted.

Notebook - 8th April:

'Finally, I came to rest opposite a superb oak that spread its roots on one side into a stream just where it sidles under a slab-bridge and worms its devious way onwards towards a belt of woodland. I do not know whether this oak has a name but it is certainly a monument of the Marches.'

H.J. Massingham: 'The Southern Marches', (p. 121)

CHAPTER 4

Notebook - '9th April: Walk with Milo.

At the site of an impressive motte and bailey fortification lying to the east of Gulible and located on a 'tump' near the junction of the Melglyn Brook with the River Monnow. The prominence of the spot makes for an excellent look-out place because it overlooks the entrance to the narrow valley of the brook, where the slopes are steep, and the Monnow on the other, as well as the southern approach to Mynydd y rhibo, which everyone here calls 'Rhibo Mountain'.

I can imagine a wooden palisade surrounding a fortified timber stronghold on this hillock when it was a frontier outpost of the Norman English. The setting was probably a landscape of large forests overshadowed by the Black Mountains - a forbidding expanse of inhospitable land. Perhaps the Welsh were still the main inhabitants of the area at that time. Now, the motte is covered in scrub and occupied by a gigantic and venerable ash tree, the largest tree of its kind I have ever seen. Was it planted in such an eminent position, or did it arrive naturally like all the other trees and bushes which are attempting to reclaim this site for the lost woodland? The tree must be over two hundred years old. Its lower limbs have the girth of the everyday ash tree found along the brooks hereabouts. It looks healthy enough, but one of the higher branches disports a bracket fungus which Milo says is Inonotus hispidus, a species crying out for a common name.

As I write this, Milo has gone off to a nearby farm to see if he can borrow a ladder - he wants to look at the lichens higher up on the trunk of the tree. So far, he has discovered some uncommon lichens on the bark, lichens which are found only on ancient trees in unpolluted areas. He hopes to discover some really rare ones - if he can get a ladder. Apparently, 265 species of lichen have been recorded on ash in Britain, and the tree is second only to oak in this respect, which has 326. According to the oddments of information Milo is passing on, some epiphytes are relics of the wildwood, the ancient forest cover of the country, and indicate continuity of woodland conditions and micro-climate. The Deer Haye, with its long history of stability, is what Milo calls a 'refugium' for epiphytes. It has over 200 lichen taxa recorded for it, many of which are the indicator species which confirm continuity. And the Monnow valley is supposed to be renowned for its flies! What next?

It is not difficult to imagine a forest scene enclosing this tump - the name used locally for a small hill. The surrounding countryside still has a sylvan raggedness which *conjures up a picture of not-so-long departed forests. There are still numerous large woods - some of them without conifers. But I can see a very large wood away to the east where conifers have made the same incursion into and among the natives that the Normans probably achieved eight hundred years ago. But the conifer incursions are nowhere near the overbearing sight that they are in Northumberland. At least, the old ash beside me has asserted the native right to regain tenure of a once conquered site.*

There is something serene about an open-grown and free-standing tree. It can be seen entirely, without any neighbouring distractions; in this case, elevated and supreme, visible and impressive from afar. Obviously, the Normans knew what they were doing when they chose this site for one of their mottes...'

Milo interrupted Owen's gathering reverie. He had been successful in borrowing a ladder, an aluminium one, from the nearby farm called Trellwyn. Hurriedly, he placed it against the tree, asking Owen to steady it at the base, and then rushed up the first few rungs. When he stopped, he peered intently at the bark, his nose making contact with the trunk. He was well equipped for his obsessive interest, carrying around his neck, on separate pieces of cord, a hand-lens, a pouch for samples, a pen and a small notebook. Owen observed him closely from below as he scrutinised the corrugations in the bark and then balanced precariously to record a find. Within minutes, he decided that it would be easier to enlist Owen's help in recording his findings. He dropped his notebook down to him and began to shout out short-hand Latin names which, of course, only he understood.

Keeping pace with such enthusiasm when it is not your own was well known to Owen; difficult at the best of times, without having to write it down. At least, it was not as chaotic as Suzy's.

There came a pause in the dictation. Owen looked up to see Milo scrambling out onto the lowest of the tree's limbs, and lying along it with one boot pressed firmly against the trunk to steady himself. There was a long observational silence - the longest yet. It was broken by a howl of delight as Milo jerked around, almost falling out of the tree, shouting loudly - "Anaptychia! I've found it! Whoopee! Owen; Anaptychia ciliaris* - a sunshine species. The rarest find yet."

After this discovery, he seemed to calm down and muttered his additional findings in matter-of-fact tones. Owen's list became a lengthy one of meaningless items, for most of the lichens did not have common names. The overwhelming complexity of the Latin versions removed any initial interest he might have had in learning some of the identities. When Milo finally descended the ladder, Owen handed him the notebook and, with a voice subdued by a drenching in taxanomic Latin, asked, "How long did it take you to learn all these awkward names?"

"Oh, I don't know. It's all happened gradually by repeated observation and osmosis. What does it matter? This ash is what matters. Its epiphytes now make it a special tree. It needs a Tree Preservation Order on it."

"It was a special tree before", added Owen, "for its history and its presence. You're probably not the first person to have climbed into it, though you're probably the first to have done it for lichens. I wonder how many people have stood on this spot, staring up into its branches..."

He would have gone on, but Milo was already pouring over the plant fragments he had collected in his pouch. So Owen kept his thoughts to himself, stepping back from the ash to get another complete view of it. As he contemplated its dimensions, he was again taken back in time. He imagined the Norman fortress in its heyday, surrounded, or not far from, ('by') countless trees of a similar stature and agedness, the guardians of the forests and the isolated woods. He had seen old trees before, the occasional ones in parkland and botanical gardens, but there was something different about this one and the ones he had glimpsed from the edge of the Deer Haye. He sank deeper into the early medieval period, imagining himself as a traveller following a primitive track through the local forest towards the fortress. Would a traveller of the time have stopped and marvelled at the old trees along the way? Or would they have been more concerned for their personal safety, being unsettled by the awesome appearance of the venerable denizens of the forests? How many of his own ancestors, he thought, had been awestruck by such trees to the point of shivering fright?

"Okay, let's go for that walk now", said a voice from the distance. "Owen!" called Milo, gathering his things together. There was another moment's silence while the medieval peasant came back to the present.

"What about the ladder?" he reminded Milo.

"Oh, yes... Then we can make our way on to Rhibo Mountain. I'm glad I found time to survey this tree instead of having to make a lichen list of a fallen butt, as I have done so many times before."

This comment intimated to Owen that there was more to come. He was getting used to Milo's conversation and the sorry tales which flavoured it with doom. As they carried the ladder back to the farm at Trellywn, Milo remembered the saga of a grove of oaks on Carling Medlar's estate at The Prospect. His inspection of the trees during a meeting of the Royal Forestry Society revealed them to hold one of the best collections of lichens in the Southern Marches. But the grove had been planted and nurtured for timber, not for epiphytes, and after an hundred and eighty years of growth had matured into what the forester called 'veneer trees', ones that were of such high quality timber that they were good enough to peel rather than plank. Of course, as soon as the forestry agent recommended the sale of the trees, and obtained a felling licence, a dispute arose between the estate and the local conservationists, led by Milo.

His plan of action had been to persuade the 'Meddling Baron' to manage the grove as an elite stand of trees, producing approved quality seed. This way, only a few of the trees - the less than perfect specimens - would be felled. When the trees were valued at almost a thousand pounds each, their fate was sealed. Although the Nature Conservancy Council were involved, eager to designate the grove as a Site of Special Scientific Interest - a triple S I in the jargon of the conservationist - all that could be saved in the end were a few trees, the ones with the very rarest epiphytes. Milo admitted that when he realised the campaign was all but lost, he performed an 'Owen Forrest' - a disappearance act. He went to stay with some old friends in Mid-Wales without telling Alison where he had gone. Until he telephoned her late the next day to explain what had happened and where he was, she was thinking all sorts of terrible thoughts. He went on, without any urging from Owen, to admit that the loss of the grove was such a personal catastrophe, it undermined the whole raison d'être for his study and for continuing his lichen searches. It was only the counselling of a mentor, a distinguished botanist who specialised in lichens, which brought him round.

The story came to an end as they deposited the ladder at the farm. Milo had become progressively more subdued in telling it and was now visibly dejected. Having known him for only a very short time, Owen was concerned to see him so despondent. As they made their way onto Rhibo Mountain, following the footpath from the farm, he tried, somewhat awkwardly, to cheer up his companion. He asked what assignment Alison had been given to occupy her day off that was better than a walk on the Mountain. The look of sullen seriousness on his face gave way a little. She was covering the sudden discovery of some prehistoric implements unearthed by a farmer quarrying stone for a new roadway. She was going to write a report for the local archaeological society, and would probably end up writing an article for the paper as well. He gave Owen some background information on Alison's archaeological connections.

Whether Milo realised it or not, the question did succeed in bringing him out of his dejection. And the subject of archaeology gave Owen the chance to enquire also into the folklore associated with Mynydd y rhibo. Milo made some disjointed comments in reply. Various mysteries were supposed to be connected with the mountain. It was reputed to be the burial place of a number of Celtic chieftains. If true, this suggested that its place in Celtic mythology was important before the local chiefs started dying. There was even an Arthurian connection somewhere.

Milo was throwing away information without really giving

any corroborating details. When Owen picked him up on this, and also asked for a translation of the name 'Rhibo', he was told to talk to Catherine Farr, who lived at Bodcut Farm. He said that she and Suzy were as 'thick as thieves'. She would know where all the details could be found because she was the assistant curator at the County Records Office.

"And she might like to meet you", he added, with a saucy grin which completed his rehabilitation.

They were now following a track, a wide bridleway bordered by hedges, which ran in a more-or-less straight direction (except for the deviations of time) up the southern ridge of the whale-backed hill due north towards its summit, where a trig point marked the height of 327 metres. As before, the massive edge of the Black Mountains dominated the views to the west. Its bareness, delimited the whole scene as a frontier country. The ragged line between the enclosed pasture-land of the lower slopes and the openness of the bracken-covered middle slopes marked the change from marginal farming to tempered wilderness. Scattered thorn trees and rowan made diminutive gestures of defiance against this wall of waste, clawing back their former ground and reaching the brown sparsely heather-clad upper slopes in the more sheltered places. The gullies on the upper slopes, high-lighted by the low angle of the sun, cut through the tawny bracken waste and disappeared into tree-lined field boundaries. The small, awkwardly shaped pastures, which had gone as far as they could go against the wall of waste, were enclosed by hedgerows whose sinuosity and raggedness gave them away as remnants of the forest cover from which they were hewn. In places, it seemed that the pastures were being reclaimed by trees. Indeed, the balance between wildness and culture seemed not to lie solely in the linear division between field and waste - it lay also in the aura of the setting and in the impact this had upon the human mind.

"And there's the cursed place", said Milo, still dwelling on the setbacks of the past, and pointing in the other direction, away to the east, beyond The Goggin — "The Prospect: the evergreen palace of the Meddling Baron. Its original name was New Buildings Farm until he bought it. You can pick it out by all the conifer plantations around it, especially those linear shelterbelts. But the real Medlar blot on the landscape is that plantation over there which disappears behind The Goggin. Before the Baron got hold of the land, it was the equivalent of the old medieval wood pasture - a couple of large pasture fields with a scattering of declining oak pollards. It was quite a striking feature from this side of the valley but more so from The Goggin. Medlar bought the land and bulldozed it clear before I got involved with wildlife conservation in this area. If the trees were good for lichens, there was no record of it. The few that are left in the hedges are not bad. Anyway, it's too late now."

Owen was not very interested in looking in that direction, nor at the distant evergreen grandeur of The Prospect. He left Milo to his regrets, for he wanted to revel in the walk; in the breeze that was stiffening as they neared the summit; in the frontier to the west; and, particularly, in the views to the south. Some of the ground he traversed walking backwards, to enjoy the southern vista without terminating the enjoyment of the climb, and without losing contact with Milo, who was surging ahead in the manner of someone who had seen it all before. The shallow upland valley that lay before him was full of striations trending across the view, field boundaries following the line of the slopes and foreshortened to such an extent that the impression conveyed was one of a threadbare forest - or a land where trees were reclaiming their lost inheritance. With an occasional squint, and the glaze of water in the eyes induced by the breeze, he could see a primeval forest before him and imagined for a moment that he was a shaven-faced intruder from the past reconnoitring new territory.

During a period of backward-looking revelry, Milo began telling him about an old small-leaved lime tree which stood near an outcrop of psammosteus limestone* below the summit, not far from the trig point. He went on at some length about the tree's age and stature, unusual leaf shape and early flowering and, of course, its lichens, assuming that his companion was listening to every word. When he came to the end of his little discourse and there was no reply, he looked around to see Owen with his back to him gazing rapturously towards the south.

"Owen; Owen! Are you still here?" he asked, sarcastically, remembering what Suzy had told her friends about her brother. Owen started from his absent-minded state and nodded affirmatively. "Have you been listening, or were you miles away?"

"Yes, I've been listening", he replied, in a not very convincing manner. "That hill away to the south is Ysgyryd Fawr, isn't it?" he asked, getting the pronouncement wrong.

Milo confirmed the sighting, adding that it was commonly called 'The Skirrid', to save the tongue being twisted out of shape. He went on to say something about the steepness of the climb onto its summit, but Owen's attention was still miles away. He was struck by the apparent timelessness of the scenes below. He felt again that this edge of England possessed an atmosphere steeped in history. Its trees and woodland remnants were closer to the primeval forest than anywhere he knew. Again, he tried to imagine how the scene would have appeared before the forest was decimated, but his musing was interrupted once more by Milo telling him that the trig point was just up ahead.

When they reached the whitened piece of concrete, the panoramic vistas and the stiff breeze aroused Owen's emotions even more. Milo pointed out the landmarks around them, beginning with the view to the south. The Skirrid was serene in its isolation. Seen edge-on as a narrow ridge, its craggy summit appeared like a buckled canine tooth. Beyond it were the hills which surrounded Abergavenny, the Blorenge and the Sugar Loaf. In the foreground in the south-east, rose up Craig Syfyrddin and the hills of Garway and Orcop. Away to the north, beyond the ridges which hid the Wye valley from view, was the distinctive but very distant outline of Brown Clee, the highest of the Clee Hills in Shropshire; and nearer, the wooded hills and uplands of middle and northern Herefordshire. Just visible in the distant east were the crumpled tops of the Malvern Hills, and this side of them, somewhere in the middle distance, the city of Hereford itself, lying low and only partially discernible.

Milo could see that Owen was enraptured for he was repeating the word 'fantastic' in soft, lengthy syllables as he drifted around the trig point taking in the panorama. His open exaltation gradually affected the analytical mind of his companion; not to the extent that he became moved by the scenery; he merely took the credit for his companion's state of enjoyment. He congratulated himself on the choice of Rhibo Mountain as the hill by which to introduce Owen to the area. Walking away from the trig point he said, "Come over here, Owen. You can see the Deer Haye clearly from here."

Moving to the eastern side of the ridge that was the hill's summit, Owen was presented with a picturesque view of the furthest reaches of the Deer Haye, its nearer parts hidden from view by the remnant forest of Coed Tirion Glas, which sheltered it from the westerly winds. Llandyfrig Court was just visible through the trees. From where they stood, the Haye could be seen occupying the undulating ground at the base of the mountain. Aged trees dotted the pastureland and climbed up through bracken-covered slopes, lightly wooded, to merge with Coed Tirion Glas. Owen was mesmerised, but Milo was already moving on from the trig point towards the upper edge of the wood and to the tree he had described earlier.

"And there's that lime, the top of it at least."

"What lime?" asked Owen.

"I thought you weren't listening when I told you about it earlier", said Milo.

"You said something about trees that come into leaf early being good for lichens", said Owen quickly to show that he had been listening, but proving only that he had not. When he saw the look on Milo's face, he continued in an interested tone: "Can we get down to it?"

Without saying anything and wearing a faint look of annoyance, Milo turned and led the way to the tree. He remained silent until they reached a point where the ground fell away steeply, revealing an outcrop of light coloured rocks below which there stood an isolated tree.

"That is one of the last ancient small-leaved limes in the southern Marches", he said, "a descendent of a long line of lime trees which, according to a bog in the Monnow valley, has a continuous history of presence in the area. One estimate puts it at over four hundred years old. It's the only one of its kind hereabouts where I've found Lobaria pulmonaria, or Tree Lungwort to you, and Caloplaca lucifugar, two lichens that are relic species of ancient woodland."*

The expression of disbelief on Owen's face was remarkable. He was staring with his mouth agape, fixed to the spot. What they were looking at was a huge tree, towering above the rocks, although its top had been blown out, and standing at the top of a denuded dingle close to a narrow coniferous plantation which fringed Coed Tirion Glas on its southern side. Like all limes, it could not be mistaken for any other species, though leafless, its crown descending to the ground in pendulous limbs. Owen was so astonished that he became alert at last, asking Milo to repeat what he had said about the tree's special features. Milo gave him another admonishing look and then said again that it always flowered earlier than any other limes in the district, even large-leaved ones and those lower down in more sheltered places like the Deer Haye, and that it had 'deviant leaves'.

"Deviant leaves!" exclaimed Owen incredulously. "How can leaves be deviant?"

"Their shape differs from the type, that's all", replied Milo apologetically, lacking the enthusiasm to explain any further. "I'll show you what I mean when it comes into leaf. Some of its leaf-buds are beginning to swell already."

He beckoned Owen to his side to show him the buds and then moved under the pendulous boughs to reach the trunk, where he broke out of his take-it-or-leave-it mien into another dry monologue about lichens. He explained that the lime had a very unusual collection of lichens on it, nothing exceedingly rare nor exclusive to itself, but a unique mixture of species not found together, to his knowledge, on any other small-leaf lime – even though limes generally were not noted for their 'epiflora'. A rare beetle was also linked with it.

"Nothing conforms to the type on this mountain. A friend of mine, who made a classification of the woods in Herefordshire, came up with four limewood types, one of which had only a single wood - Coed Tirion Glas. For some strange reason, we couldn't work out why the computer analysis separated it off from the other woods. He kept re-running the programme, but the wood always came out on its own."

Owen remained on the edge of the crown, pondering the magnificence of the tree and peering in all directions around the site. Again, the two men were poles apart; Milo absorbed in his lichens, checking the trunk once more with his hand-lens; and Owen absorbed in the presence of the tree and the ambience of its location. It was only an accidental glance at his watch which made Milo aware of how late in the afternoon it was. Without a wrench or any apparent regret, he muttered, "Come on, Owen, it's time to go back. I promised Alison I'd pick her up from the farm she's visiting."

Reluctantly, and painfully, Owen pulled himself away and began to follow, for Milo was already walking down the shoulder of the dingle. But the wrench was too much for him. Calling to Milo, who was now some distance away from the tree, he said that he wanted to stay on the mountain a little longer and would make his own way back to the cottage. Milo said something about him not getting lost and seeing him another day, and then disappeared from view. Owen returned to the tree and sat down on the rocks above it. It was not long before he was writing in his notebook again.

Ancient Small-Leaved Lime: Rhibo Mountain.

There is something strange about this tree and its location. According to Milo, it flowers earlier than other limes in the district, has unusually shaped leaves, (deviant ones!) and has a unique collection of lichens, including some species which link it with the long-lost wildwood. A pollen record of a bog in the Monnow valley proves that limes have occupied the Mountain since the time of their arrival in Britain in late Boreal times. Apparently, they have survived in ancient woods and on ungrazed scarps elsewhere in Herefordshire. A rare beetle (Ernoporus caucasicus), peculiar to lime and found locally only in the Deer Haye, has established an outpost here. And that is what this place feels like - an outpost. After only a short while here, I feel that there is more than just a strange tree in a strange place. The stillness, even on a breezy day, is so unusual that you feel compelled to listen. I do, anyway.

This veteran tree stands below an outcrop of limestone above a shallow dingle, near a spring which issues from the rocks and feeds the Melglyn Brook; defiantly close to a conifer plantation of Douglas Fir and Western Red Cedar. The vantage point is one of extraordinary vistas towards the Goggin and the south. The mountain must have been a special look-out place when the primeval forest was being opened up. The tree stands by the rocks like a sentinel, a solitary, watchful sentinel; one of the last great trees of a vanished forest, still holding a commanding position but without a great expanse of woodland below, only a remnant - Coed Tirion Glas. It now overlooks an empty dingle crowded with primroses that are squeezed into all sorts of crevices, and perched on sheep-made micro-terraces. Although rather bare, even with the flowers, the dingle is sheltered and open to the midday sun. And yet, there is something inauspicious, even ominous, about the proximity of the coniferous plantation. It is unsettling to see it there. Whoever planted it has desecrated the beauty of this place. Why do such things have to happen?

This lime is supposed to be over four hundred years old. It certainly looks venerable - well past its prime. Though even now, it rises up majestically and carries a huge crown of ascending limbs which contrast starkly with those branches blasted by age. The rock outcrop above gives a stunning view into its damaged crown. Some of the limbs display a greater purple sheen than is common for lime. One high branch has a bulbous swelling supporting a great bush of mistletoe which spreads down and around it. Another carries a tangled mass of twigs growing in all directions from a dark centre. There is historic character here.

Its trunk is immense, measuring six large paces around the base, and rising to about fifteen feet before branching. It is also completely clean of epicormic growth and has none of those great bulbous swellings commonly seen on limes which have been hacked or pleached. It is an unscathed forest giant from the past, giving way at last to decay and the chiselling of woodpeckers.

I can see I'm going to spend a lot of time here. Suzy knows me too well - I am wilting.

The Melglyn Stoggle

CHAPTER 5

'The tree which moves
Some to tears of joy
Is in the eyes of others
Only a green thing which
Stands in the way.'

William Blake

On the morning of his lunch date with the Farr family, Owen decided to set off for the engagement early, occupying a couple of hours or so on a circular journey towards Bodcut Farm via Elchon and Onen. From the Goggin, he cycled cautiously to Elchon and climbed the long haul of the spur onto the ridge, where breathtaking views rewarded him for the effort; similar vistas to those seen from Rhibo Mountain. But it was the intricate landscape of the succession of ridges either side of him which occupied his attention whenever he stopped. The way the ridges collapsed into the narrow valley bottoms, their descents accentuated by hedge lines which linked into tree-scattered defiles where brooks etched lines southwards. The narrow road, with its long straight stretches, was on top of everything, revealing the lie of the land below, as well as the distant scenes beyond: but only almost on top of everything. There was a buzzard in the sky above him surveying the same scenes below. Its mewing was hanging in the air, and dissipating gently, a sound which made the listener beg for more. He was reminded of Northumberland again. His thoughts wandered off the tarmac track...

Notebook - 10th April:

Keeping to the tops in Celtic times would not only have had the benefits of passage and surveillance. With the valleys densely wooded and impenetrable, it was probably safer, as well as easier, to traverse the country on the ridges. But the views would have been vastly different; the valleys hidden by trees, the configuration of the ground masked by a continuous canopy of crowns, smoothing and softening the contours. Climbing a tall tree would give the Celt a panoramic vista - a buzzard's perspective - and knowledge of encampments elsewhere, even of those two days' march away. How many clearings would be seen? How many changes would be observed in a lifetime? What would the surroundings feel like? Had the prominent landscape features been given names? What had the area been called...?

As Owen had begun to discover from his reading, Bodcut Farm lay on the fringes of Ewyas - an old frontier land which had given its name to a village; where the transition from Welsh to English ascendancy in farming, and from continuous forest to fields surrounded by trees were late in coming, and where the encroachments of the modern world had been delayed. It was situated on the eastern side of the valley of the Dol Barcut Brook, close to one of its tributaries, occupying a ledge of land above the dingle which carried the feeder stream. Unlike the dingle of the Melglyn Brook, trees still lined the edges of the waterway - alder, ash, maple, hawthorn, goat willow, and dead elms - those whitened reminders of how catastrophic change can be.

The ungated entrance into the farmyard was wide, with a wall against the lane on either side. Its width had saved Owen from a nastier accident. The concreted expanse which he freewheeled into was enclosed on its other three sides by buildings, the actual farmhouse itself positioned directly opposite the entrance. As stone farmhouses go, it was not all that special, except that the stones were thinly coursed greensand, very much in need of pointing up. Its most notable features were a stone slate roof and a broad front door which vied with a heavy oak lintel for supremacy of impact. There was no front garden, only a corridor of flagstones between the house and a low wall against the yard, a wall made higher by Victorian iron railings painted deep, rust-proof red. This barrier continued beyond the sides of the house, enclosing its actual garden at the back, the equivalent of a green yard. If there was a building of 'character', it was the long stone barn positioned lengthways on the west of the yard with one gable end against the lane. It, too, had a fine stone slate roof, but its finest architectural details were an open archway entrance into the farm workshop, or waste metal dump, on one side, and a flight of stone steps in the middle leading to a small doorway into the roof-space.

Owen wheeled his precious piece of metal into the workshop

- it seemed the most convenient place to leave it. He was to leave it there whenever he visited the farm in the future. Fascinated by the stone steps, he climbed them and sat down on the huge stone slab at the top. The elevated position gave a clear view of the yard, and a view south across the lane into the dingle. On the other side of the yard there stood the largest building of all, a mammoth barn divided in two by a roadway through its middle. Its lower section was of stone, the middle of timber shuttering, and the roof of metal sheeting, the last two surfaces painted black. The roadway through it turned an awkward corner before climbing up a bank onto a man-made ledge which accommodated the newer buildings of the farm, the ones constructed of iron stanchions and cross members, concrete blocks and asbestos roofing. One was a byre for the lumbering beasts of the field; another, a covered silage store. There was also a long single storey stone building behind the house on the east, and various huts in odd corners all over the place. As farms go, it did not appear prosperous, nor did it look run down; it just looked worn. Sheep were its tradition and Owen had moved to the area just after lambing time, when the noise of new arrivals was piercing the air at every turn. He could hear a chorus of motherly bleats and pathetic cries from where he sat, so many that it took him a while to realise that he was being spoken to from the yard.

It was Catherine Farr. When he turned to face her, unaware of the identity of the speaker, he was unready for what he saw. If he had a preconception of the appearance of his sister's friend, it was dispelled at once. Whatever he had expected, it was not to see such a striking face. She resembled her father in this respect - high cheek-bones, slanted grey-blue eyes, and slightly flared nostrils - sharply defined features held within a taut skin; features which projected her face, giving it resounding hints of exquisite beauty and stoicism at the same time. Her hair was short and straight, just reaching to her neck; a light shade of brown with a lustre which matched the sheen on her face. Its style of cut, and the plainness of her attire was typical of the clean, conservative country look; but her face and her youthfulness shattered any impression of staid dress in her appearance. For a moment, Owen experienced an unusual mixture of feelings.

He made a clumsy descent to the yard, but when he reached it, he was not quite on the ground. Or rather, he was unaware of the surface beneath his feet. He was not unduly shy, but in this instance, his confidence and composure seemed to be reluctant to leave the steps and join him. The introduction which took place was an embarrassing one for both of them. As they shook hands, his tentative offering went limp in her palm.

"I'm sorry about your accident. What a coincidence it was our yard? You're not still suffering, are you? Suzy said you were a zealous cyclist." The questions came out rather quickly.

"I'm alright", was the dismissive answer. "It's not the first time I've come off my bike; but it was the first time to happen in a farmyard amid such filth."

"Why haven't you got a car, or a motor-cycle?"

"I haven't needed one yet. And I haven't been able to afford one either. I can't bear the thought of owning a second-hand vehicle which calls for continuous maintenance. And I prefer to hear the countryside I'm passing through."

There was another pause in the conversation.

"Your hair is much lighter than Suzy's. Don't you inherit it from one of your grandparents? "

"Yes, from our maternal grandmother. But mine is only a watered down version. Suzy was the one to inherit the strong colour, the strong looks, and the strong temperament of Gran. You look like your father."

"I know; everyone tells me that."

There was another pause. Then she invited him into the house. He managed a smile before following her across the yard.

For some reason, there were only four of them at lunch. Catherine's brother was elsewhere. Owen was asked a lot of questions about himself, and some concerning Suzy.

"What made you become a vegetarian?" asked Mrs Farr, as Owen cut into a nut rissole cooked by Catherine.

"When I was at school, I used to stay with a friend whose whole family were vegetarians. Somehow, I came to prefer their food to ours."

"What was Suzy like as a sister when she was growing up? – that's what I'd like to know" interjected Lloyd Farr.

"Father, that's not a very fair question to ask him", interrupted Catherine, quickly.

"But it's an interesting question, isn't it Owen?" said her father, smiling at Owen.

"It's a question I've been asked before", replied Owen with a nonchalant look. "I've had to accept that my elder sister is a carbon copy of Gran, and like Gran her personality can be wearing at times. When she got too much for me, I used to absent myself. That's why I stayed with my friend and his family so much, when I had the chance. I think Mum and Dad could have done with some periods of respite as well, but they had to wait until she went off to art college. Anyway, they both had the experience of Gran to prepare them for Suzy. What are your two like as kids and companions?" he asked, turning the question around and looking at Catherine's parents with a wry smile.

"They didn't get in each other's way, only ours" said Lloyd Farr, curtly.

"Now that's not fair, Lloyd", said his wife, hurriedly. "You've spent most of your time outside – and with their help when you needed it".

"We get on alright", remarked Catherine. "Ralph has helped or hindered Dad for as long as I can remember so we haven't had many chances to get in each other's way. He's become so imbued with farming and all its jargon that we are not really on the same wavelength."

"'Imbued'? – And what does that mean Catherine?" asked her father imperiously.

"Sodden with it", she replied cheekily.

"Alright you two", said Martha Farr. "Now let's enjoy our meal."

After lunch, Catherine wasted no time introducing Owen to the current task of caring for ailing and orphaned lambs; a task he took up readily. He stayed for tea and afterwards they went outside again to check the lambs. The day was so absorbing that by the time the introduction to lambing was over, he was too weary and it was too late to cycle home. He was invited to stay overnight and to help out the next day, if he wanted to. He did. In the end, he stayed on for two days, helping the family care for the lambs, because the weather turned bad as a depression came over, bringing persistent drizzle. Another hand was sorely needed to rescue ailing, bedraggled, and improperly mothered lambs lying deserted and too weak to walk in the fields. Some ewes had aborted so Lloyd Farr was expecting the worse. Catherine took a day off to help as well. Mrs. Farr was delighted to have his help. She told him he was good at caring for lambs, as good as Catherine when she could spare the time to help. And Lloyd Farr was pleased to have an extra hand, so pleased that he asked Owen to help out on a number of other jobs in the coming weeks. He found working with Owen easy-going, which contrasted markedly with the way he got on with his own son.It did not take Owen long to realise that Ralph and his father did not fit well together, neither temperamentally nor in their attitudes to farming. He gathered from Catherine that Ralph was always talking about 'systems' of farming, and always impatient to try something new. He was forever giving the impression that he could not wait to be in charge himself, which was not only proving presumptuous to his father but also an aggravation to him.

Differences between father and son seemed to run in the Farr family. As Owen soon learned, Lloyd's father was a taciturn man who was very set in his ways and who rarely visited the farm. He could no longer bear to see the place - it was too painful a loss to him. As Owen was to discover, he was simply instilled with an ancient tradition of shepherding which he continued at Gwenynog, his retirement holding near the Melglyn Dingle, with a few sheep and his old sheep-dog. It had been the fatigue of a recurring illness, aggravated by new developments in farming, which had finally persuaded him to hand over the farm to his son and retire to Gwenynog. There, he and his wife had joined Catherine's maternal grandparents, Rowena and Jack Parry, not long before Jack, a local woodman, had died. The two couples had been life-long friends.

Lloyd Farr had rarely clashed with his father. They had not communicated well enough to clash. The old man had expected his son to pick up the job and its imperatives as he went along, in the time-honoured way, without question. If he perpetuated any of his father's traits, it was his conservatism for spending money. Other than this, he was different because the times were different and because his generation was different. He was reasonably receptive to new ideas because it was his generation which was the first to be supplied with bureaucratic and scientific explanations as to what the hill farmer should be doing and why. But he took his time getting used to the new ideas. And he was reluctant to spend a lot of money unless he was left with no other choice. Neither he nor his farm had much money to spare. In the opinion of his son, an opinion often openly and bluntly expressed, he was slow to make changes at Bodcut, and was not investing enough in the future - his son's future.

Unlike his grandfather, Ralph was as far away from being taciturn as he was from the era when the old man had acquired the farm. But he had inherited his brusqueness. He was outspoken and often in dispute with his father, which is why one day he chose to move out of the farmhouse and move in with his grandparents at Gwenynog. Though his grandfather kept himself to himself, he still expected to instil the lad with the art of his ancient tradition. Had Ralph not been the one and only son he and his father might have parted company completely. However, with the regular intercession of Martha Farr, they managed somehow to co-operate with each other, as Lloyd Farr and his father had managed to co-operate. Nevertheless, Ralph's deference to his dad was always grudging, invariably argumentative, and sometimes withdrawn in paroxysms of seemingly irreconcilable disagreement. Mary Farr and the two grandmothers were the intermediaries who appeased the situation and mended the rifts.

Ralph was particularly friendly with Carling Medlar's son, Tim, and influenced very much by the systems and attitudes which underpinned the management of the farm at The Prospect. His most recent preoccupations were with dual-purpose buildings and their flexible systems. Bodcut did not have the range of new prefabricated buildings which were present at The Prospect, nor did it have any of the very large ones present at one or two other farms in the locality. The buildings at The Prospect constituted something of a local mystery because they were hidden from view by coniferous screens and shelterbelts, and because few people ever got near enough to see them. There was no end to the stories circulating the locality about the latest happenings and developments at the place. In this respect, Ralph held a rather privileged position, and he knew it.

Currently, he was into sheep-sheds, those prefabricated aircraft hanger buildings which enable a farmer to house his ewes under one roof during harsh winters and while they lamb, instead of having to consume time checking the edges and corners of every field for new deliveries. This had been a matter of contention between Ralph and his father during the lambing. The only sheep-shed in the locality was close by on the neighbouring farm of Treribble, owned by Arnold Prosser. It was over two hundred feet long and nearly eighty feet wide, with huge galvanised doors at either end. Unlike the larger buildings at The Prospect, it was visible for miles and likely to remain visible for decades. The lightly coloured shed stood out starkly in the local scene, especially when seen from high points like The Goggin and the Ridge Road. Owen had noticed it during his walk with Milo and had tried not to see it. He had seen it from the ridge as well. In terms of scale, it was out of all proportion to the existing cluster of buildings at Treribble Farm. 'Arnold the Treribble' was quietly smug about being the first local farmer to have a sheep-shed but retorted, whenever the building was criticised, that it was not erected to look good but to serve a purpose.

The two days were very busy, especially the Monday. Catherine never left Owen's side. At the end of the day, just before tea, she made a tentative suggestion:

"Owen, can I persuade you to join me at a talk tomorrow evening at the village hall in Ewyas? It's being held by the Ewyas Arts Society. Suzy is the Society's secretary and its driving force. I've got to stand in for her while she's away and try to keep a loosely-run and loosely-supported local group going."

"What's the talk about? Could I cope with the subject?" answered Owen with a hint of disinterest in his voice.

"As you might expect, such a Society has a wide range of subjects on its agenda – anything to do with art from embroidery, corn dollies, love-spoons, and flower-arranging to drawing and painting murals, fine-printing, felt illustration, and so on. But this time, from what Suzy told me before she left, there is a chance that the subject might interest you. The talk is to be on 'Exotic Trees in Landscape Painting', maybe a subject too obscure for the local community. The cancellation of the scheduled talk has led to a contact of Mr de Bohun standing in to speak about trees. If you came, it would give you a chance to meet the illustrious owner of Llandyfrig Court. You have to sometime."

"With a subject like that, I couldn't keep away, even if my sister was there. What time does it start?"

"That's why I asked you because if you're going to be here all day helping out, you might as well stay for tea again. Mum says you can. Okay?"

"Alright, so who's the speaker?"

"I think she's a relative of Mr de Bohun with a passion for foreign trees. I also think she knows both Milo and Mr Medlar, the arch-enemies of our district. Milo won't be there but it is possible that the owner of The Prospect will turn up because he won't have Suzy to inhibit him or make him feel uneasy. Alison won't be there either unfortunately. She's attending another local meeting. So it seems that I shall have to write a short report for the local newspaper. With your interest in trees, perhaps you could help me out?"

"If you need some help, I'll do what I can", replied Owen, suspiciously.

"No, that's not the reason I suggested you come to the meeting Owen", added Catherine, hurriedly.

Owen smiled quiescently.

When Catherine arrived home on Tuesday - earlier than expected - she was surprised to find Owen sitting on the slab at the top of the steps. She expected him to be inside having tea. When he told her what was going on in the house, she understood immediately. By the time they entered the kitchen, the altercation had subsided, but the air could still be cut in two with a knife. Mrs. Farr had managed to mollify the two men and was relieved at the entrance of two other adults who could temper the situation. The meal was a strained one. Owen could not understand why Ralph was staying to eat anyway. He had a choice of places to eat and often had his tea at Gwenynog. Catherine was not disposed to be the intermediary her mother was, for she was more inclined to take her father's side, if she sided with anyone. Her usual demeanour was to treat such altercations as beneath contempt. Owen was glad when the time came to leave. Catherine tried to persuade her mother to join them but she declined, saying discreetly that she could not go anywhere until Lloyd and her son were reconciled, or at least calmed down.

When they arrived at the village hall, the guest, a middle-aged woman, was already there with Mr de Bohun. And so, Owen met the owner of Llandyfrig Court for the first time; a brief introduction at first, for the man was preoccupied with the evening's proceedings. His handshake was rather tight and bony, but there was a sparkling gaze as he looked quickly at a new face. Owen's first impression of the man was of a tall, thin individual with a dishevelled mass of grey hair, a mischievous grin, and a cadaverous handshake.

"So, you're the other half of the furious story young man? Don't wear me out will you? Excuse me while I sort out the evening's deliberations." With that, he rushed away to converse with the speaker.

Once this hurried introduction was over, there was not much he could do, except put a few chairs out while Catherine and Mr de Bohun conferred with the speaker to make sure everything was in hand, and quietly observe them. Owen soon realised why Humphrey de Bohun had a reputation for being amiably eccentric. He had the appearance of a curiously scatter-brained, but likeable man. For his size, he was a nimble man, rather nervous in his movements. He seemed to want to do two things at once; to place the lectern in two places; to say something to Catherine while talking to the visiting speaker at the same time. Catherine appeared reluctant to interfere. She was quite self-assured, but there was a respectful reserve about the way she related to 'Mr de Bohun', as she called him; an almost reverential reserve. However, it was not really her manner which Owen observed but her face. In the drab hall, it was the only compelling prospect. In the stark simplicity of the hall, her rather ordinary clothing made her face that much more exquisite in the purity of its beauty. She had already caught him looking distantly into her face on several occasions during his stay at the farm.

The talk proved to be as revealing for the nature of the audience as for its content. Catherine knew some of the audience, but it was Humphrey de Bohun who hailed the most; one in particular, whose arrival confirmed what she had expected. Making her way over to Owen as discreetly as possible, Catherine quietly explained who he was: "That's Carling Medlar, the imperious owner of The Prospect. It must be the first time he's attended one of these meetings. Mr de Bohun probably encouraged him to come, knowing that Suzy's absence would make his attendance possible." As the new landowner entered the room, he looked around combatively, expecting an eyeball-to-eyeball confrontation with Milo. Owen observed the man as closely as he could without actually staring at him. He had the bearing of a self-possessed person who was inherently aware of being both new to the area and big in the area, commanding and defensive at the same time. He was not a large man, but wide shoulders and an enlarged abdomen made him appear larger than he was. He was impeccably dressed, but the shape of his torso called for a loosely fitting jacket while his trousers were too tight for his waist. Mr de Bohun had saved a seat for him in the front row.

At first, Owen assumed that Carling Medlar would not know who he was, but then he remembered that someone on the local grapevine had special service ties with the vineyard at The Prospect - Ralph. When he drew a couple of stern glances from the man, the sort of glances that would make anyone quake on the spot, he felt known already. Was the reputation of the sister to be visited on the brother, he thought? Sitting next to Catherine and receiving friendly looks from Humphrey de Bohun was inevitably to place him in some kind of local limelight - the limelight upon which his sister thrived. He drew some other equally remote but more curious glances from elsewhere in the audience, similar to the ones he had received in the store at Gulible. For him, the speaker was the central figure of the evening, not Suzy Forrest's brother.

The speaker charted the appearance of exotic trees in landscape painting, drawing particular attention to the time it took for certain trees, especially conifers, to make their presence felt in the English countryside. She noted that it was not really until the late eighteenth and nineteenth centuries that conifers made their mark, as experiments in forestry progressed, and as the Victorians used the evergreen giants of North America to "distinguish" - in the words of an eminent contemporary botanist - "the residence of the large landed proprietor from those of his more humble neighbours".*

The fashion of the wealthy landowners to have their properties glorified in oils and water-colours was beautifully illustrated with slides. This had a particular effect upon Carling Medlar. After the talk, he was the first person in the audience to corner the speaker, wishing to know if she could recommend any artists who could paint some scenes of The Prospect for him. Innocently, the speaker said that Humphrey knew a young local female artist who might oblige. "Suzy Forrest is her name, I think." The point was dismissed out of hand, irritably, which made the speaker somewhat reluctant to recommend artists to such a bellicose man. Had Owen been close enough to hear Medlar's reaction, he would have experienced at first hand the animosity the man held towards Suzy. He knew already that it had something to do with the man's son. All he noticed at the time was that other members of the audience, eager to have a word with the speaker, were unwilling to approach too close while the owner of The Prospect held the foreground. The speaker was pleased to turn her attention to the questions of others in the audience.

Owen's patient waiting for Catherine to extricate herself from the business of closing up the meeting was rewarded in an unexpected way. Before they left the hall, Humphrey de Bohun invited him to visit the Court and promised to show him around the Deer Haye. The evening had been worthwhile in more ways than he had expected. When Catherine dropped him off at the Goggin, nothing was said by either party about their next get together.

CHAPTER 6

'You are a Gentle Son of Dyn
You hear the Gentle Trees of a passing Gentle Time
You feel the baleful anguish of my Soul
Let the echoes of Y Coed resound in you.'

Spirit of Y Coed

On the day after the meeting at Ewyas, Owen was roused at 5.30am by noises coming from outside and above. It was the wind eddying around the cottage, and reverberating in the roof-space. Groggily, he roused himself and went downstairs. The boisterous buffetings of the house while he made some tea, and the internal agitation of the pliant or loose fittings of the living room as draughts surged in from everywhere, unsettled him. He preferred to be outside to feel the wind on his face. So he decided to forego breakfast and experience this morning of atmospheric turmoil from the top of a hill, taking with him some pieces of flapjack made by Catherine's mother. Dismissing

The Goggin as the preserve of his sister, he chose to revisit Rhibo Mountain, and take in the lime tree at the source of the Melglyn Brook on his way. Ever since the excursion with Milo, he had wanted to see the tree again, but his lambing duties had intervened to keep him away.

It was not until he got outside the cottage that he realised the true ferocity of the wind. The leafless trees in the garden and along the brook were being assaulted and roared their disapproval. The wind seemed to be blowing from the south-west, which would explain why the cottage was receiving sudden blasts of air - the Goggin hill was partly in the way, and the valley of the brook was serving to funnel the wind. A hard ride was inevitable. Nevertheless, he made the journey without parting company with the bike, although he did have to swerve to avoid a branch blown down into his path.

He left the bike near Gwenynog, the smallholding belonging to Catherine's grandparents, which was located sixty metres or so from the road, at the head of the dingle of the Melglyn Brook. On his visit with Milo he had returned from the tree via Gwenynog, along the footpath which led from the holding to the summit of the Mountain. This time, he ignored the footpath and found his way to the lime by ascending the brook. Although denuded, the dingle had even more primroses in bloom than before. Their felt-like and procumbent leaves and the beauty of their yellow flowers, protected from the elements by the dingle and its irregularities, lent calmness to a morning of gusty weather. Nevertheless, he could hear the wind buffeting the hillside and the trees roundabout, and at times he could feel himself almost being sucked out of the dingle. Walking slowly up the brook, sheltered from the wind and soothed by the colour of the primroses, he did not expect to be faced with such a startling view of the tree as he approached it from below.

When he reached the very top of the dingle, where he could see the lime above him, spreading over the gash in the ground, he was shocked to see the crown of the tree moving about violently. As he approached closer, he could hear its branches clashing. Nearer still, and he could hear it groaning. When he climbed out of the dingle just below the tree, the violence of the wind hit him too. He had difficulty keeping his foothold. Everything was in motion - the conifers in the plantation, the clouds in the sky, the air, his clothes, his sinews and, notably, his heart. The lime seemed to be swaying - or was it his body that was swaying. The tree was obviously under considerable strain; so was he. With crazy abandon - or was it some other urging - he placed one side of his face and one ear against the tense trunk, and gripped the tree to steady himself. The shuddering was tremendous, increasing in intensity as the blasts tore into the crown. He thought he could feel the earth beneath his feet heaving as the tree's roots flexed to keep it upright.

Suddenly, some of the limbs on the dingle side whiplashed causing such creaking and groaning that he jumped away from the trunk. If it should shed any branches, he was safer at its base, but he merely reacted on the spur of the moment. In stepping further away from the massive butt, a blast of wind blew him back towards the dingle. He recovered his balance and withdrew down-slope, looking up into the crown. The stag-headed top seemed to be trembling as the huge limbs below it swung back and forth. He began to tremble. He could see that the tree was under great strain - perhaps anguish - as it tried to withstand the rigours of the gales. Uncannily, he had a sensation of anguish too.

It was while he had his eyes on the ragged top that the sound of cracking reached his ears. He braced himself against the wind, his eyes darting all over the crown trying to locate the limb under stress. Instead of a sudden cracking and an ensuing crash, the noise, wherever it was coming from, continued. Strangely, the agony of the tree became his agony. His body became as taut as the tree as he automatically resisted the wind's buffeting. This tension was accompanied by a growing feeling of heaviness which increased with every second. Then an almighty crack occurred, as loud as a gunshot, as a limb split away from the higher reaches of the main stem. It crashed through the crown down into the dingle, the thud of its impact on the ground echoing but being cut short by the wind. As suddenly and as violently as this happened, his heaviness peaked and then left him completely. But the consequent relief was replaced with a feeling of deep sadness; such sadness that for a brief moment he was on the edge of tears.

High up in the crown of the lime, where there had been a branch carrying an unusual swelling and a large bush of mistletoe, there was now a long gash of white wood. The tree continued to flex with the wind, but not as violently nor as agonisingly as before the crash. The wind seemed to be blowing with less vigour and fewer blasts. His dumbfounded eyes moved from the severed branch to the wound and back. The mistletoe bush was still attached to the limb it had held fast to for so long. Descending into the dingle, he could see that the bush was much larger than it had appeared when suspended above the ground. It was held fast to a swelling, about the size of a beach ball, by a stout stem that was clearly many decades old.

Immediately, he noticed that some of the golden stems of the mistletoe, many of its leaves, and some mummified berries were covered in tiny black globules. He ran his hands around the swelling and discovered that it had cracked underneath. He also noticed that some of the light green buds on the fallen shoots of the lime were breaking into leaf.

He sat on the branch beside the swelling and looked up to the tree. The wind was still disturbing its crown and creating what Owen thought was his first experience of a genuine arboreal lament. He sat where he was for some time, staring at the lime from the comparative calm of the dingle, hearing and seeing the effects of the wind but not feeling them. He thought about going up onto the Mountain, but the experience had rooted him to the spot. As before, on his first visit to the tree, he was reluctant to move. The lime was in need of company. Leaving a wounded and anguished tree by itself in order to enjoy the exhilaration of a mountain top in a strong wind was unreasonable in the circumstances. He scrambled out of the dingle and stood beside the tree. Placing one palm and forearm against its bole, he rested his forehead on the back of his hand. The shuddering had ceased. After a few minutes in this position, listening and feeling, he went up onto the rocks and sat down. Fortunately, he remembered the pieces of flapjack in his pocket. He needed one. It was ages before he moved. And when he left, he went downhill, not uphill. He did not take many strides before he looked back at the tree, a pattern of departure which was repeated as he descended the hill. It took him a while to realise that the wind had abated.

Returning to his bike, he set off down the road towards the Deer Haye, emotionally wounded by the event in the dingle.

He expected to see similar amputations there. He cycled slowly along the road against the Haye, glancing over the high paling fence of split chestnut stakes, behind which there was an internal perimeter ditch giving added height to the boundary. The stakes consisted of two alternating sizes, squared off at their tops as if miniature wooden castellations. Fallen branches and twigs were everywhere, testifying to the ferocity of the recent gale. And at the base of many of the oaks were piles of timber debris, fallen branches and dead wood in all stages of decay, neatly collected together. This was the Deer Haye of the de Bohuns at close hand.

The first major feature to attract his attention was a low hill surmounted by an old tree that was silhouetted against the sky. The tree was the epitome of the Shakespearian oak - 'bald with dry antiquity'*. It had no branches left, only spikes of various lengths, stiffly attached to a very dead trunk which ended in a sharp point. No other trees occupied the hill, but at its base and all around it there were other venerable specimens of distinctive stature, holding their own against the backdrop of Coed Tirion Glas. The leafless garb of winter still prevailed, but the onset of spring showed itself in the bright green young foliage of a number of trees scattered throughout the Haye, particularly in the distance. He thought they must be horse chestnuts to be so advanced in their leafing.

The views into the Deer Haye were so scenic that he dismounted and walked, peering between the chestnut stakes of the deer fence. To one side of the hill, the land sloped down gently to a small, shallow lake bounded on its far side by an area of carr. The echoing cry of some kind of waterfowl tested his knowledge of birds. But it was another tree which caught his eye. Standing alone beside the water, in a direct line to the carr, there was a tall tree, virtually all trunk and leaning at sixty degrees, with sharply ascending limbs which towered above the main stem. It was a poplar, perhaps a black poplar in view of its size and shape. In such an historic setting, it could not be anything else. Had the wind blown it sideways, or was that its normal angle of repose?

Ahead, there was a white house, and opposite it a gate into the park, a large gate of estate proportions. The house had an emphatic name-plate - 'Keeper's Lodge'. He looked around; there was no-one in sight. He leaned his bike against the thick oak post to which the gate was fastened. As he did so, the plaintive cry of a buzzard in the distance reached his ears. His body tingled. He had never before seen so many trees of such stature and ancientness in one place. Most of the ones in the lower part of the Haye were extremely venerable oaks, some decrepit, some dead. There were also a number of sweet chestnuts, over-mature in years, a few exceedingly tall limes, and the occasional horse chestnut, one of which stood close to the gate, a pendulous tree carrying bright young foliage. The rotting butt of another horse chestnut lay on the ground close to the ditch. And totally dwarfed by these massive hulks of ageing, rotting wood there cowered, presumptuously, a future generation of trees, standards and even smaller specimens, hemmed in by stock-proof frames constructed of chestnut stakes. In places, the bareness of the deciduous trees was punctuated by isolated conifers - a few Scots pines adding colour to the scene with the orange of their upper branches, some sombre yews, an enormous Wellingtonia away in the distance, and a young cedar beside the track which led into the park from the gate. Owen spent a long time surveying this scene of rotting history.

From where he was, the road led directly towards the Court, about half a mile away. He moved on. Soon, he saw another entrance in the distance. The road was leading towards a gateway marked by two pillars of stone, and only curved away to the right at the last moment. In the beginning, perhaps, the road might not have carried on. It might have ended at the Court; the only dwelling of any stature to have a road to it. To one side of the pillars, which must once have supported a very heavy gate, there stood a small, timber-framed gatehouse. It stood rather than squatted because it was taller than it was wide and was held together by sturdy uprights and cross-beams of oak. The absence of curtains suggested that it was not inhabited. It had an excellent view of the Deer Haye, overlooking the high paling fence which deterred the roaming instincts of the captive herd of fallow deer.

Again, he felt the auras of history around him. He was someone readily susceptible to their influence: he had never understood why. It was a feeling which came elusively and departed elusively. Romantic nostalgia was a part of it, almost as if he carried the strains of others who had seen the beauty of large trees in deer parks before.

The entrance, even with its cattle-grid, had an historic feel to it, imparted as much by the avenue of old oak trees which enclosed the driveway to the Court as by the gatehouse and the stone pillars. For the drive was a very narrow, unmetalled track, only the width of a green lane, slightly sunken, and proceeding through an avenue of trees so closely set together, and to the drive, that the impression received by Owen was of an approach to a hall of residence set in a wild fastness held by one of the Marcher Lords of the thirteenth century. Whether this aura was real or not, it could have been, for Llandyfrig Court had links with that time, and it was still a somewhat remote estate on the edge of England in an area which he was to discover had a fascinating history.

Leaning his bike against the most weathered and worn of the two pillars, he noticed a tall, but not a broad tree in the corner of the park, growing on the bank of the ditch. It stood out because two mustard coloured bunches of mistletoe were lodged in its crown. He recognised the tree as field maple, even though it was not yet in leaf. Without meaning to, he crossed the aristocratic threshold of the de Bohun family and ambled, somewhat enraptured, along the cordoned drive beneath the oaks. The Court itself could not be seen, for the drive climbed and curved towards the left, disappearing into the stalwart trees which enclosed it. Nor was there much to see through the avenue because of the closeness of the spacing. Indeed, the avenue possessed the forbidding dimensions of an arboreal corridor, and suggested that the dwelling to which it led was either the fortified residence of a Norman warlord or the retreat of a recluse. With creeping feelings of going somewhere he should not, Owen continued along the oaken tunnel. At the curve in the drive, he caught another evocative glimpse of the Deer Haye through the trees. Ahead, he discerned the outlines of a building. Then the Court came properly into view. It was true to its setting - a timber-framed mansion in an historic landscape.

The trees of the avenue gave way to a gravelled reception yard, enclosed on the nearside by some outbuildings, but open to dramatic views of the Deer Haye. Beyond the buildings, there was a wall of deciduous trees with emergent ornamental conifers rising behind them. The driveway continued passed the yard along the edge of the Deer Haye, where a deep ha-ha, and a narrow stretch of grass sporting daffodils, constituted the boundary between the game reserve and the frontage of the house.

There was no garden, in the excepted sense of the word, merely a well-kept lawn, enlivened by more daffodils and crossed by a gravel path lying at right angles to the drive; a path which was guarded by four sentinel-like, small spires of clipped box. Two were set at the junction with the driveway, and two more marked a change in level where the path rose up in steps to the terrace on which the house stood, facing out across an ancient expanse of pasture literally littered with old and decrepit trees and the detritus of their ageing. It was a compelling aspect: one that had remained changeless for centuries; an enduring English scene of aristocratic permanence. The house itself was L-shaped, its two sections being more or less equal in size, but not of the same age. The oldest part, which faced out towards the Deer Haye, appeared, by its construction, to be very old indeed. It consisted of a lower storey of stone of a grey-green hue, supporting a timber-framed upper storey of ornate woodwork. On the nearside, to the right of centre, a huge timber-framed porch, rising from a stone base, imposed itself upon the eye by being a third of the overall size of the section. The younger part on the far side was built entirely of stone, similar in colour to the other but not so well cut, nor so evenly coursed, the whole house carrying a weighty stone slated roof which was full of undulations. It looked as though the enormously heavy roof had tried unsuccessfully to squash the timbers below. It was an austere, antique home, carrying all the connotations associated with an erstwhile aristocratic seat, including the historic, the social and the financial distance. Owen did not have the audacity to venture any nearer. The de Bohun 'playhouse' could remain a stronghold until another day.

Feeling the guilt of a lowly trespasser, he made his way back down the drive faster than he had progressed up it. When he rounded the curve and had a clear view of the pillars guarding the entrance, he saw a man standing near his bike. For a moment, the man disappeared from view behind one of the stone uprights. Then he caught sight of Owen and positioned himself formidably between the pillars, standing with his legs apart and with his hands folded together on a walking stick held away from a midriff of considerable girth. He remained still and silently stern as Owen approached him. He was an elderly man, very stout and suffering from the facial signs of angina. He wore a pair of heavy twill trousers, held up by a wide leather belt falling outwards, a chequered shirt that was wide open at the neck, and a battered Barbour jacket. Owen's immediate reaction was that if the estate had a keeper, this man held the post. But the man remained silent when Owen said "Good morning – or is it afternoon?", and then passed by to reach his bike.

"Have you business at the Court, or just snooping?" asked the man turning round, speaking harshly in a Herefordshire accent, a usually soft tongue.

"No", replied Owen, as politely as possible. "I was just looking at the avenue of trees, if that's alright. I've never seen such a narrow avenue of oaks before."

"You should call in at the Keeper's Lodge down the road if you want to visit any part of the Court without prior arrangement. You're not another one of those conservation surveyors, are you?" He asked this question as if such people were the scourge of the district.

"No, I've only recently arrived in the area and happened to be passing by getting to know my way around. Trees interest me, so I stopped to look."

"Well, in future, I suggest you have the courtesy to get permission first", he retorted, irritated further because Owen was being his usual non-combative self.

"I do have permission. Mr de Bohun has invited me to visit the Court."

"Oh has he. Well I shall have to check on that. What's your name?"

"Owen Forrest"

"Any relation to Suzy Forrest?"

"Yes"

"Well, that explains a lot. Park your bike somewhere else next time."

With that he turned away awkwardly and limped towards the Gatehouse, leaving Owen to mount his bike and ride off without looking back. He set off without thinking about where he was going, cycling back along the road against the Haye, peering through the deer fence. The quietude of reflection upon trees and their past had been dashed by the short altercation with the keeper-like individual. Owen was now feeling tired and a bit fragile, perhaps because he hadn't eaten a proper meal. The sooner he got back to the cottage the better. When the southern extremity of the Haye came to an end, he realised that he had passed the turning which would have taken him homewards; how he had not noticed it, amazed him. He consulted his map to check his exact position and had another piece of flapjack. He discovered that he was not too far away from the turning, but even closer to a bridleway which, he noticed for the first time, led directly to the cottage around the base of the Goggin hill. Although it was now past midday, he decided to continue his exploration of the local countryside. He had often pushed or even carried his bike across county.

The bridleway left the road near where a stream issued from the Deer Haye, one of the tributaries of the Dol Barcut Brook. It descended through a young coniferous plantation which sloped down to the water's edge. The going was good until he approached the brook; then the bridleway became a linear quagmire as it followed the course of the stream. The shoes he had on were no match for the slippery mud. His feet squashed about and the suction of his prints not only made movement difficult but gave him problems keeping his shoes on.

It was while fixed in the mud, adjusting the position of the bike over his shoulder, that he took a long look at the plantation. Where the conifers met the water, an oak leaned out over the brook. It had been used as a straining post for the plantation's perimeter fence. And within the conifers there were other oak trees; only a few, but enough to suggest that the site had once been a broadleaved wood. But that was now gone and the conifers held the ground in their dense, serried ranks, excluding light and entry. The plantation, which was about ten years old, contained a mixture of Douglas fir, western hemlock and western red cedar.

He became downcast at seeing such evergreen colonisation

so close to what was for him a picturesque brook, and while the romanticism of the Deer Haye was still fresh in his mind. He started to feel a little cold inside which induced him to press on through the cold mud. Ahead of him, he could see that the plantation ended at the next curve in the brook. Here, his coldness was deepened by the chilling sight of a row of bird and animal carcasses hooked on to the top strand of barbed wire at the bottom corner of the plantation. Among the carcasses, which were in various stages of decay, were rooks, crows, jays, magpies, squirrels and rabbits. The victims of a mind which relished killing, or a game-keeper's tally for the winter? The view back along the brook from this aerial cemetery of bird-life gave an almost complete prospect of the plantation. The loneliness of the oaks was stark, and the scene suggested that more than just timber trees had been swept away. A foreground of bedraggled corpses only consummated the sense of change. He turned away and carried on. The cottage was now near enough to contemplate comfort.

The prospect of comfort, however, was deferred by the sight of what appeared to be an abandoned farmstead up ahead, set amongst trees against brook. The water was shallow at this point, and there were signs that the bridleway had once deviated to meet a ford. Seen through the leafless trees along the water's edge, the house and its ramshackle buildings, secluded in the dank valley floor of the brook, was cold comfort. If anyone lived there, their existence was bleak. He pressed on.Upon his return to the Goggin, Owen found a folded piece of paper addressed to him wedged between the door and its frame. It contained a scribbled unexpected invitation to join the de Bohuns for lunch the next day, and for an excursion around the Haye, and was signed by Humphrey himself. It had obviously been delivered during his absence, but why so soon? Had Catherine said something to them on his behalf? He rang her that night to check but she had gone to visit a relative with her mother. He also rang the Court to thank them and to say that he was free to come. He then made preparations to fill an empty stomach.

The Bubbling Bowl

CHAPTER 7

'The green trees when I saw them first through one of the gates transported and ravished me, their sweetness and unusual beauty made my heart to leap, and almost mad with ecstasy, they were such strange and wonderful things.'

Thomas Traherne (1636-1674), in his 'Centuries of Meditation'

———

The road he had to follow to reach Llandyfrig Court was the same one he had cycled along the day before when he had received a telling-off from the irascible keeper on his surreptitious visit to the estate. After passing Bodcut Farm, towards the southern edge of the Deer Haye, the road descended into a deep dingle to cross the Dol Barcut Brook before continuing along the eastern side of the park. The climb out of the dingle was short but quite steep and exhausting. When he arrived at the Gate House, he had time to spare, enough to push the bike the rest of the way so that he could both cool and calm down. The possibility of another meeting with the keeper never entered his head.

As he approached the Court for a second time, pushing his bike between the avenue of oaks, he was again impressed by its picturesque grandeur. But as he gained a closer view of the building, instead of seeing it from a furtive distance, and saw the timbers as wood and not merely as black structural lines, their length and thickness caused him to think about the number of oak trees used in its construction. The tragedy of the lime tree in the Melglyn Dingle was still on his mind. How many trees would a building of this stature consume in the erection of its frame, and in the internal woodwork? Perhaps he was looking at a dead small wood, a denuded dingle, a cleared hill-top. When the house was built, the estate would have had its pick of trees.

He looked away from the house into the Deer Haye, to make a random guess as to the number of trees consumed. The nearest ancient tree was a huge sweet chestnut about forty metres from the ha-ha, massive in girth rather than height, with a trunk that twisted upwards in powerful spirals of bark. His calculations were dismissed by the sight of a thin, grey haired man leaning against the chestnut, holding his hands over his eyes, counting loudly. Owen recognised him immediately. It was Humphrey de Bohun. In contrast to his appearance at the evening talk, he was dressed in casual clothes - baggy brown corduroy trousers, a loosely fitting woollen pullover and, as an aristocratic flourish, a red and white polka-dot neckerchief which, apparently, was as famous locally as his personality.

Then he saw a middle-aged woman, wearing a gardening

overall, lying down in the ha-ha. She had already noticed his arrival and was imploring him to be quiet by holding a finger to her lips. When he looked again at the tree, de Bohun was moving away from it saying loudly, "I'm coming!", and peering intently all around, obviously looking for the woman. He had not noticed Owen, and proceeded to walk towards the nearest large oak tree which stood further into the park. From there, he moved sideways towards another oak, at which juncture the woman crawled out of the ditch and crept in a hunched posture in the direction of the chestnut. Before reaching the second oak, he suddenly spun round and saw her. Immediately, she broke into an ungainly run towards the chestnut. De Bohun raced for it as well, but he was beaten to the tree. After catching her breath, and rejoicing briefly, she pointed towards Owen. Together, they came across to him, climbing some steps inset into the retaining wall of the ha-ha. Still beaming with joy, the woman said, "You can't be anyone else than Suzy Forrest's brother. Welcome to our playground. I've just beaten my husband at one of his favourite games; that's why his face is so stiff. Come on Humphrey, admit defeat!" De Bohun smiled embarrassingly, gave a bony hand to Owen and welcomed him to Llandyfrig Court, introducing his wife, Matilda; 'Matty', as he called her.

"Let's have another game Humphrey, with Owen this time. He might enjoy it as much as Suzy. Come on!" She turned towards the ha-ha and beckoned Owen to follow her. "I'll be the Searcher this time. You've got a slow count of fifty, Owen, to find a hiding place, and then you have to get to the tree before I see you and before I've finished shouting your name and tapping the trunk three times. By the way, we call the game

'Creep'. Suzy loves it. We've played it all over the Haye with her."

Almost as the last words left her lips, she rushed off to the chestnut and buried her head in her arms. For a brief moment, Owen was transfixed; he laid his bike on the ground and then scuttled away to hide behind the nearest tree. From there, he saw de Bohun creep up to the blind side of the chestnut, where he stood motionless with his back against the trunk. The tree was so huge that he could not be seen, or even sensed, by his wife. When she had finished counting, he deftly adjusted his position as she carefully looked around, moving first one way, then another, but staying close to the tree. After some seconds of surveillance, she ventured towards the tree where Owen was hidden. She had walked only a short distance when de Bohun rushed around the chestnut and shouted "Home!", leaning against the trunk and wearing a mischievous grin on his face. Matilda was livid.

"Humphrey! that's cheating!" she exclaimed. "You're just showing off." Ignoring him, she said loudly, "Come on, Owen, show him how to play the game."

With that, she stood still for a moment, facing the house and pointing her index finger in several directions, working out mentally how many hiding places were available to Owen from where he had been standing when they met him. Once more, she moved towards the tree where he was concealed. When he thought he had almost half a chance to reach the chestnut, he exposed himself, knowing that he would be beaten to the tree, which he was.

"You're not as crafty as your sister", she said to him as he conceded defeat. "She's brilliant at creeping up on people, isn't she Humphrey?" She was implying that her husband was always getting beaten. "Now come inside; lunch won't be long. Humphrey here will take you in hand. He has already dug out the map of the estate to show you what our huge smallholding consists of."

She led the way across the lawn to the huge church-like porch. De Bohun followed behind Owen, almost in the manner of a contrite little boy. The oak door was moved ponderously open to reveal a whitened interior of plastered walls and an impressive roof of vaulted timbers. It could have been the entrance to a medieval church. The door into the house was also of oak, but of newer vintage. It led into a wide, panelled hallway of equal size to the porch, where a timber staircase rose up on the left beside a literally gigantic dark oak wardrobe that was no longer rectangular but still perpendicular.

Matilda went through a door on the left, into the kitchen, while Owen was ushered towards a door on the right. De Bohun opened it and gave a little bow and a gentle wave of one hand as he entreated his guest to enter, in the manner of a servant showing an eminent visitor into the drawing room of his lord. The room he saw was unbelievable. It occupied the entire lower section of the right side of the house, being long like a true hall. Oak panelling covered all the walls, interrupted only by the space created by a large fireplace where two sculptured sandstone pillars supported an arching lintel of oak marked with motifs. The arch must have been hewn out of a massive log. But the preponderance of timber did not only include the panelling and the lintel. The floor consisted of wide oak boards, covered in places with carpets and rugs; and above everything, holding the ceiling in place, there were a series of lengthy beams running across the room, each one about nine inches square.

They passed through this room into the newer part of the house, into what de Bohun introduced as his library. The change was remarkable, not only for the increase in light but also for the lightness of the woodwork. The room had the appearance of a typical library - light oak panelling to waist level, narrow oak floor-boards polished to a golden sheen, an array of bookcases instead of walls, and a large oak table, together with an oak chest of drawers, occupying the expanse in the middle. It was on this table that de Bohun had unfolded his prized map of the estate, ready for his visitor, and beside it there lay a worn booklet carrying the title page, "A Schedule of the Trees of the Deer Haye at Llandyfrig Court". It showed signs of being regularly used.

"Is that the Deer Haye", asked Owen, pointing to an area of the map marked with scattered numbers.

"Yes it is."

"Why is called a 'Haye' and not a 'park'?"

"Well, it's been called this for centuries by my family and the local people. My father once tried to get everyone to call it a deer park, for some stupid reason, threatening to sack anyone on the estate who continued to use the traditional name, but he couldn't undo the usage of centuries."

"But why 'Haye'?" asked Owen again.

"From the French 'La Haie', it seems, an enclosure used for gathering deer together in Norman times so that they could be more easily killed, and later as places where they were fattened up before being killed and salted down for the winter. Domesday Book mentions eleven hays in Herefordshire, but does not include ours. (De Bohun opened the booklet on the table) This is the Domesday entry for one which gives a good idea of what our estate was probably like in the beginning." He read out the details as if briefing a public meeting.*

"'The same Hugh holds Bernoldune: Thorkell held it. There are two hides of land. The forest there is large, but how large is not recorded. There also is a hay, in which he takes all he can catch. The rest of the land is waste.'* - Nine-hundred year old words, my boy. And the landscape is still outside to see." He broke into some nervous movements after saying these words while standing stock still.

"Whether a settlement existed here or not at the time, it did not take long for the Normans to discover the wild and wooded wastes of Ewyas and the neighbouring district of Archenfield to the south-east. My ancestors, you know, were among the first Normans to reach this bow and arrow paradise. The original hay, which is mentioned in a thirteenth century document, was probably smaller than the area that was eventually emparked for deer. Deer parks of the spacious, landscaped kind are creations of the eighteenth century. That's when ours was given the high paling fence up the slope and along the top. Fortunately, ours has hardly been landscaped at all. But who knows how much it resembles the Haye when it was given a permanent boundary? The young trees then are the old ones now. Our complement of trees is now only fifteen hundred within 640 acres. The first owner on record is a Roger de la Haye, who owned the manor of Llandyfrig Haye. When he died in 1266, without male heirs, the manor passed into the hands of my ancestors. There you have it", he concluded, consummately.

Before Owen could ask any questions on this potted history

of the Haye, he was given a cartographic tour of the estate, a tour which gave him as much of an insight into the personality of the lord of the manor as into the topography of the manor itself. He soon appreciated why Humphrey de Bohun was considered to be a bit cranky. Even without the playing of childhood games, his behaviour was suggestive of someone whose marbles could fall out of their bag at any time. His looks only accentuated his cranky demeanour. His dishevelled mop of thick grey hair diminished the actual size of his head, making it appear small and boyish. His voice was rather high-pitched, which added to this boyishness. And there was a theatrical flourish to his manner of speaking, reminiscent of an eccentric professor expounding upon an obscure treatise. As he gave his cartographic tour, he moved about almost continuously, making small, abrupt changes of direction, nervous movements that did not synchronise at all with the drift of his discourse. Being tall, lean and wiry, his movements appeared that much more chaotic. Owen could not stop himself from imagining Humphrey de Bohun and Suzy together, playing silly games. A wry smile came to his face just as Matilda called them for lunch.

They joined her in the dining room beyond the kitchen, another room with panelled walls but a lower ceiling, where antique furniture crowded the walls. De Bohun jerked his way around the dining table, uttering disjointed remarks about the quality of the meals in "this establishment", and picking at the salads. Clumsily, he knocked a glass over as he prepared to offer Owen a drink from a jug containing a liquid tinted green and loaded with submerged pieces of fruit. Matilda calmly carried on with her preparations to serve the food. She gave the impression that her husband could throw glasses at the wall, or even hang from the ceiling, without drawing from her anything more than a request for him not to get too excited. She seemed to be perfectly attuned to his foibles, and to be occupationally adjusted to his idiosyncratic behaviour.

"We are always delighted to entertain your sister, Owen, and to be entertained by her. No-one can make things happen like she can", said Matilda.

"Or not happen", muttered Humphrey, staring at the floor.

"Suzy often thwarts Humphrey in his desire to be leader of affairs. You're bound to have a better idea than we do of the way she takes over or interrupts the course of events. But she does it in such a lovely way."

"It may have a lovely side", replied Owen, "but it can sometimes go on a bit. Escape is the only option for a break if it gets too much."

"Escaping… Is that what you used to do when you were youngsters together?" asked Matilda.

"Occasionally, if I had half a chance".

"You must have taught her a lot in escape tactics. She really knows how to lose Humphrey, doesn't she dear?"

"Only when she has your collusion", muttered Humphrey, not wishing to become too involved in the conversation.

"But you still have great fun with her. Come on, admit it. Wait until you see them together Owen. I sometimes think that Humphrey fancies her."

"That's ridiculous, Matty!" came the sudden response. "Isn't it about time we tucked into this food?"

"Before we do, we should apologise to Owen for the unfriendly reception he received yesterday from the keeper. He told Humphrey, Owen, that he'd found you trespassing on our land. He has no right to say that. We hope you were not offended?"

"Not really", replied Owen, realising that the keeper's intervention was probably the reason for the suddenness of his invitation to the Court. "I was only looking at your fine avenue of oaks."

"Which you can do anytime", said Matilda. "You can go anywhere on our land whenever you like. The keeper now knows that."

Once seated, de Bohun continued his discourse on the Deer Haye, telling Owen about its herd of fallow deer. When he learned that Owen had not yet seen any of the animals, even from the road, he was impatient to get his visitor outside to track them down. Matilda upbraided him for hurrying their guest and continued to talk about Suzy.

"Suzy often mentions you, Owen. We've heard some interesting things about you", she said with a kindly smile. "Why don't you tell us a few things about her."

"What do you want to know?"

"Anything; especially something we could tease her about when she comes back."

"Even talking about her antics wears me out" said Owen. "Why don't you tell me what stories she has told you about me?"

"You've got to the nub of the matter there, Owen" interjected Humphrey. "Matty is the best source of personal secrets like that. The two of them often get together for quiet chats in the kitchen."

"And you often get together with her in the Deer Haye when I'm not around" responded Matilda, quickly. "You don't know what she says to me, Humphrey, and I don't know what she says to you. Perhaps we should leave the espionage affairs of Suzy Forrest at Llandyfrig Court until another day."

By the time they were ready to stalk deer, Owen was well aware that the kindness being shown to him was due entirely to the esteem felt for his sister and the curiosity this aroused concerning him.

After the meal, the two men left the house through a side door which issued into a yard by the outbuildings. De Bohun donned a weathered Barbour jacket and put an even more well-used cap upon his head, his hair protruding all around it. As they left, he took a maroon recorder from one of the jacket's pockets and placed it to one side, making room for the Schedule. He had the map of the Haye in his other pocket. Together, they made their way across the yard to the ha-ha and into the Deer Haye, passing the sweet chestnut where games had been played earlier. De Bohun said that they called the chestnut the Ha-Ha Tree. On the map, it was simply Number 1. He explained that although most of the trees had numbers only some had names; names he had given them over the years.

"The very oldest trees, the really venerable ones, I call the Greybeards of the Deer Haye. They are the natural masters of the area, the descendants of the original oak woodland out of which the ancestors of Roger de la Haye carved the estate. Some of them are reckoned to be over five hundred years old. Not quite as old as the Norman genes in my body but just as decrepit. Without their leaves, they always look a bit ghostly."

Owen smiled, but the eccentricity of his host was losing out to the character of the Haye.

"I've never seen so many old trees all in one place", he said, his voice fading as he repeated the last phrase. His natural inclination was to gaze and reflect, to move about slowly, and to be quiet. De Bohun's manner and progress was the opposite. He wanted to cover the whole park all at once and was indecisive as to which tree they should proceed to next. He was quick to draw Owen's attention to the numerous miniature stockades scattered about the Haye, the stock frames which protected the young trees he had planted as the next generation of Greybeards.

"I plant a few trees every year to atone for the losses my ancestors failed to replace. If only my forebears had listened to William Watkins, a curate of Hay-on-Wye, who wrote 'A Treatise on Forest Trees' in 1753, and said, of the man who plants trees..." He held one lapel of his jacket, raised himself up to his full height and pronounced, almost by way of self-congratulation -

"'He has a healthy, innocent and beneficent Amusement; the Sweets of an undisturbed Repose, and the happy Reflection of a Life well spent'"*. It was a quotation which many visitors to the Deer Haye had heard and one of several which Owen was to hear that afternoon.

"I applaud that", he said, seriously. "What was that book again? I'd like to have a look at a copy."

"You can look at mine when we get back. You can look at all my books. My library is as open to you as it is to Milo and Alison, Catherine, and, I suppose, Suzy, as long as you don't leave it in a mess like she does; but first let me show you my wonderful trees."

They progressed deeper into the Deer Haye. Owen tried to keep close enough to de Bohun so as to glance at the map and orientate himself. It was a difficult exercise, for in introducing his venerable trees, the man moved in all directions while revealing their identities. He knew exactly where to go to point out the more exceptional or distinctive trees, and even the ones which harboured the rare beetles and the rare epiphytes (the mosses and the lichens). His Latin pronunciation was particularly good. His life-long association with the Haye and its aged denizens, and the quirks of his personality, meant that he did not give a dry catalogue of information, although what he had to say had been said to countless parties of students and other visiting groups. It was so well rehearsed in parts that the monologue was delivered faultlessly, as well as theatrically.

"And here we have one of the most ancient trees of Ewyas, a noble tree from a noble time..."

The first of these noble trees was a pollard, one of the oldest oaks in the Haye. Because of the epicormic swellings on its short trunk, and the vicissitudes of time, it was almost round in shape, carrying a mop-headed top of short branches, rather like de Bohun's mass of hair. It was, in comparison to its neighbours, a dwarf.

"This is 'The Bollard', Owen, from an old name for a pollard which has given up a regular crop of useful branches ever since achieving manhood. We have a sketch of it, done by one of my relatives in the 1790s, which shows it to be more or less as it is now. Their longevity is due to this method of cropping, which also explains why they crash out from the inside instead of falling over. According to an old family tale, this pollard, along with other trees in the Haye, was first pollarded to celebrate the beheading of a local Welsh rebel, too long ago to know exactly when. And a friend of mine reckons that pollarding trees in celebration of the execution of a famous or notorious person seems to have been a common practice years ago. He told me that all the oaks in the park on the Enville estate near Stourbridge in Staffordshire were pollarded when Lady Jane Grey was beheaded in 1554. A cart-load of oak limbs for a pretty seventeen year old Protestant neck – what Catholic carnage!"

He went on to mention the natural catastrophes which had reduced some of the more ancient trees to living ruins, and explained how the trees had changed during his own lifetime. It was apparent to Owen that the man's affinity for the place and its 'Greybeards' stemmed from his childhood days wandering beneath giant trees and probably hiding in their hollow interiors. Had he been an only child, he asked himself. Or had he had an exhausting older sister?

Owen did not say much. There was too much to listen to. Observing the man almost as much as the trees, he followed his eccentric guide from tree to tree, outwardly marvelling at the collection of arboreal giants and geriatrics, and inwardly fascinated by the identities given to them. He was introduced to 'The Thunderer', a massive tree which, according to its owner, made "an almighty row in a gale", a far greater noise than its present accompaniment to a stiff breeze; to 'The Serpent', an oak pollard with serpentine surface roots creeping outwards as far as the extent of its crown; to the 'Outpost', a stag-headed, dying oak of many dead branches, which was the favourite perching tree for some of the birds of the Haye, the buzzards, the crows, the owls, etc.; to 'The Grey Giant', a huge tree with a ghostly grey trunk covered in lichens, the tallest oak in the Haye, rising to 115 feet on a bole that was 50 feet tall and 20 feet seven inches in girth; to the 'Groaner', a tree of unremarkable dimensions which made up for its size by groaning loudly whenever the wind blew through its hollow interior; to 'The Griffin', a squat, wide-spreading oak pollard with buttresses arising from claw-like roots, named "after the heraldic griffin"; to 'The Hideout', a completely hollow oak which had been de Bohun's favourite hiding place as a young lad; and to 'The Spike', a virtually branchless tree which Owen had noticed perched upon its low hill when he first saw the Deer Haye. It had a circumference at breast height of 31 feet eight inches - swollen by protuberances which exaggerated the pointedness of its branchless trunk.

They also passed a number of impressive looking sweet chestnut trees, some over three hundred years old, which made Number One, The Ha-Ha tree, seem small in comparison. These chestnuts stood out from the Greybeards by their darker colouring and the way they spiralled upwards. And in stark contrast to these broadleaved giants, there was a Wellingtonia with a stag-head. De Bohun went out of his way to include it in his perambulation because it was the nesting site of the Haye's resident pair of ravens.

"There can't be a deer park in the country, Owen, that doesn't have one of these evergreen giants. Botanically, it's related to the great Sequoias of California, which is where it comes from."

"I suppose you call it the 'Raven Tree'", said Owen in anticipation of hearing this name.

"No way, my boy. It's been known to me from when I was a young lad simply as the 'Welly'. No-one seems to like it as a tree for playing Creep. I've never liked creeping up on it. It's too dark and forbidding for me. I prefer to look at it from afar. And Suzy won't go anywhere near it!"

These were all grand trees, whatever their state; and their names gave a peculiar flavour to the Haye itself. But this collection of extraordinary Greybeards was followed by one oak, a relatively young specimen, which stood at the intersection of two trackways, the main one originating from the entrance gate by the Keeper's Lodge. De Bohun merely introduced it in passing without stopping, although it, too, had a name. The verve in his voice subsided and its tone carried the message – "Well, I suppose I should introduce this one". It was the 'Wrong Angled Oak', a curious tree because all its limbs were horizontal, branching neatly away from the trunk at ninety degrees, its crown tapering upwards like a narrow cone. If it had been evergreen, it would have looked like a pyramidal conifer.

"'The Wrong Angled Oak'", repeated Owen, bewildered. "Why?"

De Bohun did not want to spend any time at the tree. He was walking away from it when the question was put, eager to press on. For some strange reason, the tree rattled rather than enthralled him. He stopped and turned around, but stayed where he was.

"Look at it", he said, dismissively. "All the limbs are at right angles to the trunk. It's stiff and geometrical."

"But why the name", pressed Owen again, unable to comprehend why, if de Bohun did not like the tree, he had given it a name.

"Well, it should be called the 'Right Angled Oak', but the tree is not right, it's wrong. So it's the 'Wrong Angled Oak'."

With this explanation, he turned and set off again, leaving Owen speechless.

They had now quartered the northern part of the Haye and

had reached a small lake-cum-wet-depression which collected the waters of several small streams. Here, there was a tree which, for the moment, held splendour greater than all the rest. It was a hugely spreading black poplar - the one Owen had seen from the road - leafless, but covered in the deepest red male catkins, a lot of which were strewn about the ground beneath it. The contrast between the grey, deeply fissured bark of a trunk mis-shapen by nodules, and the graceful, pendulous redness of the catkins took Owen's emotional response to trees to another high point. This was 'The Leaning Tower of Poplar' - the Leaning Tower, for short - a name which hardly registered with him, for he was so enraptured by the appearance of this crimson tree. De Bohun said something about how and when the lake was formed, but his words fell into the mire beside the tree and sank. Unnoticed by Owen, he also set off for the western reaches of the Haye, and only distracted Owen from his attention on the poplar because he altered his mind and changed direction, hurrying by muttering something about 'bubbling'.

Owen reluctantly hastened after him and was led to a superb sweet chestnut tree, the most awesome one of this species seen so far. It had an immensely broad trunk, given extra girth by a bulging mass of burrs and bosses all over its lower half. To de Bohun, this was 'The Bubbling Bole', a tree which had a circumference of over thirty feet. To Owen, the name was the most bizarre yet. He finally asked the question he had harboured in the back of his mind since reaching The Spike, a question deferred by the intervention of the Wrong Angled Oak.

"How long has it taken you to give names to these trees?"

"Oh, they have just cropped up over the years. Sometimes a name has hit me as I'm strolling round. Sometimes, it takes ages to find the right name when I think a tree needs one."

"Why should it need one?" probed Owen deftly, without seeming to question the practice.

"Why should it need one?" repeated de Bohun. "We all need one, my boy. Remarkable trees cannot be anonymous. They must have names to confirm their special character. 'A tree apprehended is a tree in the mind', said Traherne*. People have been giving names to remarkable trees for centuries. Mine are just more remarkable than most. It rounds off their identity. Instead of saying, 'I've been at that tree which was struck by lightening', you can say, 'I've been at The Blasted Tree'." He smiled. "It also helps to familiarise yourself with their inner presence."

"Their inner presence?" enquired Owen incredulously.

"Yes, my boy, their inner presence. You have an inner presence; I have an inner presence; all trees have an inner presence, and some show it more than others: that sister of yours has an inner presence, but it's one she doesn't seem able to hide."

"You mean they all have a spirit?" probed Owen again, as deftly and as innocently as he could.

"Alright, call it a spirit; I prefer inner presence. Whatever words you use, it takes a very long time to appreciate the existence of one; as it takes a long time to get to know somebody - really get to know them. Getting to know a tree takes time. That's why the names often take long to come. The trees that really give out something, I call 'Abode Trees'. The Greybeards are all Abode Trees."

"Has anyone else given any names?"

"Only Matty. She and Suzy started calling Number One, The Ha-Ha Tree one day when your sister joined us for a bit of fun. It seems to have stuck."

"Has my sister had the privilege of a guided tour of the Haye?" asked Owen, showing some appreciation of his visit while at the same time probing for some interesting information.

"Not with me. She's walked around it with Matty often enough. They usually go off to look at the horse chestnuts and the limes when they're in flower. Matty likes the horse chestnuts and Suzy the limes - so do I. We'll see some limes once we pass 'The Domesday Tree', which is just up that slope on the other side of the Cwm Brook. And we'll see some trees fitted with nest-boxes for pied flycatchers. We've been recording flycatchers here for ten years now."

After crossing the brook in two leaps, via a stone slab which in times of spate (Owen was told) created a miniature waterfall, they progressed into that part of the Haye, against the southern portion of Coed Tirion Glas, where the trees were more thickly set together, and the ground blanketed with bracken debris and strewn with dead wood. On the way, Owen received a mini-lecture on pied flycatchers. A local bird-man had approached de Bohun ten years ago about studying them, and now he took part in the job of ringing the birds.

On the boundary between the bracken and the grass pasture, they came to what did indeed look like a venerable tree, an oak shell, barely alive.

"Here it is, my boy, The Domesday Oak, the oldest tree in the Deer Haye, estimated by radio-carbon dating to be nearly eight hundred years old. It can't be anything other than the last remaining oak of the original woodland that the Normans opened up to create their hunting ground - La Haie. It is marked on old maps of the estate and mentioned in some family documents as 'The Old Oak'".

Although the tree was now derelict and decrepit, and only a shadow of its former self, Owen was told that it had once been nearly thirty-eight feet in circumference until one side had collapsed. De Bohun could remember it when it had one large lower limb growing almost horizontally outwards. This now lay rotting on the ground. Entymologists had found a beetle called Hypebaeus flavipes in the rich reddish-brown dead wood of the tree, and on a few other ancient oak pollards in the Haye, a beetle found nowhere else in Britain.* De Bohun was openly proud of this discovery, and of the tree that was the hiding- place of such a rare creature. The reigning giants of the Haye were the measure of what it must once have looked like.

"Only the imagination of one who ponders where we have come from, and where we are going to, could conjure up an idea of what it has been through in the course of the last eight hundred years." De Bohun said this in a very grave manner, holding his lapel and spreading his legs wide, as though the Haye were a stage as well as a wildlife reserve.

"Does this tree still have an inner presence?" asked Owen, continuing to probe the theme which intrigued him most in de Bohun's discourse.

"No more, no more. It has gone. It has ebbed away with the decline of its torso; emptied with the emptying of its heart." De Bohun maintained his theatrical air, the last phrase dying on his lips with a gurgle.

"Vanished, as the very woods from which it sprang", continued Owen in the same poetic vein, but not dramatically, nor so affectedly.

De Bohun frowned. He pursed his lips and tipped his head to one side and nodded, as if noting the performance of someone at an audition. The thoughtful comments of his guest were beginning to register in a mind which had appeared, initially, not to give much access to the statements of others because of the tempo of its own outpourings. For a moment, he was quiet. But the pause was broken by some deer. For it was here, on the edge of the open woodland of the Haye, that they first heard and then glimpsed a group of fallow deer bouncing away through the deep litter of leaves and bracken.

"They're heading for the ground on the south-eastern side of the Haye", said de Bohun. "I often find them there, or usher them into the Gully where they sneak out and double back on me. They like the herbage on that side." He showed where he meant on the map. "The streams which cross the Haye are all tributaries of the Cwm Brook which itself is a tributary of the Dol Barcut Brook. The first northern one we came to, we call the 'Ditch' because that's what it is; the other northern one is just 'Cwm Brook' north, and the small one which we're on our way to, is the 'Gully'. Has anyone told you yet what the name Dol Barcut means?" He did not give Owen the chance to reply. "It's the brook of the Kite's Meadow. There must have been a time when the Haye was once part of the hunting ground of kites. As an ancient opening in the forest, it might have been an easy place for them to see carrion."

"Kites?" questioned Owen, in surprise. "Still in the Haye?"

"No, no; not now. Once upon a time, in the wild and wooded days when the Welsh had the place to themselves. Hereabouts, the sky is now the reserve of the buzzard. We've been hearing the distant mewing of one ever since we left the house. It's probably The Eerie Shriek; the oldest buzzard of the lot locally. It's always nested somewhere near the Haye, if not in it. The buzzards are never far away. Nor are the owls, nor the woodpeckers for that matter; the Haye is their reserve as well. You must come in here with me one night, Owen, and listen to the owls. It's spine-chilling stuff; a hoot really."

Owen's smile turned to laughter as he watched the enjoyment of the joke consume de Bohun. Its delivery, and the lead up to it, testified to its seasoned use. The man was proving to be a hoot himself.

Only a short distance from The Domesday Oak there was another old tree located on the edge of the open woodland. It was a lime, the first one they had seen. It, too, was decrepit but not so terminally derelict nor as hollow. De Bohun did not have an individual name for this tree. All he said was that the customary name in the district for old lime trees was 'stoggles'; so this one was simply the stoggle by The Domesday Oak. He revealed that there were not many in the Haye, anyway. They occurred either in the more wooded part of the Haye, in odd places along the Cwm Brook, or in Coed Tirion Glas itself.

The sight of the tree recalled for Owen the tragedy to the lime in the Melglyn Dingle. For the first time during his outing in the Haye he spoke volubly, recounting the incident to de Bohun, who listened attentively but always on the edge of his seat, impatient to continue his own story. When he did begin again, he could not speak fast enough. Owen was astonished at what he heard.

Rapidly, de Bohun explained that the 'Melglyn Stoggle', the local name for the lime in the dingle, was lucky to be alive anyway because his father almost had it felled in 1951 when he was felling the southern edge of Coed Tirion Glas before replanting with conifers under a Forestry Commission scheme. His father's friends were ripping out woods to accommodate conifers, so the 'Old Man' wanted to show them that he, too, was into the new forestry fashions. And what a better place for demonstration than the side of Rhibo Mountain where everyone could see the change?

"My mother and I made such a fuss about it all. We didn't want to see the trees go from the Melglyn Dingle. There were plenty of rough patches on the estate where he could have planted conifers. But we could not stop him clearing the trees from the dingle and beyond, although we did persuade him to leave the lime; but only just. My mother, who was fond of the writings of Walter Savage Landor, drew the Old Man's attention to a piece of prose by Landor which asks; 'Who in the world could ever cut down a linden, or dare in his senses to break a twig off one?'* My father was not the sort of man either to be moved by emotive writing or to see trees as anything more than green things which stand in the way. Do you know those words from William Blake? 'The tree which moves some to tears of joy is in the eyes of others only a green thing which stands in the way'."* De Bohun delivered the first quote on one side of the stoggle, and the second on the other, as if the tree were a theatrical prop.

Owen had heard it before. But there was insufficient time to say 'Yes', for de Bohun continued immediately.

"It was at this time that our gardener, an old man and a very dear friend, told me about a local legend which says that whoever fells a stoggle on Rhibo Mountain will cause their family name to expire. This, too, did not have any effect when

I got mother to mention it, because the Old Man said that the trees were being felled by Jack Parry, the woodman who lived at Gwenynog. He was, indeed, the man who actually felled the trees, including the fine limes and the cherries which accompanied the oaks in the dingle. And he suffered for it because he and his wife, who still lives at Gwenynog, never produced a son, only a daughter."

De Bohun paused abruptly at this point to reflect on something, almost as though a realisation had hit him. But he shook it off and continued, moving about as he spoke, and not looking directly into Owen's face.

"It seemed that our appeal was lost until my father, after having an almighty row with my mother, stopped the felling after the dingle, and a swathe of land on this side of it, had been felled. Somehow, she browbeat or blackmailed him into calling a halt, and also into not planting up the dingle. But he had the last spiteful laugh."

He looked into Owen's eyes and made a personal admission in a quiet voice. "My father was not a nice man."

"Without telling anyone, he gave the two newly-created fields against the dingle to Jack Parry as payment for the felling and for all the arrears he owed him. It was nearly six months before we discovered what he had done. My mother didn't speak to him for a week. His riposte was to plant up the swathe of land at the top of the dingle in the following spring with conifers."

Owen was nonplussed, hearing someone he had met only twice reveal such personal matters to a stranger. He did not know what to say. Nor did he get much of a chance to put any questions because de Bohun, who had moved around the stoggle during his discourse, in all directions, looking at the ground, suddenly raced off to where the deer had fled without looking at Owen, and disappeared. Owen followed and found himself on the edge of a deep gully which carried a stream that issued from the wood. For the first time that day, he experienced the undisturbed atmosphere of the Deer Haye. There was no sight of de Bohun, nor any sound as to where he might be. He was obviously hiding, and it did not take Owen long to guess where, although the hiding place made its own impact before he realised who it concealed.

On the shoulder of the Gully, there was a grove of lime trees; a grove consisting of several trees stemming from a single, ancient, small-leaved lime. The tree may have been pollarded at some distant date, or perhaps had risen from a once coppiced stool, for its bole was very short, barely eight feet tall, and divided into three huge limbs which towered into the air and which were now dying back at their tops. A fourth limb, on the down-slope side of the shoulder, had split away, leaving a large wound but retaining contact with the tree at its base. This horizontal limb was now firmly rooted in the ground, and supported a row of branches which had developed upwards into small trees. The three other limbs each had large lower branches which arched outwards and downwards and which, on the upslope side of the shoulder, made contact with the ground, having rooted themselves and subsequently grown into what were now mature trees. These in turn were repeating this parental tendency for natural layering. The ancient lime, therefore, was surrounded by two cordons of its own offspring, and the grove was a tangle of arching connections. Even with its leaves just forming, the interior of the grove was rather murky.*

Owen knew that de Bohun was concealed in the grove. It was a perfect hiding place. But he pretended not to know where he was, turning on the spot and peering in all directions. Then, he walked away from the shoulder of the Gully, making for the wood, and passing close to the grove, ignoring it completely. Just as he passed by, de Bohun jumped out:

"Bo!" he cried joyously, wearing his usual boyish grin. "Welcome to 'Teili Junction'. You're not very good at seeking people out, are you, Owen?" With that, he turned around and disappeared again.

Owen followed, bending and easing his body through the tangle of branches until he was in the bare interior of this arboreal nave. De Bohun was leaning against the parent tree.

"I once heard an ecologist say that limes were immortal", said Owen. "I can now see what he meant; but why Teili Junction?"

De Bohun adjusted his position beside the ancient lime. "Teili is a traditional name for lime, a Germanic word, I think. I used to call this place 'The Junction' before I discovered the name 'Teili', so I just put the two together. I've spent many delightful musical hours with my recorder astride this limb here (he pointed to the fallen branch), enjoying the shade and the echoing sounds during hot summer days."

Everything was now getting too much for Owen. Throughout the walk, he had been simultaneously marvelling at the trees and listening in amazement to de Bohun's revelations, without experiencing properly the atmosphere of the Haye. Teili Junction was not a place to comprehend in one visit. He would have to indulge his propensity for arboreal reverie at some other time, on his own. For the moment, the thought of de Bohun, perched upon an arching limb playing tunes on a recorder made him wonder if the real world was still around him and, indeed, what world he had come to.

Notebook - 14th April

I shall have to go back and remind myself of all the Greybeards and their extraordinary names.

From my copy of the Book of the Tree by Georgina Mase (1927) , pp. 228-30, the mystical thoughts of the biologist E. L. Grant Watson:

'I sometimes ask myself what else there is in the woods beyond what I see with my eyes...Might it not be possible but with so little a shifting of mental capacity to perceive more than what is usually present?... Are the tales of fairies and tree spirits, which come to us from the past, but false imaginings? The men who lived closer to the earth than we, less separated from its harmony by mechanical contrivance, was their vision younger and more acute? And even now the joy of that perception may yet be within the range of our grasping, for who shall say what wonder may not be revealed, what miracle accomplished at any turn of the head or quick glance of the eye.' (Extract from English Country, 1924).

The Bollard Oak

CHAPTER 8

'...the superstitious beliefs connected with trees and plants in this county (Herefordshire) show plain traces of primitive man's animistic theory of nature. He believed every tree and plant to be as himself, the conscious owner of an indwelling spirit, endowed with power equal to or exceeding his own.'

Ella Mary Leather (1912) 'The Folk-Lore of Herefordshire', (p.17)

After his busy day at the Court, Owen was sitting by a newly lit fire in the living room thinking of Catherine. Despite his ability to cope with solitude, the last two evenings still echoed the loneliness of Northumberland. Although Suzy's friends had helped him to settle in, he was reluctant to intrude too much upon their space, especially now that the Easter break had arrived. While the fire flickered into life, he contemplated the brave action of telephoning Catherine to invite her over for a meal sometime soon in return for the hospitality at the farm.

Just at that moment, she appeared on his doorstep. His mood was such that he was more than pleased to see her, though his reserve inhibited his welcome. All he could do was stand embarrassed without uttering a word. A brief moment of awkward silence ensued.

"I hope I haven't disturbed you, Owen."

"No...no. I'm just surprised to see you, that's all. You're the first visitor I've had since moving in here. Come in. Come in."

"I've brought you a fresh loaf of bread I made yesterday and two books to add to the ones Suzy sent you. This new one is the latest hardback edition of Kilvert's Diary, which has lots of illustrations; and this is one of mine on the folklore of Herefordshire by Ella Mary Leather - Suzy has told me of your passion for folklore."

"'Passion' is a bit over the top, but then that's how Suzy would put it. Thanks a lot. I liked the bread you serve up at Bodcut."

There was another brief interlude of silence while Owen perused the books. Then Catherine pre-empted an offer of hospitality by asking if he had tried any of Suzy's herb teas. He hadn't, so she offered to make a drink. The situation became easier, but the offer left him feeling a little inadequate as a host. As she moved familiarly around the kitchen, Owen stood by the fire, idly flicking over pages.

"What sort of herb tea do you want, Owen? You have an extraordinary selection to savour. I always drink the hibiscus flower brew when I'm here, but the choice is endless - rose-hip, elder flower, lime flower, hedgerow reviver... You should have discovered these teas already."

"Maybe. But there are so many contents in that cluttered kitchen - too many to sort through all at once."

"Do you want me to select one for you then?"

"No. I'll try the lime flower, please. I've always liked the smell of lime blossom."

When the brew arrived, he could not understand why he had not tasted lime flower tea before. The tea was exquisite, soothing rather than refreshing. The lime trees he had come to know as a gardener in a botanic garden had left a lasting impression upon him. Their blossom was one of the thrills he had discovered that took the bounds of ordinary enjoyment into the sublime. And there was that one time when Suzy had taken him to a lime tree she had found to share it with him while she drew some flowers nearby. That was the day he had been stung by two bees while pulling down a sprig of blossom to take back to the house. His thoughts were interrupted by Catherine telling him that Suzy collected lime flowers for tea every year.

Sipping the tea by the fire, leaning against the wall, he said the first thing that came to him. He gave Catherine an account of his confrontation with the keeper, a subject which gave her a chance to find out what had happened on his luncheon date at Llandyfrig Court.

"Why does Humphrey de Bohun employ such a morose and unfriendly man as a keeper when his own attitude to visitors to the Deer Haye is completely different?"

"That's a long story, Owen. Old Crabface - to use his local name, which should give you an idea of his reputation in the district - was appointed by Mr de Bohun's father, and given the tenancy of the Keeper's Lodge, which is opposite the main entrance to the Haye. You must have passed it on one of your journeys. He uses the Gatehouse, where you met him, as a store. In the days of Mr de Bohun's father, everyone had to ask him for permission to enter the Haye. What you got was sour grapes from a sour face. I don't think I've ever seen him smile. When I was in my teens, he used to leer at me... Anyway, when Carling Medlar moved into the area, Old Crabface's son became the keeper of The Prospect. He spends a lot of his time over there advising his son. He's virtually only the honorary keeper of the Haye, now. Suzy hates him more than I do. When she came to see me just before she left, she bumped into him hanging dead birds on a fence along the bridleway between here and the farm. You can guess what happened."

"I may have seen those carcasses. They're a hideous sight. I suppose they're intended to frighten away the birds and other animals he considers as pests. All they do is alienate me from the individual who hung them there. If he felt the wrath of my big sister, then he deserved it. I hope she made him quake in the mud on that bridleway."

"He doesn't quake, he just seethes. You were unlucky to have met him because he had an accident recently which damaged one of his ailing legs. He is unlikely to be getting around much at the moment. Anyway, you should ignore him. Pretend he isn't an important part of the scene; he'll hate that. Now tell me, how did you get on with Mr de Bohun?"

"Oh, not bad. As a guide, he's somewhat frantic. He doesn't give you very long to ponder a place or digest what he says, does he? But I managed to keep up with him. Both the tour of the Haye, and the tales that went with it were absorbing, though digressive. He kept delivering quotations during our progress between the trees; the words of Thomas Traherne and William Watkins mostly. His memory for prosaic lines and pithy sayings adds quite a dash to his conversation, doesn't it? When we returned to the Court, he took me into his library and showed me some of his favourite books. He said I could use the library whenever I wanted to, which was kind of him. He has a remarkable collection of books. He also showed me a copy of a survey of the Llandyfrig estate done in 1583, which he said you discovered for him. Did you?"

"Yes. I found it by accident actually while looking for something else. He was so delighted when he saw it that he went into a dramatic eulogy of my worth as a curator. It was quite embarrassing. He's a leading member of the Elchon Drama Group, you know, an activity that has cast him in some ridiculous roles. In the pantomime last year - Little Red Riding Hood - he took the part of the wolf and Suzy played the lead. The play was the subject of discussion for weeks afterwards."

"Yes, I can imagine that..."

"He's renowned locally for his theatrical antics. Some people think he's a bit of a crank, but that's unfair, although I don't really know him that well. I think that his unusualness is due to an eccentric disposition and a disorganised mind. My reaction to the way his mind works in conversation is that it's like trying to make sense of research notes gathered from an assortment of disparate sources."

This rather intellectual analogy caused Owen to look askance at his visitor. It was a somewhat academic interpretation. The question then crossed his mind why his sister should know the man better than a local person like Catherine who had lived in the area all her life. Suzy's chaotic personality was, perhaps, more in tune with that of de Bohun.

Then Catherine launched into a story about de Bohun that had happened a year ago, when he was compelled to have a favourite tree felled because it was a potential danger to road users near the Haye.

"He was waiting beside the tree, a horse chestnut, early on the morning when it was to be felled, before the two woodmen had arrived on the scene. The men were not locals so their story of what happened would have gone away with them had they not met Suzy and me in the Green Man at Gulible at lunch-time. It was Suzy who got talking to them first. According to them, Mr de Bohun had been at the tree since six o'clock that morning, and remained with them throughout the felling. They said that he spent some time telling them, while they were preparing to fell the tree, how special it was to his wife and the part it had played in his life. He told them about all the champion conkers it had furnished him with, and the conker battles it had won for him. Everyone knows how enthusiastic he is about conkers because he still plays the game with local youngsters. He holds a conker battle every year in the ruins of the motte and bailey castle at Ewyas. He'll probably challenge you, Owen, if you're still around then. Is that possible?" For some reason, she did not wait for an answer.

"Anyway, after extolling the fame of the tree in this connection, he urged them to be as gentle as they could in reducing the crown, and to fell it with as little noise and damage as possible. He insisted they felled it in a particular direction to prevent the remaining limbs from shattering when the tree hit the ground. Apparently, the job called for the use of a winch, so he insisted also that they minimised the chaffing of the trunk by covering it with a sheet of sacking which he had with him. He was so insistent that they accepted his directions and went about the task with deliberate and exaggerated care. So they said. According to them, he stroked the tree and kissed it before they delivered the coup de grace. Suzy believed this but I think they were spinning a yarn by this time, although it would have been a typical gesture of his. They were full of drink and the younger one, who Suzy had got talking to first of all, was good at telling stories and he knew it. Anyway, Mr de Bohun then instructed them not to cut up the trunk, most of which was rotten, and to leave the branches in a neat pile nearby. He wanted the tree to waste away with time on the ground. It remains on the ground in the Deer Haye where it fell. At the time, Suzy contributed to their flippant tale by saying that he probably wanted to give the spirit in the tree the chance to pass away peacefully, after such a catastrophic ending."

Owen was impressed, and intrigued at this other insight into the character of the owner of Llandyfrig Court.

"So, he does have communion with his trees", he observed.

"What do you mean?" she asked, surprised by this reaction to what she thought was partly a tall story.

"Oh, Milo made a comment about Humphrey de Bohun's reputation for conversing with his trees. And after my visit, I've been wondering if he actually talks to them or just amongst them. He talked to me about 'inner presences' in trees. I know what he was getting at. It's difficult to pin it down in words, but there is something there, I'm sure." Owen said this rather wistfully, breaking into the habit he had of seeming to drift away during a conversation.

"But, surely", broke in Catherine, "what he feels and what

you feel is only a projection of your own emotions. Some people won't be affected at all, and not every tree will influence the emotions of everyone in the same way."

"Any spiritual force, of whatever kind or residence", responded Owen, shaken into a reply, "will only be detected if the individual is sensitive to its presence." He paused and looked away before continuing. "If you haven't felt such forces, then I suppose you're not receptive to them. Not everyone is. Surely, you must have felt, somewhere, the spirit of a place?"

"Yes, I have, but what has reached me has not been the presence of a spirit but the presence of the place as my cultural background and emotions induce me to feel it. I know that I see my home area rather differently to the way Suzy sees it, for example; and, perhaps to the way you see it. Your impressions must be very shallow ones at the moment."*

Owen was about to reply when Catherine asked how he had been greeted when he arrived at the Court.

Newcomers to an area are inevitably detached from its social scene and, unless already acquainted with some of the local inhabitants, naively unaware of the nature of existing relationships and contacts. Owen was still in this position, yet it did not occur to him to be anything but honest and open about what had transpired during his visit. Rather ingenuously, therefore, he began by telling Catherine how he had found the de Bohuns playing a hide-and-seek game on the edge of the Deer Haye. At first, she thought he was pulling her leg. She had never seen them playing such games, although the behaviour was true to form for Mr de Bohun, who was very fond of playing board games with visitors to the Court.

Continuing to be open with her, he mentioned that the

game was very popular with Suzy when she visited the Court. This revelation changed her demeanour completely. A look of dismay came to her face, and he finally sensed that his news was having an unsettling effect upon her. She admitted, disconcertedly, that Suzy had never said anything to her about the playing of such games. On her visits to the Court, she had never been invited to play games, except stupid board games. Her close friend, whom she knew visited the de Bohuns regularly, had kept something from her; a small matter, but one which assumed exaggerated importance in her mind.

Owen could see that he had revealed more than the idiosyncratic behaviour of a local landowning couple. He changed the subject, saying how surprised he was to find the de Bohuns so well disposed towards him, and unusually open in their behaviour towards someone they hardly knew. He was even more surprised when Catherine admitted, in disaffected tones, that they were never as open with her as they were when she was with Suzy. Her parents did not know them all that well either, even though her mother got together with Matilda on a number of local charitable activities. The undertones in this conversation confused him, but he did not delve into them. He realized, at last, that he was only on the surface of the local social scene - a strained surface in some respects. He wondered if the undercurrents involved would be understandable if he became privy to them at some later date.

For the moment, he decided to move onto a subject that he knew would interest Catherine and take them away from local personalities.

"My tour of the Haye turned up a number of local names which you might be able to explain or translate for me. I'm intrigued by the names Ewyas and Archenfield. Both Milo and de Bohun have told me to ask you for the details of the historical significance of local places."

"Yes I can, Owen, but it will be easier when I've got the right maps and my notes with me, the ones I use for local history talks. We can get together sometime and I'll give you a briefing, if that's what you want."

There was a quiet moment of direct eye contact. Although the conversation had lost momentum, Catherine's face was continuing to have its effect upon Owen. When he thought about the evening later, he was surprised at his forwardness:

"Is there any chance that you could collect what information you've got from the farm in return for a meal with me tonight? I can't guarantee that the food will be as good as the history, but I'll try."

Catherine smiled.

Later on that evening, the cottage became quite a homely place, for Owen and Catherine were both lying on the floor by the fire, surrounded by maps, drinking herb teas. Catherine had been very relaxed during the meal, but when she proceeded to answer Owen's questions her manner changed, almost automatically. He could see that he was going to get the sort of explanation usually reserved for a local history society. He settled himself against the sofa and the talk began.

She told him about Offa's Dyke and showed him on the map how much of Herefordshire was still in Welsh hands at that time.

"If we get a chance, Owen, we should go for some walks along the Dyke. All the land west of the Dyke was Welsh, and although the area between the boundary and the Wye gradually fell into Saxon hands, the territory lying to the west of the river from the Wye west to the Black Mountains and south to the River Monnow - the boundary between Herefordshire and Monmouthshire - remained Welsh for a very long time. You can see from the dearth of English place-names that the settlement history of the area is one of continuous Welsh occupation. This is where Ewyas and Arkenfield came into being."

"But Arkenfield doesn't sound like a Welsh name to me", interrupted Owen looking at the map.

"It isn't exactly. It seems to have been coined by the Saxons, whose Chronicle of 915 calls it Ercingafelde; but to the Welsh it was Ercineg or Ergyng, a name connected with a sixth century Welsh king, although it may have distant connections with the Romans whose settlement of Ariconium, near Ross-on-Wye, would transpose into Welsh as 'Ergun'".

Catherine paused briefly, not to check that Owen was following her explanation, but to give herself a moment's respite before continuing.

"I'm still with you", he muttered, giving her the cue he thought she needed to carry on. "And so is the rest of the class, I think."

Catherine pouted but continued.

She explained that by the beginning of the tenth century, the Mercians had advanced beyond Offa's Dyke, because in the time of King Athelstan,* the first king of England and the grandson of Alfred the Great, the River Wye was recognised as the boundary between the English and the Welsh. But, by the end of that century, the Saxons had crossed the Wye, advanced into Ergyng, and were making forays into Ewyas, the Golden Valley becoming the boundary between England and Wales. On the accession of Edward the Confessor in 1042, Archenfield had the status of a Welsh dependency connected to Herefordshire, but Ewyas was still a Welsh cantref. However, by the time of his death in 1066, Ewyas had become disputed territory, parts of it being annexed as early as 1046 by Frenchmen, of all people, friendly with Edward, an incursion which provoked the wrath of the Welsh, whose reprisal raids were devastating. From 1055 onwards, there were several raids by Welsh princes into Ewyas and Archenfield.

"According to the Domesday Book of 1086, which mentions both districts, the lands were 'laid waste'. An indication of the extent of the upheaval, and evidence that Archenfield was then only just within the reach of the new Norman Kingdom of William the Conquerer, is confirmed by the actual Domesday entries for the districts. There is only one entry for Ewyas, and almost nothing for the greater part of Archenfield which, when it is mentioned, is classified as being 'waste', meaning that it had no current value. The Domesday picture of Archenfield is one of a sparsely settled land where woodland and tree-covered wastes were extensive, and where the Welsh land holders paid their dues in sesters of honey. Eventually, the Normans designated it a Royal Forest, a game reserve for the King."

"Even at this time, both Ewyas and Archenfield still observed Welsh laws and customs. The paying of honey dues was one. Gradually, Archenfield was absorbed into Herefordshire, becoming a Hundred in 1125, but eventually its ancient provincial name was lost. Ewyas was infiltrated and then conquered by the Normans towards the end of William's reign, and became one of the famous Marcher Lordships, a semi-autonomous district ruled over by a Norman baron who gave allegiance to the English King. It was in the Lacy family for many years, and did not become a Hundred until the sixteenth century."

Catherine paused again, to take a long breath after this extraordinary outpouring of historical facts, which she had delivered as though speaking to a local history society. But Owen was still engaged and did not have that blank expression so often seen at meetings of local history societies, though he had moved from the floor to the sofa.

"Didn't Humphrey de Bohun tell you that he is descended from his namesake, the great Earl of Hereford, who was given custody of the Marches in the reign of Henry 111, a man who was himself the grandson of Humphrey 'cum barba' de Bohun, a follower of the Conqueror, and someone who did not shave his face in the accustomed style of the Normans?"

"No, he was too absorbed in his ancient trees and the words of bards to wander off into his own origins, although he did mention his genes, in passing."

There was another pause.

"Well; does that answer your question?" asked Catherine, knowing that she had given a consummate reply.

Owen smiled and nodded.

"Fascinating stuff, but why weren't there any illustrations with your talk?"

At this remark Catherine threw an OS map at him. She smiled, too, at last, and relaxed, losing that air of seriousness and intensity that had strained her looks during her discourse, and hardened her beauty somewhat. She enjoyed telling others about the history of her home area, and was particularly glad that Owen was fascinated by it all, too.

Relaxing further, she asked Owen about his time in Northumberland, smiling in such a way that he felt like telling her everything about himself. But he didn't. All he did was give a rather dry summary of his caravan days, touching only briefly upon the ethereal qualities of the mires and mosses, and leaving out the persistent melancholy of the winter. Before he revealed his life-story, he wanted to know how much she already knew about him. He ventured to bring the conversation round to the implications in his sister's words - that she had told Catherine everything.

"Suzy must have told you something about what I was doing", he said, rhetorically.

Catherine was not inclined to say very much on this subject. But she did say that Suzy had mentioned how depressed he had been by all the conifer plantations that blanketed the landscape in the north. This was another subject close to his heart, and one that he preferred to keep to himself for the time being. Opening-up to women was not something that came easily to Owen, though the face he now had before him was doing all sorts of things to his emotions.

Then she asked him what work he hoped to find. He had not thought about temporary work yet; he had enough money for the time being to help him settle in; but he would appreciate a lift into Hereford sometime to register at the Unemployment Benefit Office. A date was fixed. Thereafter, the conversation subsided into a casual exchange of inconsequential comments until Owen, in asking how she and Suzy had become friends, prompted Catherine to give an effusive and warm account of their friendship.

Catherine explained that they had first met over three years ago when Suzy got in touch with the Museum in town to see if it was interested in holding an exhibition of work by local artists, including herself. She happened to be in the Museum that day, taking down a display of some old documents. They got on so well that after the exhibition, which was a great success, Suzy became involved with the presentation of another display focusing on the folk legends of the County.

"We called it 'The Rediscovery of the Green Man'*. For a while, the tempo of the Records Office backroom was heightened as Suzy and I busied ourselves and enjoyed working together. That was two years ago, just after she moved in here. Fortunately, my next project turned out to be the cataloguing of the Llandyfrig Estate records. The de Bohun's asked Suzy to help me sort through the piles of prints and other artwork that lay in their library. What had promised to be an arduous task, sorting boxes and books of illustrations became a very happy time indeed. We did most of this work at the Court."

The mention of artwork reminded her of something she had promised to do for Suzy - to show Owen where all his sister's precious drawings and paintings were kept so he could ensure that nothing disastrous happened to them. Had he not become the caretaker of the cottage, she would have had the responsibility of looking after them.

Catherine took him into Suzy's studio, which was more chaotic than any other room in the house. He had ventured into it a few times already to look at the illustrations on the walls, but he had not explored any further - he was not in the habit of prying into his sister's things, and was strangely reluctant to even rummage through drawers looking for necessary household articles. To Catherine, the chaos was familiar. She knew where everything was kept and was well acquainted with the mass of illustrations she revealed. Together, like two people with a common connection, they immersed themselves in the artwork, which consisted mostly of illustrations of plants, for this was Suzy's speciality, the skill which had taken her to the Pyrenees. It was a long time since Owen had seen so many of his sister's drawings and paintings. He noticed immediately, as he perused her more recent work, that she had advanced even further in the clarity of her drawing, and in capturing those holistic qualities which plants display to the human eye but which are difficult to capture in art. One illustration in particular caught his eye. It was a very impressionistic picture of a black poplar in flower – a stark outline of the tree's structure in black with countless crimson squirls blazoning the tall crown; it was titled 'The Black Poplar in Gulible'. So far, Owen had not seen a black poplar anywhere near Gulible. He made a mental note to keep a look-out for it.

In the course of their mutual admiration for Suzy's art, Catherine became very mellow; more relaxed than she had been at any time that evening. Her mellowness may have been brought on by Owen's enchantment with his sister's creations, for they were poring over a hoard of artistic brilliance which gave them both much joy. By the time they dragged themselves back into the living room to get warm again around the fire Catherine was at ease at last. Owen made some more herb tea and then, without any prompting from him, and to his amazement, she suddenly said:

"Suzy has told me a lot about you. When we're having fun

together, she often says something like 'Owen couldn't cope with this level of activity', or 'Owen would have made himself scarce by now'. She says that your personalities are poles apart but that, despite this, you are still quite close; closer, it seems, than I am with my brother, who spends most of his time trying to introduce me to his mates - farmers' sons mostly, looking for future work-horses. Suzy says she has never been bothered by you interfering with her life."

"Huh; even if I had, I would not have known where to start or got very far. Her volubility and dynamism would have blown me away", said Owen with a shrug which added meaning to his words. "If I spend too long in her company, I flake out, even though we might be getting on alright."

"But you're not retiring and reserved because Suzy blows you away, surely? She envies your reflective nature and quietude - your 'inner calm', as she calls it. She admitted to me, shortly before she left, that she often wishes, when she is drawing nature, that she could relax as much as you do when observing it. I was surprised when she revealed one day that to illustrate plants was to dissect their wholeness and reassemble it on paper without capturing their complete beauty. I think her drawings and paintings have special qualities, don't you?"

"Yes, but there will always be a dimension which can never be captured, however good the artist. As I was saying earlier this evening, there is an indefinable element associated with plants and places..."

Owen was unwise to return to a matter upon which they seemed to hold different opinions. It undid Catherine's mellowness and reminded her how late it was. As she departed, she said to Owen that although the Easter weekend was upon them, the farm would continue to be busy and he was welcome to join them at any time. Then she paused and added, in a rather diffident manner:

"If you want to see some interesting trees and places, why don't I take you to the Hergest Croft Botanical Garden and also to Hay this weekend? Suzy suggested that I introduce you to the area."

"That's a wonderful invitation", Owen found himself saying. "Hergest was definitely on my list of places to see; and so, too, were the second-hand book shops of Hay-on-Wye. Just let me know the day."

Moments later, Owen was left eking out the dying warmth of the fire, finishing the evening as it had begun - with Catherine and her beautiful face on his mind...

Notebook - 14th April

Catherine tells me that the county flower of Hereford is mistletoe, and that the plant's association with Christmas derives from its place in Celtic mythology.

CHAPTER 9

'I fear those grey old men of Moccas, those grey, gnarled, low-browed, knock-kneed, bowed, bent, huge, strange, long-armed, deformed, hunchbacked, misshapen oak men that stand waiting and watching century after century, biding God's time with both feet in the grave and yet tiring down and seeing out generation after generation, with such tales to tell, as when they whisper them to each other in the midsummer nights, make the silver birches weep and the poplars and aspens shiver and the long ears of the hares and rabbits stand on end. No human hand set those oaks. They are 'the trees which the Lord hath planted'. They look as if they had been at the beginning and making of the world, and they will probably see its end.'

Francis Kilvert 1876
Plomer, 1964, (pp. 304-5)

Notebook - 20th April

RESEARCH ON THE AREA
FROM A VARIETY OF SOURCES

Translations of Welsh Names
(From Catherine and her sources)

The Goggin	*Unknown meaning.*
Mynydd y rhibo	*The bewitched mountain*
Coed Tirion Glas	*The wood of gentle green*
Dol Barcut Brook	*The brook of the kite's meadow*
Melglyn Brook	*The brook of the honey dingle*
Gwenynog	*The place of bees*
Bodcut Farm	*The farm of the kite*
Tre Llywn	*The homestead of the grove (The prefix 'Tre' appears in south-west Herefordshire more thickly than anywhere else in England except Cornwall)*
Treribble	*The homestead of ?*
Onen	*The ash tree settlement*
Gulible	*From Gwlyb-le: the wet place*
Elchon	*Unknown. A very old name.*
Trescoyte	*(Tre-is-y-coed) House below the wood*
Skynlas	*The amazing green dingle.*
Archenfield	*Derivation from The Place Names of Herefordshire by A.T. Bannister, 1916, C.U.P.*

380AD	*Ariconium, a Roman settlement at Weston under Penyard near Ross-on-Wye*
915	*Ircingafeldes, Yrcingafeld (from the Anglo-Saxon Chronicle)*
1086	*Arcenfelde, Arcenefelde (Domesday Book)*
1130	*Ergyng, Ercineg, Ergin, Erchyng, Erchynfeld, Urcenevelde (Liber Landavensis - The Book of Llandaff)*
1147	*Erging (Geoffrey of Monmouth)*
1550	*Herchingfield, Erchenfeld (Leyland's Itinerary) N.B. "The correct Welsh modification of Ariconium would be Ergun".*
Ewyas	*Considered to be pre-Celtic, possibly coined during the Bronze Age. It may mean 'sheep district', or it may derive from the early British word Gwys or Gwias which implies a place of battle. Both are plausible in view of the area's history. These versions of the name were used by Powell in his Description of Wales 1584 (From History and Antiquities of the County of Hereford by John Duncumb, 1804.)*

Derivations from Bannister, 1916.

1086	*Ewias (Domesday Book)*
1130	*Euwias, Euias, Ewias, Eugias (Book of Llandaff)*
c1200	*Ewias, Ewyas (Giraldus Cambrensis)*
c1300	*Euas (Black Book of Carmarthen)*
c1500	*Ewis (Leyland's Itinerary) The present pronunciation of the name is 'Ew-is', the accent being on the first syllable.*
c1600	*Ewyaslande (Llyfr Baglan by Williams)*

Notebook - 22nd April: From de Bohun's Library.

Preface to King Alfred's Version of St. Augustine's Soliloquies: (edited by Thomas A. Carnicelli, 1969).

'I gathered for myself cudgels [short, thick sticks], and stud-shafts [posts], and horizontal shafts, and helves [handles] for each of the tools that I could work with, and bow-timbers and bolt-timbers for every work that I could perform, the commonest trees, as many as I could carry. Neither came I with a burden home, for it did not please me to bring all the wood back, even if I could bear it. In each tree I saw something that I needed at home; therefore I advise each one who can, and has many wains [wagons], that he direct his steps to the same wood where I cut the stud-shafts. Let him fetch more for himself, and load his wains with fair beams, that he may wind many a neat wall [wattle and daub], and

erect many a rare house, and build a fair town, and therein may dwell merrily and softly both winter and summer, as I have not yet done.'

(Translated by Catherine's friend Colleen Powell of Ross-on-Wye Library)

Giraldus Cambrensis (Gerald of Wales) 1146-1220
The Journey Through Wales and The Description of Wales (Penguin 1978)

Ewyas: 'Those mountain heights abound in horses and wild game, those woods are richly stocked with pigs, the shady groves with goats, the pasture lands with sheep, the meadows with cattle, the farms with ploughs. All the things and creatures which I have mentioned are there in great abundance, and yet we are so insatiable in our wicked desires that each in turn seems insufficient for our needs.'(page 102)

Inquisition post mortem, 27, Edward 1. No.44. Roger de la Haye (1266).

'Inquisition concerning the lands and tenements which belonged to Roger de la Haye, to wit, how much land the said Roger held on the day he died in his desmesne as of fee to the Lord King in chief, and how much of others, and by what service, and how much they are worth in all issues, and who is his next heir, and of what age.

Made at Ewyas in the parts of Wales before the Escheator of the Lord King on the 20th day of November, in the 27th year of the reign of King Edward: By the oath of Edmund Le Galeys, Hugh de Tyberton, Walter Ragun, Hugh de Wormbrugg, Hugh Ivor, John ap Vael, Henry de Elchon, Madoc ap Jeverard, Jeverard ap Griffith, Richard de Euwyas; Who say that the same Roger de le Haye held the manor of Llandyfrig Haye, member of the manor of Euwyas, which same manor with its members he held of the Lord King in chief by barony, and did the service of two knights' fees. They also say that there is one messuage, and the easements are worth 4s. a year. And there is there one garden, and it is worth by the year 12d. And there is there one water-mill, and it is worth by the year 75s. And there is there a fishery, and it is worth by the year 50s. And there are there 410 acres of outside wood, and the acre is worth 3d. Total: #5.2s.6d. And there is there one park, and it is worth by the year as in herbage and pannage, besides the sustenance of the deer, 20s. And there are there two carucates of land, each one whereof contains a hundred acres of land by the long hundred, price of the acre 4d. Total: #4. And there are there sixty acres of meadow, price of the acre 18d. Total: #4.10s. And there are there ten acres of pasture, price of the acre 12d. Total: 10s. Grand Total: #21.17s.6d.'

Leyland's Itinerary (1534-43), ed. L. T. Smith (1910).

'*There be hills by est and southe on the right rype of Wy river, well wooddyd, and not far distant from Hereforde toune...*

Herchinfield [Erging] is a great lordship...and lieth betwixt Monemuth and Hereford abowt a ij. Myles from eche of them...Erchenfeld is full of enclosures, very [full] of corne and wood...The lordship selfe of Ewis Harold wher it is narrowest is a myle in bredthe, and moste in length 2 mile. It hath good corne, gresse and woode...'

Survey of Llandyfrig Court, 1583. (Anonymous)

'There is an Haye or Parke amonge hilles joining on the manor place. It containeth in circuit three miles, the oaken pales well repaired, the herbage goode and sweet, wherein are 180 fallow deere, whereof there are of deere of antler 60, deere of rascall 120. Within the said parke of 200 acres there are many fine oakes, young and olde, fit for timber and esteemed to be worthe 9s, some dottard oakes and also some 40 acres of wood well set with storers of oake, ash and maple, and some coppice of linden which always has been cut and sold every fourteen years, and every acre is worthe at this time 6s 8d.

The mixture of plain, of hilles, of coppice wood and of pasture, together with two plentiful springs of water, which are within the same enclosure, and a tributary of the brook Dol Barcut, afford a most pleasant abode. In winter when the pasture fails and when the snow falls, they give the deere hay and dried leaves of linden and elme trees.

The goodly manor also hath a big wood of 140 acres called Coed Tirion Glas. It containeth all sorts of timber trees but principally oake, elme, ashe and linden, especially the *latter, of which there are some very tall trees. The tree of greatest stature in the wood standeth beside the brook Melglyn above the wood reeves dwelling at Gwen y nog. It is said to flower before any other linden thereabouts and to be the best honey tree. The honey is right goode.'*

N.B. *'Rascall deere' - a term commonly used in the sixteenth and seventeenth centuries to mean 'lean animals fit neither to hunt or kill'.*

(Some Account of English Deer Parks by E. P. Shirley, London, 1867)

'Requirements of the Deer Park', Gervase Markham, 1616 (from Shirley).

'The parke would be seated (if it be possible) within a wood of high and tall timber trees, in a place compassed about, and well fenced with walls made of rough stone and lime, or else of bricks and earth-lome, or else with poles made of oake plankes. You must forsee that there bee some little brooke of spring-water running along by the place; or for want of spring-water and naturall streames, you must prepare ditches and pooles... Nor ought the parke to consist of one kind of ground only, as all of wood, all grasse, or all coppice, but of divers, as part high wood, part grasse or champion, and part coppice or under-wood, or thicke spring: nor must these severall grounds lie open, or as it were in a common one with another; but they must be separated one from the other by a strong rale, through which deere or shepe (but no greater cattell) may passe, for they must have the full liberty of every

place. Neither must the parke be situated upon any one entire hill, plaine, or else valley, but it must consist of divers hills, divers plains, and divers valleys; the hills which are commonly called the viewes or discoveries of parkes, would bee all goodly high woods of tall timber, as well for the beauty and gracefulnesse of the parke, as also for the echoe and sound which will rebound from the same... in times of hunting... doubling the musicke, and making it tenne times more delightfull; the plains which are called in parkes the lawnds, would be very champion and fruitful... for the breeding of great store of grasse and hay for the feeding and nourishing of the deere or other wild beasts... The valleys which are called the coverts or places of leare for wild beasts, would be all very thicke sprung or under-wood, as well for the concealing of them from potchers and purloyners, as for giving them rest and shadow in the day time, who cannot endure to lie open to the view of passengers, or undefended by darknesse and obscuritie... the parke is a place that must contrive all things for the good and safetie of the game it keepeth. Thus you see the parke must consist of view, lawnd, and covert, and the situation of hill, valley, and plaine... In the most convenientest lawnd of the parke, which is most spatious and fruitful, and which hath the greatest prospect into the parke, and where the deere take greatest delight to feed, there you shall build the lodge or house for the keeper to dwell in, and it shall by all means stand cleare, and open in every way, so as there may be no secret approach made into the same... and it shall stand so faire in the view of the lawnd, that from thence a man may see every way around the same, and some part up into the high woods, and other most secret parts of the parke...

Treatise and Discourse of the Lawes of the Forest', by John Manwood, 1610.

'Before this nation was replenished with inhabitants, there were many great Woods full of all sorts of wild Beasts then known in England; and after the same came to be inhabited, the Woods were, by degrees, destroyed, especially near the houses; and as the Land increased in People, so the Woods and Coverts were daily destroyed, and, by that means, the wild Beasts retired to those Woods which were left standing, and which were remote from their Habitations.

But there were still, and even in the Saxon's time, many great Woods which were not destroyed... Forests and Woods where Wolves and Foxes did harbour; which being afterwards destroyed by Edgar, a Saxon king, Anno 959, and very few remaining, the Welshmen paid him a yearly tribute of Wolves skins; and those and such like ravenous Beasts being thus destroyed, the residue being Beasts of Pleasure, as well as delicate Meat, the Kings of the land began to be careful for the Preservation of them, and in order thereto to privilege certain Woods and Places, so that no Man may hurt or destroy them there; and thus the said Places became Forests.' (From Mase pp. 33-34).

(Archenfield was one such Royal Forest).
N.B. The word 'forest' comes from the Latin word meaning 'outside of', the areas so designated being outside the common law of the land - that is, reserved for the King Francis Kilvert, Saturday, 22nd April, 1876.

The Moccas Park Oaks.

'We came tumbling and plunging down the steep hillside of Moccas Park, slipping, tearing and sliding through oak and birch and fallow wood of which there seemed to be underfoot an accumulation of several feet, the gathering ruin and decay probably of centuries. As we came down the lower slopes of the wooded hillside into the glades of the park the herds of deer were moving under the brown oaks and the brilliant green hawthorns, and we came upon... what seemed at first in the dusk to be a great ruined grey tower, but which proved to be the vast ruin of the king oak of Moccas Park, hollow and broken but still alive and vigorous in parts and actually pushing out new shoots and branches...

Notebook - 27th April: To a reader in times when pocket word processors replace notebooks. The Deer Haye of Llandyfrig Court in the spring of 1988 - from Teili Junction...

The western reaches of Archenfield bordering on Ewyas are enchanting at this time of the year, for the blossoms of the pear trees in the cottages and the farm orchards; and for the wild cherries in the woods; islands of whiteness in a scene of brightening green. Especially the single pear trees alone in the fields... They are exquisite company.

From its highest part, the plateau top beneath the cover of Coed Tirion Glas, the Deer Haye affords a fine view of this springtime setting. A field maple on the very edge of the wood above me, festooned with mustard coloured bunches of mistletoe, distracts me for a moment. The cuckoos of spring continue to resound in my ears, accompanied by the incessant tapping of woodpeckers. Around me and below, stand aged trees with rotting limbs, their backs against the mountain - in retreat.

There are decrepit oaks which stand alone in the pasture in the bottomland, surrounding the depression where water, mire and willow carr intermingle. Some of the oaks are flowering and their leaf-buds breaking. The huge black poplar is silhouetted, leaning over the pale greyish-green of the carr. Away in the distance, there is a freshly cut pile of oak fuel-wood inside the main gate, opposite the Keeper's Lodge.

Closer in the vicinity of the Ditch, on the undulating ground of the bracken pasture, the trees are more thickly set together, but barely touching. Here, some horse chestnuts, their foliage bright green and complete, stand out amongst the almost leafless oaks, which carry a hint of watery gold in the emergence of their flowers. A stately Wellingtonia, the nesting place of the Haye's resident pair of ravens, rises up above the oaks, emphatic in the intrusion of its evergreen spire. A dead larch, skeletal in its gauntness, stands in the open in the foreground at the base of the slope, together with the stock frames which protect the next generation of lonely survivors - de Bohun's future 'abode trees'.

The steep banks of the slopes below me are crowded with trees; and the tawney bracken, where last year is lost, thickens. Hawthorn trees in leaf obscure the views downslope in some directions. The Gully carves through the ground, opening up a miniature chasm below me. A solitary yew, falling outwards in decline, guards the descent into the Gully. Perched on its shoulders where I sit, small-leaved limes, with bright young leaves, surge up and out over the drop, grasping the upper slopes with their layered limbs. Teili Junction is a grand place to be - the sacred recorder grove of a latterday Norman lord.

Towards the Cwm smooth, massive beech boles, pollarded generations ago, mix with fissured oaks. Dead branches and shattered butts lie rotting on mats of dead leaves. Thick pile carpets of tightly packed bluebells are forming their oceans of colour. As yet, there is virtually nothing else, except the clustered white stars of wood anemone in the shade of the trees. Opaque beech leaves, freshly open in bunches, catch the fickle rays of sunlight, contrasting with the smooth grey boughs. One tree is bare but for one spray of leaves at the very end of a bough.

A fox creeps into view, a mere twenty feet away, sniffing a path upslope, unaware of my presence. For twenty seconds, it comes my way, then lifts its head and sees me, staring for a brief moment before running off downslope with a glance behind.

The rustling of the wind increases in the trees behind me in the wood. But the birds continue to call. The trees begin to creak. The squirrels ignore me. This is righte goode...'

CHAPTER 10

'A meditative man
Walks in this wood, and calls each tree his own:
Yet the green track he treads is older than
Recorded English history:
His feet, while moving on towards times unknown,
Travel from traceless mystery...'

From `A Proprietor' by Siegfried Sassoon

The afternoon was a fine one. Only an elusive breeze ruffled the calmness of a sunny day, and only the plaintive mewing of a buzzard somewhere in the distance haunted the quietness, which was punctuated now and then by the sound of cuckoos. The Haye was its usual self - exquisitely timeless - and the Greybeards were as seemingly stoical as ever. If they harboured spirits, these could only be in communion, filling the Haye with the aura of their silent togetherness; giving it that sense of place with which the human mind may sometimes take communion - if it is disposed to do so.

There was only one human amongst the aged trees; one whose disposition was perhaps so inclined. Owen was on his way to the Melglyn Stoggle again, but by a different route. He had been checking the tree regularly to watch it come into leaf. Matilda had told him about the path which skirted the northern sector of the Deer Haye and led to the tree through the Cwm and the southern portion of Coed Tirion Glas. It was a route which would take him into the wood for the first time.

In his quiet, unobtrusive progress between the aged trees, he passed close to several deer grazing the slopes beside the tributary stream which emanated from the northern portion of the wood, the Ditch. They seemed not to notice him. After crossing the stream by way of some slabs of sandstone, conveniently placed to constitute a ford, a vista opened up across the dingle of the Cwm Brook and on to the wood. He had not seen the wood from this angle before. The skyline of its canopy, which from all other directions was more or less in unison with the contours of the ground, presented a startling irregularity. Emerging above the canopy was the narrow crown of a single tree, a large tree and certainly a tall one. What else could it be but a lime, he thought. Using the map he had with him, he made a mental note of the approximate position of the tree in the wood - what he thought was its position - before moving on towards the narrow neck of land between the two portions of the wood where the Cwm Brook entered the Haye. The mewing of the buzzard was now more distinct. Owen looked into the sky again above the wood. He could still see the emergent crown. Then he caught sight of a buzzard gliding towards it. The bird circled the crown twice and then disappeared into its branches.

When he arrived at the high white gate which gave access from the Haye into the rough pasture enclosed by the northern and southern portions of the wood, he came to another stream, larger than the Ditch, and a bridge of railway sleepers. To the west, another vista opened up, one where the skyline of Rhibo Mountain was just visible. A cwm, with the dimensions of a tilted shallow basin, came into view, entirely enclosed by the wood and littered with trees and bracken. Here, there was a stark change in the outline of the Brook. In its course through the Haye, its banks were exposed; only single trees of immense girth grew in places along its length; there was no undergrowth. In contrast, all that could be seen above the gate was a sinuous line of tightly congregating trees and bushes, marking the descent of the brook within its cwm. There were also lines of trees across the view on the right, linking the wood with the brook, and a threadbare line of alders on the left coursing diagonally to join the brook near where Owen stood. The cwm also contained pockets of trees which, from their shape, suggested hollows or micro-cwms, and on its higher slopes, scattered individual trees. Last year's bracken covered the lowered slopes, now coloured by bluebells, expanding outwards from the lines of trees, and creeping upslope in finger-like splays. And giving the cwm edges which accentuated its shape and its seclusion was the bulk of Coed Tirion Glas itself. Woodland was not far away, neither physically nor historically.

Owen was drawn into this small, secluded valley without the guidance of the track. Alders fringed the brook on the level ground immediately above the gate. They were not single trees but the overstood stems of old coppice stools, soaking up the moisture held up upon the lip of land which marked the change from the base of the cwm to the beginning of the dingle. It was into this sylvan sponge that a stream seeped from the western portion of the wood, its course delineated by the line of threadbare alders. In fact, all the lines of trees in the cwm concealed watercourses. It was here that the track veered towards the left, crossing the main brook, again by sleepers, and heading for the wood. Upon passing this point, the sense of enclosure, of entering the cwm proper was complete, for the tributary watercourse curved upwards, its trees becoming a visual part of the southern portion of the wood. The gradient of the Cwm Brook increased also and the alders gave way to other trees.

The first main tributary of the Brook that Owen came to was quite deeply incised, the pale red earth testifying to its torrential nature in times of spate. Owen thought that this stream was probably what de Bohun called 'the Dark Dell'. Leaving the track near an oak with three separate trunks, he followed the stream, or tried to follow it, into the wood. The stream was a boulder-strewn gash in steeply sloping ground and was virtually impenetrable - a dank and slippery wilderness with dead wood everywhere, lying at all angles across the stream. The water cascaded down a rocky gully, where moss-covered slabs of stone, scattered ferns, eroding soil, and the exposed roots of trees were shadowed by the bars of rotting wood. The death of a number of diseased elms, appearing ghastly in decay, had opened up the canopy in places while closing off the dingle with debris. Limes curved upwards from the bare ground of the dell's banks, and overstood lime coppice was seemingly everywhere. Owen thought he heard the buzzard again, but there was no chance of seeing it from such a dark place. He walked back towards the track.

Notebook - 5th May: Near the Dark Dell, Coed Tirion Glas.

I am writing this while wedged between two of three sturdy stems of oak which seem to have grown up from the same stool, veering away from each other, and being devoid of any branches on the inside. In deference to de Bohun, I'll call this the Oak Triumvirate. So far, the main timber tree in the wood is oak, sessile oak by the looks of it, although there is an intricate mixing of the two native species. The oaks are only just coming into leaf, but their yellowy-brown flowers give the trees a golden sheen. I have already seen some ash, an unusually large number of field maple, the odd birch and a solitary yew, not to mention the ubiquitous hazel, but only one hawthorn. There are occasional lime trees but this species is growing mainly as straggly coppice which is layering itself, the stools looking like purple legged spiders.

There can be few places like this left in the county. A 410 acre, semi-natural, broadleaved wood, ungrazed except for the occasional stray sheep and the few deer which wander away from the Deer Haye. A Site of Special Scientific Interest: on paper, a place apart from the twentieth century woodland vestiges; supposedly `outside' the normal operations of the day, but not as exclusively outside the common law lands as the forest of the Norman overlords. For the moment, a reserve of boundless calm and peace, quietly teeming with largely unseen life.

A woodpecker has just started bashing away at a tree to remind me that other warm blooded creatures like woods, too, and the resonance they make. And another... Even before I got into the Haye, I heard a cuckoo again. I hear them every

*day, often early in the morning as I rise. How many of them
are there in this place? I hope they stay alive. The bird
carcasses hanging by the coniferous plantation have been
added to.*

*I've decided not to follow the Dell to the top; it's too
difficult, even though the map indicates that it would lead me
towards the Melglyn Stoggle. I'd rather wander around and
try to find the tall tree which emerges from the canopy
somewhere in this part of the wood - the Emergent Lime, for
want of another name. My guess is that this tall lime stands
somewhere in the vicinity of the upper part of the Dell, which
I can reach from further up the track, but it won't be easy to
find without a compass. I need a helicopter or a large bird's
help.*

Owen returned to the track, which followed a course between
the Brook and the edge of the wood. As he surveyed the scene
ahead of him, the eerie pee-ow of the buzzard returned to
capture his attention. This time, a bird was gliding above that
part of the wood which enclosed the top edge of the cwm. As
he watched it, the buzzard swooped down into the cwm and
flew over some tall trees that rose above the others marking the
line of the brook. Again, a landing was made. The young
foliage of the trees was lighter in colour than that of their
neighbours. Owen was drawn towards them. The buzzard lifted
itself out of the trees, banked sharply, and then swooped down
towards Owen. It came so close that he could see a gap in the
broad wing-tip of its left side where one of the five finger-like
primary feathers was missing. He noticed also that its belly was
as white as the blobs on the undersides of the wings. It uttered

another haunting cry, banked again into the cwm and returned to the tall trees ahead beside the Brook.

Owen approached closer. The sound of water reached his ears. The glimpses he got of the banks of the Brook showed it to be deeply incised. Among the trees clasping the shoulders of the cutting were ash, maple, hazel and elder. Further on, there was a group of taller trees. He recognised them immediately. They were limes, small-leaved limes, growing on the very edge of the deep cutting. He passed under their crowns and walked into their shade. On the opposite bank there was another lime. It was very large indeed, not as big as the one at Gwenynog but impressive, its lower limbs arching down and almost touching the shoulder of the bank. A short distance upstream, a tributary joined the brook from the right and another lime stood on the interfluve between the two watercourses. Here, the cutting was very deep indeed, perhaps twenty feet deep, a precipitously sided gouge virtually devoid of vegetation. Speckles of sunlight dashed the bare ground. The new leaves of the limes were brightly illuminated and almost transparent. The quietness was cathedral-like.

Once more, the eerie call of the buzzard distracted Owen. Involuntarily, he walked out into the sunlight to see the bird circling above the group of limes. There were about a dozen limes altogether, including a few more further up the brook. He was about to go back into the shade of the trees when the buzzard emitted another call to make him look up. It was now flying away towards the edge of the wood where he had first seen it. Without thinking, he followed, tramping through bracken and crossing the unimproved pasture. The buzzard had disappeared. Owen continued on upslope, knowing that he would come to the spot where the track entered the wood. In doing so, he came upon another lime, a pollarded one this time, growing like all the others he had seen, on the very edge of the stream's bank. Retiring primroses clung to the rumples in the ground made by the heaving of the tree's roots and beyond, the wood burgeoned with bluebells. The scene was just touching Owen's soul when he was startled by the buzzard flying out of the tree and uttering another piercing shriek.

There was a gate where the track entered the wood and beside it, an old stile, suggesting that parts of the wood had once been fenced off. In the action of skirting it, Owen again heard the mewing of a buzzard; this time a long drawn out call, seemingly coming from within the wood itself. He could not see it. Nor was there much of a track to be seen. From what Matilda had said, he expected to find a ride, for that was the word she had used. To him, a ride was a wide, well demarcated track. Instead, he could only just make out the course of a single narrow path, in places barely the width of a boot wide. Progressing along it, he thought he discerned the signs of a former ride. Some of the oak trees near the path had basal scars, evidence of damage caused by the extraction of timber. And there were stretches which appeared to have avenue-like dimensions, although now occupied by young trees and a tangle of vegetation. It was this undergrowth, together with fallen branches and some fallen trees, which obscured the course of the old ride and made the existing path deviate continuously from a regular line and in places split into two and converge later. The way forward was also confused by a succession of intersections with badger tracks, although these were so well worn and coursing away into obvious wilderness through drifts of sweet woodruff that keeping to the human way, such as it was, was not too difficult.

The effort of keeping to the path meant that Owen had to stop to allow his mind and his eyes to wander. The more he saw of the tangled world of this neglected wood, the more he dwelt upon the possible history of its existence. Since the Celtic settlement of the area, and the naming of its prominent features, many, many individuals would have walked where he now walked. Moving through the wildwood of those times must have been very difficult for upright animals with tender skin. There could be no comparison with the supposedly semi-natural wood of the present, except perhaps in the assaults made upon the skin. Why some pieces of the wildwood remained at all, when so much was lost, was a story in itself. What characteristics, ownerships, and usages kept Coed Tirion Glas together for so long? Was it a direct descendent from the wildwood as de Bohun claimed to be a direct descendent from the family which claimed it? It had the appearance of a wood that was ancient, as de Bohun had the appearance of a breed that was ancient...

The mewing of a buzzard returned. In the sunlight of a glade to his right, where an elm had died, Owen thought he could see the bird through the bright green leaves of a lime. More lime! He had reached a part of the wood where overstood lime coppice was everywhere around him. The going was better through this part, and delightful, for the play of the sunlight on the young leaves was magical; and the bluebells were profuse. Owen was uplifted. He was content to be alone and to become spellbound.

He did not see the wall of conifers until he was almost upon them. The change was dramatic and disturbing. A lime wood of bluebells and sweet woodruff suddenly giving way to a dark, impenetrable abyss of tightly packed jagged stems where there was nothing on the ground except the brown litter of needles and fronds. Owen was repulsed by this evergreen wall, but the way through it along the old ride was more clearly defined than any stretch of the walk so far, and it was bathed in sunshine. After coping with the sudden, unsettling change to his mental state, he ventured forward, down the spacious path which he knew would take him to the edge of the dingle and the Stoggle. Either side of him, the wall of conifers varied in its continuity. In such a dense plantation, he was not surprised to see a number of places where the trees had failed to grow, and where the original coppice stools had regenerated, notably the shade-tolerant limes. But they were a sorry sight; thin and straggly, and drawn out searching for the light in a dark place surrounded by invaders. One sad sight was the immense butt of an old lime, at least 3 feet across; the remains of a felled tree that had yet to die because a few straggly stems with young leaves issued from recesses in its girth.

Halfway through the plantation, the path turned sharply to the left, and the Stoggle came into view; a bright green tower of foliage shining in the sunlight. He could see the wound caused by the wind's ferocity, but the stag-headed top was obscured by foliage. The brightness of the tree was welcoming, but against the frame of conifers it looked lost. Owen quickened his stride, keeping his eyes on the crown ahead. As he did so, he heard the sound of flapping wings behind him. Before he could turn round, a buzzard flew over him closer than any bird of prey he had ever seen. It was the same buzzard he had seen all day. It swept along the ride, over the gate at the edge of the plantation, and up into the Stoggle, dropping into its stag-headed top.

He was glad to reach the lime as well, and to have the conifers behind him. He could not see the buzzard but he was sure that it was still in the tree. He tried to locate it but he was overcome by the presence of the tree. To him, the Melglyn Stoggle was such a beautifully massive bastion of stability and bower of calmness that he spent many minutes looking into its crown and peering closely at its leaves. Now that the leaves were fully out, he could see that they differed slightly from the norm for small leaved lime. They were more or less heart shaped like all lime leaves, ending in a sharp point but having two subsidiary points on their shoulders. Most of the leaves were shaped like this, although some were asymmetrical, having only one side point. He detached one or two leaves to take back with him and noticed that the side veins emanating from the end of the petiole ended in the subsidiary points. He was fascinated by these peculiarly shaped leaves and started to imagine that the tree was a small-leaved lime derived directly from a very ancient line of trees local to the area. He took out his notebook, inserted the leaves between its pages, and then slid down the trunk into the natural seat at its base. The soft light coming through the crown, and the tender greenness of the leaves above him, relaxed his mind. He slipped deeper into the seat and closed his eyes to rest. For some reason, he quickly fell asleep.

Twenty minutes elapsed before he stirred, his head rolling from side to side and upwards for some seconds. Then suddenly his head jerked upwards stiffly and stopped moving; his mouth dropped open and his eyes opened too, very widely, staring fixedly up into the crown. He remained like this for half a minute. Then, just as suddenly, his head dropped towards his chest and he woke up, breathing deeply, gulping and swallowing as if his mouth were dry. At the moment his head touched his chest, the buzzard, which had been in the tree all along, flew off and away over the mountain. Owen did not see it go. He looked about from side to side with sharp automaton-like movements of the head, and then scanned the sky. Drawing his hands up onto his hips, he took a deep breath, tilted his head to one side, and stared out into the distance beyond the dingle. He felt detached from the present. After a lengthy period of deep thought, he took up his notebook, which had fallen to one side, and began to write in it...

Notebook - 5th May Elglyn toggle.

Walked from the Court to the toggle via the route atilda told me about. The ourney has worn me out. There are some uperb lime trees beside the rook in the cwm above the Deer aye. The cwm has the appearance of a lace where oodland has not long been lost. As the 17 estate map shows it as the middle ortion of a larger Coed Tirion las, and the ithe Map shows it as almost lear of trees, I wonder when or in what tages it was leared. de Bohun might know.

A buzzard was lying around in the cwm, curiously choosing the limes as perching laces. I first saw it when it was lying over a tall tree which emerges above the anopy of the wood, and which must be an exceptional tree. I shall have to seek it out. The buzzard had a feather issing from its left wing tip, and was very white beneath. It made a soul-rending cry, more iercing than any I have ever heard before. The sound of it gave me that tingling feeling one sometimes gets when on emotional enterhooks.

Dropped off to leep beneath the lime and had what can only have been a daydream. I kept seeing a buzzard, like the one today, ircling above a wood and giving out an incessant series of calls; a rather aunting replay of the sounds of the afternoon. I woke up feeling a bit disoriented, and at first not knowing where I was. If a short walk like the one today has orn me out, there must be something wrong with my system.

Upon reading the notes through, he corrected the spelling mistakes, but they bothered him. His spelling was usually perfect. What had happened to his head?

Notebook - 6th May, 1988. The Common Buzzard (Buteo buteo).

'Dark brown hawk with barred tail. Soars on broad motionless wings, wing tips curved upwards, the feathers spread open like fingers. Tail usually spread in flight. More time spent perched somewhere - a tree, a rock, a crag, a post - than in flight. Aerial displays: soars on thermals and wind currents. In breeding season, they swoop and circle above the nest site, mewing incessantly. Nest usually in a tree. Often has a number of nests within the territory of a pair.

It does not continue on the wing for a very long time together. When not engaged in flight, it will remain, even for hours together, in the same spot - on the stump of a tree, or the point of a cliff, motionless, as some have conjectured, from repletion; and others from being on the look out for prey, at which, when coming within its ken, to stoop in pursuit. It frequents very much the same haunts, and may often be seen from day to day, and at the same hour of the day, beating the same hunting ground."

'The note of the Common Buzzard is wild and striking, its shrillness conveying a melancholy idea, though as every feeling of melancholy produced by anything in nature must be, of a pleasing kind - when heard in the retired situations in which this bird delights. One of its local names is the Shreak, evidently derived from the sound of its note.'

From British Birds by the Rev. F.O. Morris, (1850), (pp. 22-23.)

The Buzzards

CHAPTER 11

'The beauty of the view, the first view of the village, coming down by the Brooms this evening was indescribable. The brilliant golden spires shone in the evening light like flames against the dark hill side of the Old Forest and the blossoming fruit trees, the torch trees of Paradise blazed with a transparent green and white lustre up the dingle in the setting sunlight. The village is in a blaze of fruit blossom. Clyro is at its loveliest. What more can be said?'

Kilvert: Sunday, 14th April, 1872, (pp. 173-4)

"Catherine, has Owen told you that he spent part of Thursday night sleeping beneath the lime tree above Gwen y nog? asked Alison, as they prepared for a day in the Black Mountains and waited for Milo and Owen. "He told Milo that he ended up there after wandering through Coed Tirion Glas, and stayed because it was such a glorious evening. He said he fell asleep and woke up after midnight feeling heavy-headed."

"Never! He didn't say anything to me when I saw him on Friday, after he had helped my father with some more fencing. But I'm not surprised. That tree is becoming an obsession. We walked over to it last Saturday when I took him to Gwen y nog for the first time. My grandmothers wanted to show him around their place. He went very quiet when we sat by the tree. I asked what was bothering him. All he could say was to ask me if I felt that there was something special about the tree and its location."

"What did you say?"

"I just said it felt the same as being beside one of the trees in the Deer Haye - you know, dwarfed and overawed. He then asked me if I felt any different to usual."

"Did you?"

"No, of course not. He was disappointed. He couldn't understand why I was just as I usually am when he felt so different. I think Suzy has made a mistake in believing that we would get on well together.   His dreamy states are unfathomable. Suzy said that he would be introspective at times, and might even disappear if he got low, but I wasn't expecting him to absent himself while you're standing next to him."

Alison was surprised to hear Catherine divulge her thoughts in this way. She was forthcoming with Suzy - she knew that from living at the Goggin - but not with anyone else. Intrigued, she offered some more observations from Milo.

"That's interesting, because Milo has noticed him in what he calls a semi-trance like state on one or two occasions when

Owen has accompanied him on survey work. He reckons that when he goes like that, it is difficult to hold a conversation with him; that once he is turned on, he turns off as far as communicating with others is concerned. I think he is a bit like Suzy in this respect."

"Never! They are complete opposites. Their only likeness is in their looks. Suzy cannot relax long enough to become faraway or dreamy. We both know that; especially how uneasy she gets whenever she finds herself standing around with nothing to do. No, Owen is very different."

"I'm not so sure they are all that different, Catherine. When Suzy is in one of her crazy moods, it is as difficult to reach her as it seems to be to reach Owen when he drifts off. They're both escaping in a way. As, I suppose, I escape when I get wrapped up in Milo. We have yet to discover where you escape to..."

A friendly, but inquisitive, smile came to Alison's face, but Catherine was not to be drawn, whether or not she had escape routes. If anything, she was slightly discomposed by the remark.

"What does Milo think?" she asked after a short pause, preferring to keep the subject on Owen.

"He can't really make a comparison because he doesn't know Suzy very well; and I'm not sure he likes her very much: you must have realised that by now. Suzy has, hasn't she?"

This was another enquiry which Catherine preferred to let pass, asking instead what else Milo had observed about Owen.

"Um... the other day, he suggested that Owen might have a split personality, or at least a tendency to operate on two different levels; that for most of the time he is engaging, in an undemonstrative way, and very 'down to earth', as he put it.

Then, when the moment is right, he becomes - 'otherworldly'. Milo believes that this is the difference between their respective positions regarding conservation. Where have they got to anyway? They should have been here by now."

"What does he mean by that?" asked Catherine, eager to hear more.

"Well, I'm not sure, to be honest. My understanding, from what I've heard so far, is that they justify conservation in completely different ways. Milo's justification is purely scientific, whereas Owen's is - dare I say it? - romantic or possibly spiritual."

"And Suzy's aesthetic", interposed Catherine. Alison nodded, and returned to what she was saying.

"I listened to them the other evening in the Kite's Nest, discussing environmental conservation. I could have written quite an interesting article for the newspaper afterwards. Perhaps I will one day when the time is right, and I've done some more research on it - or slept with it long enough..." This aside seemed to go over Catherine's head.

"They were talking about the protection of small ancient woods, and the various factors which should be considered in their conservation - this is beginning to sound like one of your talks, Catherine." She smiled and so did Catherine, for the first time.

"Now, I must recall what was said carefully because it brought out the differences between them quite well. They agreed that the woods could not be properly protected without some sympathetic management of their wider setting - the surrounding landscape and even the watershed they exist in.

Acid rain came into the discussion, of course, as an example of how a wood cannot be considered in isolation. It wasn't long before they had descended into the depths of fundamental ecology, ecosystems, and wildlife communities. Milo had, of course, to bring his lichens into the discussion somewhere. They were a microscopic example of a community - a symbiotic assemblage of an alga and a fungus - which could be affected by changes in the acidity of the bark of a tree, in the water draining down it, or in the cleanness of the air."

"Alison, what is all this leading up to? You're sounding like Milo verbatim, not paraphrasing him. You've been inseminated with conservation jargon." Catherine had been listening carefully to Alison after all.

"Alright... I'm only trying to show you how the discussion developed. For Owen, an ecological community was more than this. It not only meant 'nutritional wellbeing', as he put it, but also spiritual wellbeing. Changes in the wider setting, in the quality of the water and the air, also meant changes in the ambience of the entire community. I was quite impressed by what he said. Milo was a little floored by this slant, and asked him what he meant. This is where the real twist came, and why I think the discussion was particularly revealing. Owen drew Milo's attention to the law of ecology which recognises that the community as a whole is greater than the sum of its parts. He contended that this greater dimension was essentially spiritual. It was at this juncture - just when I was getting interested in the conversation rather than merely listening - that Milo dropped out of the discussion by remembering my presence and asking me an irrelevant question. It was afterwards, when I asked him why he had curtailed the discussion that he said he thought Owen was lapsing into his 'otherworldly' self. I felt like getting Owen to go on, but I sensed that Milo had had enough. I'm not sure exactly what it is that gets under his skin at times like that, but I do know that Owen's other self rattles him - as I do sometimes when he can't get through to me. Maybe, it is the mind of a scientist meeting the mind of a spiritualist while both are standing knee deep in the same bog", concluded Alison, mischievously and laughing.

Catherine found the remark funny as well. It was needed to undo the seriousness and the concentration of the last ten minutes. As the thought of Milo and Owen, knee deep in a bog, discussing its wholeness sank in, their laughter increased until Alison was in tears. It was at this point that the two men walked in through the door, Milo having collected Owen from the Goggin. The two women composed themselves as the inevitable quizzical gazes came their way. Catherine had no trouble in adjusting, but Alison, on seeing the two men in front of her, was moved towards another fit of tears. She checked herself, and before either of the men could ask what all the fun was about, she raised the subject, in a trembling voice, of where they were going for their day in the Black Mountains. Catherine suggested driving into the upper reaches of the Vale of Ewyas, and doing a circular walk via Offa's Dyke Path, Hay Bluff, and the northern edge of the massif, either Darren Llwyd or Twyn Tal-y-cefn.

"Anywhere there aren't any bogs", she said. "I don't want a boggy walk."

Alison had to struggle hard to contain herself from laughing.

Notebook - 8th May, 1988.

A walk in the Black Mountains yesterday with Cath, Alison and Milo, beginning at Capel y ffin in the Vale of Ewyas. We followed the footpath into the valley of the Nant y Bwch below Darren Lwyd, climbing up to Rhiw Wen and the Twmpa, and then walking along the northern edge of the Mountains to Hay Bluff, where we had lunch. We returned along Offa's Dyke Path and the footpath which passes near The Vision Farm. Not a good day for long distance views.

I had a long conversation with Alison on the route back after she asked me what I meant the other evening in the pub, when I said to Milo that in any community the whole is greater than the sum of its parts. To explain what I was getting at, I referred to Cath's new display of old photographs at the Museum, featuring the heyday of the cider industry in Herefordshire. I said how surprised I was that she had not touched upon the spiritual connections which must have been a profound aspect of such a long-standing industry. I said that if there are economic, horticultural and cultural sides to the industry, there is bound to be a spiritual side as well which would have pervaded the whole county. A spiritual side arising from the folklore and the traditions of the orchards and the cider making; and from the reputation of the area in other parts of the country due to the involvement of migrant labour and the activity of trading itself. The display does not consider that the loss of these connections, as the industry declined, would have reverberated not only economically, culturally and scenically but also spiritually.

One feature I took to give her an idea of what I meant

concerned the place of mistletoe in the countryside. I mentioned the quote Cath has used to go with a photograph of a mistletoe possessed orchard - "Herefordshire may be considered the centre of the mistletoe district of England." (The Mistletoe in Herefordshire by Woolhope Transactions of 1852-1865, p. 338) It seems that down through the centuries, the orchards constituted a reservoir for the plant, allowing it to colonise all kinds of trees in the area, and to become a common and characteristic sight throughout the countryside. It still is a feature which conveys a particular flavour to the landscape because of the folklore and the traditions associated with it. What would its impact have been a hundred years ago when it was so ubiquitous? This conversation reminded me about the ball of mistletoe at the Stoggle. Milo tells me that the dark spots I saw on the fallen plant are the fungus Sphaeropsis visci which is peculiar to mistletoe.

As an example of this, I told her about an elderly man, named Arfin Marnur, whom I met one day on a cycle ride to Hay repairing holes in hedges, and who has been laying hedges in the area since he was a young man. He took time off from some patching to show me some of his hedges and explained the techniques he used. He had an extraordinary rapport with hedges and with the trees and shrubs in them. For him, hedge-laying was a work of art, even though he had to tear them down and start again, and was dependent for its detail upon his familiarity with each species and their particular place in the barrier he was making. He told me how the area had changed in appearance during his lifetime, especially in the clearance of woodland and the disappearance of the small farm orchards; how the smallholdings had been "gobbled up", and how the population of working people had declined. I said that it was through listening to him that made me think about all the connections - physical, cultural and spiritual - which must have existed within the traditional industries and activities of the area. Alison wants to interview the man with a view to writing an article for the paper.

Since talking to her, and after coming across King Alfred's comments on raiding woods for timber, I have had some more thoughts, especially concerning the old ways of managing hedges, trees and woods; and how wood pasture, coppice, coppice with standards, and hedgerow timber would have supported all sorts of activities and practices, and produced all sorts of articles, wasting little. All the hedges, woods, copses, groves and wooded fields that managed to survive the clearance of our ancient forests would each have had, like the many orchards, a sense of place, an identity, the character or ambience of which would derive not only from their appearance, but also from the way they were managed and from the place they held within the local community. Old trees, old woods, old orchards, old practices, all persisting within scenes changing slowly with the times, must have constituted an historical and a visual framework which maintained spiritual as well as cultural continuity, a reservoir of connections and deepened the sense of place. When overtaken by decline, or swept away, as in farm amalgamations, prairie farming, coniferous afforestation, and the spread of built-up land, the framework and the connections go as well. What is left is newness, without contact with the richness of the past; isolated fragments of lost habitats; detachment on the part of the visitor and the local inhabitant; and spiritual oblivion.

Alison asked me to write all this down, so I have.

Kilvert: 28 April, 1876, (p. 307.)

Another one of his references to Florence Hill:

'I never saw anything so lovely. A tall beautiful stately girl with an exquisite figure, a noble carriage, the most lovely delicate and aristocratic features, gentle loving blue eyes shaded by long silken lashes, eyebrows delicately arched and exquisitely pencilled, and beautiful silky tresses of golden brown hair falling in curling clusters upon her shoulders. And the loveliest part of it all was that the girl seemed perfectly unconscious of her own loveliness. Well, I thought, you will make some hearts ache some day.'

What would he have said about Catherine?

CHAPTER 12

'The New Barn meadows are fearfully cut up by the timber carriages which are hauling away the fallen giants, ash and beech. The shouts of the timber haulers are ringing hollow and echoing through the wasted murdered dingle. My beautiful favourite cwm is devastated and laid waste.'

Francis Kilvert, 26 March, 1872 (pp. 168-9)

Rhibo Mountain did not have the expansive splendour of the sombre massif which over-shadowed it on the west. It was merely a foothill in comparison: a foothill which often went unnoticed by visitors, whose attention was captured by the dominating edge of the Black Mountains. Nevertheless, it was a grand foothill, one which had impressed itself upon the consciousness of generations of local people since the time when its reputation for enchantment was immortalized in a name. It was not an austere expanse of upland where the merging of hilltops with moorland made the visual separation of named tracts of land a conceptual quagmire. It was an individual mountain, albeit a small one, which stood out in the landscape because of its distinctive shape, and because it could be comprehended in a moment: a place on its own; hence, the strength of its identity in the local mind. It may have been overawed by the wall to the west, but it did not cower beneath it. Mynydd y rhibo was an emphatic lump of earth which had made its presence felt in the past, and which continued to impress.

Owen Forrest had been impressed from the beginning. Although the Goggin Hill was base to the cottage, Rhibo Mountain had stolen first base in his spiritual resettlement on the edge of the ancient province of Ewyas. He thought it had everything: the outlook of an island; outstanding panoramic views; bastions of wood - "the force that through the green fuse drives the flower"* in Owen's mind - and an enchanting sense of place.

Once more, he was on his way up the gash in its side towards the Melglyn Stoggle, to gaze out over the valleys of the Dol Barcut Brook and the River Monnow, and at the scenes to which the Mountain gave access. On this occasion, it was mid-morning of a day that from the start had promised to be balmy. He had planned to wake up before dawn so that he could watch the sun rise above the distant Malvern Hills, as the lime had seen it rise hundreds of times. But his alarm had failed to rouse him (not for the first time). When he had eventually woken up, and realised what time it was, he had made himself a cup of lime-flowered tea, had some toast, put together a quick lunch, rushed out of the cottage, and ridden fast to Gwenynog.

Although late, there was still some freshness left in the morning, and a hint in the sky that he had missed something spectacular.

Approaching the tree, he noticed how its branches, now carrying partially open leaves, seemed even more pendulous than before, arching away from the venerable fuse and drooping down at their outer reaches under the growing weight of greenery. The brightness of the day was beginning to highlight the translucent yellow colouration of the small young leaves which dangled tenuously on long petioles, adjusted with imperceptible precision to receive the light. Such a myriad of clonal movement imparted a powerful sense of being and an inkling that a limitless force was at work. The immensity of the leafless structure which had moved Owen at the onset of spring was now almost canopied and complete. The wound and the ragged top, and the numerous other dead or dying branches, were only partially discernible, hidden by this recurrence of green life. But, sadly, it was still obvious that the tree was in decline. Even so, there was a remarkable serenity and a strange stillness about the tree, a stillness which Owen felt was its most engaging quality.

With his back against the tree, he looked at the scenes that were now familiar to him. Surveying the landscape from above had become a fascinating pass-time for him now that he could identify actual places - they loomed larger in the mind and stood out from what before appeared as a conglomeration of topographical unknowns appearing just as scenery. But the plantation loomed large as well; forbiddingly close. The pathetic remnants of the original wood, lingering on the edge of the coniferous invaders, were more noticeable now that they carried leaves; desultory thirty year old thickets consisting of regrowth from stumps and the natural regeneration of trees and bushes. There was also a rearguard profusion of vernal and early summer flowers surviving in the unusurped ground. Most of them were white, a mixture of wood sorrel, wood anemone and sweet woodruff, each in their respective huddles. A few primroses still held their own blossom in the crevices on the bare banks of the dingle, but the immediate area around the Stoggle, which must once have carried drifts of white petals to welcome the summer, was virtually flowerless. The incessant grazing of sheep since the felling of the trees had extinguished the herbal delights of the sward. Only a few isolated plants of wood sorrel persisted at the base of the tree, holding on in the ructions of soil heaved up by the roots.

Owen tried to imagine how the dingle would have appeared before the removal of its trees and shrubs. He pictured it in his mind as being like the dingles which still lay deep within the wood, collecting the waters of the Cwm Brook. As his imagination took him away from the present, he thought about the way Kilvert had been moved by similar scenes: he felt the need to write down his thoughts. He searched in his rucksack for his notebook, and then settled down into the natural seat he had discovered at the base of the tree on its south-eastern side, a seat formed by a small platform of wood linking two root buttresses, with support for the back provided by the fluting of the trunk. Some minutes elapsed before he began to write.

Notebook - 16th May 1988: At the Melglyn Stoggle.

I can see trees clasping the steep banks of the dingle, curving upwards at the base, stiff with fluted trunks dusted with Tree

Lungwort, rising into the light that they themselves exclude from the woodland floor. Some clasp small protrusions of rock, their roots enveloping these moss covered outcrops. The lighting is subdued and soft, except where breaks in the canopy allow shafts of sunlight to penetrate the restful gloom. Bare ground and exposed soil is commonplace, due to the deepness of shade and the instability of steep slopes. In response, the ground vegetation is thinly set, consisting of fragile coverings of grasses and herbs, and an assortment of ferns. Moschatel grows around the base of trees where roots hug the ground; the whorled leaves of sweet woodruff cluster together, their tiny white flowers dusting the almost blossomless deep; and a few isolated cuckoo pints thrust themselves into the scene. In places, where the light is brightest and the slopes less steep, as on the shoulders of the dingle, rampant vegetation, in the form of tangled masses of shrubs, saplings and young trees, prevails, rising out of a sea of dogs mercury. Wild service trees, maples and crab apples grow close to the limes and their companions, the sessile oaks. And, at the top of the dingle, supreme in its eminent position, is the Melglyn Lime, a true tree, not a stoggle; perhaps the wood's finest tower of green, surrounded by the company of life it had known from the beginning of its days.

As he wrote the last sentence, a sensation of tingling affected the upper part of his body, making him shiver. He was about to continue when he was distracted from his musing by a skirmish in the sky as a crow startled a buzzard and started mobbing it. He watched as the buzzard twisted and tumbled to avoid the guerrilla tactics of the crow. But it was the crow which gave up the skirmish and retreated, leaving the buzzard to settle down into a series of sweeping glides above the Stoggle. It was too early in the day for the thermal uprisings that raptors enjoy. The bird made only a few sweeps across the sky before drifting down towards the lime and landing on its stag-headed top. Owen observed the bird closely to see if it was the buzzard with the missing primary feather and the white belly. It was, but he lost sight of it as it dropped into the tree.

He returned to his notebook jottings, adding a note about the buzzard. He was impressed with what he had written, and surprised that he had remembered such a plant as Moschatel and the name of one of Milo's lichens. With his own words reverberating in his head, he pressed his back firmly against the tree and closed his eyes. He sat still for some minutes listening to the sounds around him. He thought he could hear the buzzard flapping its wings above. Had Milo had been there, he would have assumed that Owen had passed into another of his trance-like states. He had that faraway look again on his face.

Then his eyes opened wide, and he stared vacantly ahead of him. His face went pale and his mouth dropped open. He peered at his surroundings as if apprehensive of someone creeping up on him. In a state of fright, he leapt to his feet, breathing deeply and walking unsteadily away from the tree. When he passed beyond the spread of the crown, he stopped, still breathing heavily. At the same time, although he was unaware of it, the buzzard flew off its perch and soared into the sky. He sauntered about aimlessly, looking into the dingle, across the valley, and back at the tree, appearing not to know where he was. In time, he settled down, returning somewhat nervously to the base of the tree to rummage in his rucksack for a drink. A bottle of water came to hand and was swigged thirstily, in the manner of someone drought-stricken. Taking up the sack, he retreated to the limestone ledge where he scoffed his meagre lunch of banana, dried figs and apple, all the while looking intently at the Stoggle. He was noticeably perplexed. After throwing the apple core into the dingle, he took up his notebook and began to write, telling himself what had happened, and convincing himself that it had happened. As before, he made spelling mistakes but this time he was careful to correct them as he went along.

I have just experienced a weird series of sensations while sitting beside the Stoggle. They were uncannily reminiscent of the time I first fell asleep here, but of a far more intense nature. Admittedly, I went without a proper breakfast so I may have weakened my system a little; but I am beginning to think that what I felt this time was induced by my being here. This is ridiculous, I know, but what other explanation is there? As I sat with my eyes closed, half asleep I suppose, I felt a strange upwelling in my whole body, a sort of suffusion similar to the flush you sometimes feel after rising to your feet from a long-held squatting position, but ten times as strong. When I opened my eyes, everywhere around me seemed detached, as if I were levitating and drifting into another plane of existence. As the upwelling intensified, I thought the surroundings were closing in on me. Then I jumped up and snapped out of it, although I was breathless for a short while afterwards.

He stopped writing, and wondered if he had the nerve to put

himself in the same position again, now that he had eaten some food. He still felt a little uneasy, although not as drained as before eating. The day had become quite warm and the sun's rays were streaming directly onto the rocks where he sat. His freckled face never appreciated the sun when it was this direct.

Gathering his things together, he stood up, undecided as to what to do. In this indecisive moment, he saw the buzzard flying towards him from the direction of the wood. It flew past the tree, whirled about the rocks and let out a shriek which went right through him. Unafraid of his presence, it glided back to is perch in the Stoggle. Owen had a clear view of where it landed - on the top-most live branch, close to the stub of the decapitated trunk, an ideal perch for surveying the activities of rodents and other creatures scurrying among the rocks and feeding in the dingle. But the buzzard was not surveying the ground for food, it was staring piercingly at Owen. As their eyes met, the bird gave out another plaintive cry, that same soul-rending cry which had made such a penetrating impression on the day he first saw it. Unthinkingly, he was drawn towards the tree, his eyes fixed on the buzzard's gaze. As he passed beneath the outer branches of the crown, he lost sight of it, but he continued forward. Placidly, he returned to his seat beside the lime, settled into a comfortable position, and placed his notebook on his lap, making all these movements in a very deliberate manner. His eyes closed.

For the first time that day, updrafts of warm air from the dingle began to stir the young leaves of the lime into very gentle waves of movement. The ginger hair lying across Owen's forehead ruffled ever so slightly. There was a quiet mingling of sounds - intermittent bird-song, the continuous rippling of the brook, and the stirring of leaves. It was a classic balmy setting. And that indefinable quality of the place seemed to have transferred itself into Owen's face. His calm look appeared to be holding something. He could not be asleep because his head had not slumped onto his chest as one might expect it would had he dozed off. He remained in this state of arrested calmness for twelve minutes.

Remarkably, the buzzard remained in the tree during this time. But, by the end of this period of time, it became restless and began to weave its head from side to side, and up and down. As it did so, Owen's eyes opened, much wider than normal, having the raptor's quality of brightness, and he stared straight ahead in a gaze ten times as distant as his usual faraway look. Gracefully, and without moving his head at all, he extracted the pen from the ribbing of the notebook and opened the book. For a while, no other movements were made. Then, he began to write; fitfully at first, followed by spasms of scribbling, spasms interrupted by periods of time varying in length from a few seconds to a few minutes. Although his writing was rapid, he had difficulty putting pen to paper after each pause.

He had only just continued another spasm of scribbling after the longest pause of all, when the tranquillity of the dingle was shattered by the sudden roar of a jet plane which came over the Mountain from the north-west, only a few hundred feet above the rocks. His notebook fell off his lap as he was startled by the deafening noise. At the same time, the buzzard flew out of the tree and away into the wood, screeching. The fright unsettled Owen so much that, in trying to get up, he stumbled against one of the root buttresses and fell over, rolling down into the dingle, almost into the brook. He recovered himself and sat upright, gazing around in the same manner as before when he suddenly jumped up from the tree. He was aware that he was in the dingle, but he did not feel a part of it. Fright overcame him. The bare surroundings of the dingle and the hollow noise of the brook echoing around him in seemingly cavernous magnitude caused him to struggle madly up the slope, falling twice before reaching the top. Trembling, he stood near the Stoggle, unable to stand still because his balance had been affected. Another jet roared overhead, higher in the sky but loud enough to make him put his hands over his ears and hunch his shoulders in distress. He stumbled forwards to the trunk of the tree and propped himself up, feeling very, very heavy headed, and throbbing all over.

Gradually, the palpitations and the imbalances lessened. He regained some degree of composure, enough to cause him to look at his watch. He had been sitting there for over an hour. He assumed he had fallen asleep, perhaps after a disturbance similar to the one before lunch. All he wanted to do was get back to the cottage and go to bed; a simple intention in normal circumstances. But Owen was not feeling normal and the surroundings did not look normal to him. He squatted to pick up his rucksack and the notebook, which was resting beside one of the root buttresses, careful not to lose his balance and end up in the dingle again. Walking clumsily away from the tree, the sun now out of sight behind a swelling cumulus cloud, he made his unsteady way down the slope to Gwenynog, and his bike. When he reached the transport home, his condition had hardly improved. He still felt unsteady and heavy headed. Leaning his bike into his body, he placed his foot in the toe clip and attempted to ride away in the accustomed fashion, swinging his other leg over the saddle. Both the leg and his balance failed. He fell backwards, the bike landing on top of him. He did not hurry to extricate himself, but when he did get up he decided to push the bike until he thought he could ride it, and to return by the easy route via the Gulible road. At the junction of the lanes, he made a second attempt to mount the bike, which was successful, but he wobbled the first few hundred yards.

The journey back to the cottage was a strange one, for Owen could remember the departure and the arrival, but not the bit in between. Once inside the house, he could not even remember what he had done with the bike after reaching the front door. He could not care less, anyway. He had an overpowering desire just to crash into bed, but he forced himself to make a cup of tea before lifting his heavy legs up the stairs. He took the drink with him to the bedroom, and after only a single sip of the liquid, fell asleep, so fast asleep that he was not roused by the ringing of the telephone. The 'phone continued to ring at intervals until quite late into the evening.

CHAPTER 13

'Fellow-ranger of the green woods!
Painful, piercing grief affects me
Conflicts are pangs of anguish to the upright.'

Skene, 'Red Book of Hergest xxi,'
(untitled lines 80-82, p. 493)

The telephone at the Goggin was again ringing in the morning between eight and nine o'clock, but again Owen was oblivious to the noise. He did not stir until after ten o'clock, and would have stayed where he was even longer if the telephone had not rung once more around about eleven. Clumsily, he dragged himself out of bed and stumbled downstairs. It was Catherine.

"Owen, is that you? It's Catherine. I've been phoning since yesterday afternoon. Where have you been?"

Before a reply came to her question, she added - "Did you stay the night at that lime tree again without telling anyone where you were? I almost called in on you this morning on my way to work because I thought something might have happened to you. Where have you been?"

Owen was still in a dazed state from the events of yesterday, and only just awake. His discomposure was increased by Catherine's earnest expression of concern; in the background of his mind, it reminded him of the effusive, affectionate concern often shown in the past by Suzy when he returned from one of his absences, after escaping from an outburst of hectic ebullience. For a moment, he was silent, until an importunate 'well?' from Catherine made him admit that he had been at the Stoggle.

"Where do you sleep?" she asked in a tone of incredulity. "Did you have a sleeping bag with you? It rained last night - didn't you get wet? Surely, you didn't sleep through it all?"

Although Owen was not thinking very clearly, and barely coherently, he managed to put together an explanation, which he thought answered her questions, saying that he had spent the night at the tree and that his sleeping bag was drying on the line in the garden. He was not a good liar, and the thought of existing weather conditions did not cross his mind. He was just about to say that the tree had been a good shelter from the rain when Catherine interrupted."Are you alright, Owen? You sound a bit confused and tired. If you haven't had much sleep, then you should go back to bed and rest. I thought I'd come round after work to show you some photographs I've found. Will you be there?"

Owen said he would and that was the last word necessary because Catherine quickly said that she would see him later and then hung up. Putting down the receiver, he stood still for a while to contemplate his condition. He seemed to be alright, except that the stupor he usually felt upon waking up was very heavy indeed, and the events of the previous day were not easily recalled to mind. His difficulties in answering Catherine's questions, and now his empty-headedness, aggravated him. Instead of making an effort to recall what had happened, he turned his thoughts to food. But he turned away from the telephone too quickly, losing his balance and colliding with the edge of the sofa. He collapsed into the soft cushions of the sofa and rolled backwards onto the floor. Slowly, and deliberately, he stood up, getting onto his knees first, and then, with both hands resting on the arm of the sofa, pulled himself onto his feet. He stood still for some seconds, while his head adjusted to the upright position again. The room was around him, but he was not sure that he was a part of it. Supporting himself on whatever was to hand, he moved his unsteady frame into the kitchen.

The preparations for his lunchtime breakfast brought further aberrations. He could not remember where his favourite foods were kept. When the muesli was revealed, there was no milk to douse it with. Then he saw a carton of fruit juice in the fridge. For some inexplicable reason, he recalled Alison mentioning once that muesli soaked in apple juice was a religious delight of a vegetarian friend. The carton contained grapefruit juice. He let the mixture soak while he put the kettle on, and then carefully cut some bread for toast. The slices were too thick for the toaster, so he lit the grill, burning his fingertips on the match as he absent-mindedly held onto it while blowing the flames into action. When the meal was ready, he did not sit down to eat the muesli. Under normal circumstances, he might have been prepared for such a taste. In his present stupor, he reacted sharply, swallowing the first mouthful with a grimace. His hunger overcame this initial reaction and by the time the bowl was nearly empty, he had come out of his befuddled state and was properly awake at last.

At this juncture in his recovery, the events of the day before started to impinge upon his mind. Vaguely, he remembered the unusual sensations he had experienced at the tree, and that he had written them down. He decided to take the rest of the meal, and his notebook, wherever it was, back to bed. Placing the pot of lime-flower tea and the toast on a tray, he passed out of the kitchen, and was about to mount the stairs when he noticed his rucksack lying nearby on the floor. He transferred the tray into the hold of his left hand, picked up the rucksack, and precariously mounted the stairs, grasping the banister and the sack in the same grip. Without the support of the rail, he might not have ascended to the landing. Upon reaching his bed, and putting the tray beside it on the little table, he noticed the full cup of tea he had only sipped the night before. At this point, a sudden relaxation of tension made his head feel unusual. He was right to return to bed and rest.

After sipping his now favourite tea and crunching some dry toast - he had forgotten to spread anything on the bread - he took his notebook from the rucksack. He opened it and propped it against the tray. As he crunched another mouthful of dry toast, his eyes fixed on the pages in wide-eyed amazement, and his mouth fell open to reveal moistened crumbs, some of which fell onto the bedcovers. The writing was not his. It was a shaky script of words of varying sizes; some of them in Welsh. The left hand margin was as ragged as the right, and the writing ignored the lines completely, the spaces between the sentences varying in width. The levelness of the script was also disordered, some lines veering upwards, and some downwards, especially where a section of writing came to an end.

He flicked over the pages. There were scores of jottings, all seemingly disjointed and separated by gaps of different sizes. Turning back through the pages, he eventually found the entry he had intended to read, but he was now completely absorbed in the content of the curiously scripted passages which followed his own. Forgetting the tea and the toast, he began to read, or rather tried to read because the opening lines of the strange writing were illegible. The first intelligible line began:

'Only anguish makes my entry sorrowful and harsh...

Do not be disturbed
I am endlessly benign...

Be still and stay with me
Your Gentleness is precious to my Soul...

I am a Spirit of the Gentle Mingui Limes
Be still and hear my plea...

Restore me to the Deepness of Y Coed
Let my ancient spell Continue to enChant...

Through you I shall unburden the anguish of my Soul
Through you the Serpent Dyn will be denied my death

Through you I shall recover my place within Y
Coed
And dwell within another Gentle Tree...

Owain
You are a Gentle Son of Dyn
You hear the Gentle Trees of a passing Gentle
Time
You feel the baleful anguish of my Soul
Let the echoes of Y Coed resound in you

Be patient with my words
Your tongue is not the tongue I used to know
My verse is not the verse I gave the bardd...'

At this point, there was a large gap in the script, and a notable
change in the tempo of the words as the message continued.

Erstwhile Spirits of Y Coed leave behind their
hollow sounds
Lost companions in whose anguish I must
share
We are dying not deceased
Our demise is ages long
We may never gain another Gentle Tree

Lonely is my Lime beside the Melglyn gleam
Lamented is the losing of Y Coed

I know you are a Gentle Son of Dyn
You are different to the selfish ones
Who take the Serpents path
Your Soul is with the Trees
With their Canopy of leaves
You too regret the passing of the Trees of
Gentle Green
You too lament the losing of Y Coed

Restful were the Limes in the valley of the
Gwy
Resplendent was the Greenness of Y Coed...

Five Trees ago my Lime was great and tall
Y Coed stood vast and Deep
I would have grasped you Gently then
Enchantingly and long
My spell was always magical and sweet

But now my spell is weary waning and unsure
My power is ebbing earthwards with my Soul
Soon it will succumb to decay and waste away
Leaving me a woeful echo in the Cwm

Lonely is my Lime beside this barren Cwm
Lamented is the losing of Y Coed...

Owain
I cannot feel the Deepness

Nor the Greenness of Y Coed
My dingle now is hollow
Empty sadly bare
Made barren by the dreadful Serpent Dyn

I am girdled by a void of hollow ground
Where searching roots once swelled the earth
with life
Severed from the multitude of ties which gave
me strength
The pathways of existence in Y Coed

Only echoes of my ancient ties remain...

Through you I shall unburden the anguish of
my Soul
Through you the Serpent Dyn will be denied
my death
Through you I shall recover my place within Y
Coed
And dwell within another Gentle Tree...

Owain
You wonder what Y Coed and its Canopies were
like
You are wistful and desire to see the Trees
Your longing leads me back to a soothing
Gentle Time
Your longing is my longing for Y Coed...

Y Coed was always greater than a gathering
of Trees
Greater than the Spirits of a gathering of
Trees
Greater than the ardour of the selfish
Serpent Dyn
Everlasting... ever Gentle... ever Green

For Greenness was the summer joy we felt
The endless leaf unfolding
The endless flowering calm
The timelessness of tenure in Y Coed

Restful were the Limes in the valley of the
Gwy
Resplendent was the Greenness of Y Coed...

Alas... Y Coed has gone...

The spreading of the Serpent Dyn
The dreadful Serpent Dyn
Devoured the Deepness and the Greenness of
Y Coed
The vastness of the Trees was an
overflowing feast
To the Worm that is insatiable for space

Our Trees were stolen
They were slain

They were shredded
They were lopped
They were stunted and their Spirits Cut to
earth...

The Earth holds many wasted souls...

The remains you Call the green woods
Isolated remnants of Y Coed
Merely desolate and separate in space
Lonely fragments of the Deepness of Y Coed

And a Darkness has descended to feed the
dreadful Worm
A Darkness that displaces what is left
Where once Y Coed was Deep
A shadow Claims the ground
The pathways there are foreign to my Soul...

Owain
Rarely have I found a Gentle Son of Dyn
For Gentleness is not the Serpents way
The Worm has always lived in Conflict with
itself
And with the Trees
Ever since it scorched the Greenness of Y
Coed

If you will pierce for me

The sombre needle wall
The Darkness that blocks me from Y Coed
I will show you the enchantment of the Trees
of Gentle Green
I will show you the Glory of Y Coed

Through you
I shall unburden the anguish of my Soul
Through you
The Serpent Dyn will be denie.........'

It was at this point that the jet passed overhead and curtailed the communication.

Owen stared at the page until his spell-shocked mind recalled the shattering noise of the jet and realised that the plane had brought an end to the writing. Leafing through the mysterious text, he uttered aloud, in a quivering voice, a succession of questions, pausing and frowning between each one:

"Did I write this?

Why isn't it in my handwriting if I did?

And why is my name spelt wrong if I wrote it?

Is it possible for someone to write in totally unfamiliar handwriting while dreaming beneath a tree?

Or have I really been contacted by a tree spirit - one of the last ones?

Why me?

And why now?

What can I do to help?"

These questions only compounded his confusion. He closed his eyes and tried to close off his mind, hoping that when he opened them he would see everything in a more rational light. When he did open them a few moments later, it was to escape into daylight from the intensity of his thoughts. For more distraction, he turned to the statement in his notebook which preceded the enigmatic passages - his account of the sensations he had first experienced at the Stoggle. More questions struck him. Had these sensations happened because a tree spirit was trying to cast a spell over him? Or had Suzy's herb teas predisposed him to hallucinations? He threw his head back in a dismissive nod. The last thought was as incredible as the first.

He turned over the page, to be faced with the message again. This time, his thoughts fixed upon the script itself. As he gazed at the scribbled letters and words, he thought he could see familiar strokes, strokes that a graphologist might link with his own handwriting. But, then, if he wrote it, why should there not be touches of his own style?

Taking his time, he re-read aloud the tortured writing, concentrating more deeply on the meanings of the passages, and continuing to pose questions. The numerous plaintive references to "Y Coed" - presumably, the original or primaeval forest cover of Britain* - called up in his mind the plaintive mewing of the buzzard, a sound that had become a familiar strain to his soul in Northumberland and even more penetrating in Ewyas, although he was unaware of the effect it was having upon him. But why was the Welsh word for woodland used instead of the English words "forest" or "greenwood"? And why was there a scattering of other Welsh words? Mynydd Rhibo and Melglyn were familiar names, to him but not Mingui...

So the "Serpent Dyn" was Man and he, as a "gentle son of Dyn", was considered to be in sympathy with the cause of whoever was calling for help. Well, that much was true. Should it not be so, if he wrote it?

"Is this all out of my imagination? Is it possible? Has all the reading I've been doing affected my subconscious state?" These questions crossed his mind in rapid succession.

He thought that some of the passages were very lyrical and eloquent - qualities he struggled to achieve whenever he attempted to write poetry. He was never really satisfied with his compositions, and only Suzy knew that they existed. Was it possible to attain expressions of brilliance while hallucinating? If he took some paint with him to the tree, would he produce a work of art approaching Suzy's standard? Ridiculous thoughts like these continued to punctuate his attempts at reaching a rational explanation.

And why pauses in the writing? Were they there because his mind had wandered away from the message and had to be recaptured; or did the spell have to be recharged? Or does schizophrenia, in a dream-like state, move in fits and starts?

"Schizophrenia!" ejaculated Owen, closing the notebook with a thud. He would rather believe that he had been contacted by a tree spirit than be suffering from a syndrome akin to a split personality. What was happening to his head?!

The shock of this reflection had its effect. He got up, dressed, and started to formulate a plan that would prove, one way or another, what had happened. He had to return to the tree and put himself in the same position again. He was now thinking more clearly than at any time since his groggy return from the tree. His body was also feeling better, but he needed some liquid refreshment to maintain the improvement. Holding the notebook tightly in his left hand, he went downstairs for another drink, taking with him, in his other hand, his wrapped up sleeping bag, intending to put it on the line outside so that his story to Catherine would gain credence.

It was now mid-afternoon. Seated in the kitchen sipping lime flower tea, he read through the message for a third time, speaking the passages to himself as if he were the caller in distress. Again, he was left wondering if he had been contacted by a tree spirit. Was the traditional belief in tree spirits, and the folklore associated with the mysterious influences of trees, true after all? When early man held the primaeval forest in awe, was it induced by the insecurity of dark, forbidding surroundings, or was it because the tree spirits were protecting their wilderness by instilling fear? This reflection brought de Bohun into consideration. Owen became curious to know in more detail the background to the man's belief in tree presences. He had not really questioned him in any depth about this during his tour of the Deer Haye. On what pretext could he arrange an intimate meeting with him? He knew that he was welcome at the Court any time.

Deep in thought about how to open a conversation with de Bohun on tree spirits, Owen moved into the living room. Looking out across the garden, holding a cup of lime flower tea in his hand, he was still cogitating when a car pulled into the lay-by. It was Catherine. His first thought was for his notebook which he had left on the table in the kitchen. Madly, he rushed into the kitchen, grabbed it, and then froze in a fix of indecision. Where should he hide it? As he looked for possible safe places, his nervousness made him dismiss each one. In coming out of the kitchen, his eyes met the floor by the sofa. Quickly, he slid the notebook under the sofa, just as he heard Catherine's footsteps on the garden path. He had only enough time to pick up a Resurgence magazine that was lying on the sofa, change places with it, and pretend to be reading. The door opened. He turned around wearing a feigned look of surprise on his face.

"Catherine! What are you doing here so early?"

"Hello, Owen. I decided to take the rest of the afternoon off. I had some time owing to me, and I was a bit fed up, so here I am. How about making me a Suzy special herb tea while I sort through the things I've brought to show you."

As Owen concocted an hibiscus flower brew, the kind he knew she favoured, Catherine came into the kitchen with a handful of old photographs. But whatever she was about to say was stalled by the sight of the sleeping bag in one corner of the room.

"That can't be dry yet", she said, picking up the bag. "It will need longer than a few hours to dry, especially in the moist atmosphere of today after the drizzle this morning."

She was about to unravel the bag from its stuff-sack when Owen rushed forward and took it from her.

"You sound more like an elder sister everyday", he said agitatedly. "My sleeping bag is dry enough otherwise I wouldn't have stuffed it back in the sack."

Catherine was shocked by this abrupt response, which was so unlike Owen. She, too, was not in the best frame of mind for her reaction was equally as abrupt. She went back into the living room, collected her things, and left. Owen tried to say something but he could not bring himself to speak. He walked into the living room just as the front door was slammed shut. Upon hearing the car drive away, he threw the sleeping bag into the sofa, and muttered some words to himself. Moments later, he was pushing his bike towards the footbridge. He was going to punish his body in atonement. As he set off down the road, the moist air revealed that it, too, was saturated to breaking point - it started to rain.

The Thunderer

CHAPTER 14

'Your Soul is with the Trees
With their canopy of leaves
You too regret the passing of the Trees of Gentle Green
You too lament the losing of Y Coed'

Spirit of Y Coed

On his arrival at Bodcut Farm, Owen was soaked. Standing in the porch of the farm-house, composing himself - or trying to - and allowing some of the water to drain away before he entered, he looked a pitiful sight. His locks of pale ginger hair were flattened and dripping wet, hanging over his ears and his forehead. He licked his lips as the runnels of water trickled down his face. And he stood stiffly on a moistened slab of stone which seconds ago had been parched in the shelter of the porch. Bedraggled and sopping wet, inside as well as outside, he tried to calm himself and collect his thoughts. Before he was ready to touch the door, it opened, revealing the smiling face of Mrs Farr.

"Owen! Your sister would be proud of you. Her habit of turning up soaked must be a family trait. Come inside. Don't bother about the floor."

Owen shuffled in. He wiped his wet face with the back of his hand and then opened his mouth to ask for Catherine, but Mrs Farr spoke again.

"I saw you from the bedroom window as you entered the yard. I gave Catherine a shout. She should be here soon unless she's gone out to help her father with something. Here, dry yourself with this (she handed him a warm towel from the Rayburn) while I go and sort out some of Ralph's old clothes for you."

She left the kitchen and Owen heard voices from another room. Moments later, as he peered through a gap in the towel draped over his head, he saw Catherine in the doorway, staring impassively at him. He was a funny sight but, unlike her mother, she was nowhere near smiling. Slowly, he lowered the towel and his face broke into a sheepish smile.

"I've done penance for being so short-tempered. Is it enough, or shall I go round again?"

The remarks were sufficient to reach Catherine's offended depths, but she only half smiled. However, by the time her mother returned with the clothes, Owen was sitting in a chair and Catherine was drying his hair.

"It didn't take you two long to become friends again", she said, smiling at them. "Have a bath, Owen; then you can stay for tea."

He stayed the night. He did not wake up until long after

Catherine had gone to work. Mrs Farr thought he still looked tired, so she discreetly dissuaded her husband from asking him to help out on the farm. He was left alone to take as long as he wanted to over his late breakfast. Once more, he contemplated a visit to Llandyfrig Court - he was already half-way there - for he had to do something to settle the confusion caused by the message in his notebook. In his present state of mind, he did not have sufficient confidence to telephone the de Bohun's to arrange a visit. Instead, he decided to call in upon them while taking the long way back to the Goggin, as if making a casual call. Matilda often said 'Come again' after every visit. However, his departure was delayed because Lloyd Farr disregarded his wife's advice and called upon him to lend a hand unloading a vehicle delivering feed. When the job was done, it was lunchtime, and Mrs Farr insisted on putting back into him some of the energy her husband had used up. But before he got away, Lloyd booked him up to help with the shearing, which he planned to do in a few days time. It was nearly three o'clock when he set off in the direction of the Court.

The de Bohun's were pleased to see him. Suzy was always dropping by unannounced, they said. And they were the last people to stand on ceremony, the ceremony that had governed the Court for too long. He found them putting together a swing chair they had restored after purchasing it at a local sale. Matilda was glad to let Owen take her place in helping her husband manoeuvre the chair into a position by the ha-ha where they had decided to put it. They had obviously changed their minds about its final position otherwise they would have assembled it on the chosen spot, instead of having to move it. The chair was a heavy object and awkward to move about.

Humphrey had oiled the heads of the swinging arms so well that the suspended seat would not keep still.

Matilda departed knowing that, although a position was set for the moment, the exercise was far from over. She knew her husband's manner of working. Even when the chair reached the chosen spot, the manoeuvring did not end, for he could not make up his mind in which direction it should face. Owen co-operated obediently as the chair was shifted about to face in a number of directions overlooking the Deer Haye. In each case, Humphrey sat in it to experience the view, and talked his way through every adjustment. To Owen's eyes, the differences were only slight, for you could alter your position in the chair anyway to gain a variety of perspectives. He was beginning to think that the niceties were farcical when finally the man suddenly made up his mind.

As they fixed the chair in place, Matilda came over to them with some tea, smiling knowingly at Owen and saying that if Humphrey did not have a wife, he would not live long, forgetting to feed and water himself, and those in his company. She invited Owen to stay for a meal and then left the two men to recline in the chair with their refreshment. Owen had his wits about him at last and was careful to keep still, but Humphrey, being a compulsive fidget, disturbed the chair and upset his tea all over it. Almost immediately, Matilda came out again with two more cups of tea, laughing this time. She was surprised that Owen had maintained his poise.

"She knew that was going to happen", said Humphrey once Matilda had disappeared, "but I'll get my own back." He frowned a scheming frown. "Well, Owen, my boy, what have you been up to since we saw you the other day when you dived into our library again? Have you been listening to the trees instead of just looking at them?"

Owen could not believe his ears. He had already dismissed from his mind so many opening statements which he thought might broach the subject behind his visit. His reply was effortless.

"Yes, listening and wondering. I've been so impressed by all the venerable trees in the area that I wonder if any of them have had strange effects upon local people in the past. There are often local stories, aren't there, about trees influencing minds in strange ways? There can't be anyone in the area more in touch with trees than you. Are there any stories about trees having special effects?"

The enquiry was perfectly presented. Humphrey exclaimed, enthusiastically, that there were several folk stories he knew featuring trees. In trying to make up his mind, and remind himself, which were the best to recall, he listed them by talking his way through his thoughts. After a few garbled words and unfinished sentences, accompanied by the usual idiosyncratic gesticulations, he settled upon one which he described as being a "great tale". To tell it, he left his seat and paraded about on the edge of the ha-ha, another improvised stage. It was a Welsh legend about a young man - "just like Owen" - who became enchanted by the calling of a nightingale in a maple tree.

"He sat beneath the tree to listen to the beautiful strains of the bird's song, and did not move until the singing ceased. When all was quiet, he rose up with a contented look on his face, but found that the fine maple tree was a lifeless ruin, a shell, a miniature version of the Hideout. He was staggered - wouldn't you be staggered, Owen? Bewildered, he returned home, only to discover that the house and its garden were not the same as before. Instead of his parents, he found an old man living on his own and dressed in unusual clothes. Upon asking what the old man was doing in the house, he received a prickly reply. The old man said that it was his house, and then asked who he was talking to. When he heard the young man's name, he was shocked right down to his boots. In amazement, he said that his grandfather had had a son by that name who had suddenly disappeared. He had last been seen sitting beneath a fine maple tree in a meadow. After many weeks of sad waiting by his parents, his father had consulted a wise woman of the district as to his whereabouts. She said that he had been taken away by wood nymphs and would not come back until the maple tree was withered and dead. With tears in his eyes, the old man advanced towards the young man saying: 'Welcome home great uncle, embrace your great nephew'. As he took his long lost ancestor in his arms, the young man crumbled away to dust, and a nightingale started singing in a nearby maple tree."

The tale was not just told, it was acted as well, with a touch of cheeky Shakespearian gravity bringing it to a conclusion. Before Owen could comment, Humphrey carried on. Gleefully, he said, "I like the bit where the young man crumbles away to dust. His great uncle probably fainted or had a heart attack... I've just remembered another one. This is even better." Owen restrained a smile, wondering if anyone else ever got a word in when de Bohun was practising on the stage.

"And it's closer to home. It's a story about the lopping of a majestic lime tree on Rhibo Mountain; how a tree spirit exacted retribution on a local man centuries ago. One of my aunts told it to me one summer when we were over by the Melglyn Stoggle. It concerns the son of a wealthy family who lived somewhere near Gulible. He was nuts about wood carving and had paid the owner of an old lime tree for the right to lop some branches off it, much against the wishes of the tenant farmer and other local people. The tree stood in a grove which was reputed to have given new life and heroic vigour to some Welsh comrades fighting to protect their land against marauding Saxons. Their success in repelling the invaders caused them to revere the grove and its trees as a symbol of freedom and liberty. This traditional reverence was disregarded by the arrogant wood carver. All he wanted were large pieces of wood. My aunt said that he wanted to make a love spoon, but I think she got herself mixed up here, unless the fellow had a big heart or a big girlfriend."

Humphrey looked at Owen for a response. He was already grinning.

"When the wood carver and his friends were about to take their axes to the tree, intending to remove some large limbs, the young man suddenly noticed a pall of smoke rising up from the cottage which his father had given him in the valley below. He quickly told his friends to wait. Leaving the tree, he hurried home, but when he got there he found no fire. So he returned to the tree and was about to commence the lopping when the sight of smoke billowing from his house stopped him. Off he went again to put the fire out, but there were no flames to extinguish. Once more, he took his axe to the tree, this time instructing everyone not to look towards the cottage. They lopped off a number of limbs and carted the wood into the valley below. When he got back to his home, he found it burned to the ground, a heap of charred cinders. Shattered, he moved away from the area, and never got round to making any love-spoons. Forever after, it was said that whoever harmed a lime tree on Rhibo Mountain would lose his house in a catastrophe and leave the area, downcast. My aunt added that it was also said that whoever felled a lime tree on the mountain would cause his family name to die out. That was the prediction we told my father when he was clearing the southern edge of Coed Tirion Glas."

Owen was astonished. Had he been told this story on his first visit to Llandyfrig Court, he would have taken it as just another idiosyncratic twist to the de Bohun tour. His experience at the Stoggle now caused all sorts of thoughts to race through his mind. Humphrey stood in front of him, as if waiting for the applause to start. Owen disappointed him. Instead, he asked a serious question.

"Whereabouts was the lime tree that was being lopped?"

"Come on, Owen, you can't have everything. I suppose it would have been somewhere on the south or the south-western flank of the mountain, otherwise he couldn't have seen his cottage on fire, if he lived near Gulible. If it was before 1707, it might have been on the middle slopes because that old map we have in the library shows the wood going all the way around the mountain. We'll have a look at it again when we go inside if you're that interested."

"What about other tree spirits connected with limes in the area?" pressed Owen. "Do you know of any, other than the ones in the Deer Haye?"

"Owen, Abode Trees are everywhere, I've already told you that."

"What I mean is..." Owen hesitated for a second, "have you

ever made contact with an inner presence?"

Humphrey gave him a strange look. It either meant "can I trust you with my secrets?" or "what are you fishing for?" Owen could not tell which. The man was intriguing when he first met him, and was becoming more curious as the acquaintance grew. Humphrey proceeded to answer the question, choosing his words carefully, rather than rushing along as usual, and speaking in a way which suggested that Owen might be digging too deep into the man's own inner presence.

"I've been aware of them, but you have to be in a special frame of mind to feel their influence. Whenever Matty and I have a problem to resolve, I always take a stroll in the Deer Haye among the Greybeards. We haven't failed to solve a problem yet. Teili Junction is the place where I have been influenced most. That's why my ashes will be buried there when the time comes. Abode Trees are the bridges by which we pass from the mortal to the immortal world. But it's necessary to commune with the trees on a regular basis for a long time if immortality is to be assured. So start now Owen, and keep it up."

Owen wanted to dig deeper, but he did not have the nerve to ask what being influenced meant. Instead, he tentatively and casually asked if Humphrey thought the Stoggle in the Melglyn Dingle was an Abode Tree.

"It must be; but you'll have to ask Matty. When she goes off on her walks, she usually ends up there. She likes walking through Coed Tirion Glas, up onto the Mountain and back via that grand old stoggle. If we set off together, she usually leaves me at the Cwm Brook."

Humphrey was too immersed in his reply to notice how Owen reacted to this insight into Matilda's life. However, the mention of his wife made him pause and look around to see if she was anywhere near. Owen's face was turned towards the house as well.

"Are you looking for the food source as well?" he said, rubbing his hands together in a boyish manner. "Come on, let's see what's in store for us." With that, Humphrey pushed one arm of the chair backwards so that Owen received a jolt which interrupted his contemplation.

Matilda was not yet ready to give them a call, so they carried on their conversation in the library, where they looked at the 1707 map. Since Catherine's cataloguing of the estate records, it was kept in a glass cabinet in one corner of the room, away from the light. It was a map of rather rudimentary cartography, showing the extent of the estate but including little else, except for the names of the main settlements nearby. Coed Tirion Glas did, at that time, extend around the southern flank of the Mountain, as far as the stream which flowed down into Gulible. Where the stream began, there was the name Llannerch Hudol. On the other side of the Mountain, the lower reaches of the wood surrounded the place Gwen y nog. A particular feature, which stood out on the extreme south of the Mountain, was the motte and bailey castle site near Tre Llwyn, hatched in isolation and visually more formidable than the wood overlooking it. Curiously, there was the name Llwyn Beibio, as well as Castle against the feature. But the most dominant marking on the map was its title and the embellishments which surrounded it, a motif which tried to make a rudimentary illustration of the estate of Llandyfrig Court illustrious.

When supper was eventually served, Humphrey turned all his attention to the food, leaving Matilda and Owen to strike up a conversation. When he had finished eating, he rose from the table and, like clockwork, retired to his favourite chair in the long room to fall asleep, a routine that was habitual. It was not until he had absented himself that Owen considered raising the subject of the Stoggle with Matilda. But, whereas he thought that Humphrey would answer his enquiries without being curious about the motives behind them, he saw Matilda as someone who was very perceptive, almost prescient. This intuition inhibited him. However, Matilda offered him a chance to begin by asking what he and Humphrey had been talking about outside.

"What was Humphrey telling you by that chair? Was he reciting a part from one of his favourite plays?"

"Oh no; he was telling me about folk legends and the presence of spirits in trees. Your husband seems to believe that every large and venerable tree is occupied by some sort of spirit. This made me ask him if he thought the old Stoggle above Gwenynog was inhabited. He said that I should ask you because the tree is a favourite of yours. Is that true?"

Matilda looked inquisitively at Owen with a slight tightening of her eyes which was a peculiar facial detail of a gaze that for him was rather enigmatic. She came straight to the point.

"Why do you want to know? Do you think there is a spirit in the tree?"

This was the very question he did not want to answer. Nonchalantly, or with an attempt at nonchalance, he said, "If it does have a spirit, I'm not sure I could detect its presence, although Humphrey seems to consider the existence of spirits, or 'inner presences' inevitable."

"Well, I don't. His Greybeards in the Deer Haye are certainly grand and venerable, but spiritually they must be in decline. I like the Haye when the mist or the snow or the rime envelopes it, or when it rattles in the wind and echoes with hollowness. It oozes mystery and ghostliness, especially in the mist - the trees seem to move about then - but if you look at them long enough, the only reality is that they are lost. All free-standing trees, however grand or creepy, look forlorn, as if they're being watched and can't wait to get back into the wood. The Melglyn Stoggle is just more forlorn than the rest. It fascinated Suzy for a while over a year ago, when she thought the dingle might have influenced the artwork of one of Humphrey's forbears. She was convinced that there was some power in the dingle, a power to enhance creativity. She tried to see if it would influence her work, but it didn't. To me, the dingle is just one of those places where there is a special sense of place, something more than what you see; an atmosphere peculiar to it. That's why I like going there. And I like going into the wood as well. I prefer the wood to the Haye. There's a different sense of creepiness. Have you been in there again?"

"Yes, a few times now."

"Well, you're proving braver than your sister. She won't go in there, unless I drag her. She loves walking up onto the Mountain and dancing around in the moonlight, but she doesn't like going in the wood. That's why we sometimes meet up at the Stoggle after I've been through the wood and she's been on the top. We had a super time two years ago. We had a supper party at the Goggin - Suzy, me, Alison and Catherine, and a friend Suzy hadn't seen for ages - a party which had its finale at the grand old Stoggle. It was all Suzy's idea. The five of us had never sat down to a meal together before. After the spinach balls and white sauce, and the wine, which was the last of her dandelion wine of 1983 - beautiful stuff! - she dragged us all out for a moonlit walk onto Rhibo Mountain to collect flowers from the old Stoggle for making herb tea. The evening was such a glorious one. As we approached the tree around midnight, we were overcome with scent - it was delicious! The smell was heavenly and there were a few bats bombing around to keep us company.

We floated around beneath the tree, drinking in the aroma, until Suzy turned our spontaneous reverie into a sort of medieval celebration of the magic of nature. First of all, she got us to make lime flower necklaces. We hoisted her into the tree and she sent down a shower of flowers. Then, when the necklaces were made, she persuaded us to take off our clothes and to prance about half naked - well, almost half naked - beside the tree doing a French medieval circle dance." (In telling this story, Matilda discreetly scrutinised Owen's face for signs of reaction) "It was all fabulous fun, but Catherine was reluctant to let her hair down, or take off as many of her clothes as the rest of us, even in the warmth of the scented moonlit air. Your sister is quite a live wire. If there is a spirit in that Stoggle, it might not have survived the rite and the views that went with it... Perhaps I shouldn't be telling you all this. You're not embarrassed, are you?"

Owen said "No", in a way which implied that he had heard it all before, and a smirk came to his face. "I can imagine how it all started, and how her ebullience rubbed off on everyone else, especially if she was entertaining an old friend she hadn't seen for a while, and if she had wine inside her."

"We had a similar celebration last year, but it wasn't the same. Alison brought Milo with her for some reason. Anyway, when it was all over, and Suzy had collected some flowers for making herb tea, which turned out to be the best she had ever made, I walked back through Coed Tirion Glas. The others thought I was mad. Humphrey didn't believe me. That was when I saw my first Long-eared owl."

"Didn't believe what?" said Humphrey as he entered the room, stretching himself after his nap.

The Groaner Oak

CHAPTER 15

'This afternoon I walked over to Lanhill. As I came down from the hill into the valley across the golden meadows and along the flower-scented hedges a great wave of emotion and happiness stirred and rose up within me. I know not why I was so happy, nor what I was expecting, but I was in a delirium of joy, it was one of the supreme moments of existence, a deep delicious draught from the strong sweet cup of life. It came unsought, unbidden, at the meadow stile, it was one of the flowers of happiness scattered for us and found unexpectedly by the wayside of life. It came suddenly, and it went as it came, but it left a long lingering glow and glory behind as it faded slowly like a gorgeous sunset, and I shall ever remember the place and the time in which such great happiness fell upon me.'

Kilvert: Monday, 24th May, 1875 (p. 286)

On his return that night, Owen was in more of a quandary than when he set out. Unimaginable connections to what was already confusing had presented themselves. At the outset, he had expected to cope only with the spiritual beliefs of a latter-day aristocrat. Humphrey de Bohun's folklore revelations, far-fetched in content and embellished by time and play-acting, carried elements of myth, but they had given some clues which called for investigation. They might not be solely mythical, and due to fantasy. But the subsequent disclosures were not fantasy. Matilda de Bohun's connection with the Stoggle was an intriguing side issue which would have to lurk, enigmatically, in the background until he had clarified other matters and got to know her better. It was Suzy Forrest's involvement with the tree, the unexpected intrusion of his sister, which confused him most.

As soon as he got inside the house, he inspected the dried flowers in the amber jar, curious to see the actual blossom of the Melglyn Stoggle; wondering, once more, if the herb tea had affected his mind. He felt compelled to observe more closely - if that was possible - the way the flowers gave off their colour and their scent when brewed; and the way the infusion affected his body when imbibed. Whatever the effects of lime flower tea, from whatever source, it was a delicious drink that had to be re-evaluated. He made it stronger than usual.

He then sat down in a chair to await whatever noticeable changes might overtake his body. On a stool nearby, there was a poem he had started, prefaced by a paragraph from Kilvert and inspired by two impressions that were currently ubiquitous in the surrounding landscape – the call of cuckoos and hawthorn blossom. As usual, he had managed to write an opening verse and then put it to one side, unable to concentrate on the subject, probably because of the events that were now in the forefront of his mind. After reading the verse again, he took up the pencil and the rubber lying on the stool and, without any overt cogitation, began to write. In a matter of minutes, he had finished. Never before had he written a poem so quickly and without revision.

Cuckoo Calling Calm

Fine snow it seems in May on canopies of thorn
Smells out across the cuckoo-calling calm,
Creaming nose and eye rosaceously with balm,
As shivers on the skin bring shivers of communion
newly sworn.

Although last year my spring was cool, withdrawn
and dry,
Postponing the arousals that would show,
Pre-ordained displays arrive disguised as snow
As fitful smells of 'May' join fitful spells of cuckoo
calling by.

I know, inside, the way that blossom on a breeze
Perpetuates initial overflows,
Promising successive pleasures to the nose
As fragrance in the air makes fragrant inhalations
newly please.

I go outside and stray by flowers in the hedge,
Breathing there the cuckoo-courting scent,
Being overwhelmed, becoming nostril spent
As all-pervasive 'May' calls all-persuasive spirits
to re-pledge.

At last, with warm delay, a summer urge is borne;
Forgotten intimations stir and throng,
Fulsomeness emerges welcomed by a song
As cuckoo-calling calm melts blossom-coated canopies
of thorn

Upon reading the poem, Owen was pleasantly surprised, but impressed, too, at what he had achieved. Was his spring of the previous year 'cool, withdrawn and dry'? He could not remember. He thought about the tea again. Had the infusion of lime flowers made him more eloquent and fluent than usual? Maybe it had, but whether or not the tea had a new significance, he could not believe that it was responsible for his experience at the tree and his dilemma. It might possibly predispose someone to have communion with nature. If one relishes lime flower tea, then an affinity for lime flowers and, by association, lime trees, might be obvious consequences. Of course, drinkers of herb teas are likely to be nature lovers anyway. If it was potent, why had Suzy not been affected? How could he assume she had not? This likelihood was impossible. She could never relax long enough to be overwhelmed in the way he had been. Even alcohol had difficulty overwhelming her; it just made her more ebullient.

She had rarely shown any special interest in trees - she had left that to him (he had to have something to himself) - certainly not the mania she had for flowers, herbs and open spaces. She had once said that they were too big to draw; that it was difficult to get close enough to them to sketch the flowers in their most natural angles of repose. In the field, she preferred to lie in the grass or the scrub, dissecting on paper the constituent parts of the ground flora. Had she changed? Had something changed her? Had the pale yellow, perfumed flowers of the Stoggle overwhelmed her? Perhaps by their profusion and heady scent; or by some other influence? He was assuming too much in the connection. Her attraction to the tree was simply to collect flowers for making herb tea. Was the celebration the first time she had gathered flowers from the Stoggle, or had she gathered them before in the summer of the previous year?

It was late; too late to dwell upon such questions. Perplexed, he retired to bed, taking his notebook with him. However, before sleep overcame him, he read again some of the mysterious passages, sinking into sleep with the lines...

'Through you I shall unburden the anguish of my soul
Through you the Serpent Dyn will be denied my death
Through you I shall recover my place within Y Coed
And dwell within another Gentle Tree...'

The following morning found him in another disoriented state. For a brief moment, he had no idea of where he was or how he had got there. He was even unsure of his own identity.

He sat on the edge of the bed with his head in his hands. The events of the previous day were gone. His only recollection was of a dream he had experienced shortly before waking up; a vivid dream, the images of which were close enough to be the latest real events in his life. Rubbing his palms into his forehead, and his fingers into his tussled hair, he came round, blinking at the daylight flashing through an opening in the curtains. The reality of the present had arrived. The stupor of the morning was upon him. Gradually, the mental picture of naked women dancing in the moonlight by a flowering lime was understood.

On pulling the curtains, he saw that it was a confused morning. Bright sunlight was struggling to assert itself through forbidding grey clouds. By the time he had gone downstairs, he could hear the rain. Another glance through a window ended the confusion - the sunlight had disappeared; it was going to be a wet day. Another visit to the Stoggle would have to be deferred. He was not sure that he was ready to visit the tree, anyway. Breakfast was the immediate priority.

In the kitchen, he looked at the dregs of the lime flower tea. Should he continue the ritual or abstain? He was too involved to abstain. Deep down, he was worried that without daily doses of herb tea, he would not be able to resolve the mystery before him and answer a call for help – if he had received one. Whatever the effects and the consequences, the tea would be made. The supply in the amber jar! How long would it last? The jar was already only half full. Was there more? A search in the cupboards behind the open kitchen door revealed a bagful of the stuff.

The door had been wedged open ever since his arrival. It was only now that he noticed a calendar pinned to the back of the door, still showing the month of April. In shocking, felt-tip red against the date of his arrival was the exclamation: "Sweet welcome brother mine. Look after this place or else..." Was there no escape? He took it down to change the month to May, but folded two sheets back, uncovering June. The sheet was empty except for another, equally shocking, note in yellow, marked against the weekend of the 18th and 19th: "Melglyn Stoggle should be in flower - check with Matilda."

The questions of the last evening came back into his mind. With his eyes still on the calendar, his thoughts moved by association to diaries. He knew that Suzy kept a diary - she found time for everything. He could remember their mixture of scribbles and miniature sketches. The latest one would be with her in the Pyrenees, but what about the others? Were they still somewhere in the cottage? He had never before pried into his sister's closest affairs, but his predicament compelled him to investigate further.

Her desk was more or less as she had left it. He had hardly moved a thing aside on the few times he had used it. And he had not opened any of the drawers. The two small drawers on either side of the ornamental back-piece contained only pens, crayons, pencils, dried flowers and earrings. The obvious place was the stack of three drawers below the desk top to the right of the leg space. The first was full of letters; some loose, some bound together with elastic bands; but only letters. The next was full of sketch pads of assorted sizes, each one dated. He ignored the most recent one and unearthed the pad which covered the period for June of the previous year. It contained a mass of drawings and sketch details of countless objects; plants being the major subject and most of the pages dated. He flicked through it; there was nothing connected with the Stoggle, unless some of the sketches were done in the dingle. He found the pad covering the same period in 1986. It had various ideas for displays of work connected with an exhibition at the museum, and there was a sketch of a figure dressed in leaves surrounded by flowers. Then, to his surprise, quite out of context with everything else, there was a sketch of the Stoggle. He recognised it instantly and the angle from which it had been drawn. It was only a sketch, but it was good, occupying a page on its own with the words - "The Stoggle in the Honey Dingle". He had not heard that name for the dingle before. On the opposite page, there were sketches of its flowers, and details of the flower parts. The date was the 22th June, presumably, he thought, the day after the weekend supper party and the moonlit celebration.

He continued his search for the diaries. He tried the bottom drawer; it was empty, which struck him as being unusual because his sister would have used it for something, if only for some of her junk. Had she kept her old diaries there and removed them before his arrival? Wherever they were, he lost interest for the moment because he suddenly thought that she may have done an even larger drawing of the Stoggle.

He went through into her studio, which was the room looking out over the garden towards the walnut tree. He knew where to look because Catherine had shown him the cabinet where most of her work was stored. He remembered going through the work in the top two drawers with her, so he opened the third one down. Almost immediately, his hunch was rewarded. He found a series of beautifully coloured drawings of lime flowers in exquisite detail, almost pungent in their exactness; and, beneath them, an enlarged drawing of the

Stoggle, which he thought was fantastic. In that moment, his admiration for his sister filled him with warmth. He wanted to put the drawing up somewhere, so he could commune with the tree at home, but his duty to protect his sister's artwork restrained him.

After admiring the drawings for a long time, he put them back, exactly where he had found them. Replacing them, he came across another sketch of a lime, smaller and on discoloured paper; an old drawing dated 1796, signed by a Rosamond de Bohun, and annotated "The Early Flowering Linden in the Honey Dingle". A piece of work discovered when she helped Catherine catalogue the Court's records? It did not match her drawing for quality, although it was good. But it did not resemble the Stoggle. And the aspect of the dingle was not the same either. He replaced this picture as well, but as he did so the script of the title, which was in longhand, caught his attention. The writing seemed familiar for some reason.

Then his mind returned to the diaries? Where were the diaries? Repressing feelings of self-reproach, he began to search the studio. There were few places where they might be kept, unless there were secret recesses in the room. A fruitless search made him realise that if Suzy had hidden them, they could be anywhere in the cottage. He was reluctant to believe that she had hidden them; it was unlike her. That was her trouble. She wore virtually everything on her gorgeously coloured sleeves. Everyone knew her affairs, even the emotional ones, because she was always spontaneous, unaffected and publicly ingenuous. And yet, like other people there was an unreachable recess in her personality. She had inner thoughts like everyone else. If her diaries were strewn with these, then she would want to keep them out of the way; beyond the eyesight of her young brother, certainly. Owen had not lived in the same house with her for some years, but he recalled that she never left her diaries unattended for the family to read. Written in them in public regularly, but not opened them to the public gaze. Where, then, might she have concealed them? Her bedroom was the most obvious place.

Continuing to feel pangs of guilt over what he was doing, he entered her bedroom. In searching it, he made a conscious effort to divert his eyes, and to close off his mind, if he came across anything personal while rummaging for the diaries. He had been in her bedroom only twice since the first exposure to its startling decor. The clothing in the two wardrobes was equally as colourful and as shocking. She had not changed. If anything, her taste had become more bizarre, if that was possible. He smiled in brotherly amazement as the array of dresses and other garments met his eyes. The half-light of the wardrobe interior saved him from being dazzled.

He found nothing but garish clothes in the first wardrobe. The second had heavier garments and coats, and also piles of folded clothes at its base supporting shoes and sandals at all angles - an ideal place for concealment - but only for more shoes. He rummaged through the top drawer of the dressing table but found nothing except piles of gaudy under-garments, and some unexpected oddments. It then occurred to him that he could feel his way around the other drawers without looking. Unsuccessful again, he turned his eyes to the floor, looking under the dressing table, the bed and the wardrobes, before slowly making for the door while continuing to scan the room for possible hiding places. Pausing in the doorway, he glanced around the room for a last time. His angle of view caused him to notice that the stool between the dressing table and one of the wardrobes was closer to the latter. This made him look up towards the top of the wardrobe. Crossing the room quickly, he climbed onto the stool and discovered that the architrave surmounting the wardrobe concealed a recess which held seven diaries, at all angles of rest. Being careful not to disturb them too much, he recovered the ones for the last two years and then sat on the stool.

The pages in the first diary were the epitome of Suzy. Her personality leapt out at him in all manner of ways - the gargantuan handwriting which would intrigue any stranger to the point of wanting to meet the writer; the impulsive and restless nature of the entries, obvious bursts of thought scribbled down with whatever pen, pencil or crayon was to hand, producing changes in colour which reflected the cacophony of colour in the cottage; fragments of the garrulous outpourings of a frenetic person. The pages were as full, as busy, and as chaotic as the life she led. The miniature sketches that Owen remembered so well from her childhood days were everywhere. But the first noticeable place he came to in the 1986 diary was the 15 April because the pages were separated by the insertion of dried pale crimson catkins: the entry for that day was written in very dark red pen – 'My favourite black poplar on the green at Gulible has been felled while in flower! This act is outrageous! I must get Humphrey to put it in the local rag.' Now Owen knew why he had not seen a black poplar in the nearby village. The small green had only a sapling tree – an ornamental maple was all he could remember.

The initial impact of the pages upon him was similar in

effect to the very moment when he first entered the cottage. He could cope with his sister in small bursts, but not in explosions, and certainly not repeatedly. For a second, his resolve faded at the task ahead of him. But he told himself that he was in control of the situation; that he could close the diary when he wanted and open it when he wanted.

He persevered, flicking through the pages to locate the middle of June. He could not have missed the entry. For Friday, the 19th, entered in large yellow words was the statement; 'Matilda phoned - Honey Dingle lime in flower.' There was also a note that Lulu was booked in for the weekend, whoever she was. The following day mentioned the supper party at the beginning and ended with an ebullient record of the evening's rejoicing. To Owen's surprise, it revealed that 'Matty's idea to have a celebration soaking up the moonlight and the scent of the Stoggle in the Honey Dingle was the highlight of the evening. We almost overcame Cath's reserve, for she was affected by the heady perfume as well. We all vowed to repeat the celebration next year'. So it was Matilda's idea, not Suzy's. Mrs de Bohun was becoming more intriguing than her husband.

But this thought was pushed aside by the following entry on the Sunday; a terse, somewhat flat record of only one event in the whole day: 'Another moonlit night by the Stoggle. Just Cath and me, knicker-naked together. Alison preferred to be naked with Milo, so Cath stayed the night in her room.' So Catherine was inclined to let her hair down sometimes. That was an uncloaking in itself.

Turning to the diary for 1987, he found that the flowering occurred in the week beginning the 14th of June. This time, the news was more casually entered at the bottom of the page of Tuesday, the 16th: `Matilda says the Stoggle is in flower. Celebration tomorrow or Saturday'. The celebration happened on the Friday, for there was a note that - `Only Matty, Cath and I braved the breezy night. Ali stayed put in the cottage with Milo (her fault for bringing him!). Too windy for bees, but warm enough for nakedness. Cath finally disrobed in front of Matilda. My wine made sure of that. A celebration in itself. Lime flower tea, vintage 1987, collected for drying'.

Owen now knew for certain that he had been drinking tea that was an infusion of lime flowers collected from the Melglyn Stoggle. Therefore, he thought, that might explain the eloquence of the verses written at the tree and those he had composed the night before to complete his poem. He closed the diary wondering if there would be a celebration that year without Suzy. Catherine would not go with Matilda alone. It was better for him that nothing should happen. Momentarily, he hesitated to replace the diaries. He was tempted to delve into them a bit more. He resisted the temptation. He had already infringed her privacy enough. There was no need to look further, for he had discovered more than he expected - again - and answered some questions. He replaced the diaries in their hiding place, adjusted the stool, and left the room.

CHAPTER 16

Notebook - 23rd May 1988: About Lime Trees:

From A Modern Herbal by Mrs. M. Grieve (1931).

Honey from limes, 'regarded as the best flavoured and the most valuable in the world'.
Wood - the lightest of any of the European broadleaves.
Bast - the inner bark - makes fibres and coarse matting.
Foliage - eaten by cattle whether fresh or dry.

In France, the dried flowers make a tisane called 'Tilleul'.
'The flowers contain a fragrant, volatile oil, with no colour, tannin, sugar, gum and chlorophyll... Lime flowers are only used in infusion or made into a distilled water as household remedies in indigestion or hysteria, nervous vomiting or palpitation. Prolonged baths prepared with the infused flowers are also good in hysteria. In the Pyrenees

they are used to soothe the temporary excitement caused by the waters...' (And by visiting English women artists) 'If the flowers used for making the tisane are too old they may produce symptoms of narcotic intoxication.'

The weather deteriorated on the day of the diaries and continued blustery and unseasonably wet for a while. Overcast skies and frequent rain showers checked Owen in his response to the mystery before him. He spent several days in the most withdrawn state Catherine had witnessed so far. However, he found time, while fiddling with the gazebo, to visit the Stoggle and ponder on what had now become a new abode for him. By the time the weather improved, he had committed parts of the message in his notebook to memory and copied all of it into another book to ensure its survival. He felt that the period of waiting and reflection was judicious in the circumstances, for he had to be completely rational on the next occasion. However, he had discovered in his reading that Whitsuntide, which was only a few days away, was the traditional time of celebration of tree spirits.* This piece of folk-lore made him apprehensive. He knew that when someone is impatient to do something, and is prevented by the elements, the period of waiting can sometimes lead to over-enthusiastic behaviour.

When conditions did improve enough to proceed, Owen was very conscious that there was a possibility for him to rush ahead, as if released from confinement. Therefore, when, eventually, a fine day did arrive, eagerness of this kind was deliberately suppressed as he walked up the shoulder of the dingle in a measured gait, slower than his normal pace. During the cycle ride to Gwenynog, he had restrained himself from hurrying for fear of arriving in too excited a condition. He had regulated his speed so as to maintain a calm disposition throughout the journey. And now that the Stoggle was in view, he did his utmost to suppress any emotion he felt upwelling within him.

In such a controlled, unemotional state, it was perhaps inevitable that his response to the tree would be ambivalent. As he approached the Stoggle it did not appear at first to be the tree that had become so familiar in the recent weeks. When he reached it, the surroundings felt a little different, too. But nothing had changed. A subtle increase in the fulsomeness of the crown – such as it was - and in the depth of green of the leaves had occurred, but this was matched by a similar change in the appearance of the surrounding vegetation.

The atmosphere of the morning, although an expression of a fine day, was not out of the ordinary. There was no wind, either, to unsettle the air around the rocks. Only a light breeze ruffled the foliage; and the light coming through the crown was such that it mellowed rather than accentuated the interplay of leaves. As usual, he contemplated for a moment the ambience of the place. Where was the stillness, that uncanny stillness, which usually pervaded the tree, whatever the surrounding activity?

Had this tree really communicated with him? Or had he imagined it all? Dreamt it all? Where did the spirit - if there was one - reside? In the crown? - the trunk? - the base? - the roots?... Abruptly, he dismissed this line of thought. It was not conducive to the purpose of his being there. He resolved to be consistent; to be calm and open to the influence of the Stoggle's 'inner presence' - if such a presence existed.

Clutching his notebook firmly, he sat down in the natural seat at the base of the tree. All was quiet, except for the calling of some unseen birds in the vicinity, and a tractor whirring in the distance, its noise coming through the air as a tranquiliser. There was no sound nor sight of any buzzard. He stared fixedly ahead over the dingle and endeavoured to clear his mind. He had convinced himself that his head should be as open and as unoccupied as possible. It was not easy to think about nothing. In the far distance, the conifer-topped ridges asserted themselves through the haze, giving the horizon a serrated edge. He became so preoccupied with the effort of clearing his mind that he did not relax.

He did not have time to relax. The sight of a man in the distance at the bottom of the hill caught his gaze. It was Ralph, making his way towards the dingle from Gwenynog. Quickly, Owen scrambled to his feet with the intention of absconding, but Ralph waved to him, although they were still some distance apart. He resigned himself to the interruption, sitting down again and waiting.

"Another lazy day, Owen", shouted Ralph, half way up the dingle. "You could do with regular work: hard work."

Ralph's theme was becoming a persistent one. He had got into the habit of reminding Owen that there was work locally if he wanted to find it.

"I saw you go by the house while I was having breakfast. What do you come up here for?"

"The view", said Owen, curtly, unhappy that Ralph, of all people, should interrupt his mission.

"Coming up here is one of your sister's habits. You like following in her crazy footsteps, don't you?" The comment was intended to rile.

"Actually, I was on my way over the Mountain", reacted Owen, adding as a sudden thought; "I want to find the place marked on the map as Llannerch Hudol. Do you know where it is?" He got out his 1:25000 Ordnance map. He knew that Ralph was unfamiliar with maps - indeed, shy of them.

"It doesn't exist anymore", said Ralph, quickly. "I've heard the Greenways talk about it when gathering sheep on their side of the Mountain, but there isn't a place by that name."

"What are you doing up here, then?" Owen had now gained the initiative.

"Oh, Dad was bringing some sheep over after breakfast, but he's been delayed. So, when I saw you go by, I thought I'd see what you were up to. Someone's got to keep an eye on lazy off-comers." An unpleasant smile crossed his swarthy face. "What do you think of this old Stoggle, then? On its last wooden legs, wouldn't you say? Time for it to come down?" His goading was not very subtle.

"To come down", repeated Owen, shocked. "What for?"

"Well, it won't be long before it falls down, will it? It's already dropping branches. One came down a few weeks ago when we had those gales. And its top was blown out last year in those October winds. If it loses any more branches, there's a good chance one of your family will be underneath. And that will be a shame." Ralph was amused but Owen refused to join in.

"This tree has another hundred years yet. What happened to that branch, by the way. Did you take it for firewood?"

"Yes, it went for firewood: most of it. We used to give bits of lime to our neighbour at Wern y coc. He was forever whittling away at wood. He was found dead with a half finished stick in his hand. Maybe there's a wood-carver somewhere who will take this Stoggle when it comes down. I wonder how much it's worth... That sounds like Dad's Landrover. Go easy on the exercise." With that last remark, he bounded off down the slope, leaving Owen searching for one last retort.

Ralph seemed to be able to get under anyone's skin. His interruption left Owen too unsettled to continue with his mission. His best course was to go for a long walk and return later in the day. He consulted his map, on which he had marked the former outline of Coed Tirion Glas, as depicted on the de Bohun map of 1707. He had also located, on the six inches to the mile map back at the cottage, the exact position of Llannerch Hudol, no longer named on the smaller scale maps, and marked the place on his field map. It was not very far away; almost in a direct line westwards over the top of the Mountain. Giving the Stoggle a last searching look, he set off up the rocks towards the summit of Rhibo Mountain, his departure coinciding with the aerial passage of a lone raven, croaking overhead as it flew in the same direction.

The visibility was not outstanding; the features in the far distance being smeared with the same mellow glare that was the morning's backcloth to the view from the Stoggle. But the Skirrid, the wall of the Black Mountains, and the intervening scenes of the pastoral landscape of erstwhile Ewyas were as uplifting as ever. Once on the mountain top, the views and the freshness of the air were invigorating.

Rhibo Mountain was the local summit. It put someone on top of the landscape, but not beyond it. A person could still feel a part of the pastoral scenes which filtered through the tree-strewn fields, the ragged hedgerows, and the vestigial woodland onto its flanks and up to its summit. With such scenes foreshortened by the angle of view, the former extent of the wooded wastes of Ewyas were not far away in Owen's mind.

From the trig point on the summit, a sunken track descended in the direction of an anonymous stream which spilled out of the Mountain's western flank and sped down to the Monnow at Gulible. But, after the track had coursed down the steep upper slope of the flank, and was in the vicinity of Llannerch Hudol, it suddenly petered out. The way was blocked by a blackthorn brake, spreading vigorously on one side of a triangular ledge of ground set between two narrow gullies that converged to form a tributary of the anonymous stream.

Upon easing through the thicket in tortuous sideways movements, following a course marked out by sheep's wool, he reached one of those roughs, or awkward places, typical of the English countryside before intensive agriculture, of whatever kind, reclaimed - or, more aptly, stole - them from the wild. It was not completely given over to wilderness; stock were able to reach it, but it was overgrown with briars and brambles, as well as blackthorn, and an assortment of trees. Altogether, it looked and felt like a place that was declining from woodland rather than reverting to it. This was the site of Llannerch Hudol; it had to be.

From his vantage point at the upper and wider end of the rough, he could see Gulible below, the houses of the loosely huddled village individually distinct. His imagination got to work immediately. Was this the location of the lime which deluded the wood-carver into thinking his house was on fire? With eyes eager to discover clues to the ancientness of the place, he scanned the rough in all its entangled recesses. Spindly wild cherries fringed the gullies, along with ash and oak, the oaks being large and old. With his arms held aloft, he weaved and tore his way through the briars and brambles into the centre of the rough. Here, there were a number of whitened stumps, the remnants of large trees which had been cut through some two feet above the ground - dead elms, undoubtedly. Nearby, there was the crumbling core of a very large stump, the stump of what must have been an old hollow tree. A boundary tree? Another stoggle perhaps?

Beyond, towards the apex of the triangle, and the confluence of the gullies, there stood two exceptionally well-formed trees which, standing as they did against a backdrop of cherries, were not readily identifiable. Closer inspection revealed them to be wild service trees. The indicators of ancient woodland! They were true trees, not the outsized shrubs or the small trees that are the lot of the native Sorbus genera today. The grassy ground beneath them was strewn with last season's leaves, some of them yellow or turning towards that colour; and there were numerous suckers in the long grass. He estimated that the two trees were about fifty to sixty feet tall, and that one of them had a clean stem for over twelve feet. In both cases, their girth was greater than the compass of his arms. These were the biggest wild service trees he had ever seen. Were they the youthful companions to a lime that had departed?

Delighted with his discovery, he leant against one of the trunks, and recorded the find in his notebook. By the time he had finished, the company of the trees had won him over. Framed between two wild service trees, he gazed at Gulible in the valley below, a village he had visited several times, but not really explored yet. Its nearness decided his next move. Out of fanciful curiosity, he selected a house in the village, which was closest to the footpath that led downslope, pretended it was on fire, and then timed himself in getting to it. After extricating himself from the brake, he reached the house in twelve minutes, by which time his throat was dry and his thirst was raging. So he headed for the Green Man pub which, according to Milo, was Gulible's only jewel - besides the lichens on the sycamores in the churchyard. Like most pubs in loosely settled villages, it stood on its own, but at such an awkward angle to the lane that it was virtually unobtrusive.

When he came upon it, the folklore of the area impressed itself upon him more vividly than at any time so far. The sign outside, fixed to the stonework of what was only a small, though a solid, building, depicted an elf-like man clad completely in a garment of leaves, sporting a leafy hood, and poised for dancing. The leaves were the shape and the colour of lime leaves. He was enthralled; and perplexed. Even though he had not seen the sign before, it was vaguely familiar.

With a sandwich in one hand and a non-alcoholic beverage in the other - he was taking no chances - he interrogated the publican who, like everyone else in the district, looked at him with that quizzical gaze to which he had become accustomed.

"What's the story behind the sign?" he asked.

"It's on the wall over there, if you want to read about it", was the reply as the publican stared at him as a policeman might stare at someone suspected of shop-lifting.

Taking his refreshments with him, he sidled over to a framed illustration hanging on a smoke-discoloured wall. One look and he recognised the artist immediately - Suzy. It was the final version of the drawing in her sketch pad. The illustration consisted of a small reproduction of the sign, followed by its story, written in an immaculate script, the whole bordered by a motif of woodland flowers. In the bottom right hand corner were the initials, S.F. & C.F. - Suzy Forrest and Catherine Farr.

The script explained that the Green Man was reputed to have been the son of a local Welshman who fought against the Normans for the freedom of Ewyas. The Normans kidnapped the son and threatened his life unless his father surrendered himself in exchange. With the help of a 'Saeson'* lass whose English father had given her to the Norman lord of the area in return for the right to hold his land freely, the son escaped and fled into Coed Tirion Glas. His father was later killed in a skirmish at Gulible. After this loss, the son, who was still a wanted man, remained in hiding in the wood, wearing sprays of leaves - linden leaves according to the story - to conceal himself amongst the trees. Later, he was joined by the lass who had helped him to escape, the two of them becoming outlaws, living in the woods and being rarely seen. The story ended with a note explaining that, until the coming of the chapel days, it had been a local ritual in the spring for a young man to clothe himself in lime leaves, conceal himself in Coed Tirion Glas, and for all the girls in the area to seek him out.

Next to the illustration, there were an assortment of notices - cricket club and other sporting fixtures, WI meetings, etcetera, and among them a cheap looking business card thrusting forward the names Ralph Farr and Tim Medlar: 'for fuel-wood, fencing stakes, felling, thinning, and tree surgery'. Tree surgery! exclaimed Owen, mentally.

On his return to the bar, Owen asked who had done the

sign outside.

"Your sister, Suzy Forrest, the very lass who did the illustration over there." He then paused and, looking intently at Owen, said, "You are Suzy Forrest's brother, aren't you?"

"How did you guess?" responded Owen sarcastically.

"Word gets around. There have been a few people in here recently saying how much you look like a male version of your sister. The question on everyone's lips is do you behave like her?" This was delivered as a very loaded remark, intended to be forward, and followed by a wicked grin. Owen tried not to show any reaction to it.

"Like what, for example?" He threw the question back.

"Well, you should know her better than anyone else. Or did she leave home at an early age?" The wicked grin increased.

"How do I know how she behaves in her local area. I haven't seen her for ages. Come on, give me an example of what you mean. You might tell me something I don't know."

He had managed to wriggle out of giving an answer, and now dared the publican to reveal all. He kept a straight face waiting for the reply.

"Well, take what happened when she and Catherine Farr finished their historical work on our sign. As soon as your sister discovered that a local tradition had died out, she decided to revive it - for the sake of charity, a good excuse for any game. It was about this time, I think. She put a notice up in all the local pubs inviting the young men of the area to search de Bohun's deer park for the 'Green Woman'. She dressed herself up one evening in an odd garment, a loosely-made covering made from green and yellow materials that resembled leaves, and the men gave chase. They all ended up here afterwards. Your sister didn't have much on except a few remnant leaves."

The publican paused for a moment. Then, with another wicked grin, he asked: "Is that the sort of thing you get up to?"

Owen could not withhold a smile any longer. "Not really. I'm the shy one in the family. Who won the chase?"

"Tim Medlar, but he's given up the chase now. Have you met him?"

"Not yet."

"By the way, when are we going to see your sister again? I haven't seen her for a while. Hasn't she gone off to Spain chasing matadors?"

Owen smiled. "Yes, to the Pyrenees where she's chasing plants. She should be back at the end of the summer. Then you can tell her what her brother got up to while she was away." Smiling cheekily, he left the bar.

As he reached the door, the man called after him, saying that if he was on his bike he should keep on the right side of the road. The remark gave him much to think about in walking back through the village to the footpath.

On his return to the Melglyn Stoggle, he stopped for a while at Llannerch Hudol to marvel at the wild service trees. It was another intriguing place which was likely to have a fascinating history. The meaning of its name might reveal something. The thought did not last long, for the distant sound of a buzzard reached his ears from the other side of the Mountain.

On the summit, he paused to take in the views again. What a place his sister had found! Why had it taken him so long to visit her new home? He felt like staying at the trig point for a while, and might have done so, had not a buzzard's pee-ow captured his attention again. There it was in the sky, flying towards him from Coed Tirion Glas. He stood riveted to the spot, watching as it glided down to him and then swept away in the direction of the dingle. It came close enough for him to see that it had a feather missing; the call was unmistakable. It was the Eerie Shriek again. It did not dip out of sight below the hill, but banked and turned, looking back towards him as he followed. It turned several times to look back at him, each time emitting the eerie pee-ow which penetrated his body and left him tingling all over. It gave out one last eerie call after settling into the Stoggle, and then stared intently at Owen as he came down to the tree passed the rocks.

The Griffin Oak

CHAPTER 17

Hollow and sorrowful in heart
I rejoice in your return

Only Gentle sons of Dyn desire to be with
Trees
You have the heart and head of Beibio
I am glad you have returned to hear my plea...

Owain
I will tell you how the Serpent stole Our
Gentle Trees
How vehement and voracious was its fire
How the vastness of Y Coed was a store to
be destroyed
By the worm which carves a void with selfish
ire

Lonely is my Lime beside this barren Cwm
Forbidding is the dreadful Serpent Dyn...

Long ago
Y Coed kept Spirits of the Lime
The Oak
The Alder
And the Elm
Our Trees were Close
Our Souls were Close
Life was Close and Calm
The Deeper were Our ties
The greater was Our joy
Our Souls were ever joyful
And Cerydwen was glad
We mingled in the Deepness
We marvelled at the Greenness
We were safe within Our Trees within Y Coed

Long ago
My Soul was settled in the valley of the Gwy
Y Coed was then perpetual and Deep
Our Gentle Limes
Luxuriant and grand
Rose up in golden gatherings of Trees
Brightly shone their tops above Y Coed
Enchantment filled the Earth
Fragrance filled the Air
We were never ever lonely

Never ever lost
We were safe within the Deepness
Serene within the Greenness
Joyously embracing Cerydwen
The Greenness then was blithe and warm and
sweet

Contentment only comes when ties are Deep...

Owain
A Gentle Lime has always held my Soul
I would Pass into a Tree
When it prospered in its prime
Departing when it slipped away to rest
Forever grateful to exist
I would overstay my time
I always lingered long before slowly Passing
On
I was never very far from other Gentle Trees
There was always somewhere safe for me to
go

Restful were the Limes in the valley of the
Gwy
Resplendent was the Greenness of Y Coed...

Three Passage Trees were precious to my Soul
Trembling Aspens
Mellow Apples
Faithful Servins gave me rest

Each rescued me
And soothed me
Restored my wandering Soul

My Eagles and my Kites glided far for Gentle
Trees
To seek the tallest and the brightest in Y Coed
They would guide me to my Trees
They would sink into my tops
My Limes were then the eyes for all to see...

Alas
The Eagles and the Kites have vanished from
the Sky
Banished by the dreadful Serpent Dyn
The Eagles of the Gwy
The Kites of Euas and Ergyng
No longer soar above my Gentle Tree
The Kites of Mynydd y rhibo
They too no longer soar
The Buzzards are my only soaring eyes

Lofty were the Limes in the valley of the Gwy
Far seeing were the Eagles of Y Coed...

Alas
The Deepness was disturbed by the dying of
the Elms
By the Coming of the dreadful Serpent Dyn
The Hollowness was heavy on Our Souls...

The vacant spaces filled with Birch
The vacant spaces filled with Ash
Their Spirits spread amongst us in delight
And the spaces grew and grew
The Hollowness increased
The Gentle murmurs of the glade gave way to
row

Encroaching space is hollow to the heart...

Owain
The Gentle Spirits of Y Coed were made to
wail
The Lasting of Our Trees was made unsure
Passing On was hastened
Wandering was long
And Passing Out was borne
The agony of Treeless Souls began

Solitude is sad for lonely Souls...

Emptied of its searching roots
Deep fruitfulness
And Gentle shade
The Earth was grave and sad
The dispossessed were downcast
The isolated lost
For them it was no more the many Leafings
of the past
But Passing Out in charred and hollow soil
Wasting in the Serpent's empty ground

Feebleness bewilders those that flee...

Weary Trees kept weary Souls unfree to move
Their Cries of anguish wasting in the ground
Cries of Rootlessness
Treelessness
And Hollowness of heart...

Weakness is dear to those that die...

We assailed the Creeping Serpent with
Enchantment
And with Spells
With Wonders that would still all savage blows
But the Cunning of the Worm Continued to be
dire
Y Coed was hacked and burned
Cruelly downed with ire...

In time
The warring Worm Crept Closer to my Tree
Carving hollow lines of Carnage through Y Coed
Stamping on the ground
Taking space for noisy lairs
I had to leave my valley by the Gwy...

Passing On I entered Erging
My Eagles as my eyes
To dwell there for a while in Gentle Trees

The tallest and the brightest I have known
So tall and bright and high upon the Earth
The Serpent Dyn was guided by my tops
Another way was trampled through Y Coed...

The noises of the Worm confused my Soul...

In Erging
I could feel the Serpent on the ground
Crawling ever nearer in spite and selfish ire
I could feel the growing spaces
Emptying Y Coed
I could feel the empty spaces in my Soul...

The noises of the Worm will never cease...

It was then I cast a Spell
Upon a magic son of Dyn
Who was fearful of the Serpent's savage
ways
I warned this Myrddin Hen
Of the coming of a Worm
Of a Serpent stealing forth
From where the Sun is borne
Of a Serpent burning Trees and sons of Dyn...

From me through him the prophecy was told
And it came true...

The dreadful Serpent Dyn will burn Y Coed
And be
Forever fire
Forever ire
Forever dire...

At this point, the writing petered out, the word 'dire' being barely legible. The rest of the page was marked with a scattering of letters and half words, some of them Welsh, none of which made any sense.

CHAPTER 18

'Weary Trees kept weary Souls unfree to move
Their cries of anguish wasting in the ground
Cries of Rootlessness
Treelessness
And Hollowness of heart...'

Spirit of Y Coed

It was the ringing of the telephone - Catherine calling from Hereford - that finally roused Owen from the after-effects of his second communication with the Melglyn Stoggle. The ringing penetrated his consciousness as a sound within a dream; becoming louder and less distant as the stupor of sleep receded. When his eyes opened, and he realised that the sound was coming from the telephone downstairs, he was still not properly awake. He did not notice that he was still dressed in his daytime clothes and lying on top of the duvet. For a frightening moment, he did not know where he was, what day it was, or what had happened to him. The exertion required to struggle off the bed, and to clatter clumsily down the stairs, bouncing off the walls, dispelled the initial confusion experienced upon waking. By the time he reached the telephone, he knew where he was and where he had been the day before, but he was far from being coherent, a state of mind he could not conceal from Catherine, however hard he tried to be his usual self.

He was not bothered anyway. As soon as the conversation ended, what he had said, which was unclear to him already, and how he had said it, were unimportant. All he could think about was his notebook. But before he could immerse himself in its contents, he had to find it. This was, in view of his burning impatience, more irksome than the disturbance which had brought him to the telephone. It was not in the bedroom, the living room, nor the kitchen. Eventually, he realised what must have happened. On his return to the cottage, he had gone straight upstairs and collapsed on the bed. The notebook was still in the saddlebag on the bike, which he found lying on the path beside the front door. After putting together a breakfast and making a cup of lime-flower tea, he returned upstairs to rest on the bed.

The second message affected him as profoundly as the first. In each case, he had to cope with unbelievable words when his mind was still confused, the emotional upheavals they induced, and a body that was fragile to the point of crumbling. As before, he re-read the message several times. After having something to eat, and when he felt the onset of some kind of composure, he lay on the bed and read it aloud, analysing the passages as he went along.

Who was Beibio? An actual Welsh inhabitant of Ewyas in

247

times past? But which time? Was it his name which survived until 1707 in the place-name Llwyn Beibio?

Again, the point was made that Man's exploitation of the forest was inexorable and unthinking; that the Serpent, as an advancing fire, was too perverted by the ample store available to consider the consequences of what it was doing...

So there were other spirits, many of whom had wasted away in the ground. But once, they were united in their sylvan community of Y Coed - the more united, the more the ties, the deeper the being. That was a cryptic comment upon the affairs of the Serpent...

'Solitude is sad for lonely souls': the spirit of the Stoggle being one such soul. But solitude is sad for any soul. Centuries of it would be agony! And the sadness of solitude would be greatest when all connections with others were severed causing spiritual detachment. That refrain struck a northern chord in Owen's soul...

A Spirit faithful to limes - the abode trees of gentle spirits - remaining in each one for how long? And passing on via other trees to a new host, with renewals of vigour in aspens, crab apples and wild service trees. What differences between these three! Why these three? And how was passage made, via root contact? To the human mind, this was the only explanation...

So the spirit could not pass on from one host to another - thereby to endure - without the support of other trees, particularly resuscitation from trees of less stature and dominance than the main forest species. Another cryptic comment upon the affairs of the Worm...

And how fascinating that each new host spirit was re-located by eagles at first, then by kites, and now by buzzards - changes necessitated by Man's persecution of the larger birds of prey. The eagles and the kites, once a part of that golden time the Spirit laments, survived only by the buzzard, the plaintive caller which, like the Spirit it assists, has struggled through the onslaughts of the Serpent. The eerie presence of the buzzard was now explained. But how was contact between bird and Spirit achieved? By enchantment?

"Is that what has happened to me? Have I been enchanted?"

There was a long pause in Owen's train of thought as this reflection sank in. To be enchanted was one of the ultimate pleasures of life. Folk-lore was permeated with enchantment. Modern man wondered where enchantment was to be found. Had he, inadvertently, found it? It was too profound a possibility to be considered in his present state. He returned to the message.

The dying of the elms? Surely not the 'elm decline' of vegetation history? He was familiar with this event because of his involvement in the north with pollen studies. To remind himself of when it happened, he dipped into one of his books, and found a useful illustration showing the abundance of the main tree species since the Ice Age. The 'elm decline' - the very sudden crash in the population of elm trees revealed by the reduction in their pollen rain and probably caused by a pathogen outbreak - happened in the mid-Holocene period around five thousand eight hundred years ago when the British climate was changing from being warm and wet to the cool and wet times of today, a change in temperature which caused the lime to lose its ubiquitous place in the primaeval forest.* Before this change, it was the commonest tree in the forests of Lowland England, mixing with oak and elm in the West. All this occurred as early Neolithic Man was spreading into the forest, clearing it for primitive agriculture and other basic needs. It was, therefore, the dying of the elms, and the opening up of Y Coed by Neolithic peoples, which created the space for trees like birch and ash to increase their presence. The references to fire and to the mutilation of trees could only be the shifting agriculture of slash and burn, and the practice of shredding trees to provide young shoots and leaves as fodder for stock. There was a note that both elm and lime leaves are nutritious to stock, a fact which is known to have been appreciated by Neolithic peoples. This much should have resided in the depths of Owen's memory anyway. The elm decline had made quite an impression upon him when he first learned of it.

What happened to the spirits when the repeated cutting of trees by coppicing and pollarding became commonplace for centuries? Emasculation? Dormancy? Demise? - 'The Earth holds many weary souls'.

As he reminded himself of these facts, and pondered the questions they raised, the reality of history and the earthliness of existence, came to the forefront of his mind, and the idea of tree spirits having a place in the scheme of things became incredible once more. Was he really in contact with a tree spirit?

The message was there in front of him. 'The gentle murmurs of the glade were overwhelmed. Encroaching space is hollow to the heart...' The murmurs were still being overwhelmed, and the space created was proving hollow to the heart - throughout the world. The agony of tree-less souls had become, in some places, the agony of tree-less Man...

Weariness before death - the last throes of existence; a false and a terminal feeling of well being as life-lines faded away:

feebleness bewildered those who fled into the ground, and emptiness enfeebled those whose lot it was to linger on...

Enchantment and spells: so the awe instilled in early Man was a device to divert the Serpent's wrath, as in the legend of Llannerch Hudol. The folklore of tree worship was not merely pagan superstition after all...

The warring Worm carving hollow lines through Ergyng? Surely not the penetration of Welsh territory by the Romans? The time when Ariconium came into being and the Romans began to exploit the iron deposits of the Forest of Dean? What other pressing reason for leaving the Fastness of the Gwy? Owen knew, from the writings of Oliver Rackham,* that the Late Iron Age and the subsequent Roman period were the periods when man made his greatest inroads into the primaeval forests of Britain. So this assumption was not fanciful.

Would the move westwards have led to the high ground of the Garway and Orcop Hills? The modern route from Ross to Ewyas curves around this upland, passing through Llandinabo, Much Dewchurch and Kilpeck. Did it follow the line of an ancient trackway? Catherine might know...

A spell cast on Myrddin, a magic son of Dyn. Surely not the Merlin of Arthurian legend? This reflection affected him as sharply as the thought of being enchanted. The sequence of events in the message fitted with the time when Merlin was supposed to have lived - if he had ever lived. Would anyone believe this confirmation of his existence if it was offered as evidence? What exactly did he prophesy that came true? The advance of the Saxon hoard?

These musings, as absorbing and astonishing as they were, called for too much thought and concentration. There were so many questions and so much to dwell on that Owen's head relapsed into the addled state that had given the morning such a heavy beginning. He wanted so hard to think clearly; to rationalise everything; to come to terms with his predicament and see a way forward...

It was the sound of a voice downstairs which jolted him out of his dilemma. Ralph had turned up. Hastily, Owen shoved all his papers under the duvet and stumbled out of bed. At least Ralph could not tease him with lying-in because he was still fully clothed. Unaware of the noise he was making, he trudged heavily down the stairs, having difficulty staying properly upright as he entered the living room.

"You've got a hang-over!" said his visitor in disbelief. "So that's what you do all day, is it? Knock back your sister's deadly wines. You crafty bugger."

"I'm not drunk, Ralph; far from it. I've just worn myself out on a morning bike-ride... I'll buy you a drink in the Green Man if you can find some empty bottles. Go on, have a look round."

Ralph had a cursory look about the room and in the kitchen, but the smirk on his face did not go.

"Anyway, what brings you here at this time of the day - skiving off while your dad sees the ADAS* man?" Owen was not going to be browbeaten, whatever his state.

"Catherine asked me to call, actually. She's worried about you. Goodness knows why. I suppose with your sister out of the way, she hasn't got anyone to worry about."

"Well, you can tell her I'm okay, can't you? Just tired, that's all. We can't all be oxen like her brother."

"I don't believe you. I know when someone's worse the wear

for drink. You're speaking differently for a start. A bike-ride wouldn't do that. If this is the state you get in after a ride, then you won't be much good helping out with the shearing. Catching sheep - our sheep - is hard work. And I clip pretty fast."

"Don't worry, Ralph, I'll keep up with the going rate. Now then, can I get you a drink - a cup of herb tea perhaps?"

"No thanks. You can keep that stuff. I've just had lunch anyway. I'll get back and telephone my report - drunk in charge of a push-bike."

"Look here, Ralph, I'm as sober as you'll ever be. If you've come in your pick-up with all your gear, then let's see who's got the best eye. I'll get my axe out and we'll split a few hefty logs and time ourselves."

In his present state, Owen was taking a risk throwing down such a challenge. His annoyance had got the better of him. But Ralph, having seen him use an axe at the farm, was not ready to put the matter to such a test.

"No way; I'm not going to help you split your logs. Anyway, you might damage a leg, then I'll have my sister on my back. The best thing is for you to have a lie down and get ready to have my sister around your neck. She's got strange tastes when it comes to necks. See you in the pub sometime."

Ralph smiled meanly as he departed. His pick-up roared away from the lay-by with the sound of excessive revving.

Owen knew that Ralph had taken the trouble to drop in at the Goggin mainly out of curiosity - not strictly at Catherine's insistence. The two men had only her in common. Ralph was in a completely different social scene to his sister, and had already shown that he had no time for Suzy, even without the vituperative sniping of his friend, Tim Medlar. If he was going to get back to Catherine, then it was likely, more than likely, that she would hear the worse. And it would be inevitable that she would drop in on her way home from work. So he set about getting himself into the sharpest state possible in the circumstances - having something more to eat; some more lime-flower tea; and spending the afternoon on the gazebo to prove his sobriety.

Catherine caught him off-guard by turning up earlier than he expected. For Ralph had reported negatively and given her more cause for concern. Luckily for Owen, she disturbed him sawing some wood.

"There you are, Owen." She looked around the work place, but not at the progress that was being made. She was rewarded with the sight of a wine bottle in a corner - an old bottle now containing white spirit. "You haven't started drinking Suzy's wines while you're working?" Her question was clumsily put.

Owen erupted. "Catherine, that brother of yours is a useless idiot. I told him I had not been drinking, but he refused to believe me. Now, who are you going to believe - him or me?"

This put Catherine on the spot, and made her regret, immediately, that she had raised the matter so soon.

"Of course, I believe you. But why were you so dazed when I telephoned this morning?"

"I just went for a fast bike ride before breakfast, that's all, to shake off the lethargy of a short lie-in. I felt a bit groggy when I woke up, so I decided that some vigorous exercise would pull me round. You 'phoned just after I got back. Okay?"

"Okay. Now then, what are we going to do tonight?"

"Stay put and go over some more local history. Quaffing

that fascinating stuff - coming from you - is far better than Suzy's wines." He smiled.

"After a meal at the pub? We can decide what we might do for the Whit-weekend" she suggested.

"Alright..."

CHAPTER 19

*'Our Souls were close
Life was close and calm
The Deeper were Our ties
The greater was Our joy
Our Souls were ever joyful.'*

Spirit of Y Coed

Whenever the sheep were gathered together for one of the ritual treatments of the shepherding calendar, Bodcot Farm reverberated with the sounds of incessant bleating. As lambs became parted from ewes, calls for reunion filled the air, and there was pandemonium. Owen had never been so close to a mustering of this kind, nor was he familiar with the impending ritual that was the cause of all the noise. He was curious to know exactly how he was going to be used. Catherine had just said 'catching' and 'pitching'.

For as long as the farm had existed, shearing had taken place.

Even before the Celtic settlers, who had established the 'homestead of the buzzard', usurped an alderwood, and transformed a wet wilderness - a Welsh 'wern anial' - into a subsistence farm, there were sheep in the vicinity. Archeological discoveries bore testimony to the existence of Neolithic peoples who herded sheep in the Black Mountains. So the tradition was a long-standing one, carried out first for the material needs of the family and the tribe, and subsequently for an ever-growing populace.

Although the surroundings, which constituted the background to this ritual, had changed profoundly while the tradition persisted, they continued to carry a hint of those earlier times. The location of Bodcot Farm beside the narrowest of lanes, at the head of one of the secluded tributaries of the Dol Barcut Brook, recessed in a fold of land and partially concealed by hedgerow oaks and riparian alders, suggested that it was still on the edge of a rural waste. The sombre proximity of Rhibo Mountain and the Black Mountains only accentuated this impression of remoteness. As the sheep were hustled into the yard, the concrete yard which Owen knew so well in its filthiest state, the woollen mass, pattering and panting into place, brought together the countless white specks of the hillsides into a gnawing reminder of the permanence of pastoralism.

Once his role had been explained to him, Owen realised that everyone was to be involved in the shearing; that it was, by tradition, a communal effort of the extended family. The shearing itself was to be done by Lloyd Farr and his recalcitrant son, Ralph, using electric shears, not the manual clippers of the shepherding tradition. They expected to shear the flock of 300 ewes in two days. Catherine and her mother were there to wind the fleeces and to pack them into the hessian sacks known as 'wool sheets', one of which was already hanging by ropes from a beam in the huge barn where the shearing was to take place. Owen, together with Gavin, another of Ralph's sidekicks, had the dusty and awkward task of being a 'catcher' - catching the sheep for the shearers and then afterwards helping to 'pitch' them on the nape with the farm's brand before releasing them. And both grandmothers were there to feed and water the workers. The only person missing was the one remaining grandfather. His absence was a matter of course.

The conveyor belt of wool started from the yard, which had changed from being a filthy concrete expanse into a moving mass of dingy whiteness. It went through a series of gates which led to the opening in the huge barn where the sheep and the two catchers were corralled, ready for the next shout from either Lloyd or Ralph, who up-ended their charges onto the old carpets they were working on. Once shorn, and then pitched, the sheep scrambled away to the daylight beyond a side exit into a field which ran down to the alder-fringed brook. When the yard was emptied, another flock was brought forward from an adjacent field, and the woollen conveyor belt restarted.

For Owen, the two days were taxing activity. He found himself immersed in sheep; surrounded by them, deafened by them, covered in oil and soiled by them, and saturated by their smell. He was also smeared with pitch on various parts of his body, but too randomly to ensure his recovery to the right farm if he ever became lost in the mountains. The intensity of the work, and his exacting role in the ritual, left little time at all for reflections about the Stoggle. The work was so arduous that he could only concentrate on the tasks before him. The breaks hardly gave enough time to unwind; they were just as much a part of the conveyor belt as the sheep.

However, despite the difficulties he encountered in catching sheep, he managed to keep up with the conversation of the other workers and catch the interesting comments. The shearing was being done only a few days after the appearance of a notice in the local newspaper advertising the sale of some nearby farmland which lay on the other side of the lane. The almost derelict smallholding of Wern y coc, the 'alders of the cuckoo', was to be sold at last by auction. The holding consisted of unimproved pastures and meadows, and advancing thickets, and included the secluded ill-drained land wedged alongside the Dol Barcut Brook opposite the fields of Bodcut Farm. The confluence of the brook with a tributary from the farm was its southern limit, while on the north it was adjacent to the Gelli Copse of Carling Medlar, the coniferous plantation by the bird carcasses. Lloyd Farr had tried, on a number of occasions, to persuade the owner of the holding, an old bachelor, to either sell or rent the land to him. The old man had now been dead for over two years, and Lloyd of Bodcut, having failed to rent the land, now had his chance at last to acquire some extra fields. Such an opportunity to enlarge the farm had not occurred for ages, not since his father had added forty acres just after the Second World War. Owen listened to the slow interchange of comments about the sale, shouted above the noise of the shearing when the speakers could spare a moment from their work.

"How much did Mr Burroughs say the land would go for?" shouted Ralph to his father in a voice which carried a hint of regret that it was not his decision to proceed with a purchase.

"That depends", came the delayed reply from Lloyd as he

finished an awkward part of a sheep's rear end. "It might be sold in two lots - the buildings and the meadows separate from the pastures. The land alone could fetch thirty to forty thousand. Whatever the amount, I can't afford to bid for all of it; the pastures, perhaps, but not the main lot."

"Even the pastures would stretch us too far though", interceded Martha Farr, giving her husband a sideways look as she stuffed another rolled up fleece into the wool-sheet.

"I know; but we can't miss such a once-in-lifetime opportunity", said Lloyd, his reply only just audible above the noise of his shearer.

"Your father would do anything to buy some of that land", remarked Martha in a concerned aside to her daughter.

"Who else is likely to be interested in bidding, asked Gavin, Ralph's friend, "besides Arnold the Trerrible?" He had been renting the land since the death of its owner, being prepared to pay more for it than Lloyd Farr. Arnold and Lloyd had once been good friends. The land at Wern y coc had come between them.

No-one seemed to want to answer this question, except Catherine: "Carling Medlar is bound to be interested, isn't he Ralph; in the house, at least?"

"I suppose so", said her father in a rather fatalistic tone, while Ralph concentrated intently on his shearing.

"Even if he doesn't want to add to his empire of holiday homes cum shooting lodges, he is sure to consider purchasing it for restoration and resale, so that the locals can't get hold of it." This was a side to Catherine that Owen had not yet seen. But she was treading on her brother's ground, and he was quick to assert himself. His contacts with The Prospect made him think, in a self-important way, that he was a better judge of Carling Medlar's interests.

"If he is interested, he might bid for the whole lot. He doesn't do anything by halves."

In a movement of irritation, Lloyd wrenched his ewe into a new position and gripped it tightly; a response noticed by Owen because, until that moment, he had been impressed by the deft way the farmer sheared his sheep.

"It will be better if the whole place goes to one buyer, preferably someone who wants to farm part-time", shouted Catherine, keeping the initiative. "It should be kept as a smallholding. There are too few of them left." She ended up breathless but pleased to have made a point that was a long-standing bone of contention between her and Ralph. It rattled Ralph, as she knew it would, but it also increased her father's irritation.

"Farming doesn't work on the principles you get from your non-local friends", responded Ralph in cutting tones, referring to Suzy and Alison, both of whom were 'incomers'.

Catherine ignored him and directed a half-conciliatory question at her father, to show that she was not getting at him. "How many acres are being sold altogether, Dad?" she asked.

Her father's reply was given with authority, as an assertion that he had the last word in the matter. "Thirty-six in total, covering four fields; that's the two pastures on the Goggin side, and the two meadows down by the brook."

"Where you and Suzy go to admire those orchids", said Mrs Farr, in a timely reminder that whether or not the smallholding remained as a single unit, it had other features which his daughter would be concerned about.

"The pastures are more or less the same acreage as the dingle fields at Gwenynog", added Ralph, loudly, without looking up from his work, knowing that his remark would make a telling point.

"Can't you sell the steeper ground at Gwenynog to help you buy the land that's for sale?" asked Gavin who had not said a word since his earlier question had moved the conversation onto thorny matters.

This enquiry, although innocently put, had a stunning effect upon the busy family gathering, equivalent to the unexpected appearance of Carling Medlar at a parish meeting. The family reacted in the common way that insiders respond to an outsider who says the wrong thing at the wrong time. All present, except Ralph and Owen, stopped what they were doing and intimated with stern faces that the remark was ill-chosen. Although the general level of noise remained the same, the earnestness of the activity dipped, and there was a pause charged with verbal silence. Gavin glanced at Ralph and then at Owen, asking with a facial expression alone - 'Have I said something wrong?' It was at this awkward juncture that Lloyd lost hold of his half-shorn ewe, which broke loose and careered around the barn. By the time the animal was caught, the remark was lost and the conversation, such as it was, did not return to the subject of the sale.

That evening, when Owen and Catherine were alone in the 'best' room, he recalled the conversation that had eventually soured the afternoon.

"Catherine, why did Gavin's suggestion today that some of the land at Gwenynog be sold off, go down so badly? Or can't you say?"

"Yes, I can tell you, if you promise to be objective and keep it to yourself."

"I promise", said Owen, putting his right hand across his heart and keeping a straight face.

"Well", began Catherine, as a serious opening to what was for her a serious matter, "as you know already, Ralph will take over the farm when Dad retires: primogeniture and all that. But Gwenynog is to be left to me." She paused for a few seconds to look at Owen before continuing. The disclosure had not changed the expression on his face, although his internal state had reacted.

"You know that the smallholding has been in mother's family for seventy years. From what I've found out so far, it has always been a woodman's holding. Although small, it was enough to keep all Granpa's horses. He never made the transition from horse-power to tractors. Grandad provided those when he needed them. The only engine he had was the one that drove his big circular saw. If he wasn't cutting down trees, he was sawing them up. That was how he died - a heart attack while helping Ralph to lift a log onto his saw-bench." She paused again after this emotional diversion about her grandfather.

"The holding was only fifteen acres until Grandpa acquired the dingle fields from de Bohun's father, taking the holding up to thirty-five."

"De Bohun has told me about that", interposed Owen. "He said that his father owed your grandfather various payments for work done over a number of years. He also told me about the local legend which claims that the family name of anyone who cuts down a lime tree on Rhibo Mountain will die out. He cited your grandfather as an example." In the circumstances, this was an ingenuous remark, and made without any forethought.

"That's ridiculous Owen! Surely you don't believe such rubbish? De Bohun is full of stories like that."

Owen was taken aback by this reaction. Contritely, he returned to the original subject.

"What else were you going to say about Gwenynog?"

Catherine looked at him with a reproachful glare before eventually going back to her explanation.

"Shortly before Grandpa died four years ago, he and Grandma, after talking it over with Mother, decided that I should inherit Gwenynog when they passed away. Although Grandpa had close ties with Grandad, he didn't want his holding to be tagged on to the farm, as it would be if it passed to Mother. He wanted Gwenynog to remain a smallholding, and he knew that I would keep it as one. Mother wants me to have it, anyway. So a document was drawn up which transferred the property to me, leaving it with Grandma until she joins Grandpa. So when he died after his accident, it really did become mine. But I don't think of it as mine, yet. It is still the home of my grandparents and will be for a very long time, I hope."

"But why did everyone react in such a shocked manner today? Has someone already suggested that it be sold?"

"Ralph brought the matter up over a year ago, after meeting de Bohun. Apparently, he was interested in buying back the fields his father had sold, or swopping them for a parcel of land he owns near the Gelli Copse against the Haye up to the wood, but he never got in touch with us - another one of his hair-brained ideas - and Mother told Ralph it wasn't for sale. Ralph mentioned it again the other day, after Dad had heard about the sale of Wern y coc. We had a brief family discussion of the news, during which Ralph pointed out that if some of the land at Gwenynog was sold off, it would make it possible for Dad to afford the pastures across the lane."

"What was your reaction to that?" interrupted Owen, whose face was now strained with concern.

"I said that I would never consent to such a sale, which annoyed Ralph because he assumes that he will go on farming Gwenynog when it reverts to me. He thinks that because I have chosen a career unconnected with farming, the land would be of no use to me. Dad wasn't saying anything to support either of us. I interpreted this as tacit approval of Ralph's idea. The matter is not over yet. It's bound to come up again while the sale is on."

"It wouldn't matter if it did go back to de Bohun, would it?" said Owen, seriously. "He would just let it revert to woodland and merge it with Coed Tirion Glas". The plight of the Stoggle was again in the forefront of his mind. For a moment, he was on the verge of drifting far away, but Catherine brought him back to the present with a jolt.

"Don't you start as well!" she retorted, indignantly. "Just leave the matter alone. I didn't have to explain it to you. Let's change the subject. You asked me earlier to outline the antecedents of sheep farming in the area..."

"Did I?" said Owen in a disinterested muffle.

"I have to give a talk soon to the Ewyas Historical Society on the impact of the Cistercians in the area. Let me see how much I can remember without looking at my notes."

With that, Catherine gave him another one of her local

history talks; this time a succession of randomly delivered facts about the lineage of shepherding in the area. She began by reminding him that the ancient British name of Euas was held by some authorities to mean 'sheep district'. If this was correct, then the name probably derived from the mountainous part of the ancient district, for the Vale of Ewyas, and the eastern foothills of the Black Mountains were well wooded when the Norman-English supplanted the local Welsh rulers. Sheep, as well as cattle, had by tradition been given in payment for holding land, a tradition that persisted beyond Domesday, which records the Welsh custom of giving dues in sheep and also honey.

"However sheep-ridden the area at Domesday, the greatest period of shepherding in Archenfield and Ewyas followed the arrival of the Cistercian monks in the twelfth century.* By 1291, the Cistercian monastery at Abbey Dore was shepherding three thousand sheep and had established seventeen granges, one of which was The Prospect now owned by Carling Medlar. The wool from the Abbey's flocks fetched the best price of all the English fleeces in the heyday of the wool trade with the Continent. The reputation of the 'White Monks', as the Cistercians were called, became widely known, and was summarised in two famous lines centuries later by Wordsworth, who wrote*:

'Where'er they rise, the sylvan waste retires,
 And aery harvests crown the fertile lea.'"

Catherine was becoming used to Owen's liking for poetic references to woods and trees. She had already deposited a pile of books on Welsh verse in translation at the Goggin, the works of Dafydd Ap Gwilym among them.

Wordsworth's piece of romanticised history aroused him from the position he had sunk into in his armchair. He was quick to interrupt, and to point out how the interminable nibbling of sheep down through the centuries had helped to deplete the original woodland cover by preventing the regeneration of trees and holding back the forest so that clearings would eventually become fields. Catherine then surprised him with the fact that the nibbling was also done by goats, the 'mountain mutton' of the Welsh. She went on to say that the Cistercian clearances were vehemently criticised by the monks' contemporaries.

"The best source of contemporary comment was Giraldus Cambrensis, otherwise Gerald de Barri, Archdeacon of Brecon, who lived between 1146 and 1220, and who knew Ewyas well. He was very critical of Abbot Adam, the prelate who governed Abbey Dore in its heyday at the end of the twelfth century. One of his most cutting remarks was to accuse the monks of 'changing an oakwood into a wheatfield'. His writings implied that the monks assarted land under false pretences, as in their creation of openings in the Royal Forest of Treville, which lay to the north of the Abbey and covered over two thousand acres in 1213. If Giraldus is to be believed, it would seem that the Cistercians were treated as interlopers by the locals in the same way as the 'Saesons', the Welsh word for the Saxons and, subsequently, the English who moved westwards into Welsh territory after crossing the Wye in the tenth century."

"The migration of the English into old Welsh areas is still unsettling the indigenous population", observed Owen. "Ralph doesn't seem too happy about your friends, 'off-comers' as he calls them. I suppose I come into this category, too. Perhaps the Welsh blood in him - if he's got any blood in him - is still fighting a rearguard action, or perhaps it's been mixed with so many Saxon, Norman, and other off-comers that he's become confused about his own identity". Speaking from a very snug position, he broke into a weary grin and asked: "Can I go to bed now, and write my essay in the morning?"

Catherine's serious lecturing look melted into one of those rare smiles which made her distinctive face even more stunning. It made Owen change his mind about turning in and gave him the confidence to ask something which he had been in two minds about raising.

"Catherine, what's the Welsh name for the River Wye?" he asked glibly.

"Afon Gwy", came the neat reply.

"Then what does 'Mingui' mean?"

"That's the old Welsh name for the River Monnow."

"And Cerydwen?" His voice was becoming overly casual.

"I'm not sure. I think it is the name of a Welsh goddess. I'll look it up for you. Where have you found all these names?"

"Oh, I came across them in some old books in de Bohun's library. And is there a word 'Dyn' in the Welsh language?"

"Yes; it means 'Man'" she explained. Where did you see that?"

"Oh, de Bohun mentioned a 'Serpent Dyn' when he gave me his introduction to local folklore - the 'dragon Man', I suppose?"

"Not de Bohun again! Where did he get that name from? It's news to me, although there are numerous references to serpents in Welsh, Anglo-Saxon, and early English literature. The Welsh bard Taliesin called the Saxon race the 'Coiling

Serpent'* and Geoffrey of Monmouth speaks of serpents in his history of the British Isles. If you want to coil up in bed with a few serpents, you can take my copy of the book upstairs with you." She said this with a sweet smile which suggested that she would rather be the book, but Owen was too wrapped up in the answers to his questions to notice. So Catherine, wounded by his preference for serpents, tried again. "And if you want to think about serpents more than the company of your friends, then come into the office next week and I'll load you up with some more references."

The bluntness in this remark, however, had its effect. When she collected a book from the bookcase over by the window and handed it to him, he held her hands in his and kissed her goodnight. When he eventually carried his weary body off to what used to be Ralph's bedroom, he wondered where else his emotions were leading him. Geoffrey of Monmouth's History of the Kings of Britain gave him some dry reading to calm him down and send him to sleep.

The Hideout Oak

CHAPTER 20

Notebook - 7th June: From The Four Ancient Books of Wales by William F. Skene, Edinburgh, (1868):

> *'Fellow-ranger of the green woods!*
> *Painful, piercing grief affects me*
> *Conflicts are pangs of anguish to the upright.'*

Red Book of Hergest xxi, untitled, (lines 80-82, Skene, page 493)

―――――――

> *'When the Saxons repose from their serpent cunning,*
> *And the castle of Collwyn is resorted to from afar,*
> *Clothes will be smart, and the black pool clear.'*

(Black Book of Carmarthen xviii, untitled, verse xiii, Skene, page 486)

'A serpent which coils,
And with fury boils,
From Germany coming with arm'd wings spread,
Shall subdue and shall enthrall
The broad Britain all
From the Lochlin ocean to Severn's bed.'

The prophecy and fighting talk of the sixth century bard
Taliesin.

———

'The Cymry will meet the Saxons.
For various mutual consumption and resistance.
Of the excessively great army, when they have experience,
And on the hill, at the blades and shout, they will tremble,
And on the Gwy severe rencounters will follow them.
And a banner will come, rough it will descend.
And like the budded blossoms the Saxons will fall.

They will ask the Saxons what they seek:
How much of debt from the country they hold?
Whence is their route when they settled?
Whence their generation? From what land
did they come?
Since the time of Gwrtheyrn they trample on us.
Truth will not be obtained in the land of discord.
A nakedness on Cynon, Saxons will not be.'

(From the 'Omen of Prydein the Great', Book of Taliesin vi,
lines 54-60, 103-8, and 176; pages 438, 440, and 442 of
Skene)

'When the trees were enchanted,
In the expectation of not being trees,
The trees uttered their voices
From strings of harmony,
The disputes ceased.'

From the 'Battle of Godeu', Book of Taliesin VIII, (lines 57-61: nb. Skene, vol ii,) p. 399:- 'Godeu was certainly the name of a district, but the word also means trees, and the subject of the poem soon passes over into a symbolical battle of trees.'

———————

Notebook - 8th June:

The prophecies of Merlin, according to Geoffrey of Monmouth's History of the Kings of Britain written in 1152:

'In those days the oaks of the forest shall burn, and acorns shall grow upon the boughs of the linden tree.'

'In his days (the days of the Serpent of Malvern) shall the Pachaian mountains tremble, and the provinces be deprived of their woods. For there shall come a worm with a firey breath, and with the vapour it sends forth shall burn up the trees... Against him shall arise the dragon of Worcester, and shall endeavour to banish him. But in the engagement the dragon shall be worsted, and oppressed by the wickedness of the conqueror.'

*'In her days shall a serpent be brought forth, which
shall be a destroyer of mankind.'*

*Source: Geoffrey of Monmouth's British History in Six Old
English Chronicles by J. A. Giles, London, 1847, (pp. 121 and
125).*

———

*So, the 'worm' was the Saxon horde advancing from the east.
Were these prophecies allegorical, or had Merlin been
contacted, through enchantment, by a Tree Spirit and warned
of the impending Saxon incursions into Welsh territory?*

*Now if serpents have lain beneath our folklore for ages,
instilling a sense of unease, even fear, into superstitious souls,
the wrath of their reputedly evil dispositions and the fire of
their malevolent breath being the hallmarks of the
underworld which concealed them, how appropriate, in the
time of Merlin, the time of early Christianity and the twilight
of Celtic Britain, to conjure up a worm as the symbol of Saxon
paganism and rapaciousness. And how profound that the
underworld of Nature itself should conceive us as a serpent
as dire and destructive as anything we could imagine!*

———

A poem attributed to Merlin! 'The Avallenau'.

*'Sweet apple tree of delicate blossoms,
Which grows in the soil amid the trees!*

Saxons shall be eradicated, and bards shall flourish.

Sweet apple tree, and a tree of crimson hue,
Which grow in concealment in the woods of Celyddon;
Though sought for their fruit, it will be in vain,
Until Cadwaladyr comes from the conference of
Rhyd Rheon,
And Cynan to meet him advances upon the Saxons;
The Cymry will be victorious, glorious will be
their leader.
All shall have their rights, and the Brython will rejoice,
Sounding the horns of gladness, and chanting the
song of peace and happiness!'

(From 'Poems relating to the Battle of Ardderyd', Black Book
of Carmarthen xxvi, last verses, viii, ix, and x, Skene, p.372-
3)

———————

Seven score generous ones have gone to the shades;
In the wood of Celyddon they came to their end.

Since I, Myrdin, am next after Taliesin,
Let my prediction become common.'

(Last verses of a poem relating to the Battle of Ardderyd, page
370 of Skene.)

———————

The magic Myrddin = the Arthurian Merlin.

———————

Notebook - 10th June:

'"Cerydwen", Ceridwen, Caridwen, or Cariadwen is generally considered to be the goddess or personification of Nature in the so-called mythology of the Welsh. She is sometimes represented as the inspirer of poetry...'

Skene, Vol. 11, (p.324.)

'Bright are the ash-tops; tall and white will they be
When they grow in the upper part of the dingle;
The languid heart, longing is her complaint.

Bright the tops of the service tree, accustomed to care,
Is the aged one, and bees to the wild...
Except God, there is no avenger.

Bright the tops of the grove; constantly the trees
And the oak leaves are falling;
Happy is he who sees the one he loves.'

Red Book of Hergest ix. Untitled poem attributed to Llywarch Hen, 1st half of 7 century; verses i, xx, xxii, Skene, (pages 576-80)

A few days later, Owen decided to take his poetic discoveries out into the open air, and onto the summit of the mountain, where he could consider them in more scenic surroundings and make himself seen at the same time - if the Eerie Shriek was about.

The mountain top inspired and exalted his own inner presence. He knew it always would. Few people could stand on Rhibo Mountain, even after a life-time of visits, without experiencing feelings of elation, a gladness to be alive - although Milo was a little slow to respond. Some individuals might take it all in and keep it all in, the depth of their response being too profound for words. Some might burst into raptures of delight and yet, not see or feel all there was to see and feel. But they would be moved. Suzy was like this. When on the top, she was over the top. She would go haywire. But just how much did she see? She reacted so hurriedly, and so ebulliently, deluging companions with her effusive delight, and stalling their own response, that she could not possibly have received all there was to receive. This was the essential difference between her and her brother. He could take it all in, though he could not give it all out; certainly not when his sister was around to stall his soul. She was too excitable to be penetrated by buzzards. She would shriek rather then stare in amazement.

Pee-ow! Pee-ow! There it was; a buzzard high in the azure sky, clearly visible when its backcloth was a cloud, gliding above Coed Tirion Glas directly above the Emergent Lime, or so it seemed. Owen hastened forward from the northern end of the ridge which linked the mountain's bulbous halves. He had walked all the way to the northern end of the mountain and was on his way back. The buzzard was slowly losing height, descending in sweeping circles, and calling. Then it suddenly altered course, flying towards him, still high in the sky, banking over him and sweeping back to the Emergent lime, mewing piercingly. Owen careered down the slope to the wood's edge, and leapt the fence where the conifers began, using a straining-post for support.

For someone to keep in touch with an air-borne buzzard while descending a slope through a neglected plantation should be doomed to failure from the beginning. But the buzzard was no ordinary buzzard, and its pursuer was now no ordinary human being. Owen was helped by the openness of the boundary between the conifers and the broadleaves. If he could not see the bird above the trees, he could hear it, and his progress was directed more by calls than by sightings. When he reached the ride, he had to stop to listen for a call. When it came, he realised for the first time that it did not permeate the air all around to the extent that its source became obscure; it was more penetrating than ever and localised. Was this due to the lower altitude or his position in the wood? Or was it a characteristic of the call?

From the ride, he was directed away from the conifers into the oaks. He could see daylight ahead of him through the trees on the edge of the high ground that divided the waters of the Cwm and Melglyn brooks. Then the buzzard came into view flying between the crowns of two large oaks. In his pursuit, he concentrated so much on his progress across a shelf of ground, passed a crab apple, that he did not notice his arrival at a dingle until the last moment. Another call riveted him to the spot. Then he saw a huge tree ahead, to one side of the dingle on the edge of the shelf. A lime! The Emergent Lime. He reached it just as another call pierced his soul.

The buzzard was in its crown; a crown not yet graced with flowers. He could not see the bird, but there could be no other location for it. The tree was so tall, so green, and so healthy; so in the prime of life, that Owen emitted his own quiet 'pee-ow' in celebration of the discovery. But in looking around, he was subdued by feelings of déjà vu. There were two large wild service trees nearby, some maples roundabout, and another crab apple, all within the confines of the shelf. And there were limes growing out of the bare soil of the dingle banks. Without a second thought, he concluded that this would be the place to locate a tree spirit which wanted to return to a forest fastness...

Another call rang out, one that seemed to penetrate the whole place. With it there was a stir of leaves which checked him in his survey of the site and made him look up into the tree just in time to see the dark shape of the buzzard taking to the sky. He felt compelled to follow again. He knew that he was being called back to the Melglyn Stoggle...

On his return, he collapsed into the seat at the base of the tree, his legs weary from negotiating the buzzard's course to the rocks. All was still. He was glad to relax for a while to make some notes on his discovery and, perhaps, to receive another message. His body already felt heavy from the exertions of the last two hours, so he did not notice that he was becoming heavier after writing for only a few minutes. His eyes took on a languid glaze as he breathed gently through his nose, and it was not long before they closed. The transition from serene wakefulness to captured sleep occurred more swiftly and more gently than on the previous occasions. The effort of continuing to write in his notebook was equally as graceful. When his eyes opened, they were no longer languid but bright...

The next sentient moment startled him. Another face was within inches of his own, but it seemed distant and removed from the present. A hand was touching his shoulder. It was Matilda, a shadowy Matilda, bending over him. The subdued light of the evening and Owen's detachment made her appear a little sinister. His head jerked back in a momentary spasm of fright.

"Are you alright, Owen?" she asked gently, her voice expressing much concern. His only response was to look blankly into her face, speechless, slaking a dried mouth with a slither of saliva.

"I called to you from across the dingle. You were writing in your notebook. I didn't want to shout too loudly because the Eerie Shriek, or a buzzard like it, was in the top of the tree, but it flew away when I came over to you. You look as though you've been in a trance. Have you been day-dreaming or meditating?"

Only the last word of this question registered in Owen's head.

"Meditating? Err... yes, medi... meditating", he mumbled in a mono-tonal voice, without actually looking at Matilda. He was surveying the scene around and felt completely detached from it. The now familiar experience triggered some coherency in his post-contact state, which was not as fragile as on the other two occasions.

"You've roused me ...from a deep meditation... I'm a bit heavy headed."

"Sorry Owen. Had I known, I would have left you alone. But how can you write when you're meditating?" she asked, somewhat perplexed.

There was a very long period of silence before he replied.

"I sometimes write down... I sometimes write down feelings I experience during meditation... before I lose them... before I'm really here."

He attempted to get up, but Matilda urged him to stay still, saying, "Don't get up, Owen. I'll let you unwind while I enjoy the view and the stillness. Isn't it heavenly here?"

She moved away from him, uttering an "Emm!" as she did so, and then glided about, closing her eyes. Owen used her distractedness to struggle to his feet, propping himself against the trunk of the tree. He was surprised, and relieved, that he felt less disoriented and less unsteady than the time before. Regaining some presence of mind, and wanting to appear as normal as possible, he asked Matilda, as she turned back towards him:- "Which direction did you come from?"

"Oh, from the Court through the wood. Humphrey has gone off to see Carling Medlar about something. He won't be back until late, so I thought I would see if the flower buds were swelling. Without Suzy to prompt me, I sometimes forget to keep watch. Before she came to the Goggin, there was a glorious summer when the lime flowered even earlier than expected.

"Earlier?" was all Owen could say, raising his shoulders awkwardly but still using the tree for support.

"Yes, a week before I expected it to. Fortunately, an unplanned walk brought me to the tree just in time. Owen, you look a bit unsteady on your feet. Are you sure you're alright?"

"I'm okay; just a little tired, that's all", he said, as he put his notebook into his pocket.

"Don't put your book away, Owen? Can I have another glance at your writing? It bears a striking resemblance to the scrawl of a woman who lived at the Court in the 1790s. Her papers were unearthed by Suzy and Catherine."

For a moment, Owen was nonplussed. Then, falling back

on his shyness, he said: "Umm... My notebook holds my innermost thoughts. I wouldn't even let Suzy read it. Sorry."

"I understand, Owen. It's not important, anyway. You'd better get back to the cottage. You're beginning to look a little ashen-faced. Will you be alright? Or shall I come with you? I could telephone Humphrey and ask him to pick me up. Did you come on your bike?"

"Yes, I did, but I'll be alright. The ride back from Gwenynog will wake me up. Thanks for your concern, Matilda. I'll be okay."

With that, he mustered all the energy and composure he could find, and said goodbye, knowing that he would be watched as he walked away. He thought he maintained a reasonably steady gait.

That evening, the cottage was the same as before. The telephone kept ringing, and Owen was fast asleep. The cycle ride was uneventful but very tiring. All he did on entering the house was to drink some water and go straight upstairs, intending to read the message he knew his notebook contained. He had the presence of mind to take his notebook with him, but his eyes closed the moment his body touched the bed.

The Emergent Lime

CHAPTER 21

Notebook - 13th June: At the Melglyn Stoggle.

A great day! I have been guided to the Emergent Lime by the Eerie Shriek. I think – but this is only a guess so far – that this amazingly tall tree is located somewhere near the very top of the Dark Dell, perhaps between the Dell and the eastern tributary of the Melglyn Brook. It has a crab apple and two wild service trees for company, as well as maples and other limes. But the site is not the easiest place to get to, and it has a coniferous plantation nearby....

Owain be Calm
There is much for me to tell
Far more than the torment of the woods
Like Beibio you listen to my plea
Like Beibio you hear the anguish of my Soul

Lonely and bereft beside this barren Cwm
I long for ties to take me to Y Coed...

Passing out to still the Creeping noise
Unsettled all our Souls...
So many Souls were fleeing in the Earth
So many Souls were Crying out for Trees
So many Souls were Treeless and in grief

The Earth holds many wasted souls...

With Kites my soaking eyes
And Passage Trees my rest
I Passed on and Came to Euas in my search
Through them I found the Fastness
The blithe and Gentle Fastness
Of the Mynydd y rhibo Limes

Golden were the Limes of my enChanted mound
Resplendent was the Greenness of Y Coed...

OnCe more I found
A gathering of tall and Gentle Trees
My grieving Soul revived and then rejoiced
My flowers towered high
My fragrance wafted far
As Gentleness returned to soothe my Soul
The EnChantment of my Spell was great again
I was safe within my Tree within Y Coed

Contentment only Comes when Ties are Deep...

Alas in time
The noises of the Serpent seeped into my
Soul
My Spell no longer Cast them out
I was watchful
Ever watchful of the Worm...

Then a Gentle son of Dyn
A most Gentle son of Dyn
Discovered and admired my Golden Tree
The Fragrance of my Spell was his alone
He befriended Cerydwen
And came to me with Gentleness and Joy

Beibio Beibio Y Coed remembers Beibio
Oh Gentle oh so Gentle Son of Dyn...

Beibio exalted me
He kept the mountain Fastness for Y Coed
My Trees were venerated
The Earth was venerated
By Gentle sons and daughters
Of the dreadful Serpent Dyn

Beibio Beibio Y Coed remembers Beibio

But the Conflicts of the Serpent
Were never far away

It was stealing
As I knew it would
In violence from the Sun

I felt its violent tremors
As the Hollowness increased
As the Serpent sorely fought itself for space
I had never been so close to Serpent Ire

A warrior son of Dyn
Was carried to my Tree
And laid to rest beneath my fragrant shade
My Golden blossom strewn upon the ground
The noises of the Serpent Dyn
Were solemn soft and near...
Stealing life is Grief to those who live...

When Beibio
Dear Beibio
Was buried by my side
My Sorrow was a Sorrow
Unknown to me before
My anguished Soul sank Earthwards
Worn with Grief
My Gentle Tree imbibed him to its Heart
Floating Golden blossoms to the ground

Losing Life is Grief to those who live...

I lingered long with Beibio
Unwilling to depart
Staying in the Trees he called his Llwyn
Staying when the Hollowness
Edged Closer to my Trees
Staying when the Serpent Dyn was near

Beibio Beibio Y Coed remembers Beibio
Oh Gentle oh so Gentle Son of Dyn...

Sorely
And in selfish Ire
The warring Worm Crept Coldly to my side
Once more to fight itself for space
My Soul was worn
My Spell was weak
Enchantment failed to stun the Serpents Fire

As the Worm inflicted wounds
In my ageing Gentle Tree
I fled into the Earth
Another Serpent lair had rent Y Coed

The Trees of Llwyn Beibio had gone
And I had gone...
Beibio forgive me
The Serpent severs all...

Beibio Beibio Y Coed remembers Beibio

Oh Gentle oh so Gentle Son of Dyn...

To Beibio the glory of Y Coed was Cerydwen
The fragrance of his grove the scent of
Cerydwen
To you the lonely woods are Cerydwen
The remnants of Y Coeds enchanting life

Contentment only comes when ties are Deep...

The assaults upon Y Coed
By the dreadful Serpent Dyn
Diminished Cerydwen
And so diminished Life
They diminished Gentle Beibio
And now diminish me
In times to come they will diminish you

Beibio Beibio Y Coed remembers Beibio
Oh Gentle oh so Gentle son of Dyn...

The Serpent Dyn should listen to the Earth
And spare the spoiled wealth of Cerydwen
For if it Casts aside
The Imagination of the Trees
The anguish of the Earth
Will be the anguish of the Worm

An unenchanted Earth is weary death...

Owain
Tell my saga to the Gentle ones of Dyn
Tell them that the Trees will soon be gone
Tell them that the Gentle Trees
Cry Out and Call for help
Tell them that soon
The selfish sons and daughters
Of the dreadful Serpent Dyn
Will Cry and Call for help
When all the Trees are gone

Owain
I have lingered here too long
The threads of bare Y Coed
Grow ever fainter still
My isolation keeps me from the ties
That give me Life
My mountain Fastness empties to the End

Emptiness enfeebles those that last...

Owain
Mend for me the Pathway to my remnant of
Y Coed
Unburden the anguish of my Soul

Owain
Send me to another Gentle Tree.................

CHAPTER 22

'Contentment only comes when Ties are Deep..'

Spirit of Y Coed

On the day after meeting Owen at the Stoggle, Matilda was in Hereford. Being a Tuesday, she was in town to do her regular stint of voluntary work for a local charity. Shortly before one o'clock she was on her way to meet Alison for lunch. Usually, she met Suzy, sometimes with Catherine, sometimes with Alison, depending on the pressures of work. Since Suzy's departure, the luncheon dates had become erratic, but Matilda and Alison had lunch together as often as journalism would allow. Matilda had never had lunch alone with Catherine.

As she made her way towards their meeting place on a rather sullen day, she was ruminating on the differences between Suzy and Owen. Being a confidant of Suzy meant that she, like Catherine and Alison, had unconsciously pieced together a sketch of him from the casual asides and confidential reflections of his loquacious sister. And once before, on a Tuesday, she had listened to Alison giving her first impressions of Owen, and Milo's as well. Like everyone else, she was amazed at the facial similarities between the siblings, but also at their extraordinary differences in temperament. In particular, she recalled the very strange and distant behaviour of Owen during her chance meeting with him at the Stoggle.

Such was her contemplative mood when she arrived at the cafe. On this occasion, however, Alison had company; Catherine was with her. Matilda's arrival interrupted a serious conversation which had engaged the young women for some minutes. The subject was Owen. Alison had opened the conversation by asking Catherine how she and Owen were getting on. To her surprise again, the question had drawn from Catherine uncharacteristic declarations. She divulged all that was on her mind; her fondness for him and her concern for what she felt was his distant and unreachable nature; the kind of private matters to which only Suzy had access. It was obvious that Catherine was missing her one and only confidant. Alison had responded by pointing out that Owen, after emerging from the dreary depths of a lonely winter, probably had his mind on what he was going to do in the autumn. It would take him longer than a couple of months in a new place, among new friends, to settle down and to come out of himself; especially someone like him, if all that Suzy said was true. Catherine had been quick to note that he had not been as introverted when he first arrived as he had been recently. It was at this stage in the conversation that Matilda joined them.

"You two have very serious faces. Is there anything wrong?"

she asked after the normal greetings.

Catherine looked at Alison as if to say that she did not want the matter discussed in front of Matilda.

"No, no. We're both a bit uptight about work, that's all", replied Alison who, like any good journalist, was never at a loss for the right words.

"Well, it's lunchtime now, so you can both forget about work for a while. Let's eat and enjoy ourselves", said Matilda, taking a seat and picking up the menu at the same time.

With their meals in front of them - one frugal (Alison's), one semi-frugal (Catherine's), and one hearty - Matilda addressed Catherine with a question which was innocently put but, in the circumstances, full of coincidence.

"Catherine, there's something I have to ask you: how are you finding Owen? Has he settled in alright?"

Alison could not withhold a smile on hearing these words, and glanced knowingly at Catherine whose face had tightened as soon as Owen's name was mentioned. Matilda could see by the look on Catherine's face that her enquiry was untimely. Alison came to the rescue again.

"Catherine, tell us about Owen's shepherding when he helped you out with the shearing; you were going to tell me how he got on. Did everything go alright?"

"Yes, it did. Dad thought he fitted in well and did a good job. I think he prefers Owen's help to Ralph's. He wants him to help out with the hay next. It was a totally new experience for him. After two days of catching and pitching, and our weekend walk along Offa's Dyke path, he was exhausted."

"That probably explains why he was still unwinding yesterday", observed Matilda. "I found him at the old stoggle above Gwenynog late in the afternoon. He was sort of meditating. How different he is to Suzy."

"Meditating?" exclaimed Catherine, frowning in disbelief, and upset to hear of another side to Owen's character that was unknown to her. Alison's response was one of curious surprise.

"Well, that's what he said he was doing. He was in quite a trance-like state when I disturbed him. I never realised that meditation had such a heavy affect upon a person. I thought it was supposed to be calming – the Buddhist answer to chilling out." There was a hint of humour in her voice. "He looked very tired and white in the face, so I suggested he went home to rest."

"But he didn't go home", said Catherine agitatedly, unable to contain her perplexity any longer. "I telephoned him throughout yesterday evening, and this morning, and there was no reply. When he didn't answer the phone, I assumed that he was spending another one of his crazy nights at that lime tree. I thought he was only in the habit of disappearing when he had had enough of Suzy's company." Catherine could not disguise what she was really feeling. "I hope he's alright, and that nothing happened to him after you saw him, Matilda."

This tormented expression of rejection and concern alarmed Matilda. She began to worry as well, although she dismissed the suggestion that Owen might have met with an accident. "Surely not", she said, "Nothing could have happened to him, he's a strong young man, and well used to the outdoors, you know that."

"Telephone him now", suggested Alison in an effort to allay Catherine's concern. "He might have stayed at Gwenynog overnight with your grandparents if he was as tired as Matilda claims."

Catherine restrained herself from leaving the table too quickly, but she could not disguise her obvious disquiet. The nearest call-box was only a short distance away, so less then ten minutes elapsed before she returned. During her absence, Alison wanted Matilda to reveal more about her meeting with Owen at the Stoggle, but Matilda had suddenly remembered the reason why she had asked Alison to have lunch with her.

"Let's leave Owen until Catherine comes back. I must ask you something while we have the time. Humphrey discovered some news yesterday which might interest Milo. Do you both know that the land at Wern y coc, near the Bodcut is to be sold by auction next month?"

"I do, the advert was in our paper the other day, but I did not have the heart to tell him before he went off to his conference. Why, what is the matter?"

"Well, Carling Medlar has confided to Humphrey – as a neighbourly gesture but really to deter us from any involvement in the sale - his intention of bidding for the property, and its land, that unimproved land down by the brook, near his game covert, the covert which caused all the fuss between him and Milo. Is there anything there of wildlife significance? Humphrey says there are a lot of old trees beside the brook, and some old meadowland as well."

"As far as I know, Milo hasn't surveyed the place, although when he and I used to walk onto the Goggin when I lived with Suzy, he was forever saying that he should. I think that Suzy's discoveries about the botanical interest of Wern y coc, and her insistence that he should get down there before modern agriculture wiped it out, turned him off. It's good he's gone away to his conference now. The sale and Medlar's intentions will only wind him up, and he would spend a lot of the time away worrying. He's due back today, so I will encourage him to survey the place immediately. Now tell me, was Owen really meditating when you met him yesterday?"

Matilda was halfway into an answer to this question when Catherine returned.

"He is at the cottage. But I was right; he did spend the night at the lime tree, after going there in the afternoon. Did he have a sleeping bag with him, Matilda, and some food perhaps?"

Matilda was on the verge of saying something when this question was put, but she withheld it. Instead, she merely said that she could not recall what Owen had with him, other than a notebook. She knew that he could not have returned to the tree before dusk, because she had visited a friend at Dan y coed, a farm above Skynlas Dingle on the other side of the mountain, and walked home via the Stoggle, knowing that her husband would get back very late from his trip to The Prospect. The neutrality of her reply caused Catherine to go quiet. Alison had nothing to say, either, her mind was elsewhere for the moment.

"Did you tell Owen that we were having lunch together?" asked Matilda, phrasing her question as if to keep the conversation going.

"No, I was too relieved to hear that he was alright. He said he's been in bed for most of the morning. To me, he sounded very tired. I'm going round there after work to make sure he's as well as he says he is."

"And for a lesson in meditation?" asked Alison, mischievously, attempting to lighten Catherine's mind. "I can see it now. You and Owen, side by side, cross-legged on the floor, breathing calmly and chanting in unison."

Catherine's tense demeanour of the last half hour gave way to a tired smile, and she made an attempt to eat her salad.

"Do you remember that boyfriend of Suzy's who was always meditating, the one who was into Buddhism?" asked Alison, continuing in the same vein.

"Yes, I remember him", said Catherine, "who wouldn't".

"And so do I", said Matilda, her mouth full of dessert. "He and Humphrey spent the whole time one evening deep in conversation, while Suzy and I escaped to the library."

"Well, he was with us in the Kite's Nest the week before they split up. Milo raised the subject of reincarnation, asking him how you could tell which bluebells were the repository of a soul and which weren't. I think he found Milo's enquiries a little spurious and mocking. When Suzy said, peevishly, that he had probably been a lascivious monk in one of his previous lives, he retorted by saying that her karma would never be laid to rest. He slept in the shed that night."

Looking at her watch as Matilda roared with laughter, Alison realised that she had to leave for the court house. Saying a hurried goodbye, she was prompted by Matilda to remind Milo about the land sale. She then suggested to Catherine that, if Owen was well enough, they joined her and Milo in the Kite's Nest that night.

"Is that the sale at Wern y coc?" asked Catherine, after Alison had left.

"Yes, it is", replied Matilda who added, in an effort to be friendly, "Don't say that I told you but Mr Medlar seems to be interested in buying it. Doesn't your father need more land?"

"He always needs more land, but he may not be able to afford to buy any at the moment." As she spoke these words, her voice faded into disinterestedness. "I don't think I'll bother to have a drink. I'll get back to the office. Excuse me for now."

Matilda said a simple goodbye in her most friendly manner. She wanted to say more, words that would encourage Catherine to cheer up. Everyone wanted to cheer her up, but it was difficult. It seemed that the only stimulus which could bring out the best in her was Suzy, although Alison had noticed that when she relaxed with Owen instead of worrying about him, she was happier than she had been for a long time.

Matilda stayed behind in the cafe, oblivious of the company around her; dwelling on a number of matters: the implications of the sale, both for Catherine's father and for Milo; and Owen's strange explanation to Catherine concerning his whereabouts the day before. She became quite excited. Life had quietened down since Suzy's departure; there had been no mad evenings, few mad games, and no equivalent personalities to interrupt the generally hum-drum affairs of the district. There was no way that Owen was going to create the havoc that his sister caused - she now knew that - but he was an engaging man and his presence was beginning to be felt. And it was some time since there had been a local land sale which involved people she knew. If Carling Medlar was to be involved, then it promised to cause ructions somewhere. She was reminded of the last time he had purchased local land of wildlife significance, the small piece of woodland known as the Gelli Copse. The subsequent events had resulted in Milo and the 'Meddling Baron' despising each other, and clashing vehemently whenever they met.

With all these exciting thoughts on her mind, she left the cafe to return to her charitable work. Crossing the cathedral close, her composure was unsettled by someone saying her name; by an unmistakable, hectoring voice. It was Carling Medlar.

"Matilda! My dear Matilda. How nice to see you. Of course, it's Tuesday; you're a volunteer today, aren't you?"

She did not relate easily to this neighbour. That was why she found any excuse available to resist accompanying her husband whenever he chose to visit The Prospect. She also found his wife disagreeable. Her usual manner in conversing with him was to be as stiff as he was, behaviour that was uncomfortable to her; but he made her feel uncomfortable, anyway. Even before she returned his haughty greeting with a pleasantly banal one, she was inwardly relieved that her lunch hour had almost expired.

"Why, Carl", (both she and Humphrey addressed him in this way), "you took me by surprise. For you to be in Town, it must be very important business, so I mustn't keep you from it. I'm late getting back to the Centre, anyway. Excuse me for running off. Regards to your wife." To complete her escape, she smiled an insincere smile.

That afternoon, whenever she found herself unoccupied, she kept thinking about Owen's words to Catherine. All sorts of reasons for his explanation suggested themselves, but there was never enough time to think them through. An interruption would distract her. On one occasion, she did allow for the possibility that Owen could have returned to the tree when she was at Dan y coed, and then hidden upon hearing her retrace her steps; but the other reasons were more plausible than this...

While Matilda was thinking about Owen, his thoughts were centred on her. Catherine had telephoned him from the cafe when he was having his first meal of the day, after the mental exertion of going through the third communication with the tree spirit - or whatever it was that had captured his thoughts. Its ending had made a very profound impression upon him. Now, he was not only being asked for help; he was being asked to issue a prophecy himself. How could he be expected to do this? He was no Merlin; not somebody whose words would be taken as prophetic if he could compose the appropriate pronouncement. Who would listen? Who were the "Gentle Ones of Dyn", to whom the "Imagination of the Trees" would have some meaning? His thoughts focused on his new-found friends a number of times. And it was one of those million-to-one coincidences of life that when he was thinking about Matilda, she was thinking about him. But he did not feel that he knew anyone well enough to share his incredible secret, even Catherine, although her assistance was vital if he was to understand the latest succession of historical references. But for a brief moment, and for some elusive reason, he felt that Matilda might be more approachable than anyone else – if he needed assistance or support.

If he was right about the connection with Merlin, then the latest message should have taken the story beyond the Anglo-Saxon period. The identity of Beibio, therefore, and the allusions to what might be actual events, could have a basis in documentary fact - but where? Catherine might have some ideas, but how could he involve her without giving something away? Already, she was puzzled about his behaviour: more puzzled than he realised, for she had written several letters to Suzy, asking for insights into his unfathomable ways. Before he attempted to enlist her support, on whatever pretext he could contrive, he determined to use his own initiative first to discover the identity of Beibio.

CHAPTER 23

'Our Trees were stolen
They were slain
They were shredded
They were lopped
They were stunted and their Spirits cut to earth...'

Spirit of Y Coed

———— ⬥ ————

Milo was sipping his beer and waiting for a plate of cottage pie, chips and peas - mushy peas. Alison was only having soup and a roll – her evening appetite was unusually depressed. They were seated in a corner of the Kite's Nest pub away from the bar, in one of three compartments formed by six heavy oak settles at right angles to the wall. Milo was facing the bar. He was unusually withdrawn. He had returned from his conference with that glumness which was so characteristic of him when beset by a problem. He appeared to be in the sort of hole he usually retired to after being shell-shocked by another conservation reverse. Habitat losses and plant extinctions were regular setbacks in his campaign to protect local wildlife. His resilience in the face of such reversals was equivalent to the hall-mark of the resistance fighter, but it did nothing for his disposition. Indeed, when Carling Medlar was the enemy in a conservation issue, his challenge became imbued with the fervour of the resistance fighter. And his recoveries were like those of the resistance fighter - he came back in the end from the oppression of his bunker, helped by the administrations of a nurse, but not very cheerful. But the hole he had retired to this time was not a bunker, although it held the prospect of being one, among other things. Alison recognised that he was subdued but she had no idea why. He had been evasive when she tried to probe for the cause. Since he had returned from his conference preoccupied with a matter which he preferred to keep to himself, she had had second thoughts about telling him immediately her latest piece of news. Instead of revealing in detail what Matilda had said, she casually said that Wern y coc was on the market, and that it might be a wise move for him to survey the flora of the holding's land.

"The flora of the meadows might be as good as Suzy claims. You've known they could be special ever since she told you about that eighteenth century list of flowers she found for it. She kept on reminding you last year, but you forgot."

"I didn't forget. I've already looked it over. I knew the place was going to be put on the market before I went away. And without Suzy badgering me, I did it for my own reasons."

"Why didn't you say something about it, then?" asked Alison, a little rattled. Never before had he missed telling her important news or the findings of his days in the field - staccato lists of abbreviated Latin names which, though often meaningless to her, were part of the hubbub to their partnership. His response to her annoyance was to delay his reply, giving more attention to his pub meal than to her question. His coolness irritated her. It was not until he had swallowed a mouthful of mushy peas, and gasped for air, that he replied.

"I intended to, but I got side tracked by the conference, and then absorbed in the uncertainties surrounding the place."

"What uncertainties?" she asked in a tone which told him that his vagueness was irritating her. The afternoon at the Court House had been a particularly tiring one for her.

"The holding's future. Our future", he muttered, continuing to be reserved and chewing some chips in an indifferent fashion.

Confused, as well as irritated, Alison asked, helplessly, "Our future? What are you trying to say?" His puzzling comments and her emotional reaction to them prevented her from seeing into his thoughts.

"Let me deal with the holding first", he replied, in a manner which suggested that the matter on his mind had been given a lot of thought. "It's being sold in two lots. You should know that by now. One is the old house and the buildings, and the meadows beside the brook, where there are some fine trees. The other includes the fields of pasture against the Goggin. Catherine's dad will certainly be interested in those..." He paused, looked up from his food, as if calling upon Alison for a nod of understanding so far.

"He might", she said curtly, impatient for him to continue.

"No new owner is going to maintain the place in its present unimproved state. It will go the way of other such remnants of our wild flora, unless someone like Cath's dad bought the lot and managed it in a traditional way, which is unlikely. What do you think?"

"There's no way he could afford both lots", came another curt reply.

"So, if he can't afford the entire holding, that leaves lot one, the house, the buildings and the meadows..." Milo paused again and turned away from his food.

"Well?" said Alison, completely unaware, in fact clueless as to what he was leading up to.

"Why don't we think about buying lot one? We could do up the house, and protect the meadows at the same time."

Alison was totally unprepared for this suggestion. Unable, for the moment, to say anything, she just looked at him, blankly; so he continued, becoming slightly fervent in his delivery.

"We've talked in the past about buying a place together. This might be the time to do it."

Alison responded quickly, "You haven't talked about it much", she said, with considerable emphasis upon the `you'. "I've mentioned it when the burning issues of the day have subsided a little." Then she became a little caustic, "So your silence over the sale up till now is due to you reaching a decision to make a commitment at last. What tipped the balance - me, a boring conference, or the flora of the meadows?"

Milo could not stop himself from smiling. "Are you in the right mood to receive an answer?" he asked, still smiling. A pregnant pause ensued as he finished the food left on his plate. Alison sat in silent pique, knowing what the answer was going to be, but doubtful of its authenticity. She decided that the moment had come to reveal her news.

"By the way, Matilda told me today that the 'Meddling Baron' is planning to make a bid for Wern y coc, so we might as well forget about it."

"Now why didn't you tell me that earlier?" he asked, becoming disgruntled, having the aftertaste of his meal soured by a possibility which he had dismissed ever since the sale notices had appeared.

"I meant to tell you when I got back from work, but you were rather down when you got back from your conference", she replied. "Anyway, we're now quits as far as disclosures are concerned." His proposition was not lost on her, but he could have raised it in a better way, and chosen a less complicated piece of real estate on which to base it. For the moment, there was romantic stalemate, and deflation, instead of the euphoria that is supposed to accompany conversations of this kind.

It was during the ensuing, sullen pause that Catherine and Owen arrived at the pub. They, too, were not communicating very well, and were somewhat downcast. Catherine mirrored Alison's look, but far more intensely, while Owen had the face which Suzy knew so well - the face asking for an opportunity to escape. Clearly, he had not been forthcoming about the details of his latest experience. All four individuals were in need of a distraction if the evening was not to wear on. Fortunately, their sullen faces lasted only as long as it took for two new arrivals to take their seats. For then, the perfect distraction appeared at the other side of the bar. It was Carling Medlar himself, with a companion whom Milo recognised immediately as one of the land agents who were conducting the sale of Wern y coc. Deftly, he switched seats to join Alison and Catherine so that he was virtually hidden from view by the back of the oak settle. Only Owen could be seen from the bar. Milo explained:

"It's not how much money you've got but who you know. That man with the 'Meddling Baron' is Cedric Badsay of Badsay and Bragg, the land agents in charge of the sale of Wern y coc, one of Medlar's so-called 'friends'. Witness the beginning of yet another land grab." He spoke in whispers but the invective in his voice was as audible as his words. "By coming here, the baron is deliberately letting everyone know what his intentions are."

Catherine and Alison accepted the companionship, or collusion, or whatever it was, of the two men in an unquestioning way, almost as a matter of course. Owen, on the other hand, the outsider who was not yet aware of the local intrigues, the political alliances, or the lines of influence which permeated Ewyas, was merely inquisitive.

"So, what are they up to, then?" he asked, glibly.

Milo duly gave him an explanation of the collusion which he was sure was behind the ostensibly innocuous dialogue of the two men who, in taking their seats, disappeared from view. His words showed Alison that her news had reached one of the tender spots she knew he had. Whether or not she detected any disappointment in his voice at this confirmation of Medlar's interest in Wern y coc, the distant possibility of buying it had aroused her curiosity as well.

"But why is he interested in the holding?" she asked, earnestly, "The house is unmodernised and the buildings are falling down. Surely, Wern y coc is not suitable as one of his so-called `shooting chalets'.

"That can be the only reason", commented Milo, "I thought

it unlikely because there are two other, far more suitable properties, nearer The Prospect over by Elchon. Obviously, I was wrong."

"You seem to have given the matter some thought, Milo. Are any conservation groups interested in the place?" enquired Catherine, while Alison cast her first mellow look of the evening in his direction.

"Not that I know of. They've all given up bidding for land in this area. Until the 'Meddling Baron' runs out of money, no farmland or wildlife habitat stands a chance of survival. If he wants Wern y coc for his shooting parties, then he will blast its naturalness away with the same gun that killed the Gelli Copse." The bitterness and rancour in these words ran deep.

"The Gelli Copse?" repeated Owen, inquisitively again.

"Of course, that fatality was before your time, Owen. It was a nine acre, neglected coppice on the bank of the Dol Barcut Brook, not far from the Goggin. You must have walked by it when following the bridleway to Gwenynog or the Deer Haye. It was an ancient wood remnant full of lime coppice and a few old oak pollards. A local conservation group was planning to buy it until the baron intervened and grabbed it. Although the flack he got caused him to leave the pollards alone, the copse was clear felled, the stumps were treated to prevent regrowth, and he planted his beloved collection of conifers and alien hardwoods. He also renamed it the Gelli Game Covert. If you hear the sound of guns near the Goggin, Owen, it will be the baron and his cronies shooting pheasants as they struggle helplessly into flight."

"Calm down, Milo", advised Catherine, "At least it's still a wood. It could have been worse." These words had the opposite effect to that intended. They only added fuel to his growing fury.

"Still a wood!" he exclaimed, vehemently, "If that's a wood, then the Goggin is a mole hill."

Owen laughed. So did Alison. But the comment was not intended to be funny. Milo was not in the mood for jokes. Neither was Catherine; but, then, her threshold of amusement was unreachable when she was tense and not in the best of moods.

Alison, who was adept at defusing situations which might lead Milo into difficulties during conversations with friends, displayed her usual helpfulness by directing the conversation to something else, although she felt a recurrence of an earlier pain as she did so.

"Catherine, Milo knew of the sale weeks ago. He's already surveyed Wern y coc. If your father bought the property there, could he be persuaded to manage the meadows and pastures traditionally so as not to extinguish whatever rare plants remain, the ones that Suzy likes to draw?"

"Very well put", said Milo, tacitly, still seething slightly.

"He might be, if he could afford the price. His outlays on buildings and machinery have stretched him to the limit. He's fretting at the moment. He knew that Wern y coc would come up for sale sometime. Having waited two years, he couldn't delay the purchase of machinery any longer. If he buys anything, it will just be the pastures on the other side of the brook, but even those could be too dear for him."

"What did your survey reveal, Milo?" asked Owen, more interested in the condition of the property than its future ownership. Milo was peeping around the edge of the settle to catch a glimpse of adversary.

"Too much", was the opening to his reply as he swung round. Then he explained, for Owen's benefit, that the sale was to be in two lots, the thirty-six acres being sold in a lower and an upper section. He catalogued the wildlife assets of the site in a rather doomsday manner, slipping in such invectives as - "The baron wouldn't make way for an orchid unless it grew to one hundred feet and could be seen from The Prospect." It was the wet meadowland of the lower section which had the better flora, and the best trees for lichens, especially the old ashes and the sycamores along the brook. He had counted a total of seventy-nine species of vascular plants in the two meadows, including several rare ones. The fields had never been dressed with inorganic fertilisers, or drained, so the natural variations of the ground, especially in wetness, made for great variety in the swards, which were virtually the same as they were two hundred years ago. He had consulted again the species list for the holding drawn up by Rosamond de Bohun in the 1790s, which Suzy and Catherine had discovered when cataloguing the estate records. All the orchids were still there, including the twayblade, the green-winged orchid and the lesser butterfly orchid, but the globe flower had disappeared.*

"That list was one of your greatest discoveries", interjected Alison, turning to Catherine. "Tell Owen about it."

Catherine obliged, but she did not show any enthusiasm for the matter: "Rosamond was an artist as well as an amateur botanist. The meadows at Wern y coc were one of her favourite places for drawing plants. That's why Suzy spent so much time there. She was the one who discovered that the globe flowers had disappeared because Gethen Daw, the former owner, had picked the last ones to give to the girl-friend he lost to his brother."

Following this interruption to his tirade, Milo sank back into his seat, muttering cursedly about the arch-enemy - "Why can't that 'Meddling Baron' be content with the land he has? Hasn't he pillaged enough? Owen, you should know the truth about that land-grabbing demon."

Without waiting for Owen to respond, and ignoring a look from Alison to calm down, he went on: "In the seventies, Medlar's old man, finding the management of the little estate he had inherited a financial burden, agreed to leave the day-to-day running to his son, who was keen to get out of the city of London, and spend more time with his gun. Unfortunately, the decision led to the old man's death. Medlar set about changing everything, especially the woods, replacing the previously casual management regimes with intensive silviculture, opening up the broadleaved copses and replanting with evergreens for cover, and surrounding the estate with mixed shelterbelts. It seems the old man died of stress attempting to resist his son's so-called 'improvements'."

"Milo, you don't know that", interrupted Alison. He ignored her admonishment.

"Medlar removed a lot of the old oak trees, even though estate oaks are held to give status to their owners, including those standing harmlessly in the fields. He felled a fine wood near The Prospect so as to enlarge the ground around the house, which he has since planted up with a collection of rare conifers noted for height, so as to put his place on the arboricultural map. One beautiful coppice wood with standards of oak was cleared of its understorey and underplanted with western red cedar. And as soon as his father had passed away, the imperious new lord of the manor acquired more land, especially wood fragments, and neglected broadleaved woods where he carried out selective felling and introduced conifers. All of the young plantations you now see in the vicinity of The Prospect are the property of the man who would be the twentieth century Baron of Ewyas. To me, he's the Baron of tree cruelty. And that's not all..."

"Milo", interrupted Alison again, concerned to temper the venomous outpourings of her mate, "that's enough for now."

"No it isn't. Owen wants to know the entire background to that odious creep, don't you Owen?"

Owen was interested to hear more, and showed it, but he was a little sheepish in doing so. Milo continued while Alison and Catherine started their own conversation in disdain.

"He not only bought woods. He purchased cottages and other buildings, and turned them into holiday cottages or 'Shooting Chalets', as he calls them in his advertising propaganda. Your sister only got the Goggin because the previous owner hated Medlar's guts. Newly-weds, especially local people, don't stand a chance of buying a house to do up, unless the baron can be shut out. All his purchases now look the same, with the emphasis on the natural timber look. But even with his wealth of softwood he still uses tropical hardwood timber, for doors and windows, and the insides as well. He follows in the long-standing tradition of the Victorians and their immediate predecessors who raped the forests of the Empire, and whose ancestors now rape the tropical rainforests. Well, he's not going to rape Wern y coc. I'd rather have cuckoos ursurping the nests of meadowlarks than let that enemy of wildlife usurp another wilderness. He's got a real fight on his hands this time."

Alison's ears pricked up again when she heard this gauntlet drop. "Whatever he is up to, it would be useful to know more. Had we had this conversation before today, I could have asked Matilda at lunchtime for more details, if she has any."

"How does Matilda know what Medlar's up to?" asked Owen.

"Her husband told her after he'd visited The Prospect recently. She mentioned it today when Catherine and I met her for lunch - while you were recovering from your bout of meditation at the Melglyn Stoggle, Owen", added Alison, grinning at him. Milo gave Owen a quizzical look while he glanced uneasily towards Catherine, who averted her eyes.

Owen raised a completely different subject - the lichen interest of the wild service trees at Llannerch Hudol. He told Milo about them and suggested that he check them out. Perfunctorily, Milo said that the trees were already known to him. He mentioned some unrepeatable Latin names, Agaricus chimonophilus and Daedalea confrogosa, and then returned to the subject of the sale.*

Leaning forward and across Alison to see if Medlar was anywhere in view, he muttered something under his breath. The man was visible, for he and his companion were on the point of leaving. For a split second, the eyes of the two adversaries met. Their mutual hostility was evident, even in the very brief exchange of glances that took place. Milo sat back into his seat, his shoulders pinned against the settle. The other three waited for the inevitable response, as onlookers might wait when an individual has received an invitation to duel.

"People who fight rearguard actions in continual retreat, giving up ground as one setback follows another, do not become property magnates. Making laws to protect wildlife and their habitats are only the rules governing engagement; they do not place land out of bounds, and do not stop the inexorable advance..."

"Of the dreadful Serpent Dyn", interjected Owen without intending to say anything. The utterance left his lips before he realised he had spoken. Catherine gazed at him in puzzlement and frustration, the same frustration which had plagued her earlier that evening.

"Medlar's not a serpent, nor a dragon; they only gorge themselves until they can't move. Beasts like him are never satisfied", continued Milo. "If you want to draw parallels with the past then you could say that he follows in the footsteps of the Anglo-Saxons and the Norman English, whose ancestors have been wiping out wildlife since the Dark Ages. His City ruthlessness only accentuates the barbarity of the tribe."

"Come on, Milo, the man is not a barbarian", said Alison, in an attempt to defuse her partner. "Why don't we break off and call in at the Court for coffee; we could ask Matilda and Humphrey what else they know of Medlar's intentions. Shall I give them a ring?"

"A good idea, Alison", came the support from Catherine.

"Okay", said Milo.

But Owen was silent. However, his silence was not taken as dissent, or even noticed, except by Catherine, who was still trying to fathom out what was going on in his head.

CHAPTER 24

'I will tell you how the Serpent stole Our Gentle Trees
How vehement and voracious was its fire
How the vastness of Y Coed was a store to be destroyed
By the worm which carves a void with selfish ire'

Spirit of Y Coed

"Matty! The Friends of the Deer Haye are here. Come in. Come in. Owen! I didn't see you there, hiding behind Catherine. Have you joined up as well?"

The 'Friends' were ushered through the porch into the hall by a boyish de Bohun, excited at the visitation. Matilda came out of the kitchen carrying a tray of cups in one hand and a coffee pot in the other. She quickly gave the tray to Owen, smiling knowingly, and together they followed the others into the Long Room where de Bohun took up a central position beside a large armchair near the fireplace. As the visitors took to the seats which had been drawn together for the occasion,

Owen, under the guidance of Matilda, placed the tray on a low table in front of the open hearth which had a long slab of oak as its lintel etched at the edges with unusual motifs - another of the family heirlooms. Two standard lamps gave a glow to the summer evening. Matilda then took him aside, and after a few quiet words led him away towards the hall, saying to everyone that they would be back in a few minutes. Catherine was the only one to watch as they left the room.

Owen followed her into the hall and up the stairs to the landing. There, on the wall between two doorways, hung an old painting. It was a beautiful watercolour of a lime tree growing on the edge of a wooded dingle. With a gesture of the hand, she introduced him to it and then waited for his response. Although not as good as Suzy's picture of the Melglyn Stoggle, it was an impressive representation, and one that struck him immediately as having a dream-like quality to it and a weird familiarity. But he could see from the tree's position in the dingle that it was not the Melglyn Stoggle itself. While his eyes were fixed on the tree, Matilda, still silent, drew his attention to the inscription and the signature tucked away in one corner of the picture. It was a view of 'The Early Flowering Linden in the Honey Dingle', signed by Rosamond de Bohun. The writing registered instantly with Owen, but he did not say anything. He merely nodded and hummed.

"There you are", said Matilda, breaking the silence, I told you the handwriting was like yours. The artist was a cousin of Humphrey's great grandfather. All her pictures and her papers were studied and catalogued by Suzy when she helped Catherine with our records. She had two styles of handwriting, a general one for her letters and for most of her annotations, and this unusual one for her best work. Suzy believed that the dingle, or even the lime tree in the painting, somehow influenced the quality of her art. Why don't you come over here this week, and go through all her papers, and see what you think?"

Owen was taken completely by surprise, so much so that he did not know what to say. He sensed that Matilda was probing for some understanding of his behaviour the day before, but he was unwilling to show how the picture had affected him.

"I shall be in the Records Office tomorrow and probably Thursday - Catherine has some papers to show me."

"Then, what about Friday?"

"I don't know; I've got to start fixing the frame in Suzy's gazebo soon..."

"Surely that can wait, Owen. Suzy doesn't expect you to finish the gazebo by the time she returns... There is also the file concerning the great felling of Coed Tirion Glas in 1802. Rosamond was involved with that."

"Felling?"

"Yes; when the southern part of the wood was cleared and the dingle of the Melglyn Brook opened up. That's when the lime tree in the picture was cut down."

This piece of information changed Owen's mind. And it gave him an innocent reason to accept Matilda's invitation.

"Alright; I would like to find out what happened then."

"Good". Matilda's response was swift.

"What time shall I come?"

"When you like. Have lunch with us anyway. If you're here in the afternoon, perhaps Catherine would like to join us later for supper."

They rejoined the others in the Long Room just as Alison

was disgorging brown liquid from the coffee pot, its lustre merging with the colour of the wood panelling. De Bohun was ensconced in his favourite seat, a cumbersome chair, well worn in places and showing signs of having been repeatedly refurbished. Only the extremities of his gawky body were in view. His legs rose up to his knees and then fell away abruptly into his lap, which was lost in the depths of the chair, and his spindly arms rested on the broad platforms of the chair's arms on a level with his shoulders. As soon as Owen and Matilda appeared, the mop-headed face on the other side of two very bony knees uttered a rebuke.

"We couldn't wait any longer for you two, could we gang? They haven't come here for cold coffee. They want it hot, just like the information they're after."

"Come on then, Humphrey, tell them what Carl Medlar is up to", said Matilda, giving way to his pride of place. At this, he turned towards Milo, to savour the reason for the visit.

"What would you conservationists do without my connections? Eh? You should realise by now that any land within view of The Prospect that comes up for sale will be of interest to its owner. Until the other day, I hadn't heard any gossip about his intentions concerning Wern y coc, although everyone's talking about the sale. Arnold the Trerrible is the hot favourite to buy the land at the moment." He shot a quick glance at Catherine before continuing.

"And then, out of the blue, Carl tells me he wants some extra accommodation space for his shooting parties. It seems that the old house and buildings there are just what he needs. So he says, anyway. He doesn't seem to be all that bothered about the land, though he thinks the fields near the house could be turned into a game covert to link with the Gelli Copse. He says he'll buy both lots first, and then decide what to do with the land."

This explanation was sufficient to rekindle Milo's short fuse.

"I don't believe it. Everything is so simple for that man. He doesn't give any thought to the wildlife interest of a property, or how valuable it might be to the viability of neighbouring farms..."

"Or how ideal it might be for young local couples who want a start in life", interjected Catherine, nervously, with one of her burning issues, at which interruption Alison and Milo exchanged glances.

"All that matters is that it can be seen from his mansion. The shooting angle is spurious. The Gelli Copse is too small, and too close to a public right of way, for shooting to be safe; and the addition of the meadows at Wern y coc wouldn't make much difference. Why buy a derelict house when he could build accommodation near The Prospect, or even do up one of those cottages he bought last year and has left idle. He just wants to make sure he has control of the view from his mansion – the upstart lord of the manor overlooking his demesne."

"I thought the news would get you excited, Milo", said de Bohun gleefully, having listened with delight to his tirade.

"He might have other motives", observed Matilda. "Could he be intent on making sure that you conservationists don't get it? You've virtually declared war on him, you know."

"Matty! That's not fair", ejaculated de Bohun. "Why shouldn't he want to buy it, even as an investment. Done up, it will fetch a fine price from someone looking for a place with land - the point-to-pointers, for example. Anyway, you don't know him as well as I do. Shooting is not his only interest. He was talking the other day about various recreational schemes he's got in mind - to diversify his business interests. And he will never lose his enthusiasm for planting trees. While I was there, he even asked me if I would let him manage the coniferous bit of Coed Tirion Glas, or let him plant some amenity hardwoods where the conifers had blown down in last year's gale."

"You didn't tell me that, Humphrey", said Matilda, somewhat concerned.

"I know, dear, I was going to. We've got to do something with that untidy plantation. Don't worry, I didn't commit myself to anything. I just said that I would be pleased to hear whatever ideas he had on the matter. He raised the issue again just as I was leaving. He suggested that because the plantation was so neglected, it might be better to clear fell parts of it and start again. He's going to come and have a word with us about it soon."

Owen, who was sitting near Matilda, listening in that distant way of his, was shaken by this casual revelation, which seemed not to have stirred anyone else other than the person next to him. He shuffled in his seat and sat up. His first reaction was to ask de Bohun if he was inclined to accede to any one of the Medlar's requests, but he thought better of it and checked himself. But his stirring had not gone unnoticed. Catherine was sensitive to any sign which would help her understand the inner thoughts of her new friend. De Bohun thought Owen had almost dozed off and needed bringing into the conversation.

"Well, Owen, what do you think about all this? You're like me - impartial and cool-headed." Matilda smiled at this kindly remark.

Hesitating as he spoke, Owen said that the intricacies of the subject were still unfolding for him. He reserved his judgement. This was an unforgivable avoidance of commitment as far as Milo was concerned, who was about to say something when Alison discreetly laid her hand on his arm. She, too, was surprised at Owen's neutrality; but to Catherine, the pronouncement was all that could be expected. However, the faces opposite him expected more, so Owen added, by way of explanation that there were a number of conflicting interests. The survival of another smallholding was at stake, and the survival of a precious wildlife habitat was under threat. There were local farmers who, as ever, were desperate for more land, and there was a local landowner who seemed to have an insatiable appetite for acquiring land. The outcome would be decided by who had the most money.

This rational and rather dispassionate breakdown of the issue came as another irksome surprise to Milo, who could not be restrained this time.

"Alright, acquiesce Owen. Let Medlar run roughshod over the last few remaining pockets of wildlife left in the area. You're only a caretaker; a short-term dweller in these parts; we can't expect you to put your heart into our campaigns. Suzy was the same. But she went the whole hog and put her heart into The Prospect. Whatever happens, that man is not going to get his way without being criticised. And if you haven't got the guts to join the critics who are going to embarrass him, then so be it."

Everyone came to Owen's aid with a chorus of "That's not fair, Milo!" Alison responded by saying aloud that it was time they went, so that Milo could cool down. The atmosphere was not too tense, or charged up with ill-will; similar scenes had been experienced before. De Bohun almost relished such occasions. They were as good as the dramas at the theatre. He had tried a number of times to get Milo on the stage, but without success. But Matilda was feeling sorry for Owen. Catherine gave him some grudging support as Milo and Alison left the gathering as they had departed from the Court more than once before, especially during the time when Suzy had been going out with Medlar's son, Tim. After the much practiced farewells, Matilda assuaged the situation by explaining to Owen that it was not the first time for Milo to become belligerent among friends. De Bohun chipped in with various remarks about Milo's "firey nature" and his "sturdy words". It was not long before Catherine and Owen departed as well.

Owen could not refuse Catherine's invitation to stay overnight at the farm, for it was closer than the cottage, and he had already arranged to accompany her to work. She was keen that he should stay, to show her fondness for him despite their recent differences. She was also hoping that he might, in one of his affectionate sorties, divulge what he had refused to divulge during the journey to the pub earlier that evening, when she had tried, awkwardly, to raise the subject of meditation.

But she was reluctant to return to the matter. Instead, Catherine decided to pry into a more recent event. During the short drive home, she asked, timidly, "Why on earth did Matilda take you aside tonight while the coffee was being served?" Owen responded readily, because there was nothing to give away. "Matilda just showed me a painting of a lime tree done by one of Humphrey's relatives from the eighteenth century, a woman whose work apparently fascinates Suzy." To his astonishment, her reaction was a petulant one and she upbraided Suzy for the first time. "Rosamond de Bohun was an impostor who signed pictures drawn by somebody else, and made excuses to cover up her deceit. Suzy was completely taken in by it all." Her critical outburst shocked him not just because it was uncharitable, but because the subject seemed to rile her so much for some reason. He attempted to discover why, but she did not want to discuss the subject any further.

As they entered the house, they were back in the sullen silence that had prevailed upon their arrival at the pub. Tactfully, Owen decided not to mention Matilda's invitation to Catherine for Friday, or to say where he was going to be on that day. Instead, he took the opportunity to raise a subject that he knew would engage her to the exclusion of everything else - her knowledge of local history. Among the accumulating questions in his mind was the identity of Beibio. He used the reference to Llwyn Beibio on de Bohun's map of 1707 to ask her if she could explain why it was not recorded on the original Ordnance Survey maps of the area. It was a long shot, but if Catherine did not have an answer, he was lost for a lead. She found it a rather recondite enquiry, but then she was into that sort of research.

What followed went beyond Owen's wildest dreams and brought him to a marvellous peak of restrained elation. She revealed that the name Beibio was a personal one which belonged to a seventh century Welshman of some standing in the local community at that time, and that his name appeared in a Welsh charter, which she had translated, concerning land on Rhibo Mountain. The llwyn, or grove, of the 1707 map could have taken its name from him. She would show him the charter in the morning when they got to the office.

Owen was overjoyed. Putting all the other questions, which had until then preoccupied his thoughts to the exclusion of everything else, into the background of his mind, he mellowed at last. And Catherine appreciated his unsolicited protestations of affection. The sullenness of the evening gave way to romantic embraces bordering on love. She could not believe the change and, although welcome, it gave her even more to think about when eventually they retired to bed.

The Spike

CHAPTER 25

Notebook - 15th June. Records Office

Beibio!!

"Be it known that Brengi bought 3 uncias of land at Mynydd y rhibo from Mabsu and Bledrys, the sons of Morlas, with all its liberty in field and in woods, in water and in pastures, and all its woods with acorns and hawks therein remaining, for twenty-seven cows, a Saxon woman, a valuable sword, a hawk, and a powerful horse, with the consent and in the presence of King Ithael and the principal seniors of Ergyng.

With the approbation of King Ithael, Brengi granted the land to God, and to St. Dubricius, St. Tilo and St. Oudoceus, and in the hand of Bishop Berthgwyn, and to all his successors in the Church of Llandaff. Of the clergy, the witnesses are Bishop Berthgwyn, Tyrchan, Eli, Gwenog; of the laity, Ithael,

King; Gwen, the son of Llywarch Hen; Brengi, Hywel, brothers; Mabsu, Bledrys, brothers; and Brochwael, Beuno and Beibio, the sons of Brengi.

The boundary of it is:- From the crooked ditch into the Mingui at Gwlyb-le, along Mingui downwards to the influx of the brook Melglyn, along the brook to the edge of Coed Tirion Glas below the grove of tall lindens, onwards by the brook to the dingle at Gwen y nog, thence to the Melglyn spring, around the long tree, through the wood, out of the wood and upwards to the stone on the summit of Mynydd y rhibo, downwards to the wood again and on to the old linden, thence through the wood to the hunt house by the apple tree, and onwards to the copse of willows from where it descends to the ditch where the boundary began."

(Catherine's translation of the Latin record of a land sale enacted circa 600 AD. N.B. 3 uncias is 324 acres.)

From Catherine's notes on the Land Charter of Brengi:

Dubricius (otherwise Dyfrig) was the first Bishop of the diocese of Llandaff (circa 506 AD) which in his time had five hundred wards, including Ergyng and Anergyng, and the bay of Severn, and which extended from Moccas on the banks of the Wye as far as Barry Island. His grandfather and great grandfather were kings of Ergyng in their time. It is recorded that he was born at Madley, and that "he retained two thousand clergy for seven successive years at Hentland on

*the banks of the Wye in the literary study of divine wisdom...
and during another space of time, he remained with his
numerous disciples for many years, having chosen a place
convenient for wood and fish on the banks of the Wye, giving
it the name Moccas". He is supposed to have crowned the
fifteen year old King Arthur at Cirencester. He died in 512.
(Book of Llandaff, edited by W.J. Rees 1840, pp. 311, 323,
and 621)*

*Berthgwyn was Bishop of Llandaff in the latter part of the
sixth or early in the seventh century. Ithael was King of
Ergyng at the same time. The affairs of both were disturbed
by the incursions into their territories of marauding Saxons;
to wit:-*

*"And in his time (Berthgwyn), plundering, and laying waste
by the Saxons with respect to Southern Britain took place,
and especially on the borders of his diocese, so far that by
the violence of the invading nation of the Saxons, they
plundered his diocese from Mochros, on the banks of the Wye,
on one part, as far as the river Dore, on the other, and as far
as Gurmuy (the Worm Brook), and to the mouth of the Taratyr
at the river Wye." (Book of Llandaff, W.J. Rees, 1840, page
374.)*

*"Be it known that great tribulations and plunderings
happened in the time of Teithfallt and Ithael, kings of Wales,
which were committed by the most treacherous Saxon nation,
and principally on the borders of Wales and England, towards
Hereford, so that all the border country of Wales was nearly*

destroyed, and much beyond the borders in both England and Wales, and especially about the River Wye, on account of the frequent diurnal and nocturnal encounters which took place between both countries." (Book of Llandaff, Rees, p.442.)

Beibio: "the bard of the trees" according to the anonymous author of `Relics of Welsh Bardic Literature from the Marches', Cardiff, 1871, who does not quote his source. He adds that Beibio was buried above the Monnow at a place named Llwyn Beibio, circa 629.

Beuno, who died circa 642, seems to have been the religious one of the three brothers, for he was eventually recognised as a saint. Llanveynoe in Ewyas is thought to derive from his patronage.

Gwen was one of the twenty-four sons of Llywarch Hen who was a cousin to Urien of Rheged, and a chieftain of North Britain during the latter part of the sixth century; a venerable man who fled from his principality of Argoed in Cumberland to Powys when the English conquered his land. A number of ninth century Welsh poems record the tribulations of Llywarch Hen. They are all concerned with the "outcast, wanderer, or bereft one" (according to P.L. Henry in his `Early English and Celtic Lyric', London, 1966). Elsewhere, the poems are described as "the verse elements in a cycle of stories, tales, sagas, told in pre-Norman times in north-east Wales, in the eastern part of Powys bordering on England, opposite to, and perhaps including, portions of Shropshire *and Herefordshire. The prose setting has disappeared: the verse has survived in twelth-century and fourteenth-century manuscripts..." (`Canu Llywarch Hen' by Sir Ifor Williams, quoted by P.K. Ford in the `Poetry of Llywarch Hen', University of California, 1974: also known as 'The Lament of the Old Man' and recorded in the Red Book of Hergest)*

Llywarch Hen:

Gwen watched at the river Llawen last night;
Despite the attack he did not flee,
Sad is the tale at the green dike.

Gwen, warrior, my soul grieves,
Great is the pain of your death,
'Tis no friend who killed you.

Gwen of the mighty thigh guarded last night
Beside the ford at Morlas.
Since he was my son, he did not flee.

A man was my boy, fearless in justice,
And nephew to Urien.
At Morlas Ford was Gwen killed.

Fierce in spear-fight, daring in valor,
He arrayed a disciplined host against the English,
This is the grave of Gwen, son of Llywarch.

(Verses 67, 70, 71, 75 and 76 in P.K. Ford, 1974, op. cit.)

Notebook - 16th June: The Cottage

The inclusion of Gwen as a witness to the charter may be evidence that he was collecting a host of fighters together at the time; getting ready to challenge the incursions of the Saxons. Morlas is considered to be synonymous with Marlas near Kilpeck (according to A.T. Bannister, The Place Names of Herefordshire, 1916), which makes sense because there was someone called Ilias, son of Morlas, living near Monmouth in the time of King Ithael (Book of Llandaff). Perhaps Gwen was helping the sons of Morlas defend their home area. The location of Marlas today is within carriage distance of Llwyn Beibio. Ergo: Gwen was the warrior son of Dyn buried beneath the lime tree inhabited by the spirit at that time!!

Cath believes that there is a connection between the land grant and Llandyfrig Court, since the original settlement was a religious one dedicated to St. Dubricius. It is possible that Beuno had established a religious house there, and that the acquisition of adjacent land by his father was to augment the property already dedicated. Rhibo Mountain, at the time, held a special place in the minds of the Welsh, being the burial place, if not of Gwen, then of earlier chieftains; even Merlin, perhaps. The subsequent disorders in Ewyas led to the abandonment of the monastery or chapel, or whatever was there, but did not obliterate the name. The local Welsh ensured that the name survived; and the first Norman overlord to appropriate the property seems to have been Christian enough to keep the name, although Roger de la

Haye was not known as Roger of Llandyfrig Court.

Evening:

Brengi's Parcel of Land

Retraced, with the aid of two 1:10560 O.S. maps, the boundary of the parcel of land acquired by Brengi in the seventh century. When Cath did her translation, she only had a quick look at the map to check the existence of the place-names mentioned.

From the land charter, it seems that the grove of lime trees which took Beibio's name was the southernmost extremity of Coed Tirion Glas. The running together in the text of the grove and the wood suggests that the former was an integral part of the latter at the time. The dingle certainly was. The boundary from the spring near the present Melglyn Stoggle follows the course I took to discover Llannerch Hudol. In fact, the obvious course to link up with Gulible is through Llannerch Hudol. Was the single lime tree referred to growing there?

There are two settlements between Llannerch Hudol and Gulible - Ty-helfa, a derelict cottage now, and the farmstead of Trehelig, which lies close to the Monnow. These names appear in the Welsh version of the land grant - the first meaning `hunthouse', and the second `homestead of the willows'.

Did the original grove of lime trees decline to perhaps an island of meadowland within the wood, or did it become the last vestige in the vicinity of the southern reaches of Coed Tirion Glas? For how long was it a respected grove after the passing of Beibio? For as long as there was a settled population of Welsh stock? What happened to the local inhabitants and their settlements when Gruffydd and Blaen slugged their violent way through Ewyas and Archenfield to sack Hereford in 1055?

The Domesday record for both areas is of a land largely waste - producing nothing and, therefore, of little value. In 1086, there was only one manor in Ewyas, but the rest of the district could not have been completely empty of settlement. The fact that the name Llwyn Beibio survived into the beginning of the seventeenth century is testimony that its choice as the site for a Norman motte and bailey castle (now Trellwyn) did not expunge its identity in the minds of the indigenous inhabitants. The building of this castle must be coincident with the episode in the last message when another "Serpent lair" appears, causing the Spirit to pass on.

Despite the surrounding bareness of the site today, it is still possible to imagine what the grove of Beibio might have looked like all those years ago. A gathering of tall lime trees, raised above the nearby waterways by the eminence they occupied, their emergent crowns breaking the line of the forest canopy, would have been a very prominent feature, as is the old ash and its companions. If only one tree had been as grand as the Emergent Lime, the grove would have possessed a presence of place at once awesome and sublime - the equivalent in living wood of a medieval cathedral of dead wood. What is better: a canopy of gentle living green, or a crafted, vaulted roof of plundered timber? A respect for nature and its powers of re-creation and renewal, or a respect for man's image of what he aspires to be? There is a God in both...

CHAPTER 26

'But the cunning of the Worm continued to be dire
Y Coed was hacked and burned
Cruelly downed with ire...'

Spirit of Y Coed

"Look at Rosamond's papers first, Owen", said Matilda, "before
you study the felling records. She is an intriguing person, and
not an easy one to fathom out. Her home was in Shrewsbury,
so all we have to go on is what she got up to here. We know
that she visited the Court occasionally as a young girl, being a
niece of the owner at the time, a Marcus de Bohun. He was the
cause of all her troubles here because he got himself into
financial difficulties and resorted to selling off parts of the estate,
farms as well as land and trees, to keep himself solvent. In fact,
men seem to have been her downfall. Her father wanted her to
marry someone she loathed, a Black Country self-made man by
all accounts. When she was still a spinster at the age of only

thirty one, he became very insistent that she should marry."

"This was the time that she started visiting the Court regularly during the summers of the seventeen nineties. She seems to have been quite close to her aunt, who was herself in a marriage alliance which gave her cause for regret, and confided her troubles to her. The letters between them would warm the heart of any ardent feminist today. She spent her time here drawing and painting, and helping her aunt, the two of them supporting each other, much to the annoyance of her uncle."

"It was at this time, that old Marcus carried out his greatest clearance of trees, felling thousands to help pay off his debts. When she discovered this, and that one of the trees to go was her favourite linden, she went mad. She got under his skin so much that he wrote to her father telling him that she was interfering with the affairs of the estate, and asking him to call her home. She came back the next year in a desperate attempt to save her tree, but to no avail. The stress of the whole matter took such a toll upon her sanity that her father eventually had her committed to an asylum for a while."

"That's a brief history of Rosamond de Bohun, and here she is", said Matilda, leading Owen to the large oak chest of drawers in the centre of the library. "She's in the third drawer down".

Matilda pulled the drawer out completely and, with Owen's help, lifted it on to the top of the chest.

"This is the folder", she said, picking up an imperial sized cardboard jacket from among the various papers in the drawer and carrying it to the large table nearby.

"Everything should be in order according to the date of its making. Your sister did that. So don't get the papers mixed up. Suzy might not mind, but Catherine will. I'll have a quick look at them with you. I haven't seen them for some time."

With Matilda looking over his shoulder, Owen browsed, rather uneasily, through the inconsistent artwork and the accompanying notes of Rosamond de Bohun. He made only a cursory perusal of the file, pretending an exploratory look while Matilda was present. Each time he noticed pieces of familiar handwriting, he contained himself, acting as if there was nothing exceptional in what he saw. His reserve was necessary because Matilda was discreetly scrutinising his response, rather than the work, drawing his attention to the handwriting whenever she could. When he came upon a note in his sister's hand at the end of the file, she pointed out its significance quickly.

"That's Suzy's detective work. She listed all the better artwork, and the examples of unusual handwriting, according to their date and where they had been done. Although not everything was annotated, she revealed that during the years in question, the best work was done exclusively during the month of June in the dingle by Gwenynog."

"Em... That's interesting", said Owen, quietly, in a bland voice, conscious that he was expected to make some comment.

"Suzy believed that she did all her best work while under the influence of the heady perfume of a large lime tree that was growing in the dingle at the time. Catherine reckoned the warm, dry weather usually prevalent in June was the explanation, and that the dingle was just a favourite place for Rosamond for drawing. But Suzy was adamant."

"Whose side did you take?" asked Owen, again appearing to be a detached recipient of an interesting story.

"I suggested that if it wasn't the lime scent, it might have been the setting of the tree, the sheer beauty of the place, which I suppose was a position half way between the two views. It was at this time that I took Suzy to see the Melglyn Stoggle, to give her an idea of the atmosphere that would have surrounded Rosamond's 'Early Flowering Linden', which probably stood somewhere near Gwenynog."

"And how did my wild sister react?" asked Owen, showing a bit more enthusiasm for the matter.

"She was delighted; so delighted that I left her there because I had to get back here. When she rejoined Humphrey and me for supper that day, we both agreed that the secret to the matter lay with the tree that was cut down in 1802. Rosamond was obviously so moved by it that it elevated her existence, and her work, when she was near it. It could even have made her feel like another person – you know, affected her personality in some way."

Matilda looked deeply into Owen's eyes as she said these words. By way of an escape from her gaze, he stammered out another question.

"Was Rosamond around when the tree was felled?"

"Yes, she was. She made a special journey to the Court in the March of 1802, in a last ditch attempt to get Marcus to relent in his plans to fell the trees in the dingle. When she failed, she was beside herself with grief, and she was never the same again, although it has to be said that she was rather prone to periods of melancholy, as her letters show. If only we had her diaries as well. Suzy went to Shrewsbury hoping to track them down, but Rosamond's father must have destroyed all her papers when she went into hospital - the rat."

"Can I see the letters as well", asked Owen, timidly, trying not to be too enthusiastic.

"Of course you can. That's what you came for, isn't it? I'll dig them out for you now; then you can sift through the lot at your leisure. What I suggest you do is start with the letters, and lead up to the fellings. It will be heavy work, but with your sister's guidance you'll get through." This last comment was delivered with a knowing smile.

After some further rummaging in the chest of drawers, Matilda placed a package of letters on the table and a large box-file, which carried a label with the lines:

'Many are the tree-tops of the far-seen woods,

 many the tree-trunks of deep timber...'

(Edmund Price: 1544-1623: from The Mansion of the Woods)*

"Here's some paper just in case you want to write anything down. I'll call you when it's tea-time, unless you surface before then in need of refreshment. Have fun."

With that, she left him to delve into the past. But still, he went about the task with an air of casual interest. He imagined the possibility of his being watched through a hidden portal in one of the bookshelves. Anyway, he did not really know where to start. Ignoring Matilda's advice, his desire to read about the felling of the trees in the dingle drew him to the box-file first. It was not long before he was assiduously writing notes.

Notebook - '17th June: The de Bohun Library

Llandyfrig Court Estate Records

Notes made from records concerning the Survey and Sale

Notice of Navy Timber situated on the Llandyfrig Court estate in the years 1801-2. Taken from two small notebooks of timber measurement and valuation, dated 1780 and 1786 in one case, and 1796 and 1801 in the other; an account book covering the period 1791-1811; a book containing quantities of coppice and bark extracted from the woods on the estate, 1790-1808; and papers advertising the sale of timber on the estate, including tables of timber quantities and species.

The area concerned covered 402 acres in the southern portion of the estate, including the south side and the central cwm of Coed Tirion Glas, the immediate vicinity of Gwenynog, and also the Gelli Copse, which was a coppice wood at the time with some standard oaks. The account book records the incidental sale of timber, coppice, and bark from various places on the estate, including the regular disposal of wood and bast from limes. The survey and valuation of timber trees began in 1780, and was continued in 1786 and 1796 before the final assessment in 1801. The timber was recorded in 15 lots, with locations and species given. Trees were marked both for sale and for retention, more or less in equal numbers. Most of the limes were located in the Cwm and around Gwenynog. The wild service trees came from the Cwm.

The 1801 Sale of Navy Timber described the produce as being "Of Prime Quality, very great Lengths, and extraordinary large Dimensions."

The list of trees was as follows:

Species	No. of Trees	
Oak 'capital' ones	1620	*Largest 230 cubic feet*
smaller dimension	1460	
inferior quality	218	
Ash 'mayden'	796	
Linden	112	*Largest 207 cubic feet*
Elm 'whytche'	53	
Maple	14	
Birch	13	
Elms	11	
'Servin' (Wild Service)	8	
Walnut	2	
Total	3407	*(N.B. 50 cubic feet equal to one ton.)*

*The one located at the edge of the dingle near Gwenynog!

Three and a half thousand trees! What thunderous change! What scarring haulage! What devastation! What spiritual grief...'*

The impact of the box-file fellings was a profound one. Owen was astonished enough to consider breaking off and seeking a cup of tea. But he was not in the mood to face the questioning he knew he would get from Matilda. So he turned to the letters, which dealt with Rosamond's life at the Court. Other than a recurring longing, often expressed, to be at Llandyfrig instead of at home in Shrewsbury, there were few references to that part of her life which was of interest to him. Her problems with her father were mentioned all the time, confirming what Matilda had told him, and suggesting that the wife of the dastardly Marcus de Bohun was her main confidant and support in these matters. She did not mention trees or specific places on the estate, which was too much to expect anyway; and her handwriting was nothing like the script in the picture. In fact, it was difficult to read.

By the time he had peered into these recesses of the mind of Rosamond de Bohun, he was suffering from eye-strain, and something else, but he could not pin it down. He thought that it might have been his response to her personality, which had a tendency to border on hysteria and to be touched with the strains of melancholia.

Beginning to feel the impact of history, he resisted the urge to break-off, and went back to the pictures and the sketches. Those done in the field were annotated, and there were also notes on the back of the paper used. He discovered that her favourite places for sketching, besides the 'Honey Dingle', and 'The Early Flowering Linden', were the Haye, Wern y coc, Gwenynog, and Llannerch Hudol, for all of which places she had compiled a detailed plant list, like the one Milo had seen.

Suzy was right. He, too, thought that her best pictures, the ones with the handwriting which resembled his own message script, were done in the Honey Dingle; exclusively in the dingle. She must have been affected by the Spirit. But there were no messages calling for help; no actual communications; only exceptional art. Art that reminded him of the fineness of detail and colour displayed in the monastic illustrations of the Middle Ages. The difference between her normal style and her special achievements was startling. It was so much better that without the insight he had into the secrets of the dingle, he would have to conclude that two artists were involved. The quality was really too much to believe. He was now in need of a break...

A few minutes later, he was having tea with Matilda and Humphrey in the kitchen, drinking thirstily and digesting Welsh cakes at a rate which attracted Humphrey's attention.

"Hey! Owen - they're my Welsh cakes as well, you know."

"Humphrey! That's not a nice thing to say to our guest. A couple of hours buried in documents are enough to make anyone hungry."

"I was only joking, dear. Owen should be used to my sense of humour by now. But I would like some more." The inevitable boyish grin came to his face, and his wife obliged, smiling resignedly at Owen as she prepared more cakes.

"Well, Owen, what do you think?" asked Humphrey, in that dramatic way of his.

"What about?" responded Owen, in the process of making the last Welsh cake vanish from sight.

"The fellings, of course. What I don't understand is why old Marcus didn't knock down some of the trees in the Deer Haye."

"Yes, that thought occurred to me as well, because the fellings ripped the heart out of the estate's woods at the time. Maybe his wife restrained him in that respect, in the way your mother saved the Melgyn Stoggle. How did she react to it all? Is there any record of her views?"

"None at all", interceded Matilda. "All we know is that Rosamond was gravely upset by the whole episode, presumably because her favourite linden, the early flowering one, was one of those marked with white paint."

"How do you know that", asked Owen, "There is nothing in those documents which recorded her reaction."

"Oh, wasn't there a parcel of letters written by Marcus de Bohun? He wrote to Rosamond's father at the time, demanding that he take his daughter away because she was interfering with the affairs of the estate. Apparently, she hid all the white paint at one point. He wrote that she was making life 'unbearable for everyone', those were his very words, weren't they, Humphrey?"

"Yes dear, his very words, if you say so."

"It seems that he hardly wrote any letters, until he got mad about something. The few letters we have of his are all ones telling someone off, or ordering them into action. The best one is a short note to an Edmund Wildes of Hay-on-Wye, telling him not to come anywhere near the estate again."

"Who was he, then?" enquired Owen.

"Ask Catherine for the details, when she comes for supper. You are staying for supper, aren't you?"

Owen nodded, but concealed his surprise at the forthcoming presence of Catherine, unaware that Matilda had invited her.

"She tracked him down for us. He was a swarthy local man who had a reputation as an artist. Rosamond paid him to give her some tuition. She even drew his portrait, but we gave that to the old lady in Hay who is descended from him and who helped Catherine piece him together. We still don't know why he was banned from the Court."

At this point, Humphrey yawned - "If you two are going to unravel the saga of fair Rosamond again, I shall leave you to it."

With that, he retired to his seat in the Long Room for a nap. After his departure, Matilda explained:

"Humphrey got fed up with the arguing at tea times between Catherine and Suzy. Although they are very good friends, they don't always work well together. With Suzy, life is led on the spur of the moment, and she says what she feels. With Catherine, there is no spur of the moment - it all has to be arranged..." Matilda checked herself. "I shouldn't be saying such things to you. You know them both well enough by now..." She paused for a few seconds, and then changed the subject altogether. "Can I see the notes you've made?"

The question fixed Owen to the chair. His reading of the documents, and the discussion over tea, had put Matilda's interest in his handwriting to the back of his mind. Though his handwriting was normal, he was reluctant to show his notes to her. He was confused about what to do. The seconds of indecision seemed to last an eternity. He opened his mouth to say something - he had not decided what - when Humphrey ushered in Catherine, and changed the atmosphere altogether. Matilda smiled at Owen. Again, a knowing smile.

The Wrong Angled Oak

CHAPTER 27

'Our Gentle Limes
Luxuriant and grand
Rose up in golden gatherings of Trees
Brightly shone their tops above Y Coed
Fragrance filled the Air'

Spirit of Y Coed

When Catherine drove Owen back to the cottage, she stayed the night. The evening had gone well, better than she had expected. For once, she had felt a part of the social occasion; more so than when she and Suzy had dined with the de Bohuns on other occasions. To her surprise, she had enjoyed playing one of de Bohun's stupid board games. Both Matilda and Owen had brought her into the proceedings, and from the moment of her arrival, they had not disappeared together, or gone into a huddle to discuss Rosamond de Bohun. In fact, Humphrey had issued a 'Marcus de Bohun banning order' during supper, insisting that the subject of 'fair Rosamond' was not to be raised again that evening. And she thought that Owen had enjoyed her being there.

He had. But in the journey home, and in the quietness of the cottage, she sensed that he was drifting away as usual. But she did not let him. She was beginning to get to know a facet of his inner self. Whenever they were getting on well, she used whatever artifice she could to sustain the rapport. And he responded. So she stayed.

But in the morning, it was different. He was in his usual early morning stupor, and she knew that she would not get much out of him. Nevertheless, she tried by asking him what he planned to do that day, the beginning of the weekend. Stupor or not, he was awake enough to reply with a list of jobs on the gazebo, which were essential, but which he had no intention of doing. She was not deceived. She sensed that if he had any plans at all, he was not going to divulge them to her. As usual, she had a host of things to do.

While she got ready to leave, having committed herself to helping her mother prepare for a parish jumble sale, she dwelt on his stubborn unwillingness to allow her access to his daily thoughts. Owen, under the guise of his morning stupor, dwelt on a matter that had occurred to him the day before, and which (unfortunately) had been at the forefront of his mind when they had gone to bed. But he could not do anything about it until Catherine left the house. So breakfast, and the preparations of the morning, took place, as Catherine knew they would, in an atmosphere of inconsequential communication, although they did arrange what they were going to do later on in the day. And to confuse the issue even further, Owen actually walked her to the car in the lay-by. Despite his inner impatience to get back inside the house, he said a fond farewell and stood waving as she drove away. Then, instead of running across the footbridge and the garden, he ambled the distance in a further gesture of self-conscious restraint.

However, once inside the cottage, all restraint and thoughts of Catherine left his mind. He hurried upstairs to Suzy's room and her wardrobe. This time, his respect for the private thoughts of his sister was discarded. By finding out, the day before, the approximate dates in her diary he needed to check, he had done something to assuage the guilt he expected to feel. He needed only to peruse the period between April and July, 1986. Clambering onto the stool, he reached for the diaries and retrieved the one he wanted. Then he left the room to its ebullience and colour.

Finding April was easy, but finding the first reference to Rosamond de Bohun was like searching for an obscure crayon in a box containing countless coloured crayons. He tried to ignore, or pretend not to see, those entries which a quick glance revealed to be very personal or irrelevant; but, inevitably, some impinged upon his mind too impressively to be forgotten. Among these were comments about the boyfriend of the time, the aspiring Buddhist who was banished to the shed. His days were numbered as April drew to a close. There was even a touching reminder to write to Owen, "to see if he still remembers me", a poignant note written rather than scribbled in purple felt-tipped pen.

Then he came to the beginning of May. At the top of the page, by way of a reminder, was the note - "Cataloguing the Court's records with Cath". The next reference was on the first

Monday of the month. Sandwiched between a shopping list, which was itself an eye-opening entry, and an impression of Milo, whom she must have met for the first time that day, was the note - "Another boring day at the Court. Cath upset again because I kept taking breaks to chat to Matilda. She says the display work will be much more fun. It better be!"

The comments about Milo were far more engaging than Suzy's disillusionment with her research project at the Court. Owen could not resist reading all of it. He was already familiar with his sister's commentaries upon men. Few of her letters failed to mention one somewhere, but these reflections were not intended for his eyes, or those of anyone else. The insight they gave was yet another facet of the complex personality of his sister. He smiled to himself and wondered what she would have said about him if he, as a stranger to her, had started going out with Alison.

There was nothing exceptional or extraordinary in the first two weeks of May. Some of the first week was taken up with helping a Mrs. Howell organise the funeral of Gethen Daw, the last owner of Wern y coc. The second carried a note recording a visit one Saturday with Matilda to a design exhibition in Cardiff. The last scribble that day, which it was impossible not to notice because it was set apart from the visit itself, was very enigmatic: "Oh, to be as calm as Matilda, and still have fun!"

He thought about this comment for some time, before turning to the third week, which was far more chaotic than the previous two. How did she find the time for incidental writing? How did she manage to live life at such a pace? He had yet to see his sister as exhausted by her personality as everyone else.

Then he saw what he was looking for. There, in the third

week of May, recorded in shocking-pink ink, standing out from the page in a burst of ebullience, was the first of a series of relevant entries:-

Wednesday: "Amazing discovery! The de Bohun woodwork; the drab de Bohun woodwork, is artistic after all. Found drawings of local landscapes and plants galore by a Rosamond de Bohun, hidden away in a chest. Scribblings all over the place - especially on the back of sketches. Even some dried flowers, now faded, but recognisable, and some dried herbs. What a find! Matilda, and I danced around the library, while old Humphrey looked on by the door, dancing a sort of out of step hop on the spot." Where was Catherine that day? Owen asked himself.

Thursday: " Papers and more pictures signed by Rosamond, in a small box, rather dusty, but totally different. Exquisite compositions - fantastic art! Cath reckons they are the work of someone else. I'm not so sure. Detective work ahead."

A folded piece of paper carried some of the jottings of the next week:-

Tuesday: "Sorted all the drawings and paintings into chronological order. All the best ones with a date were done during June of 1798, 1799, and 1800. Why? Nearly all are sketches, plus a few watercolours, of plants, although there are some scenes of the 'Honey Dingle', and a few pictures of 'The Early Flowering Linden' growing there at the time. Some sketches have been touched up with colour, but not very well. Some of the best paintings derive from a few of the best sketches, but the artistic achievement is nowhere near as good. How strange."

Wednesday: "Made a check list of the places where the

pictures were done. The very best ones seem to have been done either in the 'Honey Dingle', or by the 'Early Flowering Linden'. Matilda says the dingle is the Melglyn Dingle near Gwenynog."

Friday: "Went to the Honey Dingle with Matilda. Cath too busy to come. Saw the huge old lime tree which Matilda loves to visit. I must sketch it sometime. They all call it the 'Melglyn Stoggle'. She told me how it always breaks into flower before any of the other lime trees on the estate, like the one Rosamond loved to visit. Why haven't I ever drawn lime flowers? Owen would love this tree. I believe Rosamond had a special place in the Honey Dingle where she sat and did her best sketches. But it was then wooded, according to the forest records Cath has unearthed, so the source of her inspiration may have gone too. Matilda wondered if the tree was descended from Rosamond's linden."

The following weekend was a busy one. Suzy was involved with a new man. Owen compelled himself to pass on, with an all-consuming glimpse, to the next week. Here, he came across another of the many pieces of paper that were either inserted between the pages or attached to them; notes and addenda to the affairs of Suzy Forrest. One was particularly illuminating:

"My intuition proved! Rosamond did receive inspiration at Gwenynog. Her own words:- "The Honey Dingle is so lovely. It is delightful sitting here among the trees and flowers. The bees are humming above me in the linden, and the scent of the blossom is all around. I feel so very happy. I do hope this will be another day when I shall receive divine assistance with my drawing." Note on the back of a sketch dated 17th June, 1800... And another discovery: Cath has found a reference, in a letter from Marcus' wife to a friend, to Rosamond's favourite herb tea, 'linden tea', made from the flowers of the limes growing in the dingle. I must make some."

Wednesday: "Cath at a conference. Beautiful day. Took the chance to draw the Melglyn Stoggle - to see if my art would break new bounds. It didn't. Ali is getting interested in Rosamond. She wants to put together a story for the newspaper, and call it 'The Divine Art of a Dead Aristocrat'. What a title!"

Thursday: "Cath furious that I'd taken the day off yesterday. Why can't she let up for once and stop taking life so seriously. She thinks that I'm wasting my time, that I've become obsessed with Rosamond and her art. Me! obsessed? What about her and her endless records? When I told her last week that almost every one of the pictures with the unusual signatures, the best of Rosamond's art, was done in the Honey Dingle, she dismissed it as being nothing more than plagiarism. It is hopeless trying to get her to appreciate that a twentieth century artist of plant life has an emotional attachment to a similar artist of two hundred years ago. Whatever she says, I still have faith in Rosamond."

There followed a succession of entries commenting upon the differences of opinion with Catherine, and the sympathetic support given to Suzy by Matilda. Alison did not feature much at all in the whole affair. Owen assumed that her time and interests were elsewhere with Milo, who did crop up again in the diary.

Sunday: "Milo and Tim didn't take to each other yesterday. I had no idea that Tim's father was such a thorn in the side of the local conservationists. Ali says that if Tim is going to be a regular visitor at the Goggin, then our respective trysts will have to be staggered. My reply was that staggered staggering trysts are not new. They are the norm... Milo would not believe or even entertain the possibility that the present lime in the old Honey Dingle flowers as early as Matilda says it does. He wasn't in the mood to believe anything. Ali must work on him. He needs working on. Remoulding I would say..."

Tuesday: "Stayed at the Court for a meal and zany games with Matilda, Humphrey and Matilda's sister, Maud. We had a chat till late about Rosamond and her art. Matilda supports my idea that a place, if it's a special one, can stir the creativity of an artist. To Cath, this is absurd rubbish. Humphrey offered his hackneyed tree spirit explanation. The Grey-Beards in the Deer Haye elevate his recorder playing, and so on... What a screw-ball he is."

Thursday carried a reminder of a meeting in Hay with a 'Jack French', whoever he was, and another loose piece of paper with a note which suggested that Suzy might have visited the second-hand bookshops in the town to check their natural history sections for information on lime trees:

"Trees and How They Grow by G. Clarke Nuttall, Cassel and Co., London, 1913: p.175. Lime flower tea used as a cure for chronic epilepsy in the medical lore of the countryside: p.176. John Evelyn recorded in the seventeenth century that the distilled water of lime berries was 'good against Epilepsie, Apoplexie, Vertigo and trembling of the heart.' There's nothing wrong with the trembling of my heart but Tim's heart would tremble a bit more freely if he left drugs alone." This reference to Tim was lost on Owen as he focused on the lime tree detail.

Then he came to Friday, the 20th June, for the second time, the scrawled yellow letters shouting that the lime was in flower. The day after was the day of the celebratory meal which culminated in the circle dance at the tree, and the collection of flowers for lime flower tea.

At this high point in the diary's colourful pages, Owen took an induced break from his sister to make himself a cup of tea - lime flower tea. Throughout the compulsive reading of the entries, and his attempts to disregard the passion, the hedonism and the secrets of his sister, his imagination and his concentration had been taken to the limit. As he sipped his tea, several vital questions arose in his mind. Rosamond de Bohun had been affected by something in the dingle - it could only have been the Early Flowering Linden of the time, not the one now affecting him. So the spirit must have moved - or escaped - before the fellings of 1802. The uncanny similarity between his and her handwriting, incredible though it was, suggested this much.

Matilda was more closely involved in the whole story, and more sensitive to its implications than her behaviour so far suggested. This realisation stirred all sorts of ideas in his mind. So, too, did the reactions of Catherine at the time, which were so much like her response to his own involvement with the tree that he now understood some of her attitudes. Certain of the entries suggested a possible degree of jealousy on her side, perhaps because Suzy was confiding her ideas to Matilda. But it was the subliminal desire of his sister to attain moments of calmness of the kind experienced by Matilda which made the greatest impression upon him. The thought of Suzy in need of an antidote to her frenetic self was unbelievable.

This last reflection was in his mind as he returned to the diary. But the thought was soon displaced by the sight of another folded piece of paper which slipped from the diary's end-pages as he flicked through them to pick up where he had left off. It was an unsigned and unsent letter to him dated the 26th June, 1986; typed instead of just written, which was extraordinary for her, and also lengthy – again unusual...

"Dearest Owen,

This is your sister speaking. Remember? You have a sister; a rowdy, lovely sister. How could you forget? Promise not to run away? Good. Writing letters used to be our best way of getting through to each other. Why have we gone quiet? Did I send too many? Lovely sisters always send too many letters to lovely brothers...

Let me start up again with a phenomenal story which even you will marvel at. Then you can send me some of your deep thoughts on it. Where shall I begin? I haven't made it up, but some of my friends find it hard to believe.

I've been helping one of my best friends, Cath, who works in the County Records Office, sort through the family papers of a local estate. The couple who own it are great fun, especially Matilda. You'd like her. Her husband is the Norman knight Humphrey de Bohun, who's been around since the Middle Ages.

I was finding the work boring until we came across the artwork of an unusual lady of leisure, a Rosamond de Bohun, who visited the estate several times towards the end of the eighteenth century. Her private papers are a jumble of pictures and jottings. If you think I'm chaotic, you should see how she describes her life. She was always going off somewhere to draw landscapes and plants, especially flowers like me (yes, flowers like me!), getting caught in the rain, getting soaked, and losing crayons. She seems to have known every inch of the estate, and all its plants. We've made a list of all the plants she found. A lot no longer exist on the estate, or in the area, any more. She wasn't a very good artist, a mediocre one really, but some of her work is brilliant. If you didn't know that the pictures were by the same artist, you would not connect them at all. I didn't at first. Even the handwriting style of her signatures and the annotations on her best work is different - very cursive and flowing, with only a hint of her normal style. But when I delved into the jottings on the backs of her sketches, and checked dates, I discovered that she did all her best pictures in a wooded dingle which was once connected to the big wood on the estate, a dingle which now contains only one tree, a large and very unusual lime. You will love it. When you eventually visit me here, I'll take you to it the moment you arrive. And then, if I can get you home, finish you off with some special lime flower tea I've made from its blossom.

Somehow, the dingle, or something in it, stimulated her to reach heights of creativity beyond her usual capabilities. She thought it was all due to divine intervention - a gift from God. Being a devout Christian, she probably thought she had been affected by the hand of God, a force which took over her mind and extended her skill. The more I talk to Matilda about it (she knows the dingle and the lime tree there intimately), the more I think that the dingle was such a beautiful place that she was artistically transported; uplifted so much that she broke through her limitations. I know this sounds a bit far-fetched, but you are always claiming that places have an extra dimension 'which elevates the mind' - your words, I remember them. I do listen, sometimes.

My best friend, Cath, says the pictures were either done by someone else or a person who was remarkably schizophrenic. It is possible, I suppose, that someone else was involved. But I think there are too many co-incidences for that to be the case. She could have been schizophrenic - her jottings suggest some kind of split personality. But, then, my jottings will make somebody in a hundred years' time wonder about me. All our personalities are split, or can be split if we let them, or if supernatural influences grab them. The unanswered question is why did she reach her peaks of brilliance only when she was in the dingle? I'll enclose a few photocopies of her work to show the difference. It's not a crazy idea to think that her surroundings may have raised her artistic standards, is it?"

Owen was particularly struck by the restrained and coherent way the letter had been composed. There were occasional hints at digression, but nothing of the kind for which her letters were famous in the family. He concluded that she had given the matter a lot of time and a great deal of thought. But why was the letter never sent? He continued his reading of the diary for clues. The next relevant entry suggested why she may have delayed sending it:

Monday, 30th June: "Confided in Matilda today after I'd had some wine. I had to discuss it all with someone. Tim might be good in bed (when he's not drunk and violent), but he's crackers if he has got himself involved with cocaine parties in Bristol. Matilda is right. I should leave him to wallow in his own stupidity. His father can sort him out, if he doesn't want a family scandal. I'm not sure he's all that gripping anyway."

Something controversial had happened in her love-life to

distract her from the mystery of Rosamond de Bohun, for there were no other references to the matter, which was a mystery in itself. Could the next entry have put the letter to him, and the behaviour of Tim Medlar, out of her mind altogether?

Tuesday: 1st July: "Tragedy of tragedies! Rosamond shattered by the imminent felling of trees at the Court, following the sale of 'Navy Timber'. Thousands of trees eventually felled, including her favourite linden at Gwenynog. Note on the back of one sketch repeats a local folk tale about the consequences of cutting down a linden on Rhibo Mountain - whoever does so, his family name will die out. Who was responsible? And what happened to him?"

Wednesday: "Matilda has found a list of names of woodmen and the individual timber lots they were detailed to fell. All the lots which carried limes, including the linden at Gwenynog, were felled by three men from Pontrilas - not local woodmen, and all English."

Thursday: "Checked the parish records for Pontrilas. Each one of the three woodmen died without siring sons. All three without sons! Cath thinks it is mere coincidence. Mere coincidence! Impossible! Folk-lore is fun after all..."

Friday: "Cath came at me today with that 'I told you so look on her face'. I knew she'd found something. So what, if Rosamond was eventually committed to an asylum in 1804, the fact still remains that she did all her best work in the Honey Dingle. Until she finds evidence that another person was involved, I shall not change my mind."

Monday: "Another piece of circumstantial evidence thrown

in my face by Cath. This time, a record which shows that Rosamond had regular lessons from a local artist named Edmund Wildes during the summers when she did her best work. Okay, Cath, you win. But all the pictures are going to be attributed to Rosamond in the display. Matilda is with me on that, unless we can track down some art-work by Edmund Wildes."

After these admissions, there were hardly any significant references to do with Rosamond and her art, merely the occasional brief note of attendance at the Court, and a succession of colourful reminders leading towards the date when the display of the de Bohun records was opened at the museum. The count down to this event, the culmination of the cataloguing, induced a simultaneous run down in Owen's interest and concentration. He closed the diary on reaching the day of the display, and returned it to its hiding place. As he left the room once more to its ebullience and colour, his face and his movements carried a conclusive air which suggested that his mind was made up and determined in its next course of action. But first, he wanted to complete his historical dossier of the saga so far. To do this, he had to get his head around a new system of dating that Milo insisted on using – Calendar Years Before Present or Cal.Yr.BP. Owen was still in the BC/AD frame of mind, but he could see that a view into the past chronology of the lime spirit was clearer if comprehended simply in number of years ago.

The Melglyn Stoggle with Rhibo Mountain

CHAPTER 28

'...goddess of the primeval forest, voice of the haunted glade, caring to answer only the last snatches of what we say; I beg you... grant me the key to these pathless tracts of remote woodland, where no axe has sounded, to the perplexed windings of this place, and to the forest lairs.'

Henry Vaughan (1621-1695): from 'To Echo', his own translation from a Latin poem (Fogle, 1964)

Notebook - June 1988:

THE SPIRIT OF THE EARLY FLOWERING LINDEN EVENTS IN ITS EXISTENCE

7800 Cal.Yr.BP *Late Boreal Times (warm/dry). Lime, a 'thermophilous', long-lived tree species according to Milo, became a common constituent of the forests in the southern* *half of Britain as the climate warmed. Mesolithic peoples on higher open ground above tree-line (500m).*

7800-5700 *Atlantic Period (warm/wet). The greatest spread of the primaeval forest, the 'Wildwood' of Britain, of which nothing remains except much altered, semi-natural, isolated remnants. Lime was the commonest tree, existing together with oak, ash, elm, alder or hazel according to site. "One of the main areas of former lime forest in Britain is in the Midlands... The very large amounts of Tilia pollen show its almost complete dominance in the Atlantic forest... The Midland lime forest appears to have had its Western boundary where the Welsh mountains begin..." (J. Grieg, 1982, Past and Present Lime Woods of Europe, p. 32.) Evidence (charcoal) of the burning of timber by Mesolithic people.*

5800-5300 *The Elm Decline, a vegetation catastrophe, and the simultaneous appearance of Neolithic peoples (5700-4500) leading a pastoral existence on the higher and drier ground, where it was easier to infiltrate the forest edge. Neolithic peoples may have contributed to the decline of elm by using its leaves as fodder for stock, and by moving into glades created by the death of trees. "In 500 years, or possibly much less, half the elm vanished from Europe without affecting other trees." (O. Rackham, 1980, Ancient Woodland.)*

5700-2600 *Sub-Boreal Period (warm/dry). Lime begins to disappear (c4200) due to climatic cooling and as woodland clearance occurs caused by Neolithic farming and Bronze Age (5000-3800) agriculture. Primitive peoples are known to have used bast, the inner bark of the lime tree, for making* *cordage, and to have used lime leaves as fodder for stock. 3800-2600: beginning of Celtic Britain and the exploitation of land in lowland regions for agriculture. 3000-2000: later Bronze Age and pre-Roman Age was probably an active period of wildwood clearance.*

2600-Present *Sub-Atlantic Period (cool/wet).*

2500-1900 *Early Iron Age and associated Celtic agriculture accelerated woodland clearance. This, and the subsequent Roman period (AD 43-410), saw the greatest depletion of primaeval forest in the history of woodland clearance. "There can be little doubt that the latter Iron Age and Roman period were the most active period of wildwood destruction in history." (O. Rackham, 1980, Ancient Woodland)*

1920 *Romans in control of South Wales (80 AD).*

1620 *Roman settlement of Ariconium (c380AD), near present-day Ross-on-Wye, in existence. Ariconium, and the Roman fortress at Abergavenny, were connected to the important borderland routeway, coursing north to south from Chester to Caerleon, which passed through Kenchester on the Wye, through the future land of Ergyng, and through the western reaches of Ewyas. A Roman road, leading to the Roman camp at Oldcastle, close to the confluence of the Monnow and Honddu rivers, was uncovered at Abbey Dore when the Golden Valley railway line was constructed. (Bannister, 1902, Note C, 'Roman Remains in Ewias', page 98)*

1700-1600 *●Approximate time when the Spirit of the Early Flowering Limes migrated westwards away from the Wye Valley towards the valley of the River Monnow and Mynydd y rhibo.*

1590 The break with Rome (410AD) as the Roman Empire declines, giving way to regional Celtic states with varying degrees of Romanization. Incursion of Saxon, Danish, and Viking immigrants into England, the Saxons eventually creating the kingdom of Mercia in the west midlands, and the smaller kingdoms of Magonsaeton and Hwicce either side of the River Severn against the Celtic stronghold of Wales.

'It is known that lime retreated mostly before the Anglo-Saxon period and has not changed much in [its distribution] in the last thousand years [being] the commonest tree of ancient woods in certain small and sharply defined areas of lowland England...' (Rackham, History of the Countryside, 1986, p.102).

'The pry tree, Tilia cordata [Small-leaved Lime], is a living link with Mesolithic limes.' (Rackham, 1986, 106).

'lind' from which 'linden' is derived is the Germanic word in Anglo-Saxon for 'bast', or inner bark.

'llwyf teil' is the Welsh for lime, literally 'elm-lime'. (Wilkinson, A History of Britain's Trees, 1981, p.29).

1558 The first Saxon revolt (442AD) following the settlement of Saxon invaders amongst the Romano-Celtic population, and their incursions into the eastern reaches of the country. Gildas (516?-570?AD), a monk of the troubled times to come, writing a century later, remembered the venom of the Saxon Worm: "The fire of righteous vengeance, kindled by the sins of the past, blazed from sea to sea... Once lit, it did not die down. When it had wasted town and country in that area, it burnt up almost the whole surface of the island, until its red and savage tongue licked the western ocean..." (Trevelyan, History of England, 1926, 183)

c500 AD *Narrative Old English poem Beowulf conceived in west Mercia. The tale of Beowulf and the Dragon states: "Well he knew that the wood of the forest might not help him – linden against flame" [and yet] "his hand seized his shield, the yellow linden-wood". (Norton Anthology of English Literature, vol. 1 pages 75 and 80).*

450-537 AD *A period of successful resistance by the British to the Saxon advance, begun by Ambrosius Aurelianus, who died circa 508, and continued by his nephew, Arthur, culminating in the victory of the Battle of Mount Badon when Arthur's horsemen routed the Saxon foot-soldiers, and fading with his death at the Battle of Camlann. (Morris, The Age of Arthur, 1973, page 43)*

The Mabinogion, a collection of ancient Welsh tales taken from the Red Book of Hergest (1375-1425) and the White Book of Rhydderch (1300-1325), first translated into English by Lady Charlotte Guest (1849), describes the hunting of a ferocious wild boar, Twrch Trwyth, in the tale of Culhwch and Olwen (c. 1100), which contains one of the earliest references to the Arthur of romantic tradition. The boar hunt could be a symbolic celebration of the victory over the Saxons:

"Twrch Trwyth went then between Tawy and Ewyas. Arthur summoned Cornwall and Devon to meet him at the mouth of the Severn... And by his council a body of horsemen was sent, and the dogs of the Island with them, as far as Ewyas, and they beat back thence to the Severn, and they waylaid him there..."

c506-c512 *Dubricius (otherwise Dyfrig), Bishop of Llandaff, a native of Anergyng who is reported to have crowned King Arthur at the age of fifteen in Cirencester. "His grandfather*

and great-grandfather were kings of Ergyng in their time..."
(W. Rees, 1840, The Book of Llandaff.)
540 *Gildas, who says that he was born in the year of the Battle of Mount Badon, lamented the pagan upheaval of the Welsh Christian tradition:*

"Every colony is levelled to the ground by the stroke of the battering ram. The inhabitants are slaughtered along with the guardians of their churches, priests and people alike, while the sword gleamed on every side, and the flames crackled around. How horrible to behold in the midst of the streets the tops of towers torn from their lofty hinges, the stones of high walls, holy alters, mutilated corpses, all covered with lurid clots of coagulated blood, as if they had been crushed together in some ghastly winepress... Of the miserable remnant some flee to the hills, only to be captured and slain in heaps: some, constrained by famine, come in and surrender themselves to be slaves for ever to the enemy... Others wailing bitterly pass overseas." (Quoted by G.M. Trevelyan, History of England, 1926, 540.)
c573 *Merlin retires to Y Coed?*

"There he lived for half a century, with no company but the trees and the wild beasts, mourning for the slaying of Gweddolau and afraid less Rhydderch should come against him. In this frenzied condition Myrddin acquired the gift of prophecy." (T. Parry, A History of Welsh Literature, translated by H.I. Bell, Oxford, 1955.)
1500-1030 *Cal.Yr.BP* ●*Spirit of the Early Flowering Limes resident at Llwyn Beibio. The last longest period of residence?*
c506 *"And in his time [Dubricius, 1st Bishop of Llandaff],*

plundering, and laying waste by the Saxons with respect to southern Britain took place, and especially on the borders of his diocese [Llandaff], so far that by the violence of the invading nation of the Saxons, they plundered his diocese from Mochros, on the banks of the Wye, on one part, as far as the river Dore, on the other, and as far as Gurmuy, and to the mouth of the Taratyr at the river Wye [the north-eastern boundary of Ergyng]." (Book of Llandaff, Rees, p. 374:- the diocese had "five hundred wards [extending from] the bay of Severn [to] Ergyng, and Anergyng, from Mochros on the banks of the Wye, as far as the island Terthi" [Barry Island], p. 311)

570-600 *Saxon incursions into Ergyng at the time of King Ithael. Moccas, then a part of Anergyng, and the northern Golden Valley were plundered and laid waste by Saxons crossing the River Wye, but the Welsh hung on:*

"Be it known that Rhiadda bought one uncial [about 108 acres] of the land Guruarch, with all commonage in field and in woods, in water and in pasture, for twenty four cows, a Saxon woman, a valuable sword, and a powerful horse, with the approbation of King Ithael." (Book of Llandaff, Rees, 435)

c600 *Morlas alive: a contemporary of King Ithael.*

629 ●*Death of Beibio and burial at the Llwyn above the Monnow – now Trellwyn.*

c600-630 *Brengi buys land at Rhibo Mountain and dedicates it to the Church.*

c640 *Gwen, son of the British Chieftain, Llywarch Hen, slain at the Ford of Morlas, and buried at Llwyn Beibio.*

c642 *Death of Beuno, son of Brengi, brother to Beibio.*

Llanveynoe perpetuates his name.

c646 Death of Llywarch Hen, at a venerable age for his time.

c700 The Saxon perception of woodland plenty:

"In winter and in summer the forest is alike behung with fruits; ne'er will the leaves fade there beneath the sky, nor will flame injure them, never, through all the ages, until a final change befall the world." (From 'The Phoenix', an Anglo Saxon poem attributed to Cynewulf, in Mase, 1927, p. xxxviii)

(Prophetic words in the light of tropical forest decimation...)

c760 Battle between the Welsh and the Saxons near Hereford. (Anglo-Saxon Chronicle) Saxon Mercia expanding.

757-796 Construction of Offa's Dyke, under the Mercian Kings Offa I and Offa II, as the agreed boundary between Mercia and Wales. The Herefordshire portion was intermittent due to the existence of large tracts of forest on the low-lying ground to the north of the River Wye.

"...the unbroken woodland cover of the Dark Ages was so extensive that it was known to the British simply as Y Coed... On the fringes of Y Coed, the great woodland of the Midland Triangle, forests... offered sites for new hamlets and new farmlands from the period of the leahs of the later Anglian colonisation to the emparkments by manorial lords from the Conquest to the eighteenth century." (D. Sylvester, 1969, The Rural Landscape of the Welsh Borderland, 95 and 101)

800-900 Dark Age darkness... Saxons and Angles continue to infiltrate into Welsh territory, and to settle on the edge of Y Coed. Woodland plenty a common perception:

"In each tree I saw something that I needed at home. Therefore, I advise anyone who can, who has many wagons,

to direct his steps to the same wood where I cut the posts. Let him fetch more for himself, and load his wagons with fair branches, so he may weave many a neat wall, and erect many a rare dwelling, and build a fair town, therein to dwell merrily and comfortably both winter and summer, as I have not yet done." (King Alfred's Preface to his translation of the Soliloquies of St. Augustine. Translated from Anglo-Saxon by Catherine's friend at Ross Library.)

Alfred, who was by reputation skilled in woodcraft and house-building, a timber engineer of his day, is apparently comparing the plentiful state of the remnants of Y Coed with the wealth that lay waiting to be used in the writings of his religion - Christianity - a metaphor which puts the Saxon perspective on the woods of the time: the wealth was there for the taking. A comment upon the Serpent's ways with trees and with minds, both to be exploited to the exclusion of Ceridwen.

One recent estimate is that the Anglo-Saxons grubbed up 32 acres of woodland per day for approximately 500 years: "...a rate which only the twentieth century has been able to surpass." (O. Rackham, op cit., 1980)

931 Athelstan, King of England, 924-940, received homage from the Welsh Princes at Hereford and recognised the River Wye as the boundary between England and Wales from Chepstow to Hay-on-Wye. (Duncumb, History of Hereford, 1804, Vol. 1, 158).

991 'linden bucklers' (small round shields) and 'shield walls' are mentioned in the Anglo-Saxon poems 'The Battle of Brunanburgh (937) and 'The Battle of Maldon (991):

"With there hammered blades, the sons of Edward

Clove the shield-wall and hacked the linden bucklers
As was instinctive in them, from their ancestry,
To defend their land, their treasures and their homes,
In frequent battle against each enemy."
(Translated from the Battle of Brunanburgh in the Parker
Chronicle AD 925-37 by G.N. Garmonsway and quoted by P.
Hunter Blair, An Introduction to Anglo-Saxon England (1970,
p.88).
Lime wood is the lightest of the European broadleaves, and
carves well. It seems that the Anglo-Saxon words for lime
tree and shield were synonymous: ie 'lind'.

"I stood under linden wood, under the light shield..."
"...hand grasped shield, yellow limewood." (Beowulf)

***c1000** The western edge of the Golden Valley had become the*
limit of the Saxon advance into Ewyas.
***1046** Beginning of pre-conquest Norman settlement in Ewyas*
with the construction of a motte and bailey castle at the future
Ewyas Harold by Normans friendly with Edward the
Confessor.
***1066** King Rhydderch reigned in Ewyas and Gwent Iscoed.*
William of Normandy defeated Harold, the Earl of
Wessex, at the Battle of Hastings, and annexed England.
***1067** Ewyas and Archenfield laid waste in August by the*
resistance movement of Edric, 'The Savage', and his Welsh
allies.
***1030 Cal,Yr.BP** ●The Spirit of the Early Flowering Limes*
migrates from Llwyn Beibio, as the Normans build their
'lair', another motte and bailey castle.

"When the Normans came to Herefordshire, they found wide stretches of woodland remaining, especially in the north-west and mid-west, and still more so south of the middle Wye. Compared with many south-eastern English and east Midland counties, the proportion of woodland was high, but compared with the greater part of the Midland Forest Triangle immediately to the east, it was only moderate. There remained, therefore, a considerable area of the county available for colonising, and even the better settled parts still carried populations sufficiently sparse to permit development. The mild climate and general air of fertility made this one of the Normans' most favoured counties and, to this day, the map and the landscape alike reflect their partiality." (D. Sylvester, The Southern Marches, 1969, pp. 356-7)

1074 *Another Welsh raid into Ewyas.*

1086 *Domesday Survey completed:*

Hays - enclosures within woodland - are recorded for eleven places in the county. Four references in the survey to 'assarts', a French word meaning the taking of land from the forest, "are unique in the whole of Domesday Book." (Atkin in Darby & Terrett, The Domesday Geography of Midland England, 1954, 85).

The picture of Archenfield is one of a sparsely settled district still recovering from the turmoil of its recent past, and with much waste land, that is, neglected land previously productive, as in the time of Edward the Confessor. Nine of the fourteen manors mentioned were described as being waste. Woodland was extensive and there was already Royal Forest, woodland legally set aside for the King. Welshmen were the main landholders and Welsh customs prevailed, their dues being rendered in honey and sheep. A total of 91 sesters of honey were paid in dues by the Welshmen of Archenfield. The waste manors, which lay in the south against the Forest of Dean, were regenerating with trees, a condition that was exceptional to the main trend in England at the time - the retreat of woodland.

The picture in Ewyas was even wilder. It, too, was Welsh but now under Norman control. Only one place was recorded in the survey. It rendered "15 sesters of honey, 15 pigs when men are there..." (Domesday Book: Herefordshire)

***1095** Hugh de Laci was given Ewyas by William Rufus, successor to William the Conqueror.*

***890 Cal.Yr.BP** •Spirit of the Early Flowering Limes ensconced at Llannerch Hudol on the south-western side of Mynydd y rhibo. The period when the wood-carver's house in Gulible was burned down?*

***1125-1132** The Book of Llandaff compiled, representing a history of the diocese of that name.*

***1147** The order of Cistercian monks establish themselves in Ewyas by founding an abbey at Dore in the Golden Valley.*

***1150** The Forest of Dean: perhaps the last approximation to 'wildwood' in the country; still with wolves and wild boar. (Rackham, 1976 & 1980) Reaching as far north as the edges of Archenfield, it would have been the largest and the loudest echo of Y Coed to be felt by the Spirit of the Early Flowering Limes.*

***1175-1230** The building of the Cistercian Abbey at Llanthony.*

***1188** The Itinerary through Wales by Giraldus Cambrensis.*

***1190-1210** Anonymous Middle English allegorical poem, 'The Owl and the Nightingale' contains the earliest mention* *of a 'linde' as a hedgerow tree: (line 1750)'The wrenne sat in hore linde' (Atkins, The Owl and the Nightingale, 1922).*

1146-1220 *The life span of Giraldus Cambrensis whose writings shed some light on the woodland history of Ewyas and Archenfield. He was Gerald de Barri, Archdeacon of Brecon and Bishop-elect of St. Davids, who travelled widely in south-west Herefordshire, and who wrote The Itinerary Through Wales and a Description of Wales. He said of the Welsh, "...they neither inhabit towns, villages nor castles, but lead a solitary life in the woods, on the borders of which they do not erect sumptuous palaces, nor lofty stone buildings, but content themselves with small huts made of the boughs of trees twisted together, constructed with little labour and expense, and sufficient to endure throughout the year." (Translated by R.C. Hoare, Everyman, 1908)*

1180 *Hugh de Lacy, Lord of Ewyas, in an edict to his people addressed it "...to my servants, whether French, English, or Welsh." (A.T. Bannister, 1902)*

1194 *Geraldus was critical of the land-use practices of the Cistercian monastery of Abbey Dore which made assarts in Treville Wood, a Royal Forest lying between the abbey and Kingstone. He accused the monks of ".changing an oak wood into a wheat field." The abbey continued to make clearances during the next two hundred years. (D.H. Williams, 1976, White Monks in Gwent and the Border.) - (Times have not changed!)*

1213 *Treville Wood covered 2013 acres, 700 of which belonged to Abbey Dore. (Williams, op cit. 1976) How loudly did this woodland expanse echo?*

1216 *King John 'burned the towns and destroyed the castles'* *of Hay and Radnor. (Red Book of Hergest, 209)*

1217 *Charta de Foresta whereby the extent of and, therefore, the authority of the Crown within the Royal Forests was recognised. The Charta was revised in 1225.*

1223 *Henry Piggott was lord of Ewyas. (Red Book of Hergest, 227)*

1231 *"That year king Henry built Painscastle in Elfael.*

Thereupon, because of the hostilities that had been bred between Llywelyn ap Iorwerth and the king, Llywelyn burned the town of Baldwin's Castle and Radnor and Hay and Brecon, and he destroyed the castles to the ground." (Red Book of Hergest, 229)

1233 *The Cistercian abbey at Llanthony in the Vale of Ewyas was burned down and later rebuilt with local timber from Ewyas and Monmouthshire.*

1238 *Humphrey de Bohun, Ist Earl of Hereford, (grandson of Humphrey de Bohun, the 'Bearded One', who attended the Conqueror and who eschewed the custom in Normandy at the time of shaving his face), was given custody of the Welsh Marches by Henry 111.*

A Peter Corbet was enjoined by King Henry III: "...to use all possible means for the killing and destroying of wolves in all Forests, Parks and other places in the Counties of Gloucester, Worcester, Hereford, Shropshire and Stafford, and to require all the King's people to assist in ridding the country of these noxious beasts." (Close Rolls 17, Henry III, Duncumb, 1804, p. 75)

1250 *Compilation of the Black Book of Carmarthen and the Book of Aneirin.*

1252 *The men of 'Irchenfeud' obtained from the king the* *deforestation - removal of Royal Forest status - of the Lordship of Archenfield, except 3 parcels of land. (J.H. Matthews, 1912, Collections Towards the History and Antiquities of the County of Hereford, a continuation of Duncumb's History, vol. 5, page 13).*

1266 Death of Roger de la Haye, owner of the Manor of Llandyfrig Haye.

1265-1300 The time of a John Tregoz, who may have owned Llandyfrig Court, briefly, and who gave a licence for someone to buy a certain burgage, "...near my wood which is called Haya". The witnesses were the Seneschal of Ewias, a John de Danhurste, and the Constable of Ewias, a Roger of Marcle. (Cartulary of the Priory of Ewias: Bannister, 1902, page 52).

1275 Book of Taliesin compiled.

1277 Humphrey de Bohun, 2nd Earl of Hereford, Lord of Eardisley, Huntingdon, and all the March between the rivers Arrow and Wye.

1280 Treaty of Rhuddlan between the Welsh and the English pacified the borderland for the time being.

1291 The heyday of Abbey Dore. A sheep flock of 3000 and 17 granges. (Williams, 1976) One of the granges now belongs to Carling Medlar who continues the time-honoured practice of the White Monks of changing woods out of all recognition. (Milo and Giraldus might have something in common when they eventually meet up)

1297 'As late as 1297 in England the sale of lime tree bark (corticus tilie) was reckoned in forest returns, and this use must have extended back into remote history'. (Godwin, History of the British Flora, 1975, p.164).

1350 Woodland in Ewyas now fragmented into the forests of Treville, the biggest, Maescoyte or Maescoed, Hene or Hamme, Monnow, and Olchon. (W. Rees, 1933, South Wales and the Border in the Fourteenth Century).

1358 The Priory of Ewias suppressed by the Abbot of Gloucester who complained to the Bishop of St. Davids that "...when monks well-trained in the life and conversation of the monastery are sent one after the other to stay at Ewias, they bring back such worldly and as it were boorish habits that, the contagion spreading to their brethren, the religious tone of the said monastery is seriously wounded." (Bannister, 1902, page 64). Since my sister wasn't around then the only distractions were lime spirits...

c1375-80 Earliest complete text of Red Book of Hergest.

1398 King Richard II was petitioned about the stealing of 94 "great oaks of the best" from 'Trivel' Forest. (Williams, 1976)

c1400

> *"The leaves launch from the linden and light on*
> *the ground...*
> *By a mountain next morning he makes his way*
> *Into a forest fastness, fearsome and wild;*
> *High hills on either hand, with hoar woods below,*
> *Oaks old and huge by the hundred together.*
> *The hazel and the hawthorn were all intertwined*
> *With rough ravelled moss, that raggedly hung,*
> *With many birds unblithe on bare twigs*
> *That piped most piteously for pain of the cold."*

(Anon. From Sir Gawain and the Green Knight, c.1375-1400, in Norton Anthology of English Literature, vol. 1, 1968, lines

526 and 740-47).

1404 *The War of Owain Glyn Dŵr: Archdeacon of Hereford wrote to Henry IV:-*

"The Welsh rebels in great numbers have entered Archenfield, and there burnt houses, killed the inhabitants, taken prisoners, and ravaged the country, to the unsupportable damage of the county. We pray to our sovereign Lord that he will come in his Royal person, otherwise we shall be utterly destroyed, which God forbid... Written in haste at Hereford, June 10th." (Bannister, 1902, page 79)

1407-8 *Prince Henry (Hal, the future Henry V) eventually subdued Glyn Dŵr, turning him into a guerrilla fugitive in the Welsh hills. He later pardoned Owain who died at Monnington in the care of his daughters. (Bannister, op cit, 81)*

1529 *Lease of a grange at Elchon stated that the leasee could have "housebote and heybote" out of the Abbot's wood at Dore, but that he was not to cut "The grete oke, linden, elm, or polle wood." (Williams, 1976, p. 42)*

1536 & 1542 *The Welsh Acts of Union which united England and Wales.*

1560 *Treville Wood down to 1000 acres in extent and about to suffer another period of deforestation and assarting. (Williams, 1976)*

1583 *A Survey of the Manor of Llandyfrig Court.*

1610 *Treatise and Discourse of the Lawes of the Forest by John Manwood.*

1648-1721 *Grinling Gibbons: famous Baroque woodcarver who worked almost exclusively in lime-wood, specialising in* cascades of natural history objects, especially flowers and fruits. His carvings adorn St Paul's Cathedral, Kensington Palace, Hampton Court, Chatsworth, and numerous country houses.

1616 *Requirements of the Deer Park by Gervase Markham.*

1667 *A Survey of the Manor of Ewyas which refers to the forests of Hene and Olchon.*

1707 *The illustrious map of Llandyfrig Court.*

1753 *The publication of A Treatise on Forest Trees, by William Watkins, a curate of Hay-on-Wye.*

"To the Reader: What gave occasion to the following Pages was the continual Devastation of Wood in this Kingdom; and... the Consequence such a Devastation would soon occasion to this Nation in general."

"There is such a vast Quantity of Timber daily cut down, and very little raised in its Stead. A very deplorable Circumstance, and must soon end in an utter Extirpation of the Species..."

1790-1802 *The period when Rosamond de Bohun made her visits to Llandyfrig Court, and came under the influence of the Spirit of the 'Early Flowering Linden'.*

200 Cal.Yr.BP ●*Migration of the Spirit of the Early Flowering Limes into its present tree, the Melglyn Stoggle.*

1802 *Great fellings of Navy Timber from Coed Tirion Glas and other places on the estate of Llandyfrig Court.*

1867 *A lamentation on the loss of trees at Harewood near Hoarwithy beside the Wye in the eastern reaches of Archenfield: "The last thirty or forty years has made a difference in the landscape that at first sight would scarcely be credited. If we may borrow a term from our geological* *pages, a 'denudation' of timber has taken place. Not alone have hedgerows vanished under the modern fiat of enlarged enclosures, but whole masses of coppice and plantation are gone; of woody knolls, and deep glen-like 'roughs', which helped to give that alternation of tangled intricacy and open glade which forms the most romantic expression of country scenery." ('The Trees of Harewood', Transactions of the Woolhope Naturalist Club, 1807, p. 111).*

1873 *Kilvert: Monday, 21st July:*

"A splendid summer's day, burning hot, sitting under the linden reading Memorials of a Quiet Life, Augustus Hare's book. As I sat there my mind went through a fierce struggle. Right or wrong? The right conquered, the sin was repented and put away and the rustle of the wind and the melodious murmurs of innumerable bees in the hives overhead suddenly seemed to me to take the sound of distant music, organs. And I thought I heard the harps of the angels rejoicing in heaven over a sinner that had repented. Then I thought I saw an angel in an azure robe coming towards me across the lawn, but it was only the blue sky through the feathering branches of the lime." (Plomer, 220-21).

Only the blue sky?...

1940-1944 *"In the Second World War, much of the native Tilia cordata and perhaps the native Tilia platyphyllos along the limestone gorges of the Wye was felled to provide plywood for Mosquito planes" (Forest of Dean, National Forest Park Guide, Forestry Commission, 1947.) 8000 Mosquito fighter-bombers were made!*

1952 *"At any rate, dragons are not extinct, for a peculiarly virulent one is, as I write, ravaging the fair county of Carmarthenshire, devouring its oak-woods, driving out its sheep-farmers, and from its scorching breath leaving devastation far and wide. But, alas, we are powerless to slay this dragon, which is of the state, not the village." i.e. the Forestry Commission. (H.J. Massingham: 'The Southern Marches', pp. 258-9.)*

1981 *Epitaph: 50% of the ancient woods - the remnants of Y Coed - have gone to agriculture or coniferous forestry since 1945. The limewoods of Herefordshire have suffered. The Spirits of the lime trees have suffered. We have all suffered...*

CHAPTER 29

'My flowers towered high
fragrance wafted far
As Gentleness returned to soothe my Soul
The Enchantment of my Spell was great again
I was safe within my Tree within Y Coed.'

Spirit of Y Coed

When Owen came within sight of the tree, he was sweating and out of breath. He had bounded across the fields from the smallholding, covering the distance twice as fast as usual. With the Stoggle in view, he reduced his pace of movement. Though still at the bottom of the dingle, he could see that the venerable lime was now fully in flower. Its crown was tinged with a pale yellow sheen which brightened erratically in the changing sunlight. This was the day he had been waiting for. None of the other small-leaved limes in the wood, nor in the district, were in flower. Their flowers were only just forming. Owen was unaware that they usually came into flower at the beginning of July.

Moving forward briskly, he sniffed deeply, curious to know how far afield the aroma of the flowers wafted. He should have realised that the scent was more likely to rise above the dingle than sink into it on such a warm day. He stopped a couple of times to sniff in long, deep inhalations. The way he cocked his head, advanced, and cocked it again, carried a hint of the jerking movements of de Bohun. All he had to do was talk to himself and the transition would be complete. But words were impossible while sniffing and at the same time stooping to cope with the steepness of the climb.

As no smell assailed his nostrils, he gave up. For the last fifty paces, he inhaled normally, knowing that something subtly delicious would soon be detected. But, instead of being overcome by scent, he was assailed by the communal movement of a multitude of bees, sucking one of their favourite nectars. Scent or no scent, he was mesmerised by the sound of humming; by the intensity of it as he drew closer to the tree; and by the incredible number of bees combining in unison as they drifted amongst the flowers.

It was at this point that the fragrance of the flowers reached his nostrils. He inhaled slowly and deeply through his freckled nose to enjoy the smell to the full, but it was intermittent and variable in its strength. Either the light breeze or the thermal up-draughts from the vale were affecting the movement of air about the tree. Or was it that the flowers were only profuse on one side of the lime, the southern side, where the blossom and the blade-like bracts created the creamy sheen he had seen from below? Elsewhere on the crown, the flowers were sparse and recessive against the backcloth of leaves.

While not as profuse as in the past, in the days when the tree had its entire crown, there was sufficient blossom for rejoicing. In a spasm of elation, Owen almost broke into a celebratory dance around the trunk. He checked himself, and looked about to ensure that he was alone. Inwardly, he went into raptures of delight. The aroma lifted his head and his legs made a swift recovery from the exertion of the climb. He glanced down at them in surprise at the lightness of his contact with the ground. The delicacy of the blossom's lemon colouration softened and lightened his being as well. The gentleness was ethereal. And it was familiar. He was reminded of two things: the feelings he experienced when the Spirit floated to his soul; and the flavour of lime flower tea.

Once accustomed to the pungency of the moment, his mind came back to the other reason for his presence at the tree. He had time to spare; enough time to see if anything could happen when so many bees were busy draining the tree of its energy. Automatically, he settled into the seat at its base. In a token gesture of intent, he read aloud some of the passages from the last message. The haunting lines and the refrains blended well with the bees and the scent, but they did not remove him from the present. Nor did any tingles or feelings of floating claim his attention. Gradually, the droning and the occasional surges of scent made him drowsy. Then, when he felt his body relaxing during a brief moment of absent-mindedness, he jumped up for fear of being overtaken by the Spirit before he was properly ready. Although the buzzard was not in the tree, nor in the immediate vicinity, he had yet to learn if the blossom alone could induce a communication from the Spirit,

Keeping what he thought was a safe distance from the Stoggle he walked about, climbing onto the rocks, trying every angle to find the best wave of scent while continually looking across the dingle for the person he had arranged to meet. The raised platform of the rocks was the sweetest vantage place. There were moments when he glanced at the tree and wondered if the whole experience was real or imaginary. He had to arrest himself from these thoughts as well.

Twenty-five minutes elapsed, during which time he became progressively more apprehensive. He had arrived early because, after deciding to confide in someone – a decision which itself had taken an entire day of difficult thought - he had become restless and impatient waiting for the appointed hour. Once he had made the decision, the process of deciding what to say and how to go about saying it, had occupied another day of indecision. As two forty-five approached, his mind wandered off into second thoughts; thoughts which he arrested and cast aside, telling himself that the decision had been made and had to stay. Arranging to meet someone at the ultimate moment in the yearly cycle of the Stoggle was perhaps a mistake after all. Or was it? For the umpteenth time he looked across the dingle. No-one was in sight.

The appointed hour passed. Second thoughts intruded again. Once more, he asked himself the questions he had toiled over in the previous two days. Why shouldn't he be believed? He had the Spirit's messages and pleas, written in handwriting which bore a startling resemblance to the script of Rosamond de Bohun who, in Suzy's view, had been affected by a lime tree in the same dingle. He had corroborated, from reputable secondary sources, the various people, places and events referred to by the Spirit, none of which had been known to him before. How could he not be believed? But was it a good idea to divulge the secret to someone in front of the Spirit? Would it know? Could it see what happened around it only through the eyes of the buzzard? Or did it feel the presence of humans - the trampling of their feet upon the ground; emanations from their minds?

He looked again across the dingle at the forestry gate and the plantation. There was still no-one in sight.

"Looking for someone, Owen?" came a familiar voice from behind him.

He spun round with his heart in his mouth, spluttering as he said, "Matilda! How did you get here?"

"I came another way, up over the mountain. That's why I'm a little late. I thought you might hide until I arrived, so I thought I'd creep up on you. Anyway, it's the best approach to the tree when it's in flower. You feel the full strength of the scent... Are you alright? You've gone very pale."

"Yes... yes... I'm okay. You just startled me, that's all."

"I know I did", said Matilda, gleefully, in the manner of her husband. "Suzy used to hide whenever we arranged to meet here. One time, she hid amongst the rocks over there and kept making funny noises while I waited for her. This reminds me of my meetings with her. She always had something incredible to tell me... Isn't this scent heavenly? And the tree - how beautiful it is? Aren't we lucky to be here? Now then, what have you got in store for me?"

This series of questions by Matilda gave Owen a chance to compose himself. His heart was back in its right place, his throat had moistened again, and he had ceased trembling.

Taking a deep breath, and then walking a few yards to the rocks above the tree, he prefaced his explanation by first asking Matilda to come and sit down. She came over to him wearing a friendly wide-eyed gaze of curiosity, and sat down in front of him on a slab of rock, breathing in the scent, her eyes closed. He stepped to one side, looking down at the ground, and began, sparing only the occasional quick glance into her face.

"Do you recall that when we last met here, you asked to see my notebook?"

"Yes, I do", she replied, smiling at the seriousness of his whole manner.

"Well, here it is. I want you to read the pages that I have marked. Only those pages, not the ones I've joined together with paper clips. It's important that you look at nothing else, and I must have your word on that".

She gave it with a kindly smile and a nod.

"And here is another notebook which you can browse through after reading the first one, which is the most important. I've marked the critical passages. I'll go for a short walk while you're reading. It should not take you more than about thirty to forty-five minutes, but I'll stay away for longer so you can mull it all over. All you need to know is that the passages written in the handwriting which smacks of Rosamond were written while I was at the base of the Stoggle over there, and that I did not know I had written them until after it had been done. And on each occasion there was the same buzzard in the tree - the Eerie Shriek. You will realise the significance of this when you have read everything. All the entries written in my normal handwriting are what I have subsequently discovered or surmised. Okay?"

Matilda nodded, and uttered a quiet "yes", completely

baffled but excited by the mystery of it all. After taking Owen's telephone call in the morning, she had been intrigued but had never expected anything like this to happen. She stood up as he handed her his notebooks before walking off towards the summit of the mountain on his way to Llannerch Hudol and back. She watched him walk away. Outwardly, she had remained calm, as calm as ever, but inwardly she was experiencing the excitement she often felt when Suzy had concocted something. She kept the notebooks closed until Owen was out of sight, not because she did not want him to see her relish the opening, but because she wanted to savour the mysteriousness of the moment alone. She had no idea at all what he had in store for her. It was to eclipse anything Suzy had concocted...

On his return, Owen resorted to furtiveness too. He crept up on Matilda by way of the same descent from the summit that she had taken to surprise him earlier. There was little to conceal him as he drew closer to the rocks, but he hoped that he might get a chance to see her manner before she saw him. Approaching quietly, he saw her standing beneath the Stoggle gazing up into its enormous crown of waning limbs, holding one notebook open in her left hand. Drawing even closer, without being detected, he could just make out the sound of her reciting one of the refrains from the Spirit's second message:-

The dreadful Serpent Dyn will burn Y Coed
And be
Forever fire
Forever ire
Forever dire...

The words were uttered slowly and profoundly, with a touch of sadness, and far more sensitively than her husband might deliver some grave lines from a Shakespearian tragedy. Intuitively, Matilda sensed that someone was nearby. Calmly and unhurriedly, she closed the notebook and turned around. Owen was only a few paces away from the rocks.

"Owen, this is incredible. It's beautiful", she said, holding the notebooks in the air. "I knew I would miss Suzy's engaging fantasies this summer, but I never expected to be presented with such an enchanting story as this during her absence."

"Fantasy! Enchanting story!" exclaimed Owen. "Is that all you think it is?"

Matilda attempted to undo the misunderstanding, and moved to retrieve the situation, but Owen continued before she could reply, his response a mixture of disappointment and tension.

"It's a true story; and I'm going to do something to help the Spirit return to what is left of its original wilderness, if I can. I chose to confide in you because I thought you would be as sensitive to the Spirit's plea as I am."

"I know its true, Owen. I do believe you. And I am as sensitive to it as you thought I would be. But it is also enchanting. It's meant to be enchanting otherwise we mortals wouldn't want to help. I believe it all completely, and I can't tell you how honoured I am that you have disclosed the secret to me. I believed it immediately, when I read the messages and saw the handwriting."

Owen became reassured by these remarks, but it took him a while to settle down. Matilda's gentleness in putting him at ease helped to soothe the tension which had built up inside him during his absence, but he was not quite ready to respond. Matilda continued to reassure him.

"When Humphrey talks about tree spirits, I always take it with a pinch of salt because he is forever talking to trees, using them as the audience for his theatrical performances. I have preferred to listen to our trees and to feel their presence. And there have been times when this place has had strange effects upon me. I have stood here more than once wondering if there is someone with me - an invisible being. Your revelation has only tipped a mind that has been primed already by a lifetime of listening - to trees and to Humphrey; listening which has made me wonder if my soul is being heard. The years have shown me that Humphrey's mental state is improved when he talks to his trees, although he has never actually said that he has been contacted. Whether or not Humphrey is capable of extra-sensory perception, I know that you are. Suzy told me you were."

"Suzy said that!" exclaimed Owen incredulously. He was so astonished by this disclosure that he experienced a curious relief from the pressure of confiding in Matilda and from doubting her sympathy. While he stood motionless for a few moments, she moved back to the rocks.

"Let's go through these entries in your notebooks together, Owen. Let's sit here on the rocks. You should appreciate that I am just as intrigued by it all as you must have been when it first happened. Oh! That scent." She closed her eyes again.

They sat together and Owen took her through the entries stage by stage.

"I came up here one day after Milo had shown me the Stoggle at the end of his introduction to the Mountain. It's an ideal place to repair to, you know that. I sat down at the base of the tree on its lower side where there is a natural seat, a very comfortable seat with a clear view over and down the dingle. I often become a bit dreamy when I take myself off to what my sister calls my 'retreats'. You now know what my initial thoughts were at that time, and the strange feelings I experienced. When I exposed myself to the force a second time, I was completely overtaken. My next awareness of my surroundings was the sound of a jet roaring overhead. I had been sitting and writing beneath the tree for almost two hours, totally unconscious of what I was doing. When I got up, I was dazed and very unsteady on my feet, as I was when you disturbed me. When I saw what I had written, I couldn't believe it."

"You must have been bewildered. What an experience!" exclaimed Matilda.

"When you disturbed me here last week, I had not been meditating; I had just received the third message from the Stoggle's Spirit. That's why I looked a little unsettled. And there is more to come for the Spirit's story has yet to recount the modern phase of its existence. So far, all that has been related to me is completely new to my understanding. None of the story could have come from deep-seated knowledge. I've checked the authenticity of the names mentioned, the personal names and the place-names, and also the events touched upon. It is obvious that 'Y Coed' is the original forest cover of the Marches. I found the reference to it in one of Catherine's books. If you understand any Welsh you might know that 'Dyn' is man; so we are the Serpent. Catherine has unwittingly translated all the Welsh names for me, and has guided my researches, although I haven't revealed these secrets to her yet."

"Why haven't you told her?" asked Matilda, interrupting again.

Owen had expected this question to arise and had not really sorted out in his mind how he was going to answer it. He side-stepped the question by simply saying that he would come to it later, and then carried on with his explanation.

"I have yet to understand why most of the names used are Welsh. I can only assume that it has something to do with the special contact, which seems to have lasted for a long time, between the Spirit and Beibio; or, I suppose, because this area has been Welsh speaking longer than English has prevailed. The Spirit admits that it is not used to my tongue.

"The coincidence of the name Beibio with Llwyn Beibio - 'the Grove of Beibio' - which is the site of the motte and bailey castle near Tre-llwyn – the 'Homestead of the Grove' - is irrefutable evidence that the story is true. So is the fact that Beibio, as one of the sons of Brengi, who owned land on Rhibo Mountain in the seventh century, actually existed. The warrior, who was buried beneath the limes at the grove, must have been Gwen, the son of Llywarch Hen, a more or less contemporary British chieftain. Gwen was slain at the Ford of Morlas, which is thought to be Marlas near Kilpeck. The grove could have been a sort of sepulchre, a place of spiritual significance locally, and even regionally, in view of Gwen's burial there.

"Before the Spirit occupied the grove, probably around the beginning of the seventh century, it could have resided anywhere in the western reaches of Ergyng, or Archenfield as we know it. Wherever it was, it must have been close to one of the main thoroughfares of the time, which would explain the connection with Merlin. The old lane on the ridge which Cath says was a

Celtic trackway linking the provinces of Brechiniog, Ewyas, and Ergyng, may be the thoroughfare.

"I had not heard of the two prophecies, attributed to Merlin, in Geoffrey of Monmouth's Histories of the Kings of Britain - more irrefutable evidence that the messages are real. I've tried to find a reference in old local documents to a 'Merlin Tree', but I have not been successful - it's probably too far back in time. But Catherine dug up a reference to the Latin 'Tilia' for me in an almost contemporary Welsh version of the history.

"Anyway, when the Spirit was at Llwyn Beibio, the site would have been a very special part of a more extensive Coed Tirion Glas - a forest full of gentle limes, as its name implies. If there were other spirits then their existence may explain the name given to the Mountain - 'Bewitched'."

Owen wanted to continue but he had to pause for a break, which gave Matilda another chance to interject.

"Bewitched, and also haunted by the owls and the buzzards. Describe the buzzard to me, Owen."

His description of the bird and its call confirmed to Matilda that it was the Eerie Shriek. No other buzzard had such a strange mew. She said that Humphrey believed it was the parent of all the buzzards on the Mountain.

"An enchanted mountain; an enchanted bird; and now, an enchanted tree. How beautiful..." said Matilda.

Owen now accepted – or thought he did - that Matilda genuinely believed in the existence of a tree spirit in the Stoggle. She kept repeating how she had always felt that the Stoggle and the head of the dingle were somehow more than special in the earthly sense of the word. She told him that she and Suzy had often talked about this "specialness", as she called it, but could never touch it, or even define it - they just revelled in it. On several occasions, they had felt light-headed, and could not understand why, although the perfume from the flowers had a tendency to be uplifting before inducing drowsiness if too much of it was inhaled. The more she harked back to her own experiences at the tree, the more enthused she became; and the more Owen heard, the more secure he became in his choice of confidant.

After almost an hour of intense discussion, during which he gained insights into exactly how she had reacted to the entries while he was absent, Matilda came out with the inevitable request:

"Can I see if you will be contacted today? I could let you know how it all happens."

This was another of the questions he had anticipated. He accepted that if he was going to confide in someone, the ultimate proof of his experiences lay in an observation of actual contact. But he was not sure if the presence of another person would permit contact to take place.

"Yes, I would like you to witness the receipt of another message, but I'm not sure that contact will occur with you beside me, or if contact is possible with such buzzing activity in the tree."

"But I don't have to be beside you, Owen. I could position myself discreetly on the other side of the dingle, or in the dingle itself, where I would be below the roots of the tree."

"It might be better if you hid altogether, because contact has occurred so far only when the buzzard is in the tree, and it might not land if you're here as well. Anyway, I'm not even sure that I will be able to put myself into the right frame of mind to be contacted. I have to be receptive, the buzzard has to be present, and the Spirit has to be moved enough to reach me. The chance of all three occurring today is unlikely. You know, it's taken a lot out of me telling you this secret. I put myself in a position to be contacted before you arrived, but nothing happened. Let's leave it till another day."

"Alright, I understand. My enthusiasm got the better of me. But I hope I can see it happen soon. Now then, what assistance do you want from me? What plan have you devised to help the Spirit get back into the wood? Or haven't you decided yet?"

"Yes, I've got some ideas. Though the Spirit is separated from its natural environment by the bare space of the dingle and the gloom of the conifers, I believe that the surviving lime coppice in the plantation, if allowed to grow up properly, could provide a pathway of root contact for it to migrate into Coed Tirion Glas. Some of it has already recovered after the gale of last year."

"But where would it go?" interrupted Matilda, earnestly.

"That has been solved for me by the Eerie Shriek. As in times past, the eagles, the kites, and, latterly, the buzzards, have scanned the woods in search of new trees for the Spirit to inhabit. Its current scout, the Shriek, actually took me to the next tree - guided me to it with its call and its flight. There can be no other lime to match it for suitability. I haven't seen another like it in the wood or anywhere else. I've called it 'The Emergent Lime' because it's the one whose top rises above all the other trees in your wood. You must know the one I mean?"

"I do. It's the one below the path, somewhere near the top of the Dark Dell. It's a superb tree. I first visited it to collect some flowers for Suzy, but it's rather difficult to get to, and its branches are far too high for that. And now you mention it, Humphrey and I have seen The Eerie Shriek circling above it countless times, and even landing in it. In fact, Humphrey concluded one day that whenever the buzzard glided above the wood, its circles, however large, were always centred on that tree. What a coincidence..."

"There can't be any other place. I knew the moment I found it. I had seen it all before - a lime tree, a dingle, wild service trees, an apple tree. I had seen it in my mind; it was so familiar, uncannily familiar. It has all the ingredients; the same ingredients I wrote down when I first sat beneath the Stoggle and tried to imagine what the original forest cover would have been like. Isn't that uncanny?"

Matilda was enthralled; so enthralled, and intent on listening to Owen, that she urged him to continue.

"Though the lime coppice could be revived, there is the problem of the gap between the tree and the plantation - the 'void of hollow ground where searching roots once swelled the earth with life'. The aspens, which have grown up on the edge of the conifers, could fill this gap, if allowed to - if their suckers were protected and permitted to extend around the top of the dingle. What is needed, therefore, is a fenced enclosure to encourage this to happen, and the thinning of the conifers to favour all the surviving broadleaved trees, and to give the lime coppice free rein."

"Is that why you have revealed everything to me - to get the plantation managed appropriately?" asked Matilda, continuing to delve into the reasons why Owen had chosen her.

"No", said Owen, quietly, fidgeting. "I could... I could have kept the whole matter to myself, but I wanted to involve somebody else. Even though I think I know what to do, the impact of the responsibility has made me restless. The Spirit needs my support, and I need support as well. Obviously, your help in getting the plantation sorted out will be essential. But I didn't plan it that way."

Matilda wanted to ask how he had planned it, but she was aware that Owen had been unsettled by her question, so she did not press her enquiry any further for the time being. Instead, she turned to the other essential link in his proposals.

"How are you going to get Catherine and her family to control the grazing in the dingle – to enclose it?"

"Simply to ask if the Melglyn Stoggle - my obsession, as everyone knows by now - could be reunited with the wildwood. It's only the top part of the dingle which needs to be enclosed. If you and Humphrey agree to return the plantation to its broadleaved state, then my concern - or rather, my hair-brained scheme - will be even more plausible. They will all think I'm crackers, but then, if it's linked to something Humphrey wants to do we might be seen as little boys playing with trees."

"You might indeed. So what do you want me to say to Humphrey? Have you thought that far ahead, yet?"

"Yes. I want to reveal to him that I think the Stoggle has a spirit, but without revealing what I have disclosed to you, and without showing him the messages. I'd rather keep that a secret between you and me until later. He will believe me, won't he?"

"Yes, he'll believe you, but he might be a little put out by a new boy like you poaching on his territory. But he likes you, which will, I'm sure, secure his help, although you might have to do a deal in return. He needs a diversion at the moment - he hasn't stopped speculating on the outcome of the sale of Wern y coc. I suggest that you ask him to change the plantation rather than leave the request to me. You approach him as if I'm completely in the dark. He'll like that. Then, when he tells me, I'll agree that it's a good idea. It will be fun to see how much time passes before he brings me into the conspiracy, and how much he tells me."

The look on her face reminded Owen of the time he had first seen her, crouching in the ha-ha, playing games. He had often thought about the relationship between Matilda and Humphrey, how they seemed poles apart at times while at others locked together in fun. With these thoughts rekindled, he gazed into Matilda's eyes searching for an answer; a stare which lasted longer than he realised. A wry smile from her, hinting at the thoughts in his head, caught him off-guard and caused some embarrassment, which he attempted to disguise. Quickly, Matilda filled the gap.

"You'll have to wait a while, though. Humphrey's going to a workshop over the weekend on directing, and he won't be back until next Tuesday, the last day of the month. That gives you plenty of time to prepare yourself."

"My time's going to be occupied soon because I shall be helping with the hay-making at Bodcut, so everything will have to be delayed."

"Anyway, Owen, why didn't you approach Humphrey first? Why me instead of him?"

Owen had expected this question as well, and like the one about Catherine, he had not resolved how to cope with it. Her earlier probe concerning Humphrey's involvement had not been direct enough to put him on the spot. But now, he had to explain himself. It was now Matilda's turn to stare at him, outwardly as calm as ever, but inwardly longing to know why she had been chosen. Although she could see by the lost expression on his face that the question was as awkward as the one about Catherine, she continued to look for an answer. A moment of suspended heavy silence ensued as Owen's mind raced through numerous past episodes of thought. The silence and the stare eventually tumbled him into a beginning, a very hesitant one.

"Em..." He hesitated. "I wasn't sure... eh... what response I would get from Humphrey. He is so... em... Tree spirits are so peculiar to him that I thought he might resent me intruding into his domain in such a dramatic way. I wasn't sure that he would believe me if I came out with a true story... well, one so unbelievable..."

"And me?" probed Matilda again.

He hesitated again. "I felt that, well... because you are so close to Suzy, that you would understand the predicament I face... I mean... I thought I could trust you more than anyone else. This whole experience; this appeal to me for help, is the major event of my life so far. I had to tell it to someone..."

"Then, why not Catherine? She is very close to Suzy, and you are very close to her, aren't you?" asked Matilda, pressing even deeper.

"Too close... You know the tree very well, perhaps better than anyone else. You've seen me behaving strangely beside it. And you showed me the handwriting of Rosamond de Bohun."

"But the tree belongs to Catherine. Isn't she going to inherit Gwenynog eventually? And she knows just as much about Rosamond as I do."

Owen almost said, 'Not as much as Suzy does', when he

checked himself. Then he became emphatic, feeling that he had said enough to escape from the question.

"I know, but the solution also rests with you and Humphrey. The plantation and the wood are yours. Only you can safeguard the future existence of the soul that's in the tree over there. I couldn't have spoken to Humphrey first. I wanted to speak to you. I didn't want to tell Catherine, Milo, or anyone else."

Matilda feigned satisfaction. She accepted some of the commonsense in Owen's explanation, but her wily intuition sensed that what she had been told was not the entire case. In letting her read his notebooks, including some of his own observations and inner thoughts, Owen had opened up more than ever before. He had given a prescient woman an insight into more than he realised. His insight into the workings of her mind was shallow compared to the insight she had gained into his.

CHAPTER 30

Notebook - 22nd June (1988): Bodcut Farm.

If I didn't have the Stoggle on my mind, my first experience of hay-making would be immensely enjoyable. And being continuously busy, doing arduous physical work as part of a family team, could be a distraction, but for one person - Ralph. He knows that his father has a better working relationship with me; a realisation which gets under his sarcastic skin. He not only continues to make me feel like an incomer, he treats me like an interloper as well.

Mrs Farr is treating me more and more like a potential son-in-law!

Notebook - 23rd June (1988): Bodcut.

Wern y coc is still proving a touchy subject for Lloyd, although Ralph has gone ominously quiet on the matter.

When I dared to ask if they were going to bid at the sale, Lloyd was unusually sharp with me. Mrs Farr apologised for him afterwards, saying that he was going through mental torture over the sale. When I asked Ralph the same question, privately, he just said that I will have to wait and see. He replied with that wicked smile of his. Then I got it in the ear from Cath tonight for raising the subject in the first place.

Notebook - 25th June (1988): Bodcut.

I've just about had enough of Ralph. Every chance he got today to say something while we were hauling or stacking the bales, he had to mention his tree-felling exploits and his fuel-wood business. He boasted about the extra work he and Tim have sought to contract out as woodmen - and even as tree surgeons! I'm convinced that he does it purely out of spite, knowing my affinity for trees. I'm also becoming wary of his intentions towards the Stoggle. There is something going on in his mind which is evil. I can sense it. I must be vigilant.

Two shots rang out from somewhere in the Deer Haye. It surprised them both because it was not the season for shooting deer or game. Since taking over from his father, de Bohun had outlawed the use of guns in the Haye, except for the supervised culling of deer, after seeing the Keeper shoot a fox one summer with his stalking rifle.

"That could be the Keeper, Owen. He knows Humphrey is away and that I should be in Hereford today. As he gets older, he becomes ever more difficult. We know there are times when he shoots rooks and crows on the edge of the Haye, but we have yet to catch him at it inside the deer park. We're afraid that one day he'll shoot the ravens by mistake. We are looking forward to his retirement. It's a wonder we've kept him on this long."

Matilda and Owen had arranged to meet in the Deer Haye at the Wrong Angled Oak, a follow-up meeting which had been delayed by the hay-making at Bodcut Farm. After some prompting, and further words of reassurance, he had agreed for her to witness an attempt at contact with the Spirit before he approached Humphrey for his support. He was due back later that day, a Tuesday. Matilda was free because she had exchanged her day at work in Hereford so that a colleague could attend a funeral on Thursday.

The Wrong Angled Oak was a convenient place for an early afternoon rendezvous, standing as it did on a junction of tracks, one of which linked with the bridleway to the Goggin. It could also be seen from various sectors of the Haye; not as an eye-catching feature like the Spike or the Leaning Tower of Poplar, but as a tree visually apart from the other oaks, although surrounded and dwarfed by them. It lurked in the ground instead of commanding it, as the other trees did. It was almost sinisterly different. Matilda confirmed that it had been the bane of Humphrey's early life, adding that it was a Quercus robur brought back from the Continent and planted by his grandfather.

The day was different, too. The sky was a confused one as the area of high pressure which had facilitated hay-making gave way to a depression from the north-west, bringing with it some churlish winds. Stirring leaves and creaking limbs were the background noises to their progress through the Haye. The warmth and tranquil air of summer was absent. There was a feeling of changing times. When quiet, the Haye was immutable. But when stirred into motion by swirling air masses, it had that feeling of impending alteration. It was disturbed; and its human interlopers were unsure of their feelings towards the disturbance. The Wrong Angled Oak was awkwardly stiff and resistant to the wind, unlike many of the other trees, which flexed with the buffetings and roared their disapproval. But it was now behind them, for they were on their way towards the Cwm and the entrance to Coed Tirion Glas. They heard the gunshots just as they passed through the high white gate out of the Haye.

They had decided to approach the Stoggle from this direction so as to allow ample time for the Eerie Shriek to see Owen. After leaving the Wrong Angled Oak, he had progressed alone, some distance ahead of Matilda, who maintained a very discreet presence. They came together at the gate to confer, for they had yet to see a buzzard, and the noises in the Haye had limited the chance of hearing one.

"How do you think we should proceed from here, then", asked Matilda.

"It might be best if I wander around in the Cwm for a while to make myself seen. If nothing happens, I'll set off through the wood. You'll just have to follow on out of sight. I'll sit down at the Stoggle if I think the Shriek is about."

Owen wandered around in the Cwm for three quarters of an hour, visiting several solitary limes, which were only just coming into flower, and climbing up the open slope to expose himself to view. Two buzzards did appear high in the sky, wrestling with the air, and could be heard, but the sound was not the familiar pee-ow of the Eerie Shriek. In the end, he entered Coed Tirion Glas and set off along the overgrown ride for the Stoggle. It was possible he had been seen without knowing it. He hoped so. Despite the piercing nature of its call, and those strange eyes, it was exciting to be swooped down upon at close quarters. He heard the flapping of wings in a tree behind him. He swung round, but it was only a pigeon. Matilda was not in view either.

There were few flowers in the wood; some red campion and foxglove spires on the edges of the old ride and, in places, the soft pinkness of dog roses. The luxuriance of the summer had arrived. Despite the wind, the wood was quietly fixing energy as only woods can - at an elevated level in the canopy, beyond the appreciation of the lowly wanderer in its shady, subdued interior. The many layers of vegetation - the mainstorey, the understorey, the shrub layer, the dwarf shrub layer, the tall herb layer, the herb or field layer, and finally the ground layer – gave so many habitats for so many niches of life, and so many unseen creatures most of which was hidden from the average human being, who usually sees only tree trunks, irksome brambles, and barriers of dead wood.

But Owen was different. He appreciated it all. As he made his devotional way up the slope into what he knew was only a pale reflection of the real wildwood, his thoughts delved into what was there and what it would be like if left alone for another forty, or eighty, or one hundred and twenty years. His mind was elsewhere, as usual, but poised for penetration if the buzzard should call. He could not enter the wood without musing on how happy the Spirit would be if it were back amongst the other limes and the wild service trees, away from the bareness of the dingle and the grim wall of the conifers. As he drew closer to the edge of the plantation, he avoided looking towards it, keeping his eyes to the right and the left, and on the ground; keeping the ambience of the wood and the future of the Spirit in the forefront of his mind. But the wind was an unsettling factor.

He did not notice the change in the plantation until he was almost upon it. Someone had started to clear the storm damage and to brash the remaining conifers. The impenetrable tangle of interlocking dead branches, which had made access difficult, had been cut away, the debris lying flattened against the murky brown floor of decaying needles and fronds. It was totally unexpected and ominous; and it cut away everything else from his mind. Disregarding the planned approach to the Stoggle, he quickly inspected the plantation to check on the broadleaved regrowth. It had not been touched - yet. He came back to the path just as Matilda was passing.

"The plantation's been brashed!" he shouted to her. "And some of the storm damage has been removed. What's going on?"

Matilda was also shocked by the neatness of the serried ranks of trees, as tightly packed together as ever but all trimmed to above head height. Her innate calmness restrained her response.

"There can be only one explanation for this. Carling is involved here. He has been trying for some time to persuade Humphrey to let him manage the plantation. He approached us last year with an offer to buy it, but I was adamant that we should keep it. Humphrey surprised me by being undecided at first. I knew he had something to tell me before he went off to his workshop, but he said he would tell me the outcome of his latest conversation with Carl about the plantation when he got back. All he could talk about was either his preparations for the workshop or the impending sale of Wern y coc. When he gets excited, it's difficult to keep his attention."

"Well, it looks like Medlar hasn't wasted any time if he's arranged to help out. This brashing is only a few days old. If this plantation is to be managed along forestry lines, then the Spirit's chances of returning to the wood are gone; gone forever..." Crestfallen, Owen's words trailed off into a particularly strong rustle of leaves.

"Don't be upset, Owen. I'll sort it out. Have they touched any of the broadleaved trees?"

"No. I checked that before you came. But if they intend to thin it, they're bound to clear out the 'scrub', as they call it, including the lime regrowth. Whoever does the work will have to leave the place 'clean', as the forester says in his house-keeping jargon. And if Tim Medlar and Ralph are involved, the place will be blazed as well as cleaned."

Matilda smiled. "Leave it to me, Owen. Nothing else will happen, I promise you that. I'll talk to Humphrey when he returns this evening. I can't believe that he has given Carl a free hand to do what he wants, not without talking to me about it first. Let's continue with our trip to the Stoggle. I'll wait here for a while to give you time to settle in. Off you go."

Matilda was a very calming person. She had to be to live with a man like de Bohun. Her calm was one of the qualities which had influenced Owen in deciding who to share his secret with. But he hesitated to move. There were other things on his mind which had been there ever since she had asked to observe the Spirit contacting him. The changed state of the plantation, and its effect upon his equilibrium, brought them to the fore.

Matilda could see that he was still bothered, and reluctant to continue.

"Free dinner for your thoughts", she said, amiably, as he stood there sullenly in the shadow of the conifers. The sun was in the wrong quarter of the sky to bathe the ride in sunshine. "Or do you give precedence to mind over edible matter?" The friendly question brought a half smile to Owen's face. He relaxed a little. But he did not speak for some seconds. Matilda was on the verge of speaking again when he broke the silence, choosing his words carefully.

"I've been wondering if the Spirit will contact me when another person is present. The merging of our souls does not happen every time I visit the tree. The buzzard has to be there, but even then contact may not be made. And the wind won't help." He paused.

"Well, what do you think determines the chance of contact, then?" asked Matilda, gently, endeavouring to dispel his reservations by encouraging him to be more open.

"It must have something to do with the state of the Spirit. I'm sure of that. Its power is waning, and it might not always marshal enough energy. It has already said that its spell is not what it used to be. My own state of mind also has something to do with creating the right conditions for contact." Owen was loath to mention the possible affect of lime-flower tea.

"I think your own state of mind has everything to do with the fact that you've been contacted. I've been alone at the Stoggle on countless occasions, and Suzy has spent a number of hours beside it, but we have not been asked to help. Unless the Spirit is a male chauvinist, it seems to be a very careful judge of character, which is not surprising if its future existence depends upon the person chosen to liberate it..."

She was interrupted by the faint mewing of a buzzard. They both thought it was the cry of the Eerie Shriek, but the disturbed air did not allow it to linger.

"At least let us try, Owen - for my sake. I'll help whatever happens; you know I won't let you down."

Matilda's words persuaded Owen to continue with the original plan. He set off down the grassy ride, shivering a little, having cooled off in the shade of the wood, and against the darkness of the conifers. Matilda waited behind.

When he came out from the plantation, broken sunlight affected his eyes, causing him to squint. The grandeur of the Stoggle, sighted after the gloom of the conifers and through the glare of fitful sunshine, made it appear for a second as though blazing with light; golden light. It was spectacular and arresting. When his eyes adjusted to the brightness, he noticed that the flowers were in decline. The nascent fruits, closeted by their pale, creamy-green bracts, twisted as the now heavy, folded leaves, drooping together, moved in swathes. Some bracts were now scattered on the ground beneath the crown. The colour and aroma of the week before haytime had gone. But the strange pendulous heaviness remained, in defiance of the wind. Beneath the tree, in the deep shade of its crown, any movement above was muffled.

The dull mewing of a buzzard reached his ears. It sounded like the Eerie Shriek, but it seemed different, less sharp and not as strong. A bird was not in view but he was sure, almost telepathically sure, that the buzzard was not far away. He was still unsettled, but at the same time, he had a feeling that something might happen. So he took his seat at the base of the

Stoggle, looking, as he sat down, for Matilda. She was not in view either.

With his notebook on his lap, he focused his eyes upon an interlocking spur in the dingle where the darkened brook, changing direction and level sharply, became agitated and glinted in the occasional sunlight. Warm air swirled upwards to him in rapid draughts, in contrast to the churlish winds that had beset them when they set out. But the draughts were as faint as the buzzard's call had been, and gone before he could adjust to them. They seemed not to be synchronised with the external noises, or the muffled movement above. A sharp draught touched his face just as he heard the muted cry of a buzzard again. He recognised the call, for it was now part of his soul, but the bird was still not in view. However muted and indistinct, it was unmistakably the call of the Eerie Shriek. But its penetration was missing; that piercing quality which usually went right through him to leave him tingling. He felt its edge, but not the penetration.

Nothing had felt right since his rendezvous with Matilda at the Wrong Angled Oak. But her urgings and her help had induced him to make an attempt at contact. He owed it to her, as well as to the tree, to try. As usual, he concentrated his thoughts on the forests of yesteryear, this time dwelling on the depletion of trees in 1801, when Llandyfrig Court and Rhibo Mountain suffered more than a scenic unclothing. At that time, the dingle would have been a deep and integral part of the forest; the Stoggle, a young tree growing in its prime; the Spirit, cautiously inhabiting the 'Early Flowering Linden', somewhere below.

Arboreal thoughts drifted through his mind, and he

attempted to relax, but he did not become detached, nor did he feel any inklings of change, only inklings of air - the wind had subsided in the lee of the wood.

Further thoughts of the valley below as an unbroken tract of woodland, undisturbed by the dreadful Serpent Dyn, took him to the verge of something... The snap of a brittle twig recalled the present. He turned towards the plantation, but Matilda was not visible. Assuming that she could see him, he nodded from side to side to indicate that he was still in the dingle of today. Then his head stopped still and his eyes widened in alarm. Coming into view over an intermediate rise below, he saw three men walking along the perimeter fence of the plantation. They were engrossed in a conversation which expressed its content in the sweeping gestures one of them was making towards the conifers and over the dingle. It was Carling Medlar, accompanied by Ralph and by someone Owen had not seen before, a man carrying a clipboard and wearing a light brown jacket with leather shoulder pads. He did not have time to move or even to gesture to Matilda, so he pretended to be asleep. His presence was soon noticed by the trio. They stopped and went into a surreptitious huddle around Ralph, emerging from it seconds later and progressing onwards, furtively this time, towards a straining post in the fence where they crossed into the plantation.

In pretending to be asleep, Owen had not positioned his head so that he could follow their progress. When he dared to move, in a spasm of sleep, they had gone out of sight. Instead of jumping to his feet, he made a pretence of waking up, stretching his arms and gradually scrambling to an upright position without looking towards the plantation. When he did look across the dingle, there was still no sign nor sound of the trio. Nor was there any sign of Matilda. Gathering himself together, he ambled up the dingle along the narrow path which led to the gate, still pretending to be unaware of the presence of others, but carefully scanning the way ahead for any sign of them. He climbed the gate and proceeded along the ride, casually peering into the packed stems of the conifers. The fact that the plantation was now partially brashed increased the internal visibility considerably. And it meant that any movement off the path did not have to be restricted to those parts where the failure of the conifers and the resurgence of broadleaves made progress easier. However, the brashings had to be negotiated without making a noise. Was it possible?

He decided to be cautious. Instead of risking everything on the avoidance of brittle twigs, he hurried along the ride to enter the wood proper, to approach the interior of the plantation from the cover of the straggly lime regrowth. After penetrating about fifty yards or so into the plantation, he guessed he was somewhere near the crab apple tree. There were a few purple legged spiders ahead, and some daylight. He was right. But as the crab came into view, so did the trio. They were standing beside it, Medlar expounding enthusiastically while the anonymous man interjected when he could.

Owen crept within earshot, moving deftly across the ground, knowing that if they looked backwards from where they stood, he would be seen. He felt particularly wary of Ralph. He need not have been, for the errant son of Lloyd the Bodcut was too engrossed in his own self importance to act as a look-out man. The abatement in the wind had restored some of the vaulted quietness of the wood, making sounds other than rustling leaves audible in all directions. His nerve was rewarded by the proximity of an old saw-pit which he slid into, and from where he listened...

"If you want to convert this plantation into a mixed stand of amenity trees, Mr Medlar, it will have to be done carefully in case of wind-throw. So I suggest you create only a limited number of openings once you thin it, small enough to take groups of five or at most nine trees. And then create more openings after the next thinning. It would make sense to base some of the initial openings on the places where the old coppice has maintained a foothold. Clear away the lime regrowth, treat the stumps with herbicide, and fill up the spaces." These were obviously the words of a traditional forester.

"My son Tim, and Ralph here, can do that. They've already done some of the brashing and started to tidy up the storm damage."

"We could start with the removal of trees like this old crab apple, which would create a sizeable opening, wouldn't it?" interjected Ralph.

"It would", agreed the forester. "I suggest that something is also done about the few old shells and hulks of trees we've seen so far. If left, they will only harbour pests and disease. What other trees do you have in mind to plant besides the amenity conifers you mentioned earlier, Mr Medlar?"

"It's a long list. I'll show it to you when we get back to the Grange. I want to plant as many different oaks as I can, especially the ones noted for autumn colour, and an assortment of other amenity hardwoods... What was that?"

"What?"

"I thought I heard someone."

"We're alone Sir. It was probably a squirrel", said Ralph to get in on the conversation.

"I don't have to remind you to keep them under control", said the forester, "otherwise your planting efforts will be wasted. They're particularly fond of hardwood sap. With a broadleaved wood so close by, you're bound to be plagued by them, and by stray deer."

"That's no problem. My Keeper is also the keeper for the wood, so we can be comprehensive in our control measures."

"May I ask why you have taken on the management of this plantation when it isn't yours? Are you being paid to do it?"

"No. I'm paying for the privilege. The Mountain could do with a well managed feature of interest instead of this neglected place. I've acquired carte blanche management rights in return for donating one of my old buildings in Elchon to a local theatre trust. My patronage is well known in the district."

"You're a very generous man, Mr Medlar; very generous indeed. A building for the privilege to manage an unkempt place like this. Em... Why not own it?"

"Well, there is the eventual possibility of that, but it will take time to secure." Medlar looked askance at Ralph, who smiled knowingly. "It's rather confidential at present, if you don't mind."

"I understand. Now let me have a look at the rest of this plantation, although I think I've seen enough to determine the management it needs."

"Let's follow the line of this coppice regrowth and then double back across the bottom of the plantation to Gwenynog", said Ralph, asserting his role as guide.

As the name of the smallholding died in the air, Owen was

left out of earshot, and dejected. He had heard enough. For a while, he remained in the saw-pit, staring at the crab apple through the now tidy mixture of crowded conifers and surviving regrowth, his head muddled with all sorts of matters. Was Matilda being honest with him? Was Humphrey being honest with her? Where had she got to? He rolled out of the pit onto his feet in one movement, and retraced his steps to the ride and the Stoggle without bothering to be quiet. Medlar and Ralph in collusion - what next, he thought?

And there she was, waiting by the tree.

"Owen! Wherever did you get to? Did you see Carl Medlar, Ralph, and that forester?"

"I've just followed them into the plantation to find out what they're up to."

"Oh, I can tell you that", said Matilda, indignantly. "I could hear what they were saying as they came up the dingle. When I left you, I followed one of the badger tracks to the middle section of the plantation. I intended to find a good place inside the fence where I could watch you. When I saw them, I had to scramble into a ditch - that's why I'm so dirty - but I heard everything they said as they went by. They were talking about removing the fence along the edge of the plantation, felling trees to alter the line of the conifers, and planting trees in the dingle. Who does he think he is? Humphrey hasn't said anything to me about changing the plantation; certainly not with Carl's involvement - and certainly not with Ralph's help!"

"Did he say anything about the Stoggle?"

"If he did, I didn't hear it. But then, they went out of earshot. What happened? When I hid from them, I lost sight of you. And when I surfaced again, you weren't there!"

"Oh, I pretended to be asleep, so they ignored me and carried on. Then I went all the way back to the wood, so as to enter the plantation from the other side as discreetly as possible."

"You followed them! Suzy would be proud of you. That's the sort of excitement she likes."

"Hardly excitement. They're planning to remove most of the surviving lime coppice and the other broadleaved trees, including a crab apple, to make way for the introduction of amenity trees - Medlar's so-called amenity trees. It seems that Ralph and Tim will do the necessary felling work. They were the ones who brashed it. Medlar also said that he was paying for the privilege to manage the plantation."

"Paying for it!" exclaimed Matilda.

"Yes. He said he had acquired carte blanche management rights in return for donating a building in Elchon to a theatre trust."

"So that's it. What will Humphrey get up to next? That must have happened just before he went away, because he hasn't said anything to me yet. Don't be dispirited, Owen; Humphrey wouldn't make that sort of a deal without discussing it with me first. I'll find out what is going on. He wouldn't allow Carl to interfere on the estate against my wishes. Believe me. Everything will be alright. Let's forget it for the moment and try to contact the Spirit. I thought I heard the Eerie Shriek a few moments before the interruption of that little threesome."

"I thought I heard it, too", said Owen, disinterestedly. "But it wasn't nearly as piercing as normal... There it is again; almost straining to escape. The omens are not good, Matilda; I've sensed that all along today."

"Oh, please let us try, Owen?" implored Matilda. "I'll watch from the edge of the plantation." She started to move away, but Owen's face held too much anguish. She could see that she was asking too much of him. The events of the last hour had put his mind beyond reach, as far as he was concerned. He did not expect to be contacted, even if the buzzard did fly in.

Another call reached their ears, closer than before. They scanned the sky to see if the bird was visible. Then they saw it, perched on a straggly ash which was leaning out from the edge of the plantation where there was a pocket of regrowth, close to the point where Owen had first seen the trio of men. It gave out another cry, an agonised shriek which faded on the air instead of piercing the whole dingle. It lifted its broad wings and pushed weakly out of the ash, as if to make for the Stoggle. Instead, it hung briefly above the dingle before dropping limply and clumsily to the ground. Without even a glance at Matilda, Owen raced down into the dingle, sliding the last few yards to the brook. The buzzard was writhing on the edge of the water. Its belly was bloodstained and half shot away. Matilda was at his side within seconds. They exchanged glances, knowing what must have happened. At least one of the shots they had heard when they set out for the Stoggle had been fatal - and, perhaps, fateful, too.

The Eerie Shriek was dead before they reached Gwenynog. Matilda's hope that they could get it to the vet in Ewyas in time delayed the true impact of the bird's injury upon Owen's soul. Catherine's grandfather not only pronounced it dead when Matilda asked to borrow their vehicle, he expressed amazement that the bird had not died at the moment of being shot. He was shocked even more when Owen, still clutching the bird, suddenly rushed away, heading for the bridleway and the Goggin.

Matilda shouted after him, asking if he was going to be alright. He did not reply. She wanted to follow him, but she knew that he needed to be alone. His anguish, coming as it had after disturbing discoveries, hardened her resolve to tackle those matters over which she had the greatest control. Catherine's grandparents were disappointed when she refused their invitation to go inside. She usually had time for everyone...

The Outpost

CHAPTER 31

'I know you are a Gentle Son of Dyn
I am a Spirit of the Gentle Mingui Limes
I know that you believe me
The softness of your Soul can help me thrive'

Spirit of Y Coed

Late that afternoon, the telephone was again ringing to an empty house at the Goggin. Matilda had given Owen a while to settle in before calling to check that he was alright, and to offer to do what she could to assuage his grief. She began to worry. Catherine, on the other hand, knew, or thought she knew, where he was, and was irritated.

He had got only as far as the bird carcasses on his return from Gwenynog before being snapped out of his fit of utter dejection and hopelessness. Seeing the ghastly remnants of the Keeper's tally for the winter made him stop and collect his thoughts. Why was he taking the carcass of the Eerie Shriek back to the cottage? There could be only one resting place for it.

He skirted Gwenynog on his return to the Stoggle, and was careful in his approach to the tree. If Matilda was there, he would resolve what to do when the time came. She was not there. And the stillness was its solemn self, undisturbed by unsettling winds and by scheming pseudo-foresters. He had the place to himself.

The day had matured into a very fine one. A breeze was all that was left of the aggression of the morning. Sunshine and haze gave an indistinct glare to the glory of summer. The scenes below and away in the distance carried that inevitable hint of nostalgia - of warm times in the pastoral past. He spent several minutes on the edge of the dingle, staring into the blue sky and into the hazy distance, on the edge of reality, seeing imaginary buzzards whirling on updrafts.

Finally, the wetness of blood seeping through his shirt onto the skin of his stomach brought him back to the present. The blood had discoloured his notebook. With the aid of a sharp stick he had collected along the way, he dug gently into the soil below the tree, on the shoulder of the dingle, and used his hands to excavate a grave. He did not have to dig down very far to reach the uppermost roots of the Stoggle. Carefully, he loosened the soil and freed some roots, and then dug deeper. When the hole was ready, he collected together handfuls of the spent flowers and bracts which lay strewn on the bare ground below the crown. Would these be the wreckage of the Stoggle's last summer, he asked himself, plaintively? He covered the base of the hole with these floral remnants, creating a cushion for the bird's body, and then he searched the lower branches of the tree for late blossom. There were still a few flowers, although they were almost past their best. As he laid the buzzard in the grave, he uttered the words:

"My Gentle Tree imbibed him to its Heart
Sending many many blossoms to his grave
Leaving life is grief to those who live."

He repeated them as he sprinkled the flowers over the bird's shattered breast. Then he spread the roots over the breast, added some more flowers and uttered more of the Spirit's words before filling the grave with earth. Lastly, he concealed the place by covering it with leaf-litter and more floral remnants.

As he stood up, the sorrow of the ceremony unsteadied him. Abjectly, he leant against the trunk of the tree, his head resting on his forearm. In that moment of grief he felt an upwelling of intense sadness through his whole body, culminating in a suffusion of tears which were unstoppable. For some minutes, he was overcome by a sorrow which was greater than anything he had experienced before. Then the tears and the quick breaths ceased, as suddenly as they had begun. He looked up into the graceful crown of the tree, at the shafts of sunlight which could enter where the foliage was sparse. As he did so, a shower of petals, some of the last to be discarded, floated down around him; a few nestling in his hair, the pale colour of their afterlife blending delicately with the soft ginger locks; a few clinging to his face in the briny smudge of tears. His legs gave way and he slid down to the ground, ending up in the seat at the base of the tree.

He was aware of what might happen, but he was feeling very weary, a condition which blurred his existence. Although he felt that the chance of contact was remote, and although the future - whatever it held - felt bleak, he assured himself that it was his duty to be in attendance, whatever the outcome, and to continue to attend as regularly as before.

An hour transpired, during which he imagined all kinds of intimations of contact, passing in and out of a fragile state of awareness. His unsettled condition, and the uncertainties connected with the Spirit's power, introduced such confusion that contact, if it were possible, was unlikely to occur for long. Eventually, he lifted his weary body out of the seat, glanced down at the grave, and left. As he did so, his notebook dropped to the ground, and he noticed his pen lying beside it. He was in too much of a far-away state to even think about why this should have happened. He merely picked up the two precious items and tucked them away in his blooded coat. The journey home was slow and sad...

Catherine reached the Goggin on her way home from work just as Owen passed the bitter sight of the shredded bird carcasses. Upon finding the cottage empty, she expelled a few words of disappointment beneath her breath, with resignation. Hurriedly, she wrote him a note, which he found on his return. His name was squeezed between exclamation marks:-

'!Owen! Must see you. Have some fantastic news to tell. Phone me at home tonight before seven. I've got a meeting to go to. Love C.'

A communication from or with Catherine was the last thing he wanted. In the agony of the day's events, his thoughts had barely strayed from the mission of the day, wandering at times onto the approach he had yet to make to de Bohun. Nothing else had intruded. In an aftermath of mental tension, he could hardly cope with another development. So he put the note aside and made himself a cup of lime flower tea. He drank it thirstily as the beverage calmed him down. Did he want to hear some fantastic news? Could his already overtaxed brain cope with romance as well? All within was grey matter calling for rest. Forgetting the stains of blood on his clothes he slumped into the sofa and pulled his legs up, placing his booted feet on the attractively embroidered coverlet of the broad arm-rest, and subsided very quickly into sleep...

"Owen! Owen! Wake up, Owen! Are you alright?" said Catherine, as first she shook his shoulders and then lifted up his chin in a grip that was prompted more by agitation than by tenderness. "What's all that blood on your coat? Are you hurt? What have you done to get into such a messy state? Suzy will be indignant if you've stained her sofa. Come over here to this old arm-chair."

Owen came alive, but only slowly, aware that Catherine was beside him, but unaware, for the moment, of the identity of his surroundings and of the thoughts which had caused his mind to give up for the day.

"I'm okay. It's the blood of a bird. I'll tell you about it later."

Catherine could now see that he was tired and somewhat disoriented, so she helped him to the chair more tenderly than she had roused him. She knew very well that it would take some minutes for him to come round. Resigned to a wait, she made him a cup of herb tea – lime flower tea.

When she returned to his side, he was reclining backwards, his head arching over the top of the back-rest, his heavy eyes half open, his mouth ajar.

"Your favourite tea, Owen", she said, pulling a small table up to the side of the chair and placing a two handled cup upon it, impatient for him to respond. "Is everything alright? Your eyes look sore."

"What time is it?" he asked, continuing to peer blankly at the ceiling, unmoved even by the clash of gaudy colours.

"Just after nine. I've come straight from my meeting because something terrible has happened. Owen! Open your eyes properly and look at me. Are you alright?"

"Yes, I'm okay", he said, lifting his head upright and staring into her face, but realising that he felt unusually detached. "The keeper shot the Eerie Shriek today, the bastard. I buried it this afternoon, that's why my coat is stained."

"But that alone couldn't have made you look so awful." Owen's plaintive stare made her realise the insensitivity of her remark, so she handed him the cup of tea and then broke into the news she was so eager to tell.

"Carling Medlar has asked Dad if he would be interested in exchanging the dingle fields at Gwenynog for the pastures at Wern y coc – once he has bought them. He assumes that only he will buy them. He said that he intends to buy Wern y coc but isn't sure if he needs the pastures. But he will buy them and decide afterwards. That man is despicable! I thought Dad would be completely shocked by the proposal, but in the exchange of words which followed between us, he revealed that that Meddling Baron approached him last year with an offer to buy the dingle fields. My fields!" This was all uttered in a gush of sentences which finally roused Owen into a sensible state of awareness.

"This is all falling into place, now", he said, fatalistically, awakened by the news, his mind back on the problem that had soured his day.

Catherine ignored the import in his words and continued.

"Dad couldn't explain why he didn't tell me. Perhaps because he's been presented with an easy way to get his pastures. He tried to convince me tonight that I won't need the land when I move into Gwenynog. I only found out about all this today when I got back from work. Mother told me. Dad and I had our worst argument ever, until she sorted us out. Even she is wavering. I don't want to lose any land from the smallholding. None! And Dad shouldn't consider selling any while my grand parents are still alive."

"You don't have to. Gwenynog is legally yours, isn't it? All you have to do is say no to an exchange. Did you say no? Did your father actually ask you to agree to an exchange?"

"Not directly, but I did make it clear to him that I was against the proposition."

"Medlar is trying to undermine the opposition, Cath, and win them over, at the same time. He's a calculating man; a businessman who knows how to conduct a ruthless campaign of acquisition, whatever the goal." Owen's own mind was beginning to tick over. "If you only found out after work, why did you leave me that note?"

"Oh, that was because of the first piece of news to shatter my day. Alison told me at lunch that she and Milo have decided to bid for the house and the meadows at Wern y coc. She took me into her confidence at last, perhaps because she's missing Suzy. Milo is treating it all like a crusade, a last ditch stand against the marching acquisitiveness of the Meddling Baron.

She wanted someone else's confirmation that it was worth the effort. But their decision doesn't solve my dilemma. Just before I left home for my meeting, I asked Mother if Dad would agree to me helping to buy the pastures at Wern y coc. She said it was worth a try, but she wasn't very encouraging or supportive. I wanted to see what you thought before I went back home."

In the time it had taken Catherine to pour out her news, Owen had revived to the point of movement. He was on his feet walking about the room, sipping his tea agitatedly. He was properly awake at last, but the events of the day were again piling up against him. He could not disguise his mood.

"Did Medlar say why he wanted the land?" he asked, in a tone of voice which implied that he was going to answer his own question.

"No, because he said he hadn't made up his mind whether or not to keep it with the holding."

"That's just a ruse to let your dad know he's going to be bidding, and to make the offer of an exchange without appearing to be too interested in it. The truth is, he wants the dingle fields because he's scheming to get de Bohun's coniferous plantation as well. He wants both so he can create the equivalent of an arboretum on the side of the Mountain; an arboretum visible from The Prospect, and to everyone in the valley. Then he will have left - or rather, stamped - his mark on the local landscape."

"Owen, that's crazy. I would expect that sort of explanation from Milo, but not from you... What's got into you?" asked Catherine, in shock.

"Gavin's remark during shearing wasn't accidental. I was at the Stoggle, today, when Medlar turned up with a forester and

- guess who?"

"Who?"

"Your brother." Catherine's eyes squinted as her head jerked to one side. "Yes, your brother. I managed to conceal myself from them and overhear some of what was said. Ralph, because of his working partnership with Tim, is virtually in league with Medlar in his scheming to get the dingle fields, and is already helping his son manage the plantation for de Bohun."

He looked towards Catherine from the other side of the room. She was shaking her head in disbelief.

"That can't be true. Ralph can be objectionable but not deceitful."

"It is true, and he is being deceitful; treacherous, I would say. Your brother is more interested in his partnership with Tim Medlar than anything else at the moment."

"Well - he's had it now. Ralph is going to get a piece of my mind."

"That won't do any good, Catherine. If you want to thwart him, as I do, you must be as devious as he is. You could start by being resolute in your opposition to an exchange of land. If Medlar gets hold of the dingle, the Stoggle - your ancient lime tree - will be lost; either felled or surrounded by a motley collection of amenity trees. You're right to oppose an exchange of land. Medlar should not get anywhere near the Stoggle."

"The lime tree! The lime tree! That's all you ever think about. The tree is irrelevant as far as I am concerned. I would sacrifice it to keep the dingle, if necessary. If Medlar wanted the dingle fields just to get his hands on that tree so that he could have his effigy carved in its wood, I would let him have it. It's the smallholding that is at stake. My grandfather's smallholding.

My smallholding. Can't you see that? Anyway, I'm going to my building society tomorrow to see about a loan. Then I will try to persuade Dad to let me help him buy the pastures... By the way, Alison asked if we wanted to join her and Milo at the Green Man tonight after nine. You might like to go."

With that curt ending, she left. Owen made no attempt to detain her. The oblivion of lime flower sleep had not disposed his state of mind towards redeeming such a fraught situation. Catherine's complications only aggravated the ending to a day which held so many misfortunes that he was still on the edge of despair. Her abrupt departure merely tortured an already tortured soul. Her company was not the answer. Nor was escape the answer; where was there to escape to? At that moment, he needed to have his mind diverted onto other things.

Ignoring his heavy state, he stripped down, cleaned himself, and changed his clothes. He then telephoned Milo to arrange to be picked up so that he could join them in the pub where he knew the food was good enough to restore his energy.

"Owen, where's Catherine?" asked Alison as Owen came over to her with Milo. "We thought you would be coming together."

"She couldn't make it in the end", was all he said as an explanation, collapsing onto the settle, but this attempt at lying did not deceive Alison, although Milo accepted it without a second thought. Before Alison could enquire further, Milo launched into the plans they were making to buy Wern y coc.

"Owen, we're going to make a bid for Wern y coc, and we thought that you and Cath might be able to help us because no-one else must know."

With that, he revealed that they had been thinking of buying a house together for some time, although not one which needed so much building work. It was when he discovered the importance of the meadows that they decided to take the plunge. They had already negotiated the necessary mortgage, but still had one problem to solve - how to make a bid without the Baron knowing who was bidding. Milo knew that if he came in as a buyer, Medlar would be even more determined to acquire the property. They were investigating a way to get someone else to bid on their behalf. This was the reason why they had suggested a meeting with Owen and Catherine. They thought Catherine's father might bid for them. They had even considered asking Owen to bid by phone.

"Me! Why me?" he spluttered in surprise.

"Well", began Milo, "It needs to be someone who would give him no reason at all to link us with the bid. That could be Cath's dad. If he won't do it for us, then an anonymous bidder might be the only answer."

"Obviously, you two are unaware of the latest development", said Owen, shifting in his seat as a prelude to what he was about to say. "Medlar has revealed to Cath's dad his intention of buying Wern y coc, and has offered to exchange its pastures for the dingle fields at Gwenynog. Catherine told me tonight. She is dismayed that her father is showing some interest in the deal, and confused because she knows how much he needs more land. And it seems to be Ralph who suggested the idea." He could have revealed more but he preferred not to.

Alison's mouth dropped open. In a spasm of automatic movement, she turned to reach for the notebook she usually kept in her bag, checking herself immediately. Milo's exclamation was not audible to others sitting nearby, but the impact of his fist on the table did attract some attention.

"The conniving creep", he said with gritted teeth, releasing the anger he felt through his arm.

"Is that why Catherine didn't come tonight?" asked Alison.

"It was part of the reason", admitted Owen. "She is so incensed that she is considering raising the money herself to help her father purchase the pastures."

At this point in the evening, with Milo and Alison shocked by the news and not really clear as to what it meant, Catherine herself appeared. She had entered the pub, bought herself a drink, and then walked over to where they were sitting before they noticed her. Her face was the one that had left Owen so abruptly almost an hour earlier. He turned to greet her with a half smile.

"I've just told them about your latest discoveries; I hope that's alright", he said.

"And we're wondering why and what it means", said Alison.

Owen was about to offer his explanation, but Catherine was first to speak.

"It means that I am determined to get a loan and to make a partnership bid with my Dad. I might even bid for the pastures myself. Then Dad can rent them from me, if he wants to." Her fit of pique had not subsided. If anything, she was more intense than during her altercation with Owen. Alison and Milo exchanged looks.

"We've just been telling Owen that we want to disguise our bidding so Medlar will not know we're interested. We thought your dad might bid for us, but that solution now seems to be too complicated", probed Alison.

"If my father and my brother are prepared to alienate me over this sale, then I don't suggest you take either of them into your confidence", said Catherine, bitterly.

Alison looked towards Owen, while Milo sat there ruminating, staring ahead and still gritting his teeth.

"I'll do the bidding by phone if you think it will help", said Owen, generously. "Or Cath and I could do it together. That might confuse the issue a bit." He looked at Catherine as he raised this alternative and attempted a smile. Her demeanour did not change. Alison and Milo exchanged glances again. Milo broke his silence.

"The fewer people who know about this the better. Maybe if we absent ourselves from the sale and leave the bidding with you two, Medlar will be confused and not riled. But we must keep everything to ourselves. I still think that someone unconnected with either of us would be the safest way to bid."

"Then why not a solicitor?" asked Owen.

"No way... It has to be someone we can trust completely. Let's leave it for the time being. Alison and I have to give it some more thought."

The evening did not wear on for long. With Owen eating some food at last, the quartet became introspective, reflecting on what seemed to be another fait accompli for the Medling Baron. Inwardly, Milo was so crestfallen by what had at first seemed a worthwhile crusade that his mind was wandering everywhere. Owen was similarly distracted, but his preoccupations were unknown to the present company, although Alison sensed that something was amiss between him and Catherine. Catherine always behaved as though she had important matters on her mind. Only Alison attempted to improve the atmosphere of the evening. She failed, and the gathering broke up before closing time.

When the two couples went their separate ways, Catherine assumed, in her own way, that she had apologised to Owen for her behaviour earlier that night. But he knew that in the intimacy which was to follow, he would have to be careful not to divulge any details concerning the plight of the Stoggle. Their growing friendship and their evenings together, were making it difficult for him to conceal from her the major concern of his life.

Owain
Through you I shall unburden the anguish
of my Soul
Through you the Serpent Dyn shall be denied
my death
Through you I shall recover my place within
Y Coed
And dwell within another Gentle Tree...

Like Beibio my Lime tree calls you back
Like Beibio your heart receives my Soul
Like Beibio the Spell of Mynydd y rhibo
Rests in you...

My soaring eyes you laid to rest
Beneath my fragrant shade
My Golden blossom strewn upon the Earth
I know you know the place where I should be

Owain
I still can feel the faintness
Of fibres in the Earth

Of Gentle ties once long and sweetly Deep
If only I could reach them
Enchantment would remain
Enchantment would be yours
Mend for me the Pathway to my remnant
of Y Coed

Contentment only Comes when ties are Deep

Owain
As you have Cherished me
And the Buzzard of my Spell
Nurture all my Passage Trees to link me
to Y Coed
Protect for me my seedling life
Restore a place apart
Recreate the splendour of the Mynydd y rhibo
Limes

Immortal is my Spell when Gentleness is near

Owain
I know you are a Gentle Son of Dyn
I am a Spirit of the Gentle Mingui Limes
I know that you believe me
The softness of your Soul Can help me thrive
Beibio...Beibio...Y Coed is safe with Owain
Oh Gentle oh so Gentle Sons of Dyn

CHAPTER 32

Notebook - 29th June:

'*Wildlife habitats, as fragments in isolation, are like lonely individuals, separate from the world at large; from the world which gives them life and being. And, I suppose, like lonely individuals they eventually succumb to oblivion unless reconnected to the community of life (the habitat) from whence they spring. Until recently, such habitats included tentacles of arboreal life on the edges of the Serpent's tortured spaces - linear belts of self-sown trees, ancient hedgerows, tree-lined watercourses, copses, roughs, carrs - the remnants of the onslaught of man, surviving while connected together. Sadly, these connections are now wasting away. Increasing isolation is reducing their richness and their spirit to survive.*

By how much have the pathways and the echoes of Y Coed declined in the last sixty years as a consequence of the hedgerow clearances, the ancient woodland clearances, the spread of coniferous plantations, the break up of communities, the spread of unemployment; since the catastrophes of two world wars and the catastrophes of technology? By how much has the hollowness increased? The Serpent continues to isolate wildlife as much as it isolates itself...'

The narrow avenue of oak trees exerted its influence once more as Owen dismounted his bike at the entrance to Llandyfrig Court. Slowly and thoughtfully, he pushed the quiet vehicle along the rutted track beneath the arch of oaken limbs, his head twisting up at acute angles to view the grand arbour around him. The rehearsals of what he planned to say to Humphrey that had occupied his mind on the journey until his arrival at the Deer Haye were forgotten. They had given way to reflections that were now his second self.

Again, he wondered if any of the trees around him were inhabited by spirits; if the closeness of trees in an avenue resulted in such an interlocking network of roots that it constituted a retreat harbouring a single spirit. He knew that the individual trees were of the same age and more or less the same size, although some were more vigorous than others. With such uniformity of growth and coalescence of identity, the avenue could accommodate only one spirit. Then he reminded himself that it had been planted; that it was an artefact of man, a baronial feature of the past. Spirits were unlikely to enter trees set in the ground by man. However evocative, however inspirational, however romantic, it could not replace a vestige of Y Coed. Therefore, it was unlikely to succour a tree spirit, unless an isolated one had been given no choice but to retreat into it.

When the 'abode trees' in the Haye came into view again as he emerged from the avenue, he was filled with the same mixed feelings. It was a stirring place that exuded a powerful, indeed, awesome sense of being by its permanence and apparent timelessness. But it, too, was a baronial feature of the past, albeit with ancient connections to Y Coed in its oldest trees. As a cameo of arboreal beauty, it epitomised a part of the English pastoral scene in a land once Welsh to its roots; the sylvan idyll of the romantic poets - a place of old trees and old times, where deer roamed free; a place which remained unchanged while all around the landscape altered in appearance. Only latterly had it been recognised as a rare enclave for wood-boring insects, other barely noticeable invertebrates, and the equally anonymous lichens and mosses. But it was only the accidental home of these organisms, and an artificial home for the deer. It was one of the few places where they had survived. However ancient, however idyllic, it was not Y Coed. And there was the possibility that its surviving wildlife was experiencing a phased delay into extinction. The very existence of its lingering creatures depended upon agedness, stability, continuity; not upon romantic notions, nor idyllic isolation. Only real connections with Y Coed, not imaginary ones, could ensure their survival; connections which, if severed, could not be replaced unless the Serpent Dyn was itself replaced. And even then, some organisms would be lost forever. It was fortunate that their hold upon life, albeit tenuous and doubtful, was supported by a vestige of Y Coed, the neighbouring 'Wood of Gentle Green', which if allowed to 'linger long would help them linger on'. But could Coed Tirion Glas give sustenance to every micro-moth, to every beetle, to all the miniature, barely visible creatures and plants which fought to linger on?...

Suddenly, Owen was standing at the impressive porch of the Court. His wandering mind, and the cavernous journey through the avenue and into the Haye, had reached reality. The porch was as immutable as ever - darkened oak and shadowed whiteness; the huge door ponderously shut. Pinned to it there was a fragile note of wispy paper, cringing at the edges, as if overawed by the weighty structure to which it was attached:-

"Owen. Find me in the Deer Haye - if you can! Humphrey."

He knew that Matilda was in Hereford for the day, having again switched her duty, so the house was empty. He had expected to see her before his meeting with Humphrey, but a morning phone call from the wiry denizen of the Court had delayed everything until the afternoon. He placed his bike against one side of the porch and strolled to the edge of the ha-ha. Standing beside the refurbished swing chair, he could see nothing but grand old trees with wizened, greying limbs piercing heavy crowns of green: and a herd of deer in the distance. Humphrey could not be in that quarter, he surmised. Teili junction was the most likely place. With a short run, he leapt across the ha-ha and settled into a brisk walk.

His thoughts returned to the script he had been rehearsing earlier. He repeated quietly to himself the opening gambit - 'Humphrey, I need your help. I want to save a tree spirit. You're the only one I can turn to because you understand trees...' These words fell slowly and hesitantly from his lips as he passed one huge tree after another - the Thunderer, the Serpent, the Grey Giant, the Griffin - each one causing him to break off his speech while he touched them, or stopped for a moment of reflection.

He had to concentrate hard after each interruption in order to regain his train of thought. In the end, the frequency of the distractions made him give up. But his mind remained with the lord of the manor. If Humphrey was at Teili Junction, then he, himself, would soon be in view. The brief message on the porch door flashed across his mind; so, too, did the time when he first saw de Bohun playing the game of 'Creep'. He should conceal himself now and attempt to surprise him by creeping up on him. He thought that such an approach might distract his mind until the moment of his proposal.

By stealth, he reached the rougher section of the Deer Haye, and the edge of the bracken, where the slope increased and where the trees were more numerous and closer together. The Domesday Oak was up ahead and, beyond it, one of the Stoggles. The lime trees of the Junction could just be seen, grouped together on the lower slopes of the Cwm, the yellow sheen of their emerging blossom marking them out. Furtively, he moved forward from bole to bole, scanning the view ahead while at the same time working his way around to the left so as to come upon the Junction from the other side. To an onlooker, he might have been stalking deer, or creeping up on woodpeckers. His progress was that measured and careful. The new growth of the bracken was tall enough to conceal most of his body but not dense enough to impede his movement. Some foxglove spires challenged the dominance of the bracken in places on the slope where the soil had been disturbed. But the musty odour of bracken spores in the air irritated his nose.

He crossed the brook half way up the slope and made his way around the top of the cwm, knowing that the only view into the Junction was from the top below the woodland edge.

But the top was strewn with dead wood, and the bracken gave way to the detritus of previous seasons, especially crackling leaves. He managed to reach a fallen log, smothered in moss, just as a blackbird squawked in retreat. He dived down against the log.

He allowed a minute or so to pass before peering towards the Junction. Still lying on the leaf litter, he wriggled his way to the end of the log and edged one eye beyond it. He was right. Humphrey was in his favourite place. From his position, two hundred yards away, he could see him walking theatrically to and fro within the confines of the Junction, holding a book at arm's length. He watched as Humphrey walked one way, then another, talking to himself and stopping occasionally to peer through the cordon of lime trees in the general direction of the Domesday Oak, to see if anyone was coming. Realising that the man was not expecting an approach from the top, he crept forward, carefully slipping from one piece of cover to the next - a gnarled trunk, a foliaged bough curving down to the ground, a horizontally spreading hawthorn - moving each time the Junction's occupant was turned the other way looking for him, or immersed in the text he was reading aloud.

Finally, he was within earshot, crouching low against the shattered and tangled remains of an old yew, now split into halves, one of which was rotting away on the ground. He listened. Humphrey was reading a Shakespearian play, one that was not immediately familiar to Owen. Smiling, and wondering how this real character ever managed to divest himself of his idiosyncratic mien before acting a part on the stage, he prepared to move to a closer position from where he could suddenly reveal himself. In making the lunge towards another screen, his shirt caught on a sharp stub of the decrepit yew and heaved him backwards, ripping the cloth and leaving him prone beside the rotting half. Humphrey's head turned slowly round over his left shoulder at the sudden swish of noise, the rest of his body remaining still. His movement could have been rehearsed and part of the play. When he saw Owen rising to his feet, he turned round completely, smiling broadly, saying loudly:-

"Good try, Owen; but if I was a deer, I would have smelled you ages ago." He put one finger in his mouth, moistened it, and then held it up to the air, cocking his head as usual. He did not lower his finger until Owen was only a few feet away, wagging it admonishingly at him.

"What a dramatic coincidence, my boy. I was just thinking about you for a role in our next play, 'As You Like It'. I'm directing it and playing Touchstone. How would you like to play Jacques? I'm thinking of holding some trial performances in the Haye for originality. Here, read this passage that I've just reached." He handed Owen the book, pointing to the part, and then folded his arms and leaned back in expectation.

Owen smiled at the man's incorrigible manner, glanced at the text, and then at him.

"Come on. Let me hear some agile words from the star of our next show."

Owen obliged:-

"A fool, a fool! I met a fool in the forest,

A motley fool; a miserable world!

As I do live by food, I met a fool;"

Owen paused and smiled as he realised the double meaning in the words.

"Who laid him down and baskt him in the sun,

And railed on Lady Fortune in good terms,
In good set terms, and yet a motley fool.
'Good morrow, fool', quoth I. 'No, Sir', quoth he,
'Call me not fool till heaven hath sent me fortune':
And then he drew a dial from his poke,
And looking on it with lack-lustre eye,
Says very wisely, 'It is ten o'clock:
Thus we may see', quoth he, 'how the world wags:
'Tis but an hour ago since it was nine,
And after one hour more, 'twill be eleven;
And so, from hour to hour, we ripe and ripe,
And then, from hour to hour, we rot and rot;
And thereby hangs a tale'."

"And thereby hangs a tale", repeated Humphrey, unfolding his arms and opening them up to the audience of trees. "Audition over!" he exclaimed. "You've got the part, Owen. With a little practice you'll learn the lines, and you might become the best Shakespearian actor on the Goggin."

Owen could not fail to smile at this remark, but his mind had already passed from imaginary to real drama.

"Matty says you've been looking a bit dejected lately. A bit of acting will cheer you up. We start casting in two days time. What do you say?"

Owen abandoned the original script of what he had proposed to say.

"Yes, alright; but will you do something for me?"

"Of course, dear boy, of course! Anything to help you out. Matty thinks there's a problem that's getting you down. How can I help?"

Matilda had prepared him well.

"I have a problem to solve which must be kept a secret. No-one else must know. Your help would be critical for various reasons..."

"And you want to know if you can trust me with it", interrupted Humphrey. "Of course you can. I wouldn't let you down. Not Suzy Forrest's brother. What do you want me to do? I hope some intrigue is involved."

Owen hesitated for a moment.

"I'm worried about the safety of a tree spirit. You're the only person who can help because you understand trees and their spirits."

"Which tree spirit?" interrupted Humphrey again. "Mine are safe enough. It can't be one of mine", he added, implying that nothing could be amiss without his knowing.

"No, it's not one of yours. It's the one in the Melglyn Stoggle above Gwenynog. I'm sure it's inhabited; an abode tree like yours in the Deer Haye. I've got a plan to save it, but I must have your support and your help to do it."

Humphrey was somewhat flummoxed by this request. For a brief moment, he was agape, until he reverted back to acting. Then, stifling a stutter, he said:

"Of course, the one in the old Stoggle. You've got it, my boy... I mean, my help. What do we have to do?"

Owen explained that he felt there was a spirit in the tree which wanted to return to Coed Tirion Glas. He did not reveal that the Spirit had contacted him, nor, to his surprise, did Humphrey ask how he knew the Spirit wanted to move. He merely listened attentively, making facial gestures, as if cognizant of the problem and a seasoned adviser in such matters. Owen went into detail about his plan to physically link the Stoggle to the lime trees in the wood, via the surviving broadleaves in the coniferous plantation, by encouraging the regeneration of trees at the top of the dingle so that the Spirit could migrate into a younger tree.

"Migration! Yes!" interrupted Humphrey, once more. "That's why I've planted so many young trees near the old ones in the Deer Haye, so that my spirits can move. You're a shrewd lad. But what about the dingle? We might have problems getting the Farr family to enclose an area around the tree at the top of the dingle. Or have you won over Catherine, em? Won over Catherine, have you?" he enquired, with his eyes sparkling.

Owen became a little embarrassed, and stalled for a moment, turning his head to one side. Humphrey leant forward, pursing his lips and peering through raised eyebrows.

"No... no... There should be no problems, only a lot of persuasion, that's all", stammered Owen, unwilling at that time to raise the uncertainties surrounding the future of the dingle fields.

"Right, then. What's keeping us here? Let's go over to the plantation and the dingle and draw up some plans. Come on."

With that simple instruction, Humphrey changed the tempo of the discussion and strode off his stage, leaving Teili Junction peremptorily, without his usual farewell oration or recorder cadenza. Owen was left behind wondering why the purpose of the meeting had been achieved so easily, so far; and why nothing had been said about Medlar's involvement in the management of the plantation. Had Matilda persuaded Humphrey against it?...

As the conifers came into view, Owen hesitantly broached the subject.

"Who brashed the plantation? You ask. Carl Medlar had it done for me one day. He said that he had a gang brashing his own woods, and that they could do mine as well."

Owen was prompted to reveal the real identity of the gang but, for the moment, he thought better of it.

"Just like that? Does that mean he actually manages the plantation for you?" he probed, cautiously.

"Well, he does help me out, now and again. He's got a bee in his flat cap about the plantation. He's been on at me for years to get the place managed - 'to improve its appearance', as he says, 'before it's too late' – whatever that means. He once offered to buy it from me, but Matty and I rejected that proposal. Now, he's offered one of his redundant buildings in Elchon, the old Methodist Hall, to our Theatre Trust - the Gulible Theatre Trust which I set up with some friends last year - if I let him manage it on our behalf. It's too good an offer to refuse. He says we can have the building on a long lease, for the 'good of the local community'. He likes to act the part of a benevolent overlord, you know. Our committee's been angling for the old hall for months. As always, Carl Medlar has chosen the right time to meet our needs. Obviously, we're all cock-a-hoop."

"Have you agreed anything; I mean…in writing?" asked Owen, tentatively and quietly, continuing to put his questions as delicately as possible.

"Almost. Carl Medlar has written a letter to the Trust's secretary - that's me - saying that he proposes to place the Methodist Hall in the keeping of the Trust. And I've said verbally that I am prepared to let him help me manage the plantation, and have a say in the choice of trees that are introduced. He wants to look across the valley from The

Prospect and gaze on some red oaks or colourful maples in the autumn."

"Does Matilda know?" asked Owen, trying not to be nosey.

"She does now", replied Humphrey, hunching his shoulders and breaking into his impish grin. "She doesn't really like Carl Medlar all that much and would rather we had nothing to do with him on a business level. But she can't stop this deal going through - it's too good to refuse. Anyway, he's only going to help me manage the plantation, not keep it. I'm not being benevolent; I'm just returning a favour."

Owen had become disturbed by these admissions, but was trying hard not to show how he felt. He wanted to impress upon Humphrey the importance of a management regime which would not harm the existing broadleaved trees, but while he was finding the right words to begin, the impish man continued.

"But Matty is insisting that we place some limitations on any management agreement, if we let Carl become involved. She would like to see the plantation gradually converted back into being a part of Coed Tirion Glas. Mr Medlar wants to introduce broadleaved trees, anyway. What do you think, my boy? As our new friend, and with your interest in trees, Matty reckons you should be involved too."

Matilda had saved Owen again.

"Well, the type of management is critical to my plan to save the Spirit. Let me show you what I mean."

He led Humphrey off into the newly brashed plantation, earnestly eager to show him what must not happen if a management plan were finalised - and hoping that his own ideas could be adopted.

"You see, there is so much lime in amongst the conifers here growing up from the old stools that given room they will flourish. Their root systems will revive and provide a pathway for the Spirit to migrate into the wood. If any management is done, it needs to free the broadleaved growth at the expense of the conifers, not eliminate it, and permit indigenous trees to return. Mr Medlar will want to keep the plantation 'clean', as the foresters say, and remove any 'weed' trees – the ones like birch, willow, hawthorn and rowan - to make way for timber or even amenity trees." Owen was becoming insistent.

"Yes, yes. I can see that. I never really noticed all these thin and straggly limes before. You're lucky we neglected this plantation after my father died. Had we kept it 'clean', there would be no 'weed' trees left, and all the gaps where the conifers have failed would have been 'beaten up'. I like that forestry term. The idea of beating up open spaces with trees tickles me." Humphrey broke into one of his boyish grins.

To Owen, the remark was not a capricious but a profound one, but he was not going to reveal his thoughts on the matter.

"So what trees should I insist on being introduced as replacements for the conifers that are removed, Owen?"

"They should only be trees indigenous to Mynydd y rhibo, shouldn't they", replied Owen, careful to leave the decision with Humphrey.

"Of course, my boy, nothing else would be right."

"Let me show you what I mean", said Owen in the urgency of the moment, leading Humphrey towards a mass of tangled foliage.

"There's a large native crab apple over here which is about half-way between the dingle and the wood. It should never be felled because there's a chance its apples will provide seeds for others. And it's ideal as a resting place for the Spirit, if the journey is an exacting one." Immediately the words left his mouth, he realised what he had said. Before Humphrey could question the remark, Owen added, hurriedly: "Do you know of any other species that tree spirits like to rest in, Humphrey?"

Cleverly, Owen had stretched the man's affinity with tree spirits to the limit. The wiry denizen of the Court was caught on the hop. It took him some seconds of feigned deep thought to reply.

"Well... There are a number of small tree species which have always made me wonder why they have a strange appearance, or seem to be different in some way. Owen, you've given this matter a lot of thought, haven't you? And you've already surveyed the plantation in detail. I didn't even know that this crab apple existed. What else have you found?"

"Um..." Owen paused because he was about to divulge the whole plan. "From the dingle to the wood, there is a continuous, although a rather devious, line of broadleaved trees of all sizes, beginning with the aspens on the edge of the plantation and continuing through the attenuated limes that wander a sinuous course to this crab apple. From here, there are several straggly limes close enough to give a subterranean route across the rest of the plantation to its boundary ditch where there is a twinned stemmed wild service tree to complete the link up."

"And where do you think the spirit will go from there?" asked Humphrey, fascinated more by Owen telling his secrets to him than by the actual solution to the Spirit's plight.

"There can be only one tree that it will make for. The tall

lime in the middle of the wood not far from the top of the Dark Dell, the one whose crown emerges above the overall canopy of green..." Owen stopped abruptly.

"'Canopy of green'! What prose, Owen. I was right about you having leanings towards the Shakespearian stage."

Owen coloured up, embarrassed by his accidental slip of the tongue, and a little shocked that the Spirit's words were becoming second nature to him. With a genial smirk on his face, Humphrey said that he thought he knew which tree Owen meant.

"In honour of your passion for names, Humphrey, I've called it the 'Emergent Lime'", said Owen.

"Not bad, not bad", judged Humphrey. "It must be the one that Matty took Suzy to see last year; after persuading her that nothing would jump out at them from behind the trunks in the wood. That sister of yours is scared stiff of dark places. I gave them a head start and then raced off to the wood by another route. It was great. I hid behind a big oak tree near the path, a little way into the wood, and waited. And then, just as they were going by, I jumped out like this, screaming." He gave a demonstration, which was so crazy that Owen smiled for the first time since spying on him at Teili Junction.

"What happened?" he asked, knowing that Suzy would have been livid.

With a boyish grin wider than any grin so far, and moving about even more than usual, Humphrey explained, delightedly:

"Your sister went berserk. I've never seen her so frightened. She flew into Matty's arms. And then when she saw it was me, she shouted all sorts of abuse, some of it very naughty. I had to keep outside clouting distance."

"Did you go with them to the tree?"

"No fear! I wouldn't have come back alive. I just made myself scarce. That's what we should do, my boy. It's getting a bit spooky amongst these conifers."

With that, they left the plantation and reappeared beside the Melglyn Stoggle, where Humphrey, leaning irreverently against the trunk of the tree, immediately raised the question again of how Owen was going to get the Farr's to agree to an enclosure at the top of the dingle.

"I have never got Lloyd Farr to agree to anything yet. It was much easier dealing with his father. With inside help though, Owen, you may be successful." Another glint came into his eyes as he said these words.

"That's not really the problem."

"No. What is, then? Fallen out with Catherine have you?" The impish grin returned.

"Not exactly, although she is not very happy at the moment. She has let me into a secret which I must divulge to you, but in strict confidence. I will be on the end of abuse, otherwise." He stared at Humphrey for an indication that the secret would be respected.

"You can trust me, my boy: with everything. I won't tell a soul; not even Matty." He crossed two fingers on his left hand.

"Mr Medlar wants to do an exchange of land with the Farrs once he is in possession of Wern y coc – did you know he's going to bid for the place at the auction?. He's already approached them. The pastures at Wern y coc for the dingle fields. A deal which, if it goes through, will give him the Stoggle..." Owen's concern carried a hint of sadness, but it was lost on Humphrey.

"What a sneak! He knows that..." Humphrey checked

himself. "It doesn't surprise me. Rhibo Mountain is what he would really like to own. He's often told me how lucky I am to be the landlord of a mountain. He's even offered to buy one of my lordships, the Lord of the Manor of Ewyas, but I'm keeping it, otherwise he might stop my conker battles in the castle. I suppose the dingle fields would give him a toe-hold on one side of the Mountain. It does surprise me though that he has revealed his designs on Wern y coc; he's usually a very secretive man when it comes to the acquisition of property." He paused to think for a moment. Owen offered his views on the matter.

"I think his interest in your plantation and the dingle fields are linked. With control of both, he would be free to fashion an arboreal folly between the Goggin and the Mountain which would be visible from The Prospect, as well as increasing his ownership of land."

"Owen, you're a bright lad. But do I detect a bit of Milo in your words?"

Owen was quick to answer this: "None. He doesn't know anything about this, and I don't want him to know, even though he's a friend." This remark made quite an impression upon Humphrey, as a confidence between two boys might make when a mutual friend was being excluded, but Owen was unaware of its impact.

"Isn't Catherine the owner of the dingle fields, or is it just the dwelling at Gwenynog?" asked Humphrey.

"Yes, the fields are legally hers", replied Owen, not wishing to get too deeply into this aspect of the matter.

"Then, won't she have to agree to an exchange?"

"Yes", said Owen, tersely.

"Well, you can persuade her not to agree, can't you? A

young suitor like yourself. Perhaps the future master of Gwenynog..." Humphrey was more interested in mischief than the serious side of the issue.

"No. I cannot guarantee it."

"Owen! What an admission. You should have more sway than that with your women friends." This was a fine remark coming from someone whose life was held together by his wife.

"So, how do you propose we thwart his plans? Or should I say - his conniving? Don't worry, Owen, you can tell me all. Carl Medlar has never had my complete trust, and what trust he has diminishes with every sneaky move he makes. And this isn't the first, although it is the sneakiest."

"I don't know. I was hoping that you might have some ideas. I fear that the exchange will take place unless someone else outbids the man, which would be good for the Stoggle but not necessarily good for Catherine's family. If only we could work out a way to save the Stoggle and also let Cath's dad have his extra land..."

Owen was about to continue when Humphrey held up one hand and gestured him to stop, implying that he needed time to think. He cocked his head to one side and pursed his lips, his eyes darting about quixotically. Then a series of poses followed - hand on chin; hand on forehead; hands on hips; shoulders pulled back - all done while he moved about on the spot and interrupted twice by a hand held up towards Owen to tell him to wait. And all the time, he looked everywhere but at Owen. How did the local acting group cope with such thoughtful twinges? Then, at last, he spoke:

"Now then, Medlar has been the detonator of business bombshells in this district for too long. It's about time someone else made an explosion. Why don't I defuse his bomb and explode one myself?"

The question was clearly rhetorical, but even so Owen could not respond. How could he, when Humphrey was in this sort of vein? A bewildered look crossed his face while the man smiled mischievously, and continued.

"What if we bought the land at Wern y coc and then leased the pastures to Catherine's father? The dingle fields would be safe: the Stoggle would be safe. And I would have the land back my father gave away. With Catherine's permission, you and I could plant it up with lime and oak and cherry and maple... How about that?!"

Owen was speechless. He just stood on the spot, wide-eyed and open-mouthed.

"You didn't expect that, did you my boy? Carl Medlar is not the only real estate tactician in these parts."

Ignoring Owen's stunned state, he continued.

"I've already got the details of the sale. Matty picked them up the other day so we could see them. Come on, Owen, get excited my boy; we've got some scheming to do."

Owen did not know what to say. All manner of thoughts were rushing through his head. Was Humphrey serious or play-acting? Had Matilda discreetly prompted the whole idea? Did he mean, buy Wern y coc as a whole?

"You mean you're prepared to buy the entire holding?" He asked, tentatively.

"Oh no, Owen; only the pastures. We couldn't afford the whole place. Anyway, that's all we need, isn't it? Now, how long have we got to write the script for this piece of property intrigue?"

Owen did not hear this last question, for he was in the process of formulating one himself.

"If someone else put up the money for the house and buildings and the meadows, would you bid anonymously for them so that Medlar would not know who was bidding against him?"

"Aha! So you're not a destitute young man after all."

"No, I mean yes... No, I don't want to buy Wern y coc, but I know someone who does. They don't want to do it openly because it would infuriate Medlar and make him even more determined to buy the place."

"Oho! This is getting exciting. Now let me guess who the unknown bidder might be. Someone who would infuriate Mr Medlar. That could only be Milo, if it is someone you know. Am I right? I must be."

Owen went quiet for a moment. What should he say?

"Another secret, Owen? Come on, you can trust me. Is it Milo?"

"Yes, but it's a secret, a very precious secret, which I shouldn't have divulged to anyone. Milo and Alison have decided to buy Wern y coc, keep all its traditional features, and save the meadows. They're afraid that if Medlar finds out, he will be hell bent on buying the holding. If you were to bid for the pastures openly and the rest anonymously, he will not know what is going on. You could attend the auction and enjoy the action.

"A conspiracy! A conspiracy! And it will explode another bomb. Yes, yes, I'll do it. My solicitor is squeaky clean and unknown to Carl."

There was another pause, enlivened by twinges, as Humphrey thought for a brief moment. Then his face broke into a Machiavellian grin - almost a leer - before he uttered, in Shakespearian tones:

"The Wern y coc Cabal... I like it! Let's go back to the Court and conspire there, my boy." His eyes were now brimming with moisture and he began to set off. But Owen checked him.

"What are you going to do about Medlar's involvement in the management of the plantation? What if he gets 'his gang' to start thinning the plantation and 'cleaning' it up. He didn't waste any time getting it brashed. What if your actions upset him and make him think twice about leasing the hall to your Theatre Trust."

Humphrey halted. "Don't worry, my boy. I'm already formulating a plan in my mind to control that." He trudged around on the spot in his usual fashion, cogitating, again holding one hand up in the air towards Owen - this time with its index finger prominently pointed.

"What I will do is delay him in doing any more work until we've agreed the details - that is, drawn up a management plan. And my critical condition will be that he converts the plantation back into being a dishevelled wilderness like the wood. But first - and this is where I'll cut off his retreat - I will publicise the fact, as I said I would to him, that he has been generous enough to donate a building in Elchon to the Gulible Theatre Trust. And then, I will disarm him by writing in the local rag that he is also making an expert contribution to the protection of wildlife on the Llandyfrig Court estate by using his considerable forestry skills to convert the plantation back into being a part of Coed Tirion Glas. How about that!"

Owen was again speechless.

"Come on, my boy. We've got a script to write. We can't

hang about here."

With that, he strode off his stage beside the Stoggle and headed for the path through the plantation, with Owen having to catch him up. But Owen did not go far; he found an excuse not to return to the Court.

The Doomsday Oak

CHAPTER 33

'Trees should bear leaves together,
Safeguard the trees at your side;
The grove, would all were pleasant,
Is a grim grove without love.'

From 'A Plea for Peace' by Tudur Aled (1480-1526), lines 121-124, in Clancy (1965) Medieval Welsh Lyrics

---

"How did you get on with Owen, today, Humphrey?" asked Matilda as she prepared their supper. "Why didn't he stay for some food? You did invite him, didn't you?"

"Yes, yes; of course I invited him, but he had to rush off to a tryst with Catherine. I wonder how those two will get on when Suzy returns. Those siblings are so different, you know. Will a quiet, thoughtful young man like Owen cope with life at the Goggin in the company of his excitable sister? If he comes to need an alternative living space, we could let him stay in the

Gatehouse, in return for bashing it into shape, couldn't we? I'm sure it's still habitable."

This question was put in an off-the-cuff manner, while he was facing away from Matilda. During his journey back to the Court, he had mulled over a number of ideas involving Owen. Matilda was accustomed to hearing her husband's brilliant ideas, few of which ever came to anything. But there were so many that some had to succeed. This latest one was particularly thought provoking.

"I think Suzy expects, or assumes, that he will move away when she returns. Has he said he intends to stay?"

"Not in so many words, but he has accepted a part in our September play, so he must want to stay on for a while before he goes off to study again."

This, too, was said facing away from Matilda.

"Humphrey! How did you get him to commit himself to that? Suzy's the one for the stage, not Owen!" Matilda was taken completely by surprise.

"I have my ways", said Humphrey, turning round and breaking into a mischievous grin. "I thought the effort of learning some lines and cavorting with others in a comedy would cheer him up a bit. You did say he was in need of cheering up."

"Yes, I did; but not that sort of cheering up. Is he doing it of his own free will, or have you put some unkind pressure on him?" Matilda knew that her husband's passion for the stage had a tendency to make him overstep the mark – or even swap unwanted antiques for performance roles...

"Now Matty, that's not fair. He was pleased to accept my offer of a part."

"So, what else did you two get up to today, then?"

Humphrey ignored this question completely.

"I even thought we could offer him some work as a part-time estate handyman; a day or so a week. The work is piling up, Matty. It will give him jobs to do during his forthcoming academic career."

Again, his words were said facing away from his wife.

"Yes, I know it is; and that's a very nice thought. Have you asked him yet?"

"No", came the answer from the other side of the room.

"Then what have you been chatting to him about all this time, besides play-acting?"

Humphrey began to fiddle with various items as he shuffled around the kitchen. He was not all that good at keeping things from his wife, despite a life-time of acting. She could see that he was going to be evasive.

"Oh, I thought he might have got into a twist with Catherine, but he didn't really want to talk about her, although she's got something to do with his sad state, I can tell. That's when I got him interested in our next play. I gave him a short audition at the Junction. He's not bad."

"Where else did you go?" probed Matilda.

"Only up to the coniferous plantation. He wanted to know what my plans were now that the clearance work has been started."

"And?"

"Well, I told him that we have decided to convert the plantation back into a broadleaved wood, and that Carl is going to help us do it."

"Now, Humphrey, that isn't true, is it? Carling won't be at

all pleased when you tell him that he cannot do what he likes with our plantation - which is what he thinks at the moment. We shall have to be extremely diplomatic with him, and also very firm. We should let him know as soon as we can that you have changed your mind - we have changed our mind - before he gets too engrossed in his arboricultural dreaming. Have you thought about that yet?"

"Yes, Matty, I have," he said, looking right into her eyes.

"Then, how are you going to do it?"

"I'm keeping that a secret."

"Humphrey! This is no time for games. I do not want that man dictating to us what we do on our own land." Matilda became uncharacteristically agitated. She had had a difficult day at the Centre, covering for someone else, and she was tired. Her lack of confidence in her husband's ability to rectify his occasional lapses in good sense did not help.

"Matty, I've got a plan which will leave him with no choice but to adhere to our wishes. But I want to surprise you. And you will be surprised; I promise."

"Humphrey. There is a lot at stake in this matter. Do you realise that? The smoother everything goes, and the clearer the arrangements, the better. The last thing we want is an irate neighbour on our doorstep. We must be careful exactly how and when we involve him. He could well take his annoyance out on some of our trees. If we must involve him, we should insist upon penalties for any damage done to existing trees if he organises the thinning. For heaven's sake, Humphrey, why did you agree to his involvement in the first place?"

"You know why, Matty. And it was a good deal. A one in a million deal. But it has yet to be finalised and put in writing.

What I propose to do should keep the deal intact, and also ensure that the plantation is managed in the way we want, not as he expects. I promise you that."

"Alright, but I want to see any written agreement before it is signed, and if it starts to go wrong afterwards we shall have to be very firm indeed; ever so firm." Matilda restrained herself from pressing him further. She knew that he would reveal his secret plan sooner or later. Anyway, as always, she was beginning to formulate an alternative strategy to fall back on. She had already contacted Suzy to seek her help.

"By the way", remembered Humphrey, conveniently, "I had a word with the keeper this morning. He did shoot the Eerie Shriek, the idiot. He said he had had enough of its shrilling cry, and should have shot it years ago."

"What did you say to that?"

"I sacked him."

"You what?!" exclaimed Matilda, dropping a piece of crockery into the sink.

"I sacked him. I told him that shooting buzzards was illegal and that the penalty was his notice. I said that I wouldn't report him to the police unless he did something else foolish. "

Humphrey was enjoying every minute of this piece of news, delighted that he had caught Matilda - and the Keeper - on the hop. He felt that he was getting his own back for the dressing down she had given him upon his return from the directors' workshop.

"What did he say, for heaven's sake?"

"He got pretty mad. I thought his face was going to explode; it became so red. If his gun had been beside him, he might have shot me too. He said he would leave immediately, and that he should have left when father died. I told him to get his junk out of the Gatehouse, because we had other plans for it. That's what led me to think that Owen might like to turn it from a keeper's den into a cosy cottage again."

Matilda was flabbergasted. She had lost control of the situation. And she was growing concerned. Whenever her husband displayed confidence of the kind she now faced, he tended to become hasty in his actions, as in his treatment of the Keeper, but the outcome was not always so simple in its consequence. Normally, she could sense when his confidence was about to spill over. The lead up to a play would get the adrenalin going, and the excitement would bring about surges of over-confidence. The only explanation for his present behaviour was the meeting with Owen. Were she not one step ahead of him in this regard, she might have pressed him again to reveal his scheme to extricate them from the deal with Carl Medlar. Again, she restrained herself, although it was more difficult this time.

"I think Owen will be delighted at having the option of moving into the Gatehouse when Suzy returns. He has become extremely attached to this area. I'm sure he can co-exist with Suzy in the same valley - they're not as incompatible as everyone thinks. We should encourage him to stay. So your suggestion is perfect, although I'm sure we haven't heard the end of the Keeper's wrath. Did you say anything to him about his tenure of the Keeper's Lodge?"

"No. He rushed away too fast. I think we should consider re-letting it, while we sort out the future maintenance of the Haye."

"Humphrey, that's ridiculous, and you know it. This is

certainly not the time for embroiling ourselves in such a dispute."

"Alright... alright. I'll let him cool off and stay where he is for the moment. But he's not getting another chance. You didn't want to be accommodating the last time he annoyed us."

"I know... I know. We're better rid of him, but we should let him have the Lodge for as long as he wants it. He has lived in it for over twenty years. Now let's eat and turn to other things. What shall we do tonight?"

Humphrey did not reply to this question until he had settled down to the table and looked up from his plate of food. Continuing in his boyishly buoyant vein, he surprised Matilda even further.

"With all this fuss over the keeper, why don't we bring the books up to date, and take stock of our financial circumstances. You were on at me the other day about making an appointment with the accountant."

This suggestion was so uncharacteristic, so unexpected, and so inexplicable, that Matilda couldn't believe her ears. Even when adrenalin was not coursing through her husband's wiry body, and enthusiasm not promising to engulf him in crazy antics, book-keeping was usually the last thing on his mind. His suggestion was consequently enthralling, having the effect of engrossing Matilda in a game of unravelling why her husband should want to discuss money matters. What else had happened, besides his meeting with Owen, to interest him in their financial affairs?... She knew that it would not be long before she found out why.

Owen had not had to rush away to meet Catherine. Once they

had reached the deer-fence gate at the base of the Cwm, the inner thoughts of both men made them realise that it was better that they went their separate ways on this occasion. Humphrey knew that he would be interrogated by Matilda on his return, and that he could cope more easily with her questioning alone. He was relieved, therefore, when Owen suddenly pretended that he had a meeting with Catherine. Upon leaving the wood, Owen knew that he wanted to spend time enjoying the calmness of the Deer Haye and the Cwm, and to check on the flowering of the limes once more. He had visited the Stoggle as often as possible during its flowering, and wanted to repeat the experience with the limes of Llandyfrig Court.

The days of hay-making at Bodcot Farm had curtailed his freedom to go where he pleased when he liked at a critical time for him. And it had also presented him with some personal difficulties, one of which had been working long hours with Ralph. And when not encumbered with Ralph, he had been encumbered with endless time to contemplate the fact that the Stoggle, during its flowering, had only contacted him briefly, and might never contact him again now that the Eerie Shriek had departed. Ralph's collusion with Carl Medlar also aggravated an already fraught situation.

In the back of his mind, he felt that the calming effects of the Haye, blended with the blossoming splendour of the limes, might predispose his soul towards receiving a communication from the Stoggle - if such an event was ever to happen again. Matilda would not have wanted him to be around, anyway, when she discussed the day with her husband. But he did walk part of the way back to the Court with Humphrey, until it occurred to him that he could leave his bike where it was for the time being. Humphrey had agreed to store the bike in one of the many out-houses at the Court.

The two men had parted near the Wrong-angled Oak. From there, Owen went to the best of the lime trees in the Haye, a tree in its prime, located at the edge of the deer fence on the southernmost stretch of the boundary on the footpath route home. It stood on the lower part of a wooded bank, overlooking a secluded field. There was nothing between it and the fence save dense growths of bracken, hiding noxious stinging nettles, and a ride which had been mown recently to maintain access to the stile out of the Haye. A badger track emerged from the bracken at one point and led to the base of the tree. Nearby, on the other side of the fence, there was the bleached butt of a felled elm, testifying to the erstwhile existence of a huge tree which had been cut through twelve feet above the ground after succumbing to the virus carried by one of its beetle lodgers. Black blotches and streaks of a sooty fungus contrasted starkly with the seared whiteness of the tough elm timber; and, as an almost wreath-like reminder that life continues, this monument to sudden arboreal death supported a small clump of rose-bay willow-herb growing out of its rotting top, and a solitary thistle in flower. Opposite the butt, and to one side of the lime, the bank was clear of trees except for some hidden transplants, holding their own against the bracken within the protection of Humphrey de Bohun stock frames. A colony of flowering fox-gloves enlivened the fetid and monotonous green of the rampant fern, their red spires swaying in the breeze.

He had concluded that the tree was a large leaved lime, not a natural hybrid between the two native species.* Its flower stalks carried three to five flowers apiece, and it had been the first tree to blossom after the Melglyn Stoggle, so it was probably Tilia platyphyllos. Half of its flowers were fully open and gay, while the rest were already over or in decline. Some bracts were beginning to fade in colour and go brown at their tips, and the ground beneath the tree, which was divided by moss-covered surface roots into sectors of bare earth and fragile leaf litter, carried a scattering of discarded bracts. Bees of all kinds, and flies of all sizes, made their repetitive visitations. A very dull hum was audible, although the dominant sound was the wind in the other trees on the bank - the oak, the sweet chestnut, the beech, and the horse chestnut. A delicate fragrance floated elusively about.

For Owen, the sight, the sound, and the smell, merging together in the mind, induced that much sought after emotion - the eternal desire of the human psyche - of being glad to be alive. But the feeling stirred up other thoughts. How supreme the Mountain must have been when its lime trees were undisturbed by man; that golden time of eagles, kites, and Ceridwen. A mountain clothed in lime trees, blossoming together. Or would their spirits have flowered in succession, instead of all at once, each racing to be the first? The fragrance of the trees in the clearings of the wildwood should have been enough to make early man rejoice in being glad to be alive. Or would it...?

From here, he climbed the wooded slope back towards Teili Junction, passing another large-leaved lime in flower near the Gully. As he arrived at the Junction, a tawny owl vacated the spreading arbour. The lower flowers, the ones he could see clearly, were only just opening. So there was no scent to indulge in. However, the views into the lower reaches of the Haye were ample compensation for the stiff climb. Although the lime blossom was the only current flowering in the Haye, there were other details to catch the eye against the heavy greenness of summer growth. Yellow-green and, in some cases, deep red lammas shoots tipped the edges of the oak crowns.* Developing flower spikes made the sweet chestnuts appear as star-spangled plumes - the prelude to a symphony of blossom which would give a crescendo of individual colour to compare with the horse chestnuts in the spring. Yet these migrants from the Balkans - the de Bohun conker trees - were continuing to make their presence felt. Collapsed clusters of dead leaves, reddish-brown in their premature demise, appeared in the distance like festival tassels. In the satiety of this summer vegetation, the gaunt skeleton of another dead elm, unharvested by man, was the only stark feature.

He moved on to the Domesday Oak and re-entered the cwm through the gate, ascending the slopes where the flowers of some small-leaved limes were more advanced than those at the Junction. The yellow blossom, mixed with the pale cream of the dividing bracts, was beginning to push the floppy leaves into the background. Here, in the shelter of the natural bowl, the fragrance of the limes was heady. Sinking evening air gave ephemeral stations where nostril breathing was delicious. He moved between the trees, checking the fragrance of each one. There was little difference between them: variations in pungency but not in flavour. But the aroma was not the aroma of the Melglyn Stoggle. It was lime, and it was sweet, but it did not compare either in pungency or in fragrance with the Stoggle. Neither did the large-leaved limes lower down. The Stoggle was in a class on its own. A dying class...

Looking down into the Cwm from the edge of the wood, the lime trees in the mini-cwms and beside the brook now appeared subdued and lonely. The ageing evening darkened their forms and merged them with the ground. Away to the east, wisps of mist were forming in the distance, twisting tenuously through the lines of trees in the lower Haye and in the valley beyond. He decided it was too late to include the Emergent Lime in his circuitous route to the Stoggle. A daytime visit would be better in view of the difficulties in finding the tree. Rhibo Mountain was, perhaps, the best place to be on such a summer evening. So Owen made his way to the summit. The panorama of south-western Herefordshire, and beyond, made its moving impressions once more.

Owen watched the sunset develop to its climax - to a sky reminiscent of Chinese lacquer: very luminous, almost phosphorescent. It was almost a turquoise sky with rose-pink striations of cirrus clouds radiating across the source of light, spreading over the Black Mountains to the Wye Valley. In the east and in the south, the sky dulled to a light grey-blue, except where a belt of white clouds on the eastern horizon made the English summer heavens unreal in both directions. He wished he could wave a wand and bring Catherine to his side to enjoy the sunset with him. And then wave it again to send her away so he could continue his journey to the Stoggle. He was so elated that he covered stretches of the journey in reverse, watching the sky wane. A feint misty glaze covering the scenes below was real, not an impression induced by the moisture in his eyes. And the darkening canopy of Coed Tirion Glas accentuated the grandeur of the Emergent Lime, its elevated crown silhouetted, at one point, against the white clouds in the eastern distance.

The enchanting evening sky and the symbolic view of the Emergent Lime had its effect. His longing - the longing of the Melglyn Stoggle to be reunited with Y Coed - welled up within him. His fervour to bring about the move, whatever the obstacles, returned to the forefront of his mind. His thoughts changed from elation at seeing an enchanting Chinese lacquer sky to sadness at the Spirit's ancient call for help. The intricacies of his rescue plan, and the accessories to its implementation were given repeated analysis during the last stages of his journey to the Stoggle...

What if Medlar was stubbornly intent on acquiring Wern y coc? Could he be routed at the auction? Could Humphrey raise the necessary cash to buy the pastures? Would he pull it off or get sidetracked by acting out the part? Was it all a game to him? Was Medlar more interested in the pastures than the holding? If pressed, would he bid and bid and bid until they were knocked down to him, whatever the cost? Could anyone challenge such acquisitive intent? As a financier, he would be an expert bidder. If only they knew what his real financial circumstances were. They had to be as confident as he appeared to be; resolute in their stand; and have something in reserve. What, for heaven's sake! And the vital question of all. Could Catherine resist the pressure from her family to accept an exchange of land? And how much influence did Ralph have; that was an unknown factor?

Owen had still not decided what was best to do - encourage Catherine to join forces with her father, or persuade her to remain firm in her apparent resolve not to give up any land at Gwenynog. She had to accept, sometime, that buying the land herself was a pipe-dream. If she and her father, or else Humphrey were successful bidders, then there would be no uncertainties concerning the safety of the Stoggle. If only she were adamant in her resolve not to agree to an exchange, all would be safe, whatever the outcome of the sale.

Why could he not tell Catherine what was going on? He wanted to, but there was an intangible barrier between them which made it impossible. There were too many complications; too many uncertainties. She would never believe him. And yet, as the legal owner of the Stoggle, her consent to an enclosure was vital. He should have raised the matter again. Her reactions, so far, to his 'obsessive' interest, were not good omens in this respect. Should Humphrey win the pastures, bringing down upon her the same pressures she was under now to accede to an exchange, and should she become aware of Owen's collusion, would she forgive him? If she could not believe him, how could she forgive him?

Owen lapsed into a sadder state as he dropped off the summit towards the rocks and the dingle. It was now ten o'clock. The sight of the Stoggle's declining top aroused an assortment of feelings connected with the experiences and thoughts of the evening. As he circled the rocks, and came within full view of the tree, his mind suddenly emptied and he stopped in the action of taking a stride. Fate was testing him to the limit.

Catherine was walking around the Stoggle, staring up into its ageing crown. Her movements were like those of a tree surgeon inspecting a suspect tree, looking for tell-tale signs which would give away its condition - indications that would explain what was wrong.

He could not believe his eyes. Nor comprehend why she should be there. To his knowledge, she had shunned the dingle, ever since the excursion with him when they had differed on the subject of emanations from natural objects. The only time she had passed near the Stoggle since then was when they had gone for a walk together onto the Mountain from Gwenynog. On that occasion, she had deliberately kept to the footpath route to the summit across the dingle fields, keeping the brook between them and the isolated tree.

For that frozen moment, he was love-lost as well as shocked. Her exquisite beauty and the splendour of the lime tree were juxtaposed; but they did not unite. Seeing the two so close together was more than unusual; more than striking; it was incongruous. They could not come together, because in Owen's mind they were separate and incapable of unison. And yet, Catherine contained in her face certain indefinable qualities or ingredients of the countryside. Were they qualities acquired from generations of lives in Ewyas that were inbred? Or the brightness of generations gladdened by the sweetness of Ceridwen? There was a connection here which lay at the heart of his affection for her; a connection which had captured his attention in the beginning. But the Melglyn Stoggle and Catherine could not meet, nor could they merge, within his mind - he thought he was sure of that.

Suddenly, the thought struck him. Was her presence at the tree part of a tour of the dingle fields to decide their fate? Was she still wavering in her resolve not to give in? Had she finally realised that the cost was too great for her to bid alone? From the initial mixed feelings of shocked surprise, being glad to see her, and confusion at her very presence beside the tree, he became extremely apprehensive. Whatever the reason for her presence, he knew that such a meeting place was wrong for both of them.

When she saw him coming down from the rocks, she was as undecided in her own mind as to how to greet him as he was in his. The dingle and the Stoggle had become his place of retreat; a private part of his life in Ewyas; a part that perplexed her. Her efforts to gain access to it met with difficulties even on neutral ground. The ground she now occupied was not neutral; spiritually, it was his; legally, it was hers. She was more accustomed to legality than spirituality. But this was not the reason for her holding back.

They both smiled - the smiles of a couple meeting to undo a misunderstanding. Their whole relationship so far had been a mixture of intimacy and a series of misunderstandings. Their initial contact was restrained - a coming together, but nothing more.

"I hoped I would find you here. I've been at the trig point watching the sunset develop. Hasn't it been glorious? I can't remember such a colourful sky. Suzy would have gone mad over it."

Her words were said with the controlled excitement that was Catherine.

"Enchanting: I'm glad you saw it too," said Owen, quietly. His unreachable emotions seemed further away than usual.

"I telephoned the Court from the Goggin. Matilda said you must be lingering somewhere on the Mountain or in the Deer Haye after your afternoon with her husband. What have you two been up to?"

She asked this question in a nervous voice, by way of

continuing the dialogue, such as it was, but unwittingly getting to the heart of Owen's whereabouts before and since his parting from Humphrey. He did not want to stall, as he had often done in the past when she interrogated him on his daily activities; nor to lie; it was not in his nature to be dishonest. In the tautness of the moment, he felt there was no harm in revealing part of what had transpired that day.

"We've been discussing the management of the coniferous plantation over there. How it might be converted back into being a part of the wood. Humphrey wants to draw up a plan for it."

"And did you?... draw up a plan?"

"Sort of; the principles of it, at least. Then..."

Owen paused as he thought quickly about the wisdom of raising a matter which he had briefly raised before: a matter which, he had concluded earlier that evening, he should have raised again. But, as with all delicate proposals to Catherine, it was a matter which had to be put at the right time. But time was running out.

"Then Humphrey and I talked about the possibility of linking the Stoggle here with the wood. He knows I'm attached to the tree but he also revealed that he knows who owns it – you." Owen paused again. "Would you consent to an enclosure at the top of the dingle here so as to allow the natural regeneration of trees and to link the Stoggle with the wood?" He finished his request knowing the reaction it could induce, but hoping that Catherine was amenable this time.

She gave him a questioning look pregnant with undertones of annoyance. He was about to add an explanation when she replied.

"Why, Owen? Why is this tree so important to you? Here we are in the run-up to a sale that is of heart-rending importance to me, and all you can think about is this tree." She waved her arm towards it, dismissively.

There were some seconds of stern silence before Owen answered her question, and the importunate look which went with it.

"I'd just like to see it surrounded by other trees instead of it being forlorn; bare of company - that's all. Forgotten. Don't you think it would look better?"

"It looks alright as it is. Is this another of de Bohun's hair-brained schemes?"

"No. It's one of mine", said Owen, defiantly. Then he added, as an afterthought – "If Matilda can respect Humphrey's hair-brained ideas, I thought you might be able to respect at least one of mine."

For a moment, Catherine was caught off-guard by this comment.

"Well, it will have to wait until the sale is over. If I'm still the owner of these fields after the auction, I can consider it then."

"What do you mean, 'If you're still the owner'? You will always be the owner unless you decide to give them up."

"I can't afford to bid for the pastures. They're expected to fetch forty thousand pounds."

"Then, why don't you go halves with your dad?"

"He refuses to accept any help from me. His stubbornness is what infuriates Ralph so much. Anyway, I'm beginning to think they're right. A smaller Gwenynog would suit me better. The whole family, including my grandparents, think the opportunity is too good not to miss."

"So you're giving in to an exchange of land with Medlar?"

The disgust in Owen's voice brought a quick retort from Catherine.

"I'm not giving in. I've just accepted that it would be the best thing in everyone's interest. But it's not certain that Mr Medlar will win. He can't purchase every property that comes on the market, however much he wants them."

Owen's face expressed the depth of his dismay. Catherine ignored his pallor and continued to be unsettling.

"I suppose de Bohun as well is more interested in his trees than the sale." The remark was rhetorical, but none-the-less cutting.

Owen recaptured some degree of composure, and sought refuge in reasonableness.

"No. On the way back to the Haye we got talking about the auction. He is not very pleased that Medlar is ready to pounce on yet another piece of property." He paused for a moment. Despite her chagrin, Catherine's face was resonant in its usual beautiful way. It distracted his thinking enough for him to hesitate before he revealed more of his discussion with de Bohun. "I told Humphrey that Medlar has offered to exchange the pastures at Wern y coc with your dad in return for your dingle fields. He was a bit rattled that Medlar should be so presumptuous. So he has decided to bid for the pastures himself and, if successful, to rent them to your dad. That changes the whole situation, doesn't it?"

"Yes, it does. Is de Bohun going to let my father know? This whole sale is now becoming rather complicated."

"I'm sure he will let him know that an alternative

arrangement might be on the cards instead of an exchange with Medlar. Humphrey and Matilda have a generous reputation as landlords, don't they? And there's been another development. I don't know if I've done the right thing or not, but I asked him, without mentioning any names, if he would bid at the auction on behalf of someone else, so as to keep their identity a secret. He guessed straight away who it was, and said he would be delighted to do the bidding for them."

"He would", interposed Catherine, breaking into her more normal voice, the intonation in her words carrying the disapproval that was inevitable. "Role-playing is his speciality. You should know that by now. It wasn't a very advisable thing to mention, was it? But that's really between you, Alison and Milo. You had better tell them as soon as you can. Tonight, if they're in."

"Why is it not 'advisable'?" In a burst of concern caused by his interpretation of Catherine's mood, Owen emphasised the word she had used. She had lapsed into her local government language, and was opting out. Her tendency to look at life in terms of advisability was one of the essential differences between them. It was the tendency which had overcome her initial reluctance to comply with the family's wish for an exchange; a tendency which made Owen wonder how she and Suzy managed to get on so well. Little in Suzy's life was advisable. But, then, did he really know his sister? How well, come to that, did he know Catherine? He continued without waiting for a reply.

"If Humphrey does bid for them, Medlar will be outmanoeuvred; so, too, will all the other local bidders at the auction"

"But what if he acts the part to distraction, and misses a vital stage in the bidding? You haven't seen him on the stage yet, have you, overacting and forgetting his words?"

"He won't. Matilda will make sure of that. Anyway, he is as eager as we are to see Wern y coc go to Milo and Alison."

Catherine did not want to prolong the matter. "Have you finished on the Mountain?" she asked, making it clear that she had. "Can we go back now? I'll wait a few moments if you want to say goodbye to your tree."

"I never say goodbye to trees", was the muttered reply Owen made. "Anyway you seem to be making pretty sure that my bond with this special tree will be broken."

As they turned their backs on the Stoggle, he decided not to discuss the sale any more. Catherine, pretending that nothing untoward had happened, preferred to talk about Suzy and her imminent return. She had not heard from her friend for weeks and had no idea of the date of her homecoming. She wanted to organise a grand reception for her. But she did not divulge this to Owen as they made their way back to Gwenynog where she had parked her car. Owen was equally in the dark; but, whereas Catherine was impatient for a reunion with her friend, he needed as much time as possible free from the presence of his sister. The two close friends were at odds again.

And Owen's mind was going elsewhere. Catherine's decision to acquiesce in an exchange of land, which was now a strong possibility, had affected him more than she could see from his guarded behaviour. Being an outsider in the district, an itinerant one at that, he was beginning to feel helpless. Why had he been chosen by the Spirit in the Stoggle to help it to safety? Why not someone from the locality? Someone whose attachment to its heritage was long-standing? Why not Matilda, if she had known the Stoggle for so long? Why not Suzy, even? She had influence with Catherine, influence which would secure an enclosure overnight. It seemed to him that between them, Suzy and Matilda had unassailable influence locally; greater influence even than the 'Meddling Baron'. Why, then, had he been chosen? Had the Spirit in the Stoggle made a mistake?

CHAPTER 34

'So the lord in the linden wood leads the hunt...'

**'Sir Gawain & the Green Knight' - circa 1375 – 1400
– Part 111. Norton Anthology, p. 1178**

Time was now running out for Owen, or so he thought. The forthcoming sale was scheduled for Friday, 15 July. He had over a week to kill. There was little he could do to occupy his hours except to make the gazebo look like he had given it his undivided attention. While attempting to do this, Matilda telephoned, suggesting a meeting to discuss the next stage of their collusion, and saying that Humphrey was busy putting his own plans into action. Owen was certainly in need of such a distraction, for Milo and Alison had responded to his news in a positive way, although sceptical at first. Milo had spoken with Humphrey on the telephone; and they could not wait to get together with him to discuss the bidding. Everything was happening so quickly. It was arranged, therefore, that all five of them - including Catherine, if possible - should meet on the Sunday coming for lunch, five days before the sale, to finalise matters. When that day came, Milo and Alison picked Owen up from the Goggin so that they could question him about Humphrey's magnanimous gesture before meeting him.

"Are you sure Catherine doesn't want to join us Owen", asked Alison as they set off.

"All she said was that she had to help her mother do something at the church", replied Owen, knowing that Catherine would rather keep away from a discussion that had already become too sensitive for her.

"Is Humphrey really serious, Owen?" asked Milo, repeating the question he had already put during their telephone conversation. "Medlar is bound to find out what's happened, if it succeeds, and will want to get his own back somehow. Is Humphrey aware of the possible recriminations?"

"Yes, he knows exactly what he is doing, and he relishes the prospect of it", replied Owen, his mind elsewhere, as usual.

"But is he treating it like a serious favour to us or a chance to add some drama to the auction?" asked Alison. Her question made it clear that she, too, like Catherine, was unsure of the man's motives and the likely success of his performance.

"I'm sure he knows what is at stake; hasn't he known Medlar long enough?" Owen said this less convincingly than he intended. The doubts surrounding Humphrey's performances had sub-consciously entered a mind that was already plagued with doubt beyond the understanding of his companions. He made a suggestion to reassure himself as well as Milo and Alison. "If you have your doubts, why don't you impress upon him the seriousness of the favour and the consequences for him if it should succeed. Anyway, Matilda will make sure that his role is discharged without mishap."

Matilda, indeed, was the key to the whole affair, in more ways than one. As they neared the Court, Owen's decision to confide everything to her came to the forefront of his mind for the umpteenth time. Milo and Alison had noticed when they picked him up that he was 'day-dreaming' again. Now they noticed that he had absented himself in his usual endearing way during the short journey.

The prestigious owner of Llandyfrig Court was sitting in his swing chair surveying his domain when they arrived. His whole manner of greeting confirmed that the adrenalin was flowing in anticipation of the auction drama. He jumped up, causing the chair to swing behind him as he rushed across the lawn beaming with confidence. He lost no time in getting to the point.

"We've got this auction sown up. Your money and my guile will make my scheming neighbour become a recluse for a while. Come inside gang and let's put some camouflage on the conspiracy of the 'Wern y coc cabal'."

The prospective house purchasers were not encouraged by this excited and theatrical welcome. Their doubts increased. And Owen's tentative reservations were given more substance when Humphrey dismissed him from the proceedings.

"There's no need for you to be in on the detail, Owen. Go and keep Matty company in the kitchen. We'll be in the Long Room."

It was not until he joined Matilda that he realised it was all her idea for her husband to take Milo and Alison aside. She wanted to confer with him alone.

"I can delay lunch until Humphrey's tummy interrupts his scheming. Now then, I hope you weren't too upset last week when you rushed away from Gwenynog with the poor Eerie Shriek?"

"I'm sorry to have just abandoned you. I had to be alone, and I knew that there was only one resting place for the buzzard – at the Stoggle, which is where I buried it.

"I understand, Owen. Has anything else happened that I should know about?"

Owen pondered for a moment. "Yes. After I buried the Shriek, I received a brief message from the Spirit which I'll let you read sometime." And to get the subject of the conversation off the message he asked: "Has Humphrey let you in on all of the details of our conspiracy yet?"

"Oh, yes; he did that the day after his meeting with you. I knew he couldn't keep it to himself for long."

She explained that he had revealed everything, including his ruse to compromise Carl Medlar into accepting a public fait accompli on the lease of his building to the theatre trust, and his intention to let Lloyd Farr rent the pastures. But he had enjoined her, in his most serious manner, to maintain absolute secrecy on their revised management plans for the plantation. She was not to tell a soul, and to be doubly careful of giving hints away to Owen that she knew of his belief in a resident spirit in the old Stoggle. She smiled, and her face glowed with the specialness of their friendship.

"Will it work? Will Humphrey's devices to thwart Medlar's plans for the plantation succeed? It is all too simple."

"It has already succeeded to some extent and should be succeeding right now."

"How?" asked Owen, surprised.

"Oh, I'll let Humphrey reveal that to you. It's his scheme. He has got something else to reveal to you as well concerning your future in this area, so get ready for a number of surprises. By the way, it's a shame that Catherine couldn't join us."

"Even if she had been free to come, I think she would have been somewhat ill at ease, whatever the welcome. She was waiting for me at the Stoggle after Humphrey and I had had our meeting at the plantation. She virtually admitted that she is prepared to go along with an exchange of land with Medlar, if he acquires the pastures."

Matilda could see that Owen's confidence in helping the Spirit, a confidence which had not been strong from the beginning, was weakening further. His lack of faith, and its affects, prevented him from seeing Matilda's slight reaction to the news. In her usual way, she endeavoured to lend support.

"I expected that all along, if you don't mind me saying so. The pressures on Catherine are too great, I realise that. But it doesn't change things. Humphrey and I have looked into our coffers - we can cope with whatever Carl Medlar can offer. We have even decided to sell one of our valuable, but rather ghastly, antiques to ensure that we have something in reserve. As far as I am concerned, the man has lost already."

Owen was reassured for the time being. Matilda's emphatic dismissal of Medlar's chances was timely and well put. He returned to what he knew was at the back of her mind.

"As the auction has approached, I've been finding it difficult to relax to the point of being susceptible to the Spirit's messages - if it has the resources to contact me."

"I understand that as well. Our main concern is to safeguard the dingle. When that is done, the resulting calm and certainty will relax your mind, and we can try then. Now let's eat."

Matilda was as good at restoring confidence as she was at defusing over-confidence.

Just as Owen's mind relaxed, the door burst open and Humphrey appeared.

"It's all settled. The plan of campaign has been drawn up. Our arrows are primed, or feathered, or whatever it is. All we need now is to see the smooth suit of our adversary. Then we can shoot him up the backside." His own eyes were sparkling.

Milo and Alison were standing behind him in the doorway, smiling ambivalently...

A meal at the Court was always an occasion, whoever was to be fed. The behaviour of the lord of the manor promised to provide some diversion while Matilda always produced delicious morsels - another of the capabilities which kept the Court running smoothly beneath antics, games and drama practices. But it was not only the personality of the host, and the food, which made the meals memorable. The setting of the dining room added its own dimension to the event. For the room was more intimate than the Long Room; a little darker due to the smaller window area and the darkness of the oak furnishings, but relieved somewhat by the lightness of the upper walls above the panelling, and the colourful curtains and other fabrics roundabout.

Predictably, it was the dominance of the oak furniture which impressed itself upon the eyes most of all. Corner cupboards occupied the three corners away from the door, perched above the panelling, antiques which had hung on the walls of the room since the early eighteenth century. There was a unique dresser, almost as old, wide and tall, its upper shelves carrying samples of the family's crockery heirlooms and other culinary oddments. But it was the table which really caught the eye, being the centrepiece of the room, and the event. It was another manifestation of a craftsman's response to a perceived over-abundance or unlimited supply of local oak timber. It was so ponderous - a thick table top of four boards, almost two inches thick, surmounted on broad pillars of wood connected by stout horizontal bars below the top and above the floor - that it was probably capable of supporting all the venison in the Deer Haye, not merely a haunch. For Owen, though, the room held more interest in the few framed pictures of vanished local flowers, painted by Rosamond de Bohun, which hung meekly where space allowed: flowers of broadleaved woodland in the inanimate company of oak boards.

The Friends of the Deer Haye experienced that recurrent feeling of reserve peculiar to a place displaying the wealth and plenitude of an aristocratic past; that reserve which seems to quieten - or is it cower? - the ordinary person in the street. In this case, the effect occurred even in the presence of a clown and a woman who could make anyone feel at home, anywhere. It lasted only until a de Bohun antic shattered the conservatism of the room, while Matilda was absent collecting the main dish of the day - smoked venison and a chestnut burger for Owen.

In the relaxed atmosphere, Milo suddenly remembered something in his pocket - a copy of the parish rag, otherwise known as Llandyfrig Lines, which Humphrey edited. It was as hot off the press as the meal out of the Aga. Humphrey had distributed it in the middle of the week having had it in preparation for a while.

"What's this about the Meddling Baron helping to convert your coniferous plantation back into a part of Coed Tirion Glas? Is this part of a game to spot the mistake, or the joke of the month?"

Milo's usual tactless manner did not disturb his host.

"Oh no. It's genuine parish news, my boy. Carl Medlar's kindness has excelled itself. He is going through a benevolent phase, leasing property to our theatre trust, and resurrecting conquered woods. The details have yet to be worked out but most of the plantation will be regenerated with native trees while the south-eastern corner, which faces The Prospect, will be planted up with whatever Medlar wants – a sort of arboreal nicety." Humphrey was in his element and delighted with himself. Craftily, he winked at Owen who, not having read the latest edition of the parish rag, became a little uneasy.

"I don't believe it. There's got to be a catch somewhere. Can a man who is preparing to extinguish the wildlife of a traditional small farm be involved with such a conservation exercise? And all for a small personal arboretum?" Milo's suspicions of Medlar ran deep, so deep that the man was beyond redemption.

"I didn't believe it at first", said Owen, a little falteringly, "but it's true. You're underestimating Humphrey's influence with the man." His intervention was awkward, and not all that convincing. His acting life for the local drama club had begun. Nevertheless, whatever its effect upon Milo, Humphrey enjoyed this example of covert support from him. The conspiracy within a conspiracy was underway.

Alison's response was to ask her host if he could spare the

time later to give her the details, for the newspaper, of the theatre trust's new acquisition. Humphrey was only too pleased to oblige.

"If Carl's been to church today, I'm sure he will have received the approbation of a number of prominent parishioners", said Matilda, knowingly, having primed various local people during the week when she helped Humphrey circulated the rag; late as usual but, in the circumstances, helpfully late.

"And the blessings of the vicar", added her husband. "He's our stage manager. Carl Medlar will also be congratulated today by other eminent locals who support our dramatic productions; congratulations he knows he deserves. It will mellow him for the auction".

"Some hope!" was all Milo could say.

"But won't he retract his generosity if he finds out, as he is bound to do, that you have bid on our behalf?" asked Alison.

"No. If he does find out, it will be long after the event. Anyway, his magnanimity is public knowledge now. To retract would be to lose face. The man has lost enough of his face already through business escapades in the City. He couldn't bear to have more of it blemished, especially locally."

Humphrey was in fine form. Even Owen's preoccupation with his burden gave way at this jibe, and he broke into nervous laughter, to the surprise of those present. His host took it as another sign of the pact they had made. But Milo and Alison, although appreciating the joke, were becoming uneasy again. They looked to Owen for some reassurance. He was not any help. Matilda read their looks and was about to repair the damage, but her husband carried on.

"Don't worry, you two. You'll be the next owners of Wern y coc. If I'm wrong, we'll give you the old ruin at Gyffyliog."

This time, Matilda was taken completely by surprise, so completely that her calmness left her, briefly. Her husband continued without looking for her approval.

"You can have that heap of rubble for yourselves. But you won't have to put it all back together again. Have faith, my friends. The stars are with us. And although I know I have the mind of a weak and feeble latter-day aristocrat, I have the heart and stomach of a knight in shining armour." Humphrey had gone over the top.

Matilda reigned in her husband. Then she reassured the young couple that their formidable neighbour was not the all-powerful landowner of his reputation. He was vulnerable, like most people, especially in respect of his standing in the community. He was a ruthless business-man in the open market, but there was more to his life than just business. Her words were more than reassuring - they brought the matter to a calming close.

Now then, Humphrey, haven't you got something to tell Owen?" she reminded her husband.

"Oh, yes. Owen, my boy, now that you will be around until the end of September..." (He checked himself for an explanatory aside to his guests) - "He's going to be one of the stars of our next play - you might want to let your sister have the Goggin to herself." This was tactfully said, Matilda-like in its delivery. "So how would you like to move in to the Gatehouse in return for doing it up, a bit of estate work and giving me a hand in the Deer Haye? I've a lot more trees to plant this autumn. All this might help you finance your future university work."

Milo and Alison were the first to react. They turned in unison to look at Owen, their faces breaking into smiles as they did so, more in relief that they were not the only ones to be granted the eccentric favours of Humphrey de Bohun, than in approval. Owen's initial reaction was to look at Matilda, whose eyes confirmed the proposal. Then, in a wide-eyed state of pleasant shock, he spoke.

"I don't know what to say. I haven't thought about what I will do when Suzy returns. I have to finish her gazebo before I embark on other tasks, although I don't have to live at the Goggin to do that. Thanks, Humphrey. That's extremely kind of you. I'm overwhelmed. But I thought the Gatehouse was a store-house for the Keeper."

"It was until I found out that he was the one who shot the Eerie Shriek last week. So I've sacked him and he won't need the place anymore."

At this news, Owen was more than overwhelmed. Events were moving along too fast - at the de Bohun acting rate. The arrangements with Matilda, the sale, the collusion with Humphrey, the hood-winking of Medlar, the prospect of being on the stage - a prospect he pushed further and further back in his mind - and now the offer of work and alternative accommodation... The future of the Spirit in the Stoggle was enough.

Milo was also surprised at hearing this news and in a spasm of delight was about to offer a toast to mark the Keeper's going when Matilda interjected.

"You don't have to commit yourself yet, Owen", said Matilda, coming to his aid. "Decide when Suzy returns."

"When is she coming back, Owen?" asked Alison, "I haven't heard from her since the postcard she sent at the beginning of June."

"I don't know. In her last letter to Catherine she said she was going to spend some time in Dorset on her way back with one of the photographers on the expedition. But no dates were given."

"What did she say to you the other day, Matty, when she telephoned you from Lourdes?" asked Humphrey to keep himself in the conversation, surprising everyone, including Matilda who suddenly had three expectant faces directed at her, especially Owen's. For once, she was not quite ready to reply.

"Only what she said to Catherine, that she was going to stay with the photographer in Dorset for a while, returning sometime in early August. She is going to ring you, Owen, when she arrives back in this country to let you know her whereabouts and the precise date of her return. I meant to tell you." She did not say this last sentence with the sincerity that Owen had come to value.

Alison asked the question that was stuck on Owen's lips. "What did she phone up about, Matilda? Is everything alright?"

"Yes, she's fine." There was a pause. An explanation was expected. "I hope this doesn't embarrass you Owen. It was her second call since going away. She was checking that you were okay, and that there were no problems. I told her not to worry, and that you were fine." Everyone, except Owen, accepted the explanation in its entirety.

Alison then asked for more news of Suzy's sojourn in the Pyrenees. While Matilda replied with a few abbreviated tales, Owen only half listened, wondering to himself why Suzy should have called upon her, rather than Catherine, to check on his well-being; and why she had bothered, anyway. Matilda's enigmatic side engrossed him again. She and Suzy were as close as all the previous signs had indicated. It seemed that whatever the situation, whatever the company, there were connections, subtleties, unseen affairs immured within Matilda's mind. She exuded an omniscience which put her beyond the meaning of any one moment; certainly beyond his understanding of what was going on. He knew that, but it was part of the reason why he had confided in her in the first place. For she exuded, also, fairness, honesty, benevolence, and dependability, which he believed made her his staunch ally in the task he had before him. Nevertheless, he continued to ponder...

Milo, however, who was sitting on the edge of the conversation for the moment, reflecting on the possibility of owning Wern y coc, was thinking about the problems of restoring old buildings. Subtleties in human affairs were not his strong point. Ignoring the news about Suzy, he asked Humphrey how much work was needed on the Gatehouse to make it habitable - the possibility of collaborating with Owen on renovation work had entered his head.

Humphrey was again back in the limelight. Rather than comment on the condition of the Gatehouse, he suggested that they all went down the drive to inspect it, and then go on to Wern y coc for a secret preview. He had not visited the holding for years, not since going with his father's foreman to see Gethen Daw about doing some maintenance jobs in the Haye. He was now impatient to see what he was going to bid for. Matilda, on the other hand, had accompanied Suzy on several occasions to gaze at the orchids in the meadows, but she had not seen the inside of the house. Suzy was one of the very few local inhabitants in the valley who had been welcomed at Wern y coc by the old man whose home it had been for fifty years. She had the words and the way to talk any man into letting her draw what she liked - or get what she wanted. But the moment called for caution.

"Humphrey", said Matilda, "It is hardly a sensible idea for all of us to be seen loitering at Wern y coc prior to the auction. Let the three youngsters go alone."

"Oh, I suppose so", replied Humphrey, dejectedly, disappointed at having got something wrong and having to miss out on a piece of adventure.

It took Humphrey some time to find his key to the Gatehouse. The delay allowed for lunch to be concluded and cleared away, and for Alison to casually remind her hosts that she could remember when they had offered Suzy the tenancy of the Gatehouse, before she bought the Goggin, at another time of trouble with the Keeper. Matilda's alliance with Suzy went further back than Owen had calculated. In the course of an after dinner conversation, the Gatehouse had been transformed, in his mind at least, from being a part of the entrance to the Court, of secondary, almost incidental importance to the oak avenue, into a prospective place of residence, and another place of associations with his sister. Its position, overlooking a corner of the Deer Haye, protecting the oaken corridor to the Court, aroused an assortment of spiritual feelings. But it was really quite an ordinary place, if one viewed it from the ground.

Wherever Owen's mind was located as the key was found had to make a sudden adjustment because at that moment they were all surprised by the unexpected arrival of Catherine.

"I'm sorry Matilda to have missed your kind offer of lunch but Mum needed me to help her at the church. There were so many parishioners wanting to talk to Mr Medlar that we were delayed in putting up a display of locally made stain-glass work."

"Never mind, Catherine, you've come at the right time", said Matilda. "We're all just about to set off for the Gatehouse to show Owen around."

"And you'll never guess why", interjected Humphrey with a chance to claim pride of place again. "Matty and I have offered it to him as a place to live if he wants some independence when Suzy returns."

Catherine's reaction reflected that of Owen. As they all left the house and walked towards the oak avenue, she and Owen lingered together. He had some explaining to do and some questions to answer. Fortunately for him, the inspection of the Gatehouse interrupted their colloquy.

During the real lord-of-the-manor years of Humphrey's father, the Gatehouse had held a central place in the affairs of the estate, being used as an office and the official point of contact for all visitors to the Court. In the eleven years since the demise of that officious lord, it had declined from being the public hub of estate affairs into an untidy keeper's den. Only a few elderly survivors of the estate's old workforce closeted an image of the office in its heyday. However, though cluttered with junk of all kinds, and a dirty shadow of its former busy, spotless self, it was at least dry and of sound construction. Wern y coc, as Alison and Milo knew only too well, was dilapidated and leaking water everywhere - down from the roof as well as up from the floor. And yet, it had been vacant for only eighteen months; although anyone who had ever met its previous occupant would not be surprised at its condition. When they finally left the Court, with Owen in Catherine's car, she gave him some information about the previous owner of Wern y coc. He wanted to ask her how her father had reacted to Humphrey's offer of the tenancy of the pastures, but he thought better of it.

Gethen Daw had been a confirmed bachelor all his life, ever since his fiancée had run off with his elder brother to Australia. His subsequent lonely existence and frugality was eked out through part-time farming and hedge-laying. Occasionally, he had helped Jack Parry in his forestry work. On his death, his holding had passed to his sister, a widow who lived in Gulible. With help from friends, she had arranged for the sale of all his equipment, such as it was, and also his stock, though the price the animals fetched was paltry. There had been little of value in the house itself. Most of his belongings were taken outside and burnt.

The status and condition of the holding were reflected in the approaches to it, for there was no easy access; there never had been. A rutted, shallowly sunken track across the pastures from the lane carved a way for hardy vehicles, but there was no signpost against the road to name the existence of a settlement. Visitors to Wern y coc had been rare, and the track, like the holding, had never been improved. The best access on this occasion was from the Goggin via the footpath which led to the now shrivelled up bird carcasses, and the Gelli Copse. The route was also the most discreet. The agents' permission to view had not been obtained. Although Milo had taken an early chance to look around with a friend on the pretence of his friend's interest to buy before making his suggestion to Alison, and she now knew the condition of the place, Owen and Catherine did not know what to expect. As they neared the holding, Alison and Catherine became perturbed at the prospect of being seen. It took much persuasion from Milo and Owen to get them to go along. Owen had passed the holding on many occasions but had not ventured inside. Catherine was really more interested in the pastures.

In sympathy with the suspiciousness of the occasion, the day had produced a sultry afternoon with all the signs of an impending storm. A friendly sky in one direction was giving way to an ominous one which seemed to have appeared from nowhere. The darkest heavens were gathering over Elchon in the east. There was a freshening breeze, too, but in the lower land of the brook the air was heavy and somewhat stagnant, masking the usual sweetness of the stream. Gradually, the secluded location of the holding was helping to concentrate the smells of a left-over life. One heap of manure testified to the old man's failure to spread the muck of several years, while others testified to the uncollected muck from his last winter, which still festered in the stalls and the standings of the collapsing outbuildings.

The house stank, too. Dampness seeped from all its mouldering parts, and the interior was pervaded by the cold darkness of a departed life. Its small windows were so unclean that the darkening light outside hardly penetrated the glass. Rotting window frames, caked in the accumulated dirt of decades, were green with moss and the current year's plant life. Filthy wallpaper, dating back to the beginning of paper coverings, was peeling off at last, freed by the all-pervasive damp from the primitive pastes which had held it fast for so long. The dark green enamelled range was still in good repair, in contrast to everything else, the centrepiece of the main downstairs room. An ownerless pipe lay on the mantelpiece above, beside some brown and discoloured photographs of a young woman, both items covered by the accumulating dust. Strangely, no viewers of the property had disturbed the prints from their resting place. The flag-stoned floors downstairs were layered with grime and the remains of linoleum. All that remained passing as furniture could have been mistaken for firewood. The ceilings were the ageing floorboards of the rooms above. Their dominating feature was a huge central beam in both downstairs rooms, supporting subsidiary rafters, crumbling with decay, which sloped downwards to the outer walls.

Upstairs, in the converted loft-space, where the mouldy plaster was detaching itself from the split hazel laths, the wide floorboards, which ran parallel to the main beams, were being eaten to pieces by woodworm. Where they had crumbled or flaked away, metal sheeting and even cardboard covered the missing parts. In each room, there was a prominent central ridge - the beam - from which high point the floors fell away to the sides. The only item of note was a metal bedstead, showing rust through its last coating of black paint. In place of brass finishes that must once have sat at its corner posts were elevated grotesque carvings in wood, done by Daw, depicting what could only be ewe's heads. They were good, in a rough sort of way, but they disturbed the onlooker by the leers on their lips, and by their devilish eyes. They did not encourage an approach to the bed - perhaps this was their purpose.

It was obvious, to an abject extent, that the previous occupant had done nothing whatever to maintain the place, either inside or out. His idle hours, if any had occurred, might only have been given over to peering into the faces of sheep and cattle and whittling away at wood cut from the trees along the brook. Other than the removal of the old man's possessions, no-one had taken the trouble to give the house a good clean prior to viewing. It was too filthy. Neither Gethen Daw's sister nor the agents had seen any point in attempting to tidy up the place. The overall impression was one of a dimly lit, primitive dwelling, unchanged for decades, within view of the beaten track but stubbornly apart from the modern way. How was it to be taken out of the past? How was the place known as the 'alders of the cuckoo' to be brought into the decade of the nineteen eighties? As a shooting chalet or sort of second home, or as a home for a local couple?

"Are you sure we're doing the right thing?" asked Alison.

"Yes", said Milo emphatically. "This place has as much potential as we have."

Owen and Catherine exchanged glances, but neither smiled.

For Sale by Public Auction

At Elchon, Hereford

Lot No. 1. Wern y coc, Onen.

A Freehold Smallholding secluded in a peaceful valley with 14 acres of meadowland.

Lot No. 2. Land near Onen.

Accommodation Land extending to 22 acres.
Badsay and Bragg
Offer for Sale by Public Auction

(subject to conditions of sale & unless previously sold)

At the Castle Hotel, Elchon

On Friday, 15th July, 1988

At 3.00pm. Prompt.

Solicitors:
Messrs. Redbourne and Dredge,
Bridge Street, Elchon, Herefordshire.
(Tel: Darren 333)

Auctioneers:
Messrs. Badsay and Bragg,
The Cut, Elchon, Herefordshire.
(Tel: Darren 400)

Remarks

Lot No. 1. Wern y coc.
Situation: Recent years have seen an increasing demand for properties of this kind. Wern y coc enjoys an idyllic setting near the spectacular Black Mountains, in beautifully contoured countryside completely dedicated to agriculture and forestry. It has the added attraction of being bordered by the delightful Dol Barcut Brook, which flows into the River Monnow. The property is ideal for those seeking a country retreat, or equally suitable for a family which enjoys walking or riding.

The House: Wern y coc is a deceptively spacious, unmodernised homestead contructed of mellowed stone under a pitched slate roof. The house is worthy of complete modernisation. It has tremendous potential for refurbishment.

The Buildings: A stone-built barn divided into a cowhouse and hay-store. A timber and galvanised iron open-fronted implement shed. A timber and galvanised iron tractor shed. A stone-built pigs cot.

The Land: The land comprises two former meadows of six and eight acres respectively (O.S. parcels 5153 & 5154 on the attached plan), which provide an excellent opportunity for those wishing to keep stock and horses. The meadows offer great scope for sward improvement. On the east, the fields are bounded by the delightful Dol Barcut Brook, and by several fine trees along the water's edge.

Services: It is understood that a private water supply is available from a well on the property. The purchaser will be responsible for providing a new drainage system to a septic tank, and for the connection of electricity.

Outgoings: Payable to South Herefordshire District Council.

Rateable value: To be assessed.

Viewing: By appointment only via the sole agents:-

Badsay and Bragg, Elchon.

Auction Contract: The Auction Contract and Conditions of Sale will be available for inspection at the Vendor's Solicitors and the Auctioneers at least ten days prior to the sale. A purchaser shall be deemed to have notice of the conditions of sale, and of all the terms thereof, and shall be deemed to bid on those terms whether he shall have inspected them or not.

Lot No.2. Land near Onen.
Three fields of sloping pasture adjacent to and with access from a single track lane, as shown on the attached plan for identification purposes. The fields are shown on the map as O.S. parcels No 5150 (8.1 acres), No 5151 (7.25 acres), and No 5152 (6.65 acres). Water is available from the rivulet in parcel No 5150.

CHAPTER 35

Humphrey and Owen were not the first to arrive at the Castle Hotel. A few other people had taken seats early. Matilda was not with them because she had gone off to collect the necessary letter from the bank validating their deposit. Catherine was at work, intending to come along if she could get away. She had suggested that Owen accompany her parents to the sale, a suggestion that had presented him with another difficulty from which to extricate himself. Peevishly, she had refused his offer to reserve a seat for her. He expected her not to come.

He thought no more about her until the interior of the hotel reminded him of their discord. They had had a meal there on her mother's birthday in June. The resonance of her face on that day came back to him. Humphrey's haste curtailed the reflection, but the after effects of it were not so quickly dispelled. Feelings of guilt about not taking Catherine into his confidence had torn deeper into his soul ever since her acquiescence over the exchange of land. Before her change of mind, he had been uneasy. Now, her stance in support of the family - a defiant stance in his eyes - virtually eliminated his hope. Only Matilda's support kept him together. And since Catherine's capitulation, her beautiful face seemed to have lost some of its brightness. Long faces worn by friends can be poignantly saddening: long beautiful faces can call up disarming sympathy. To Owen, the mental video of Catherine's beauty was a painful reminder of her family predicament, his guilt, and her sadness. The auction was a trial in itself without the confusions of love, or whatever...

Humphrey knew exactly where to go. The room where the auction was to take place was well known in the community for its use by local organisations. It had the same kind of status as a village hall. The Theatre Trust used it for their meetings; and everyone, except Owen, had attended a meeting there at sometime. Cheap availability and the ready offerings of heady refreshment were its recommendations. It had nothing else to commend it. Like most auction rooms tucked away in the countryside, it was nondescript; merely a place of convenience where the business in hand could be enacted whatever the decor - even in a barn, as had happened in times past. Auctions were usually fast and furious, and over in very short passages of time, so there was hardly any need for interesting decor.

The only features of note in the room were Hogarth-like prints on the brown walls, depicting congregations of poor homeless folk having simple fun. The walls themselves were ghastly, covered in chocolate-brown anaglypta wallpaper - like dripping dirty chocolate because of the wavy corrugations. Gaudy red and green curtains hanging beside the tall windows, and sporting imitation Chinese motifs of dragons and gnarled trees, completed the `decorations'.

For the occasion, an imitation velvet curtain hung behind the table at one end of the room where the proceedings were to be conducted; an ordinary, vinyl finished table, pretending to be wood. On it there was a black and white name-block set neatly in the centre towards the front edge, freshly polished, throwing out the name Badsay and Bragg.

Five rows of chairs, mainly empty except for a few at the front, were the vacant audience, but the room was not without some noise. Three men in suits were huddled in a corner beside another table, a smaller one without a name-block, only a covering of royal-blue washable cloth. They were talking quietly, almost furtively, as though a trial was about to commence. The entry of Humphrey and Owen caused all three to turn their heads slightly towards the door in a sideways glance, which could have suggested that the relatives of the suspect had arrived. Humphrey ignored them completely, although he did know them, surveying the room as though they were not present, deciding where best to sit. Owen had expected him to insist upon turning up at the very last minute, so as to make the dramatic entry of the central figure in the event. He should have realised that the man's attendance would be noticed by more people if he was already there, prominently positioned, than if he entered a packed room. He chose to sit in the back row, on the inside of the central aisle, where everyone making for a seat would be sure to see him. Whether his scheming extended any further or not, the seat was also a good position for keeping an eye on other bidders.

It was not long before others arrived. The next to enter the room were an elderly lady and a gentleman of sagging middle age. Humphrey stood and nodded politely to the woman as she passed and exchanged a glance of mutual recognition with the man, who ushered her to a seat at the front, had a few words with the three men by the table, and then disappeared. It was clear from the lady's dress, as well as her timidity, that she was not used to such events. She sat very still, peering straight ahead, her hands gripping the handbag which rested on her knees. She might well have been at church waiting for the service to begin. Her best clothes were especially clean and neatly ironed, but her hat gave away the secular nature of the occasion by being bold enough to qualify for the Hereford Races in the 1960s. She was the vendor, the sister of the deceased owner of Wern y coc.

Soon after her arrival the ingress of people became a steady flow which quickly consumed the portentous emptiness of the room. But the original hush remained. For as they entered, the auction-goers, many of whom were elderly local folk, hardly spoke to one another, except in whispers. The gathering which developed smacked of a school assembly where silence was not golden but imperative, and where the headmaster was known to be an ogre. There was reluctance by some to occupy the seats available. Instead, they gravitated to the edges or the rear of the room, finding places to press their backs against the walls. In fact, the wall spaces were taken sooner than the seats. The natural insecurity of the Serpent Dyn was there for all to see. And as the emptiness of the room vanished, in the way that time-lapse photography shows the disappearance of open space in the countryside, it was replaced by a loud atmosphere of inhibition and apprehension, with an undercurrent of covetousness and hope...

Before all the seats were taken, Arnold Prosser of the

Treribble made a stern entry, full of intent, followed seconds later by the Farrs, both older generations of the family. They entered wearing faces which said that they were only present because they had to come. Ralph was already there in the company of Tim Medlar and two vacant-looking girls, all with their backs to a wall. Owen thought he recognised other farmers in the crowd at the back of the room. There were actually quite a few, including retired ones. There were certainly some builders for, in contrast to the farmers and other locals, they had not taken the trouble to change for the event. One had his cheque-book hanging out of the back pocket of his soiled trousers. Close to the appointed hour Milo and Alison slipped into the room; her pen and notebook prominently visible so as to place as much emphasis upon her role as the local journalist as possible.

Carling Medlar delayed his arrival until the last moment, entering seconds before three o'clock. His solicitor, one of the three men present from the beginning, had saved him a seat at the front. His overbearing air of victory was intimidating. His arrival was noticed by many, whether they knew him or not. But his was not the only threatening presence. There was another pompous man who had arrived early, to be sure of a seat, and who displayed the wealth he had, or presumed to have, in his dress. His dark suit, black slip-on shoes, and black plastic briefcase matched his glistening black hair. The woman beside him was made up to the nines. Now that the room was full, they stood out like a pair of magpies in a flock of pigeons searching for seed in a field of stubble. The nouveau riche was present in the suburban brand as well as the landed kind.

A gaudy, empty room had been transformed into a stifling

and somewhat sinister hidden ferment of expectation that was oppressive. Owen had already been there too long. It was his first auction. He had not expected such tension, although he was himself tense and had been so from the beginning of the day. Matilda had not yet arrived to exert a calming influence. Nor was Catherine there for him to look into the face where he knew he could get lost - if he wanted to.

The intentions of those present were typical of an average auction for the disposal of property. There were those for whom auctions were regular affairs - the builders and speculators who had money and perhaps some skill to invest if the price was low enough, or if the property had the potential to be turned into a ridiculous prize for the wealthy buyer. Although their heart rates might beat faster during the bidding, experience and, no doubt, business acumen, had taught them to be cool and calculating. There were probably those who had been searching for a second home for some time, who had attended, unsuccessfully, a number of auctions, and who had learned through bitter experience not to invest too much of themselves in the event. They would attempt to remain calm, and to restrain their emotional involvement. And there was sure to be a young couple, like Milo and Alison, who wanted a home, who saw Wern y coc as the ideal place for them, and for whom an auction was an unknown event; therefore, a trial. They would have invested heavily in the property already, in terms of emotional commitment. The Wern y coc of the future, not the Wern y coc of today, was the property for sale. For them, failure was a grim prospect.

The development in Alison and Milo's lives to buy a home, and to see Wern y coc as this ideal, rendered them, perhaps, the most vulnerable clients at the auction. They had spent many hours discussing what they would do with the house and the outbuildings. Alison had become quiet and mellow, unusually introspective and publicly closer to her partner. Milo's fervour for wildlife conservation had made the meadows a priority issue in his busy life of campaigning for the protection of semi-natural habitats. For him, failure would be another gruelling defeat; yet another stressful episode in his zealous campaigning. He knew that if the meadows were used for accommodating horses they would be overgrazed and coloured only by ragwort. However, at this particular public gathering the usual ardent commitment visible in his face had given way to an affected laziness; and yet, there was still a tension over his eyes, and he looked in pain. For them, the auction of Wern y coc was not just an auction of another unmodernised dwelling in the countryside. It was an auction of a way of life; an auction of a wildlife habitat; an auction of a piece of love.

Tension in the room increased, and heartbeats quickened when the auctioneer, Mr Bragg himself, the man who had seen the vendor to her seat, took charge of the proceedings at the appointed hour of three o'clock. He came to the table as a headmaster might go to the rostrum in his assembly hall. And, unlike any stern headmaster, the ensuing hush was gradual rather than instant. Momentarily he was silent, indulging in the importance the sale gave him. Pushing his pigeon chest out and raising his bony shoulders as he took in stale air, he began:

"Ladies and gentlemen - It is good to see such an attendance; an attendance which confirms my own view that the properties for sale today are valuable indeed. They are worth much, mark my words. We have two lots to dispose of; the holding of

Wernicock, and some accommodation land nearby. They come on the market due to the unfortunate death of their late owner, and are brought to your attention on the instructions of the vendor, Mrs Howell, who is kindly present with us today." He gave her a perfunctory glance and carried on. "I shall take lot number one first - the house, its buildings, and the two meadows, amounting to fourteen acres, which go with it.

"This sale is a rare opportunity, believe me, a very rare one to secure a property in a beautiful part of the countryside. Planning permission would not be granted for such a house under normal circumstances. As you will know, if you have the details to hand, the property is very close to the Black Mountains, which are a part of the Brecon Beacons National Park, and its position in the landscape is truly delightful. Make no mistake, ladies and gentlemen, this property is for sale, and it will be sold today. Are there any late questions regarding the conditions of sale? None. Right, then I will open the bidding at fifty thousand pounds."

There was no response.

"Forty-five thousand?... Forty thousand?"

Many in the room looked around to see if hands or fingers were going up.

"Thirty-five thousand? Ladies and gentlemen, we have seen dilapidated cottages without land going at that price." There was some impatience in his voice. His eyes scanned the room and he looked towards a colleague near the door.

"Thirty thousand?... I have a bid at thirty thousand."

Everyone, or so it seemed to Owen, looked towards him to see who it was. Humphrey's solicitor had started the thousands rolling on the telephone.

"May I have thirty-one please?"

Someone at the back of the room made a counter bid.

"Thirty-two?"

"Thirty-three?" From the telephone bidder again.

The thousands fell very quickly as Humphrey's solicitor competed with one of the builders at the back of the room. Within a few minutes, the bidding had reached forty-four thousand, at which price there was a pause as the builder nodded his head, declining to continue.

"Forty-five? Can I have forty-five please."

"Thank-you sir. Forty-five bid."

The man in the shiny black shoes had raised his hand above his head. Inadvertently, Humphrey turned his head towards the door. His theatrical self-assurance was now in the hands of his solicitor. Owen sensed the pressure on Humphrey increase. There was a script, but someone else was reading it. And Matilda had still not arrived.

His solicitor continued to bid, while Humphrey became disturbed by the rather evil appearance of the competitor. He had expected a duel with his neighbour. The Wern y coc Cabal were surprised that Carl Medlar had not yet entered the bidding for Lot One.

The duel with the man in the shiny black shoes took the bidding towards the maximum amount entrusted to Humphrey's solicitor.

"Fifty thousand. I have fifty thousand pounds bid."

The man in the shiny black shoes did not respond. There was a halt in the bidding as the auctioneer called for fifty-one thousand.

"Fifty thousand is not nearly what this property is worth.

And it is for sale, ladies and gentlemen. Mark my words."

Humphrey smiled at Owen victoriously, who could not resist this time a quick glance towards his friends. Their heads were down.

"Fifty-one thousand? Is there a bid for fifty-one thousand." The auctioneer scanned the room, and waited. The silence was intense. "Fifty-one thousand. I have a bid at fifty one." His voice exploded again. No member of the Cabal could see who had entered the bidding. The fear was that Medlar had made his inevitable move.

He had not. A young man, probably in his middle thirties, sitting with a nicely dressed women wearing a Laura Ashley outfit was the bidder. He was, perhaps, the calmest person to bid so far. There was yet another moment of explosive silence. But before the auctioneer felt the need to call for a bid of fifty-two, the telephone bidding continued. Owen was not privy to the maximum bid entrusted to Humphrey's solicitor, but he did see the reaction from Milo and Alison. They were trying to communicate something.

"Fifty-two thousand. Fifty-three. Fifty-four. Fifty-five. Fifty-six."

The flow of thousands stopped as Humphrey endeavoured to look calm and not towards the owners of his auction coffer. They were nodding dejectedly.

"Fifty-six thousand. I have fifty-six thousand bid, ladies and gentlemen. Fifty-six bid. Fifty-six thousand for this extra-special property. A bargain at this price, ladies and gentlemen. Mark my words."

Humphrey remained calm but not triumphant: he looked towards Medlar in the front row. The young man leaned towards the woman sitting beside him. They had a very brief and seemingly awkward discussion together, after which the man shook his head in the direction of the auctioneer.

It was at this critical point that Carl Medlar joined the bidding. His manner suggested to the assembled audience that the property was his by right.

"Fifty-seven thousand bid. Any advance on fifty-seven. Fifty-seven thousand?"

There was no response from Humphrey's solicitor.

Fifty-seven thousand then. Going at fifty-seven thousand pounds. For the last time, ladies and gentlemen. Fifty-seven thousand. Sold at fifty-seven thousand pounds to Mr Medlar."

His hand came down on the table with a metallic thud. Whatever was in the palm of his hand had sealed the fate of Wern y coc, and ended the hopes of Milo and Alison. The future of the meadows was not to be in their hands. Their future home had been taken from them. The sale had transpired in less than ten minutes; a sorrowfully long time.

With the sound of the auctioneer's metalled palm upon the table there followed a unanimous expression of relief across the room. A sudden relaxation of tension occurred which converted the charged atmosphere into hubbub within seconds. Alison fled from the room, pursued by Milo. Humphrey stood up to stretch his legs and to look for his wife, who had still not arrived.

"Where is Matty?" he said petulantly to Owen, irked more by failing to win Wern y coc for the young couple than by his wife's absence. "She should be here by now. Where is she, for goodness sake? They'll start the next sale soon." He was now desperately in need of his wife's support.

Owen could not reply. He, too, was on his feet, shocked by

the suddenness of the ending to the first sale, but knowing that the next lot to be sold was, for him, the more vital one of the two. If Medlar could be so self assured in his acquisitiveness, then what hope was there for Lot Two? He, too, like Humphrey was concerned that Matilda had not joined them. She had never failed either of them before. Where was she?

The hiatus did not last long. The auctioneer announced the sale of Lot Number Two, the twenty-two acres of pasture, or accommodation land, as it is called in the jargon of the land agent. He started the bidding off at thirty thousand pounds, coming down to twenty thousand in two steps before a bid was offered. Arnold the Trerrible could not wait. Forlornly, LLoyd Farr replied, and the two neighbours took the price up to thirty thousand, at which figure Lloyd dropped out, and Carl Medlar stepped in.

"Thirty-one thousand bid. Thirty-two. Thirty-three. Thirty-four. Thirty-five."

There was a break. Arnold Prosser had reached his limit. In the ensuing pause, while the auctioneer scanned the room for another bidder and Humphrey awaited the intercession of his solicitor, there was a commotion at the back of the room. Two women were hustling their way through the throng. One of them was Matilda. The other, upon reaching the top of the aisle, interrupted the sale. Directing her words at the auctioneer, she said:

"Please will you excuse me Sir, I have an urgent message for Mr Medlar: a very urgent message of utmost importance."

Carl Medlar stood up and turned around. His reaction was like that of a debtor apprehended by bailiffs, for the pallor of his face changed alarmingly as he recognised the woman. She was a young woman of remarkable appearance; bronzed and with an explosive shock of dishevelled red hair. It was Suzy Forrest. As all eyes in the room fixed upon her, especially Owen's, the speedy retreat from the sale of Tim Medlar, followed by his girlfriend, went unnoticed. Ignoring both Humphrey and her dearest brother, she walked down the aisle, unperturbed by the stern looks of several people, and gave her message to Mr Medlar in whispered tones; a rather long message in the drawn-out drama of the sale. The auctioneer put his hands on his hips in helpless disgust at this intrusion into his arena. Carl Medlar attempted to receive the message in a calm manner but he could not disguise the emotional impact it had upon him. He sat down rather clumsily.

Suzy then apologised politely to the auctioneer for the interruption and retired to stand beside Matilda behind Owen and Humphrey. She smiled a sisterly smile at her bewildered brother and winked at him. He could only manage a weak cheek movement in response. Her sudden appearance at the sale had astonished him. He was now even more uptight. Matilda's late arrival was now explained, but Suzy's presence was not.

The auctioneer duly apologised for the interruption, hinting with the tone of his voice and with his eyebrows that it should not have happened, and sending identical looks of reprimand to both Suzy and Carl Medlar. He then resurrected the sale.

"Thirty-five thousand pounds, ladies and gentlemen. The land is worth more than this. Is there a bid for thirty-six? Yes, I have a bid for thirty-six."

Humphrey's solicitor had joined the bidding, at which point his composure returned. He and Matilda exchanged confident glances.

"Thirty-six thousand. Any advance on thirty-six?" The auctioneer looked down at Carl Medlar, who was peering straight ahead, sternly, while his solicitor looked sideways at him in disbelief, and asked a question that was curtly rebutted.

"Thirty-six thousand pounds I'm bid for Lot Two. Are there any other offers. Thirty-six thousand pounds. Going at thirty-six thousand. For the last time. Sold at thirty-six thousand pounds at the back of the room."

His hand made another echoing thud on the table. Immediately, Carl Medlar said something to his solicitor, rose from his chair and left. His solicitor, who looked stunned for a moment, did not follow him but went up to the auctioneer and took him aside. Medlar walked passed Suzy without flinching and without a glance in her direction, but he did glower at Matilda. Seconds later both Suzy and Matilda were in the arms of their respective relatives. Owen was overwhelmed by his sister's effusive attention. He did not welcome her or smile; all he could say was: "Whatever was the message you gave to Medlar that stopped his bidding?"

"Don't ask me about that now, Owen. I'll tell you later. Let's celebrate our victory."

As the room cleared, Milo and Alison reappeared. Alison's dejection was relieved as she greeted her friend. Suzy then took Milo and Alison aside to explain something quickly. Their faces became enlivened. Owen was also standing to one side, exchanging glances with Matilda as she spoke to her husband. What had happened?

CHAPTER 36

'Let us pierce and cast aside
The sombre foreign wall
Remove the crowded Darkness from Y Coed
Let us overwhelm the Hollowness with Trees'

Spirit of Y Coed

There was no immediate need for the Friends of the Deer Haye to remain at the hotel. Negotiations for an agreement with the auctioneer over the pastures were in the hands of de Bohun's solicitor. So Matilda suggested that they all gathered at the Court to relax after such a turbulent afternoon. Owen felt a compulsion to talk to the Farrs, but when he looked for them in the room, they had gone. For a moment, he was unsure of where he should be.

"Owen", said Suzy, "go off to the Court with Matilda and Humphrey while Milo and Alison take me back to the Goggin with my things. We'll join you later."

In the hotel car-park, Milo transferred Suzy's holiday gear from Matilda's car to Alison's while she opened up to her friend.

"When I knew our bid had failed, I felt lost and empty; so empty Suzy, that I could have been told I would never bear children. I just had to leave the room. Tears were impossible at first because I felt so drained."

"Ali, dear, don't talk like that. You can bear children, you know that; and you will have a new home. Wern y coc is not lost; wait and see.

"If the place is not lost what has happened, Suzy", asked Milo aggressively, "to make it possible for us to buy the holding now when it is owned by Medlar?"

"Relax, Milo, all will become clear when we get to the Court; just wait a while. Another piece of uncertainty won't harm your tortured body. First, let me tell you about the mountain meadows I've been rolling around in."

Milo and Alison could only sit and listen in the front of the car as Suzy's words came at them from behind in a torrential flow. When they reached the Goggin, Milo had had enough. He took his time unloading the car. Her belongings had increased two-fold since the outward journey.

"Home at last! Oh, to be back among my flowers. Your flowers, too, Ali. You helped me plant a lot of them. And I've brought back some ideas on what I can keep in my new gazebo – especially colourful climbers."

As she uttered these words, her first impulse was to rush around to the other side of the house to look at the gazebo. The sunshine of the Pyrenees had convinced her more than ever that such an extension to her home was essential. All that greeted her was an unfinished timber shell - a Western Red Cedar shell

- but there was promise in it. Her brother had actually created something that had promise.

"Ali", she cried, "look at this." As her friend joined her she exclaimed, "Owen! This is wonderful... I never thought he would get going on it, Ali. And he's doing it the way I designed it. What an obedient man!"

As she spoke in her soprano-like voice, her thick red hair harmonised with the reddish sheen of the cedar structure. It was a tangled mass of hair enveloping her head and covering part of her face with tight shining curls disappearing into matted redness. Her hair was intensely auburn-red, not the pale ginger of Owen's. Her tanned, weather-beaten face, its freckle colonies pushed into the background, could have originated from a cross between a Spanish flamenco dancer and a Scottish brock builder. As could her stocky, buxom body, which was clothed in turquoise cotton trousers and a flaming blouse purchased in a Pyrenean market place.

The immediate impression – other than her hair - the one which tended to mark her out from the beginning, at any gathering, was that of a strong woman, physically and mentally strong, outwardly formidable. But first impressions, of course, usually call for reflection. She was more comely than formidably beautiful - if such strength of appearance is consistent with comeliness. And her bearing, as the audience of the day had seen, was of a dynamic kind - if that, too, is consistent with comeliness. Her dynamism was such that she seemed to carry with her a larger persona - a persona which took only some of its impact from her hair. Radiance is the word often used to describe such a glow, but it was more than this. It derived as much from her movement as from her appearance. For she was perpetually ebullient; active to the very brink of collapse; except, of course, when engaged on her art. How she managed to divert her energy into still-life drawings was, as everyone agreed, her greatest skill. The drawings, themselves, gave out a perfection that attracted special attention whenever they were displayed to the public, a public who could not believe that such a person as Suzy was the creator of such delicate and painstakingly constructed pictures. Her art was, perhaps, the way her heart, her head, her body, her very soul, relaxed.

With exaltation, at seeing the unfinished gazebo, ringing in her body, and with Alison still subdued, they went back to the car to help Milo move the baggage into the house. Suzy's belongings were already in the living room but Milo was nowhere to be seen.

"Ali, where's he gone?"

As Suzy spoke, she touched Alison gently in an attempt to motivate her friend to recover from the day's events.

"He's probably gone off for a short walk along the footpath to get away from you and me – he won't be long."

"Oh, I must tell you this, Ali. One fellow on the expedition made a secret collection of photographs of me. Yes! Of me, lying at all angles, in awkward positions, properly and improperly dressed, taking shots or sketching plants. He showed them to everyone at the end of the trip - the rogue. We had a breaking up party, complete with a Spanish guitarist. I've got some of his shots with me. The best ones. I'll show them to you, Cath and Matilda, when the men aren't around. We must have an evening together on our own, so I can tell you what I got up to, and the fun I've had. I've also got some beautiful shots of Pyrenean peasant men. Dark faces with dark eyes and dark hair - and mysterious depths. I drew some of them; and danced with them. Oh, the dancing! Stomping and gliding all in one..."

Her words had some effect, for no-one could remain unmoved by Suzy's ebullience. It was catching, although for some it was wearing because it seemed never-ending. There were signs that it ebbed and flowed with her menstrual cycle, but it was always present in some form or other. Her downcast states, like her vulnerability, were rarely seen. Somehow, she managed to burst out of any failure, setback, or sadness. Anyone who could cope with her pace of life, her radiant energy, her ebullience, her chaos, her self, found themselves riding high; taken out of their accustomed realm of existence; absorbed in fun, elation, excitement, endless activity. Anyone who could not, retired or escaped, or prepared themselves beforehand, as some did, to be taken over for a given period of time. And yet, she had a powerful way to help others to safety.

In the case of men, she moved from one to another as though nothing had happened. Usually, any venturesome male was either burnt out or switched off, and so was replaced. They were the vulnerable ones. If Tim Medlar had not sought solace in Suzy's arms, and exposed his weaknesses, his behaviour might not have backfired on his father. It was his need for a heightened personal existence that had got him involved with unsavoury people in Bristol. His father's isolated cottages had made all the rest inevitable. Tim Medlar's other life of heightened experiences was a crazy contrast to the Buddhist boyfriend whose idea of heaven was making love all day long within the aroma of joss-sticks.

Alison coped because she could outlast Suzy in any day. Her

normal bedtime was often as late as one o'clock in the morning. So she was sure of an ending without her friend; a time when she could unwind, if she needed to. And she could look forward to a beginning without her, for she would sleep in while Suzy rose early.

Catherine coped because she had nothing like it in her own personal repertoire - she was the perfect foil or complementary character in temperament and emotional make-up. Quiet, undemonstrative, emotionally fragile... And yet, in her own way, she, too, was a striking woman, although she was the kind of person who at a party evokes the comment from men, 'where did she come from?', whereas Suzy's arrival would be noticed from the outset.

How Matilda coped was a totally different matter, for Suzy's whole pace of existence was stilled when in her company. There was something uncanny, almost psychic in the way Matilda affected both Owen and Suzy...

As Suzy rummaged in her belongings for something to show Alison, another car pulled quietly into the lay-by, but they did not hear it until a door slammed shut. Suzy made for the front door, followed by Alison. She had forgotten about the photographs already.

"Cath!"

She rushed over to her friend who was halfway across the footbridge. The two women embraced each other on the edge of the lawn, beneath the shade of the mammoth oak tree. Suzy was effusive in her expression of joy. Catherine was in tears. Alison was alone for the moment.

"Cath, darling. How I've missed you." She hugged and kissed her friend, and then held her at arms length. "Cath, you jezebel! What have you been doing with my little brother. You were only meant to look after him, not seduce him." She was being playful, but there was a certain amount of self-congratulation in her enjoyment.

Catherine wiped away her tears, but she did not smile.

"I knew you two would see limpid pools in one another's eyes. How many times have you lost him in the trees? How many times has he run away?" Though flippant, her words were unintentionally hurtful. They only exacerbated her friend's anguish and puzzlement over Owen's behaviour.

Catherine had gone home quickly after work to comfort her mother, who had telephoned her after the auction to tell her the news about the sale and Suzy's sudden appearance at the auction. She knew her mother would have a trying time assuaging the stress her father had been under. But she also wanted to get away as soon as possible to see her friend. She had entered the house shortly before tea-time, just as Humphrey was telephoning her father to confirm that he could rent the pastures. On hearing this news, she felt relieved that an exchange of land with Mr Medlar was off.

But the saga was not over, nor was the stress which had plagued her for weeks. Humphrey had not only offered the rental in return for the management of the dingle fields; he had added, much to the Farr's surprise, as an extra inducement, the ownership of a piece of ground close to Gyffyliog - land which Arnold the Treribble had sometimes used for hay – in return for ownership of the uppermost part of the Melglyn Dingle where the Stoggle stood. Coming from Humphrey, rather than Medlar, the offers were easier to accept. It did not carry the bitter aftertaste of a deal with an outsider whose affairs were seen as interfering with the old order of the local community. The Farrs thought that their daughter would be more approving in the circumstances. She was not. Not because the deal was anathema to her, but because it incriminated Owen. He had withheld even more from her. His distance seemed more distant than ever. While Alison felt she had lost a future home, Catherine felt she had lost a future love - if she had actually found one.

"Cath? What's up? Has something happened at home between you and your Dad?"

"No. I'm just pleased to see you, that's all. You've been away too long. Why didn't you let me know when you were coming back?" As she said this, Catherine cast an unhappy eye towards Alison who responded by saying that she would go and look for Milo.

"Cath; you know me. I didn't know myself when I would be back. I was going to stay for a while in Dorset with one of the men on the expedition, helping to sort out all the photographs, but his girlfriend, whom he hadn't said anything about, was livid. Some men! So I retreated from the fracas to stay with friends of Matilda's nearby in Somerset, from where he and I could sort something out. But I didn't have much time for photographs because Matilda told me about what was happening here, and how concerned she was. I told her not to worry because I could return in time for the sale and put some pressure on Medlar. You know, remind him of what happened when I decided that Tim was a lost cause. That's why I came back so suddenly. I had to make sure Medlar didn't buy the pastures at Wern y coc and switch them for your dingle fields. The thought of that man anywhere near Gethen's place, or your's is abominable. Now isn't it?"

"Of course it is. And it has worried me sick for weeks. But I'm still losing control of the fields – not that I ever had control. Mr de Bohun is going to take over management of my fields in exchange for the pastures. Did you know that he was going to buy the pastures?"

"Only when I spoke to Matilda on the phone. I realised, then, that I had to act. For your sake; for your father's sake; for my sake; and for Owen's sake. That Stoggle is too precious to let Medlar get anywhere near it."

"You seem to be very well informed about what has been happening here since you left us." Catherine uttered these words with a hint of spite.

"Catherine. The issue of whether you should continue to own the dingle fields or exchange them for the pastures to help your dad is secondary; isn't it? Whatever happens, the fields and their trees, and their plants, are safe. I think you should give your blessing to the switch. It will make your father, and your mother, happy. It will get Ralph out of your hair and give him less reason to hang about at Gwenynog. It will occupy Humphrey so much that Matilda will have more free time. And it will give you a fixed address for Owen so that you can find him whenever you need him; a fixed address which just happens to be on the doorstep of your future home. Now isn't that convenient?"

Suzy's characteristically bold assessment of the situation surprised Catherine. She now knew that others had apprized her best friend of the relevant facts; and that perhaps Suzy knew even more than she admitted. She did not feel it was the right moment to spill out to her friend all the questions she had concerning Owen's behaviour. She was not sure she wanted to divulge any of it. Suzy, too, was seen to be not as close as usual. So she made no response to her friend's wise words. But, then, she had always valued her advice and support...

Alison called to tell them that she had found Milo.

"Relax, Cath. Let's celebrate - my homecoming; Milo's apparent commitment beyond the call of lichen duty; your entanglement with my cherubic brother... you haven't changed that sad face of his yet, though. Matilda has gone back to the Court to prepare some food. Owen will be there celebrating with Humphrey, the old mop-head. Now that Milo has reappeared, we can set off. Ali, why don't you two tell me about all the exciting events I've missed; and all the gossip. Has Cynthia Prosser reappeared, yet? Has Sally Redway managed to exist without letting Keith Peacock crawl back to her again?"

Suzy was back. And her remarks were typical of her. Alison knew that her coolness towards Milo had not changed. She was not hurt by it. Indeed, it presented a kind of security. She had two distinct friends who were unlikely ever to become close friends themselves. This reassurance revived her a little. She was more forthcoming in response to Suzy's questions than Catherine, who had yet to be reassured of the friendship of both Suzy and Owen Forrest. Indeed, of the friendship of anyone.

When the three women and one man eventually arrived at the Court, only Matilda was there. Owen and de Bohun were already planning the reafforestation of the dingle while waiting for the Friends to arrive. During Humphrey's call to the Farrs Matilda had explained to Owen what their solicitor had achieved. She knew that he was in need of an explanation, but it did not cover the intervention of his sister. As soon as the foursome arrived, the play-actor of the Haye and the quiet man of the woods reappeared, with the self-appointed leader of the cabal eager to reveal all.

The buffet meal which Matilda had ready was taken as they all sat in the lounge looking out over the Haye. Before Humphrey expounded on what they all wanted to hear, Matilda told him to wait until their guests had food on their laps.

"Right, gang, the news is that my cunning neighbour has failed completely in his devious pursuit of Wern y coc. My solicitor was not only successful at bidding for the pastures, he has negotiated a price for the holding as well. Mr Medlar, for reasons known only to himself – and Suzy, I suppose - withdrew his offer and told the auctioneer that it was impossible for him to proceed with the purchase."

Milo and Alison looked at each other in disbelief. Suzy smiled in a self-congratulatory manner, but restrained herself from getting too excited. Owen merely lifted his cheeks because he knew the outcome already, although not the cause. But Catherine did not respond at all, nor did she look towards Owen or Suzy.

"How has your solicitor done that?" asked Milo. "We could only afford fifty thousand."

"Yes, there is still a little complication, but that can be solved. Matty and I had something in reserve; that's why my solicitor carried on bidding, but we could only go so far. When Carl Medlar stormed in, I thought, like you, that we had lost. What's happened is that once Medlar withdrew his winning bid, the auctioneer contacted my solicitor, unaware of who he represented, because he was the next highest bidder. Now then, you two, the place is yours if you can come up with an extra six thousand pounds. Being generous buddies, we can probably lend you half that amount at a reasonable rate. What do you say?"

Matilda interjected at this point. "Let them eat their food first, Humphrey, and ponder on it. A final decision and the deposit can wait until tomorrow."

Even with Suzy present, the room went very quiet as a celebratory meal lost some of its flavour. In the circumstances, it was not appropriate for anyone to change the subject, except to say something quietly to the person closest to them. Milo and Alison exchanged a few comments in whispers. Suzy leaned over towards Owen, who was sitting with Catherine, and said – "Great shell you've constructed for me; we must meet on site as soon as possible before it blows down again". The beam on her face drew no response from her brother. Catherine was silent.

The awkward session of eating was finally interrupted by Milo. "We definitely want Wern y coc, so we shall now do what we were reluctant to do - that is appeal to my father in London. Once he knows that Alison and I want to make a home together, he will lend us the money, I'm sure."

At this, their future prospects revived and the gathering finished off the food on their plates with the usual appreciation of Matilda's menus. As she took their empty plates from them, Matilda suggested that Milo call his father from the Court. Fortunately, the news from London was favourable, and the two home-makers returned to the lounge relaxed and smiling.

Humphrey was delighted. "The Wern y coc cabal is victorious and our little valley has two excellent new residents. Come on gang, let's drink to their success." He rushed away to get some more wine, and was soon topping up glasses. "Owen, you'll have to help yourself to apple juice."

Just as they were about to raise their glasses, Alison chipped in with the remark: "And let's celebrate the homecoming of Suzy as well." Her thoughtfulness was a kind reminder that her friend had been on the sidelines for a while. But, although innocently put, it connected two subjects in the mind of her partner, whose usual tendency for speaking without reflecting first broached the matter that had yet to be explained.

"And you seem to have been a key factor in our success, Suzy", said Milo. "What you said to Medlar stopped him dead in his tracks. What was it, because if he can be so easily pushed aside like that, the local wildlife trust need not fear him in future?"

This was the question that had occupied Owen's thoughts ever since his sister's intervention at the auction. He had intended to ask it himself when he eventually had a quiet moment alone with her. Catherine was regretting already that she had not attended the auction. Suzy glanced at Matilda and then answered Milo, as if programmed to do so.

"When Matilda told me about what was going on back here, I knew I had to act. And I've been waiting for an opportunity to get that man to regret one of his most dastardly deeds. Remember, Milo, the glorious black poplar that once stood on the green in Gulible; the beautiful tree that suddenly got felled? The parish meeting which took the decision to remove it was not attended by all its members and the subject of the tree was not on the agenda. I knew that there was a group of silly ladies, led by Cynthia Prosser's mum, who were disgusted by the yearly sight of red catkins covering the green, and that they had talked about removing it. But I didn't know that Mrs Medlar was on their side and that she told them how easy it would be to fell the tree and replace it with a more decorative one. Everyone thought at the time that it was Mrs Prosser who had arranged for the deed to be done. She took the flack the felling caused because the tree upset her so much – how ridiculous! But once the fuss had died down, I began to make some discreet enquiries among parishioners who felt the loss I felt. It was only recently I discovered that it was Medlar himself who had organised the felling, paid for the job, and the planting of a suitable replacement tree. So I told him at the auction that unless he stopped bidding for the land and the holding at Wern y coc, I would let everyone in the community know that he was the guilty party. The felling outraged a number of respectable people, so he knew that his reputation was on the line. I didn't have the time to reveal any of this before I went away to the Pyrenees, or to think about what I was going to do. I just knew I had to find a way to make Medlar feel more than sorry. His desire for Wern y coc made it possible for me to get my own back without upsetting parishioners by causing a public scandal."

"And the man caved in that easily because you threatened to ruin his reputation? I don't believe it. There must be more to it than that?" Before Suzy could say anything further, Alison intervened. "Okay Milo, I think it's time we retired with Humphrey and got ready to sort out the details of our purchase tomorrow." There was more to what Suzy had said to Medlar, of which only Matilda, Catherine and Alison had some inkling. Suzy did not want anyone, other than Medlar and his son, to recall the details of it.

Humphrey took Milo and Alison in to the Long Room, which left Owen alone in the lounge with three women, only one of whom he felt at ease with at that moment. It should have been patently clear that Catherine wanted a private word with Owen and Suzy separately – but Owen most of all because she already had a reliable friendship with his sister. Owen began to feel a little uncomfortable when Suzy said:

"Owen, why don't you help Matilda in the kitchen so that Cath and I can have a quiet word together?"

"A good idea, Suzy", said Matilda. "Come on, Owen, let's leave these two girls to renew their friendship."

Their absence gave Suzy and Catherine another chance to converse together privately. It did not take long for Catherine to empty her heart to her friend.

"Suzy, why didn't you tell me you were going to turn up at the auction? You could have telephoned. So much has been going on between Owen and the de Bohuns even before the sale, around the sale, and now afterwards. I've only heard about important developments at the last moment, including yours — and I'm more local than anyone! How do you think I feel?"

"Okay, Cath. Yes, I could have rung you, but you know me – everything was happening so fast. I only just made it to the auction in time. There's a lot about what's been going on that I don't know yet. What is important to me is your friendship with Owen. I certainly haven't done anything to mess that up, have I?"

"Suzy, your brother has a whole part of his soul closed off to others, especially me, however close you get to him. And we're supposed to be lovers. Yes, lovers. And you needn't smile like that."

"Cath; Owen has always been closed off to others in some respects. Closed off to me - I've told you that already - and rather enigmatic. Everyone says that. In this case, he's got wrapped up in the fate of another tree. He's for ever doing it. So wrapped up that he doesn't have time to think about other things, or anyone else, come to that. Whereas I draw nature and put all that I can see on paper, Owen becomes a part of it; taken over by it, if you see what I mean. At least, that's how I see things. If trees had spirits, then Owen would communicate with them in preference to communicating with mortals, especially female mortals. Perhaps his elder sister has driven him into the woods. He always knew he could escape from me there. Once we became thinking adults, instead of squabbling kids, I tried several times to broach the subject of our relationship, but he retreated every time. It wasn't until we started writing to each other that we began to communicate properly. Why don't you write him a romantic letter asking him to say why he prefers the company of trees to women?"

Suzy smiled. The comment was intended to help her friend relax, but Catherine was in no mood for flippancy. Suzy was quick to continue.

"Shall I have a word with him, for you?"

"No! Not so soon after all this fuss... I feel that the old Stoggle - that a mere tree - has come between us, and that's ridiculous. A tree coming between two people who are supposed to be more than just fond of each other. I feel he has become more involved with that lime tree than with me. He hasn't taken me into his confidence at all on a number of occasions. Matilda seems to know more about his mind than I do."

"Dont't be so silly, Cath. Matilda always knows what's going on. She has a natural capacity to sense affairs. If she has helped Owen in any way, it will only be out of kindly support. Remember, she has not got a son of her own. You should get to know her better; then you'll see what I mean. If you were more open with her, as you are with me, you'd find her a wonderful friend. As for the Stoggle, it should bring you two together, not divide you. His attachment to it was inevitable from the moment he saw it. I love it, too. Matilda loves it. And at last, Humphrey recognises that special trees exist beyond the confines of his Haye. He and Matilda now want, together with Owen, to make sure of its safety. That's all that's happened. Owen has always had difficulty talking to anyone, even his family, about his love of trees and things natural - and with a sister like me! To talk to his girlfriend about such things - now that is expecting too much too soon - from him, anyway. Remember, Cath, you've only known each other a few months. And I've known him twenty-five years!"

"I know. But I would have listened."

"Did you give him a chance? Never mind that for now. He is going to move into the Gatehouse. That pleases me no end; and it should please you. Go out to him, Cath, as you go out to me. Tell him you're pleased that the dingle fields are going to be taken back into the wood - that dark, dank place. Ugh!... Tell him it is good that your family are going to make the switch. He might then go out to you as he has never gone out to a woman in his life - not to my knowledge, anyway. Ask him, when his arms are wrapped around you, why the Stoggle has become so special."

While this conversation transpired, Matilda was setting

Owen's mind at rest.

"Don't worry, Owen. That look on your face is unnecessary. Suzy doesn't know everything, and she never will, unless you tell her. Your secret soul is safe with me. And I won't pester you to share it with me. Only share it if you want to. All I've told her is that the Stoggle has become a special place of retreat for you, and the details of the plan you and Humphrey have concocted to save it. Not the reason why you want to save it. My involvement is as secret as yours. If we tell everyone, all our friends, our mutual secrets, we have nothing left to share between ourselves separately. Suzy and I have secrets which you will never know. Humphrey and I have secrets which Suzy will never know. You and Catherine must have secrets which none of us will ever know. You and I have secrets which we will, I hope, share forever. I promise."

When the four came together again, it was not for long. Catherine sought the loo, and Matilda went looking for Humphrey to see how he was getting on with Milo and Alison. Suzy lost no time in upbraiding her young brother.

"You do realise, don't you Owen that Catherine is in purgatory over you?"

"What do you mean?"

"You know what I mean. And we both know why. She can't fathom you out. Who can at times! Your confidential scheming with Humphrey and Matilda has put distance between you. And you know it. Your behaviour towards each other reveals that much. She feels rejected. I would, too, but I know what I would do. But I'm not Catherine... Where was I?... Just how much love do you feel for her?"

The question went to the proverbial heart of the matter, as

well as to Owen's reticent centre. It was the sort of question which Suzy was renowned for and which had, in the past, caused her young brother to retreat. On this occasion, he surprised her.

"A lot. More than I have experienced before."

"Then show it, brother, or you'll lose her altogether. You have a comfortable phase in your life ahead of you. A place to live. A job. Just the right job to satisfy your soul. Me close by to help you discover all the retreats of Ewyas, to stir you into action, and to love. Trees by the hill-full. And a beautiful girl within shouting distance of your favourite retreat. And a favourite retreat within sound and contact of a beautiful girl. Now what more could you ask? Go out to her Owen; or at least hint that you will in time. Mum and Dad eventually made it..."

When Catherine returned so, too, did the Wern y coc cabal. Alison and Milo were ready to leave, which prompted Catherine to offer Suzy and Owen a lift home. Humphrey reminded Owen that his bike was still in a safe place at the Court. Matilda's parting words helped the departure to be a mellow one.

Upon reaching the Goggin, Suzy left the car quickly so that the other two could be alone. As they stood together in the lay-by in private for the first time that day, Catherine suddenly put her arms on Owen's shoulders, kissed him, and then said:

"Owen, everyone seems to have got what they wanted out of recent events, except me. I'm willing to go along with the arrangements for the pastures and the dingle because all I want is to be with you. But to be with you, it seems that I have to share you with a tree. I cannot love you wholeheartedly if you keep a part of yourself hidden from me. If we are as close as I want us to be then Gwenynog and the Stoggle are as much yours as they are mine. If you want my affection as much as you want to be with the Stoggle, then help me to understand what has been going on and why."

"There is nothing I would rather do than bare my soul to you about how the last few months living here have affected me. Such places as Rhibo Mountain, Coed Tirion Glas and the Haye have had a profound impact upon my soul as never before, and you have turned my head by your beauty and something else that I can't explain as never before in my life. The two are separate in my mind at the moment, but I want them to come together in the future. They will come together in the future but you will have to be patient while I sort myself out. I have found two kinds of bliss here – you, Catherine, and a link with nature that I will share with you one day, I promise. But you will have to get to know me better, and we will have to become closer, because what I shall reveal will test your affection for me to its very limit. My strange behaviour will make sense to you, especially you, I know it will. But until I'm ready, why don't you help me by becoming an accomplice to my strange behaviour?"

"And how am I supposed to do that?"

"Don't ask for an explanation yet, but I want to spend another night at the Stoggle – tonight; so I will need to go into the house and get my sleeping bag. If you come inside with me and we say that we're going back to your place, Suzy will know why she won't see me again until tomorrow. And if you keep her talking while I get my things together in a small rucksack, then I'll be ready – that's if you would also give me a lift to Gwenynog. Trust me."

The endearing way that Owen uttered these last two words, had its effect.

"Okay", she said.

CHAPTER 37

'I am longing to enchant another Gentle Tree
The Eerie Shriek revealed where best to go
For everlasting Rest.'

Spirit of Y Coed

———— ✦ ————

The lime-flower tea was cold. It had cooled in the flask he had taken to the auction. He had expected the sale to be a protracted affair, one where a soothing drink would be needed. The brevity of the occasion, and the excitement of Suzy's return to Ewyas, had pushed the tea, along with everything else, onto the sidelines. There was also a piece of flapjack in his pocket which he had forgotten about since leaving his bike at the Court. It was sufficient to break his fast beside the tree.

At last, he had woken up before the dawn. On all previous occasions he had spent a night at the Stoggle, his slumbers were too deep and prolonged to welcome in the day. Putting his sleeping bag to one side, he fumbled in the rucksack for his pen and notebook. He then clambered onto the rocks and watched the red, bleary orb of the sun roll over the Downs at Bromyard and rise into the sky above the Malvern Hills, becoming orange and then yellow with altitude.

It was times like this, in the certainty and in the comfort of an eternal event - the dawning of a new day - that he felt, for a moment, unfettered by the exigencies of life. The event in the eastern distance was more than the inception of a new day; more than the instinctive appreciation of being a part of another precious gift. It aroused unfathomable yearnings. But the sun could not rise without other shapes rising too - and thoughts...

He knew that the Melglyn Stoggle had a deep appreciation, far deeper than any human, of the goodness and the gladness of Ceridwen. From the sylvan comfort and, latterly, the austerity of the dingle, it had rejoiced in the unerring gifts of the sun for perhaps four hundred years: two centuries in the Melglyn Stoggle and two more in the Early Flowering Linden - from the sylvan comfort of Rhibo Mountain, for several multiples of this order of lasting.

In the brilliance of such mornings, during the splendour of summer, its gentle leaves, at first limp and curled from the coolness of night, would waken gladly to the life-blood of the sky. Distant hues of red, dissipating in the lightening sky, were the harbingers to life-action, inducing an imperceptible stirring of organic achievement; the growing tissues releasing auxins, the hormones of the tree, to give it life and being. Another day of arboreal upwelling had begun...

Why should there not be a presence when the whole is greater than the sum of the parts? Chemical reactions in the leaves at the onset of light, the stimuli of auxins, the cell division, the passage of nutrients, the suction of water, the strength of wood; combined with the clasp of roots in the ground, a towering enclosure of pendulous limbs, the shade, the ambience, the prospect – all contributed to a Spirit of Place...

The tea was as subtle as the feelings induced by the sky. It lost nothing for being cold. But the flapjack was stale, and cloying in its passage to the stomach, leaving an aftertaste. It was only an emergency ration. Though it met his immediate need for food, the discomfort that it caused was translated as the cloying taste of Man in the mouth of Nature. He was sure that Ceridwen would enjoy lime-flower tea, but not flapjack. He finished the flask of tea, swilling his mouth to remove the taste of the food, regaining the subtle sweetness of the lime flowers, a transitory flavour.

The day he had welcomed looked like being a good one. He was not disposed to move from his seat upon the rocks, although he felt a need to loosen up. Parts of his body were still a little stiff. Half-heartedly, he considered climbing on to the summit of the Mountain and wandering around the trig point for a while. But his body, for all its stiffness, preferred to stay near the tree. The urge to loosen up was rational enough - a natural response - but he could not leave the Stoggle. His whole purpose for being there was to let it know that the ground was safe; that he had begun to arrange for its reunion with Y Coed; that the days of the coniferous plantation were numbered.

As he reminded himself of this, the trust placed in him by the Stoggle got mixed up with his own doubts of being able to succeed in creating the right conditions for the migration of a tree spirit. If it was the last tree spirit of Rhibo Mountain, failure would be abject. He became restless. If the Stoggle had not taken up the news during his sleeping hours, or during the early part of the morning, then he had to render himself receptive, and linger.

The bird-song of the dawn had settled down; the sky was clear, and the morning light was mellow. The Stoggle just below was as captivating as usual. Although its leaves were moving gently, it appeared still. For him, it was the only tree harbouring the erstwhile enchantment of Rhibo Mountain. He surveyed its crown, as he had done so many times before, from the vantage point of the rocks. Then he himself went still; for there was something in the uppermost branches, something only partially visible. An owl, perhaps. Deftly, he inched his body sideways along the rock ledge to get a clearer view. No! It was a buzzard! He experienced déjà vu. It was almost a repeat of the first time he had seen the Eerie Shriek in the Stoggle. The bird was staring at him through the leaves, rolling its head from side to side.

"Pee-ow", it called twice; a call so like the Shriek's that the sound was eerie for being similar. He tingled.

Without taking his eyes of the bird, he felt in his pocket for his notebook and pen. Calmly and quietly, he lowered himself off the rocks and stepped the few paces to the tree. Then he slid down the trunk into the seat at its base. In his mind, as he settled down, was the thought that it was too early in the day for proper contact to be made, but his knowledge might be understood. Even if he only made an unintelligible scrawl in his notebook, he would know that his news had been received.

He tried to clear his mind of extraneous thoughts by looking fixedly into the sky at the feint blue ether and the patches of cirrocumulus clouds - the 'mackerel' sky which is so good for contemplation. The clouds were very distant, high above him and high above the Malvern Hills. And the sun, which was now somewhere over the Cotswolds, was warm. As he lifted his head backwards to gaze up into the crown, his solitude and that of the tree were one. There was not even the suggestion of other human life; no cars, no tractors, no chain saws, no banging sounds, no planes - just birds, an occasional rustle of leaves, and the brook.

He closed his eyes and began to explain in his mind, slowly, deliberately and repeatedly, the plans he had made for the Stoggle's safety, and the timescale involved - his timescale, of course. The repetitions eased his concentration. His shoulders relaxed. Then his eyelids opened rapidly to reveal a wide-eyed gaze. He blinked. His eyes were brighter than normal; alert like a buzzard's; limpid and keen. His perception of the scene around him had changed. The dingle was deeper and closer than usual. He was no longer a part of what his half-awareness saw. The trunk of the Stoggle was no longer against his back; it was enveloping his back. His legs, which felt unconnected to his body, were changing shape, assuming the outline of roots. A wave of warmth, arising from the base of the tree, coursed through him, rolling upwards. The last sensation he felt was the wave reaching his head...

Reunion of Gentle ties is sweet
Reunion with Cerydwen is Life...

Owain
I have missed your thoughtful Soul

This barren Cwm is Hollow to the Heart
The hopes you hold for me
Renew the hopes of Beibio
Far-Feeling thoughts give succour to my plight

Owain
You are Gentle
You are Caring
You are kind
Like Beibio you tend and mend the Earth
Like Beibio the Spell of Mynydd y rhibo
Rests in you
Your Gentleness is precious to my Soul...

Beibio... Beibio... Y Coed remembers Beibio
Oh Gentle... oh so Gentle Son of Dyn...

Through you I will unburden the anguish of
my Soul
Through you the Serpent Dyn will be denied
my death
Through you I will recover my place within
Y Coed
And dwell within another Gentle Tree

Hollowness recedes when hope is near...

You were kind to let me touch
My soaring searching eyes

My Buzzards
Like the Kites and the Eagles long ago
Must sometime Come to Earth
And stay
You were Gentle in laying us so Close

Buzzards are my knowledge of the remnants
of Y Coed
Buzzards are my links with Cerydwen
Without them I will perish
Waste away and die
And Cease to see the Gentle Sons of Dyn

Parting with Far-Seeing eyes is Grief...

Another Buzzard now is soaring on my Spell
A daughter of the one you laid to rest
I need Far-Seeing eyes to shine my Spell
to you
I need your Gentle Soul to reach Y Coed

Let us pierce and Cast aside
The sombre foreign wall
Remove the Crowded Darkness from Y Coed
Let us overwhelm the Hollowness with Trees
And Cerydwen
And leave my Gentle Lime to linger long...

The roots of Life are endless while they live...

Owain
I am ready to descend into the Earth
To reside again in Passage Trees and Rest
To wander through the Trembling Ones
The Mellow Ones
The Faithful Ones
To be restored Resplendent in Y Coed

I am longing to enchant another Gentle Tree
The Eerie Shriek revealed where best to go
For everlasting Rest
Your Emergent Lime will blossom with my Spell
And you will see the Greenness
You will feel the Deepness
You will know the Glory of Y Coed

Owain
We will pass into another time
To see Euas when Y Coed was vast and Deep
Our Souls will know the vigour of another
Mingui Lime
Enchantment will be yours for long to keep

Beibio... Beibio... Y Coed is safe with Owain
Embracing Cerydwen until the End...

Owain
Gentleness is yours forever more
And Cerydwen is yours forever more

As long as Cerydwen is ours forever more
As long as Cerydwen has Life forever more
As long as Cerydwen has Life forever more
As long as Cerydwen has life forever more
As long as Cerydwen has Life.............

ROGER V CRAWLEY

ENDNOTES

Chapter 1
1. Palynologist: a person who engages in pollen analysis (palynology) to ascertain vegetation history. Plant reproduction creates pollen grains and spores that may become preserved in lake muds, peat bogs, other sediments, and also anthropological remains. Their age, distribution, and identity enables historical profiles of vegetation succession and cultural development to be reconstructed for specific sites and, by correlation, across specific areas and time spans. (See N. Roberts, *The Holocene: An Environmental History,* 2nd Edition, Blackwell, Oxford, 1998, pp. 29-37).

2. Woodland clearance place-names: *ley* or *leigh* from Anglo-Saxon *lēah* for a clearing in a wood. *Roding* and its variants *ridding, redon, reed* is cognate with German *roden* meaning to grub out woodland. *Assart,* a Norman-French word, is a legal term for an encroachment into woodland or forest. (See Oliver Rackham, *Trees and Woodland in the British Landscape*, Dent, London, 1976, pp. 55-57).

Chapter 2
1. W.H. Davies (1871-1940) from '*Trees*' (verse 2) in Ruth Alston Cresswell (1947) *Spirit of the Trees* (see Bibliography).

2. Nature Conservancy Council: then the statutory body responsible for overseeing nature conservation and officially designating sites such as Sites of Special Scientific Interest (SSSI) and National Nature Reserves (NNR). Natural England now has this responsibility.

3. Lichen: a plant form consisting of a symbiotic relationship between fungi and algae, the latter providing nutrients to the whole by photosynthesis. Lichens inhabit a wide range of bare surfaces from tree trunks to rocks. Together with mosses, lichens are described as 'epiphytes' – plants growing on other plants but not parasitic (see Harding and Rose, 1986, pp. 35-37).

4. William Wordsworth (1770-1850), 'Lines Composed a Few Miles above Tintern Abbey, on Revisiting the Banks of the Wye During a Tour, July 13, 1798' (lines 15 and 16), from *Poems of the Imagination* (see Bibliography).

Chapter 3
1. From Chapter V on 'The Black Mountains' of Massingham's *The Southern Marches* (1952), where he describes the valley of the Grwyne Fawr.

Chapter 4
1. *Psammosteus* limestone: a thin concretionary limestone or 'cornstone' in the Old Red Sandstone geological strata at the boundary between the Downton Series and the Ditton Series. (See J.R. Earp and B.A. Hains, *The Welsh Borderland* (British Regional Geology, HMSO, London, 1971, pp. 72-80).

2. Epicormic growth: dormant buds on the bole or trunks of trees that give rise to new shoots. Such growth is typical of lime (*Tilia*), especially at the base of a tree, sometimes creating a mass of closely entangled branches. Dormant buds are activated by a number of factors, notably increased light. Such shoots produce knots which may coalesce to form burrs, as is notable in the case of walnut. (See T.T. Kozlowski, *Growth and Development of Trees*, Vol. 1, Academic Press, New York, 1971, pp. 197-8).

3. *Ernoporus caucasicus*, a bark beetle that feeds on dead wood, is a Red Data Book species which has been recorded at Moccas Deer Park in Herefordshire and is specific to lime (see Harding and Rose, 1986, p. 23).

Chapter 5
1. J.C. Loudon (1854), quoted in Exotic Forest Trees in Great Britain, Forestry Commission Bulletin No. 30, p. 32, 1957.

Chapter 6
1. Lines 104-5, Act IX, Sc. III, from Shakespeare's *As You Like It*, some of which is set in the Forest of Arden in Warwickshire.

Chapter 7
1. 'Hays, or enclosures, in a wood, are mentioned in connection with eleven places in Herefordshire…The various entries show that a close connection sometimes existed between hays, woodland and waste…': 'Herefordshire' by C.W. Atkin (pp, 57-112)in Darby and Terrett, 1954, p. 89. Four references in Domesday to woodland in Herefordshire also mention assarts

(clearances), references which 'are unique in the whole of the Domesday Book'. Ibid. p. 85.

2. See *Domesday Book / Herefordshire*, 1983, 29/16.

3. William Watkins (fl. 1750-1762), curate of Hay-on-Wye, was the first Welsh author to publish a treatise on the selection, plantation, and management of trees for the 'public and private Oeconomy' (see Linnard, 1982, pp. 106-7), and Watkins 1753.

4. Thomas Traherne (1636-1674), from *Centuries of Meditation*, quoted by Mase p. 60.

5. *Hypebaeus flavipes*: bark beetle breeding only on dead wood in Moccas Deer Park, Herefordshire, a Red Data Book species (see Rose and Harding, pp. 46 and 80).

6. Walter Savage Landor (1775-1864), from *Imaginary Conversations* by Landor and Marchese Pallavicini, in Mase p. 96.

7. Dyson (1890), p. 112, cites an old lime at Knowle in Kent which had set a circle of young trees which in turn had set offspring in the same way: 'Thus one tree makes quite a grove by itself'.

8. The whole letter of the 23 August 1799 to Trusler is in *The Penguin Poets: William Blake*, edited by J. Bronowsky 1958, reprinted 1968.

Chapter 8
1. King Athelstan (reigned 925-939), was the son of Edward the Elder and nephew of Ethelred of the kingdom of Mercia. All five of the reigning Welsh kings agreed to pay him an annual tribute. No battles occurred between the Welsh and the English during his reign, perhaps because Athelstan had the Welsh kings submit to him at Hereford.

2. Mitchell, in the *The Earth Spirit* (1975) p. 74, observes: 'A person today who holds conversation with trees is liable to find himself under medical supervision far removed from sylvan influence. In the ancient world however, and throughout the greater part of history, trees were considered the most respectable and enlightening companions, and it was the custom to ask their advice on the highest matters of state.'

3. The 'Jack-in-the-Green' tradition, which is mentioned by Frazer in *The Golden Bough* (1957) pp. 169 and 394, is commonplace in English folklore and is still celebrated today in rural festivals.

Chapter 9
1. Although profound in its contemporary conception of woodland clearance, this statement is a metaphor: 'But the chief interest of the book [*The Soliloquies*] lies in its Preface, in which Alfred represents his own literary work under the symbol of a man collecting timber in a great wood, where others, like himself, might find materials for every kind of building. The metaphor is the only sustained piece of imaginative prose in Alfred's writings.' F.M. Stenton (1971), *Anglo-Saxon England*, Oxford, p. 275.

2. Passage adapted from an actual Inquisition in the Appendix, Note R. 'The Herefordshire Lands of Ewias in 1300' of Bannister's *The History of Ewias Harold*.

3. Passage composed from a description of a deer park, derived from Gervase Markham (1616), and quoted in Shirley (1867) pp. 234-5.

Chapter 10
1. *Selected Poems* (1968) p. 77.

Chapter 12
1. 'The force that through the green fuse drives the flower / Drives my green age; that blasts the roots of trees...': Dylan Thomas *Collected Poems*, 1952.

Chapter 13
1. 'the unbroken woodland cover [of the Midland Triangle] of the Dark Ages was so extensive that it was known to the British as "Y Coed"': Sylvester (1969) p. 95 (see Chapter 28 here).

Chapter 18
1. Lime (*Tilia*) flourished at a time when the summer temperature was 2° C warmer than recent times, hence its thermophilous status.

2. ADAS: a now defunct government agency which provided agricultural advice to farmers.

Chapter 19

1. The Cistercians were a Catholic religious order of monks who came into England from France. Their habit was white – hence the title of Williams study (1976), *The White Monks in Gwent and the Borders* - although their scapula was black. Their life was one of self-sufficiency, with a traditional association with manual labour and agriculture. Dore Abbey in Herefordshire was founded by some French monks from Morimond, with the support of Lord Robert D'Ewyas, in 1147. Its daughter house, founded in 1226, was at Grace Dieu in Monmouthshire on the northern edge of the Forest of Dean. Abbey Dore acquired 300 acres of the Royal Forest of Trivel in 1198 and deforested it, which was the reason for the remarks by Giraldus. The reputation of the Cistercians for deforestation also prompted Wordsworth's lines (13-14) in Ecclesiastical Sonnets (No 111). According to Williams (p.33), a survey of Trivel in 1213 put its extent at 2013 acres.

2. For the 'coiling serpent' of Taliesin see the references to Skene (1868) in the next chapter.

Chapter 23

1. Latin names of orchids in order of listing: *Listera ovata; Orchis morio; Plantanthera bifolia*. Globeflower (*Trollius europaeus*) is in the buttercup family of plants.

Chapter 25

1. Passage composed from actual grants of land given in The *Book of Llandaff 1132* by Rees (1840), especially pp. 317-8, 418, 435, 447, and 451.

2. 'Moccas', or its old name of 'Mochros' (from the 6th to early 8th centuries), is Old Welsh for 'moor or marsh of the swine', denoting pasture woodland with oak trees where pigs could feed on pannage (acorns, etc.). Moccas Deer Park (SO340425), which is close to the River Wye on the Moccas Estate, is a National Nature Reserve (see Harding and Rose, 1986).

Chapter 26
1. Edmund Price or Prys was a Welsh poet about which little is known. The lines quoted are from the poem in Jackson, 1971, pp. 84-5. Another piece of verse by Price, 'A Welsh Ballad' which also celebrates trees and nature, is in the anthology by Gwyn Jones, 1977, pp. 81-3.

2. Taken from the Whitehouse Estate Records, 'Account Book 1791-1813', and 'Timber Sales 1797', Hereford Library.

Chapter 28
1. In 1820, in the primaeval forest of Lithuania, a record was made of a lime tree bole with 815 rings, which puts its first years of growth around 1005 AD. See Schama, 1996, p. 50.

2. According to Michael Baxandall, in *The Limewood Sculptors of Renaissance Germany*, New Haven, 1980, p. 31, 'linde' was the early High German word for 'limewood' and signified a sacred grove as well as the tree itself. See Schama, 1996, p. 99.

3. See note 1 in Chapter 9.

4. Heybote and housebote were the less valuable small-sized timber obtained from coppicing: the former for use in hedging; the latter for use in such small-scale house repairs such as lathe and plaster walls. Pollewood was timber from pollarded trees and therefore wood of larger size.

Chapter 33
1. The natural hybrid between the small and large-leaved limes is common lime (*Tilia vulgaris*).

2. Lammas shoots are late summer growth traditionally associated with lammas-tide, the period of harvest festival.

Owen's References (A select bibliography)

(Including Catherine's sources, Hereford City Library, De Bohun's library), Milo, and Hay-on-Wye second-hand bookshops.

Landscape and Landscape History
Bradley, A.G., (1913), *Herefordshire* (Cambridge County Geographies), Cambridge University Press, Cambridge.

Darby, H.C. (1951), '*The Changing English Landscape*', The Geographical Journal, Vol. 117, Part 4, pp.377-394.

Davies, Lewis, (1912), *Radnorshire* (Cambridge County Geographies), Cambridge University Press, Cambridge.

Earp, J.R. and Hains, B.A., *The Welsh Borderland: British Regional Geology* (1971), (Third Edition), Natural Environment Research Council Institute of Geological

Sciences, HMSO, London.

Hooke, Della, (1985), *The Anglo-Saxon Landscape: The Kingdom of Hwice*, Manchester University Press, Manchester.

Hereford City Library, '*Collection of Maps and Plans*'; and 'Whitehouse Estate Account Book 1791-1813', Hereford.

Jones, Percy Thoresby, (undated), *The Welsh Marches and Lower Wye Valley*, (Crypt House Pocket Series), British Publishing Co., Gloucester.

Massingham, H.J., (1952), *The Southern Marches*, Robert Hale, London, 368pp.

Millward, Roy and Robinson, Adrian, *The Welsh Borders* (1978), Eyre Methuen, London, 256pp.

Lord Rennell of Rodd, (1958), *Valley on the March*, Oxford University Press, Oxford, 280pp, illustrated.

Rowley, Trevor, (1986), *The Landscape of the Welsh Marches*, Michael Joseph, London, 257pp.

Schama, Simon, (1996), *Landscape and Memory*, Fontana Press, London.

Shirley, Evelyn Philip, (1867), *English Deer Parks*, John Murray, London.

Sylvester, Dorothy, (1969), *The Rural Landscape of the Welsh Borderland: A Study in Historical Geography*, Macmillan, London, 548pp.

History and Archaeology

Ashe, Geoffrey, (1968), *The Quest for Arthur's Britain*, Pall Mall Press, London.

Atkin, C.W., (1972), '*Herefordshire*', in Darby and Terrett, The Domesday Geography of Middle England, 2nd edition, Cambridge.

Bannister, A.T., (1916), *Place Names of Herefordshire: Their Origin and Development*, The Author, Hereford.
(1902), *The History of Ewias Harold: Its Castle, Priory and Church*, Bible and Crown Press, Hereford, illustrated.

Blair, Peter Hunter, (1970), *An Introduction to Anglo-Saxon England*, Cambridge University Press, Cambridge.

Bradney, J.A., (1924), 'Ergyng (Archenfield)', *Transactions of Woolhope Naturalists Field Club*, v-x.

Charles, B.G., (1963), '*The Welsh, their language and place names in Archenfield and Oswestry*', in Angles and Britons, O'Donnell Lectures, University of Wales Press, Cardiff.

Coplestone-Crow, Bruce, (1989), *Herefordshire Place-Names*, B.A.R. British Series 214, Oxford.

Darby, H.C. and Terrett, I.B., Eds., (1954), *The Domesday Geography of Middle England*, Cambridge University Press, Cambridge.

Davies, Dewi, (undated), *Welsh Place-Names and their meanings*, The Cambrian News, Aberystwyth (published before 1990).

Dillon, Myles and Chadwick, Nora, (1973), *The Celtic Realms*, Cardinal (Sphere Books), London, 430pp.

Duncumb, John, (1804), *Collections towards the History and Antiquities of Hereford*, 2 Vols., *Hereford; Continuation of Duncumb's History* (1912), J. H. Matthews.

Ekwall, Eilert, (1960), *The Concise Oxford Dictionary of English Place-names*, Oxford University Press, Oxford, 4th edition.

Fox, Sir Cyril, (1954), *South Wales and Monmouthshire: Regional Guide to Ancient Monuments No. 4*, HMSO, London. (1955), *Offa's Dyke*, Oxford University Press, for the British Academy, London, 317pp, illustrated.

Geoffrey of Monmouth, (1152), *Histories of the Kings of Britain*, Everyman, Dent, London, 1912.

Giles, J.A., Ed., (1848), *Geoffrey of Monmouth's British History in Six Old English Chronicles*, London.

Honourable Society of Cymmrodorion, (1959), *The Dictionary of Welsh Biography Down to 1940*, Blackwell, Oxford.

Howse, William Henry, (1949), *Radnorshire*, E.J. Thurston, Hereford, 347pp, illustrated.

Jackson, J.N., (1959), 'Some Observations upon the Herefordshire Environment of the Seventeenth and Eighteenth Centuries', *Transactions of Woolhope Naturalist's Field Club*, 28-41.

Marshall, G., 'The Norman occupation of the lands in the Golden Valley, Ewyas and Clifford and their motte and bailey castles', *Transactions of Woolhope Naturalists Field Club*, 141-158.

Meisel, Janet, (1980), *Barons of the Welsh Frontier*, University of Nebraska Press.

Merlen, R.H.A., *Some thoughts on the motte-and-bailey castles of the Welsh Marches*, Tortoise Shell Press, Ludlow.

Morris, John, (1973), *The Age of Arthur: A History of the British Isles from 350 to 650*, Weidenfield and Nicholson, London.

Pugh, T.B., (1963), *The Marcher Lordships of South Wales 1415-1536: Select Documents*, University of Wales Press, Cardiff.

Rees, William, (1924), *South Wales and the Marches 1284-1415*, Cardiff. (1932), *Map of South Wales and the Border in the Fourteenth Century*, Ordnance Survey (in Hereford City Library).

Reeves, A.C., (1983), *The Marcher Lords*, Christopher Davies, Swansea, 171pp.

Robinson, Rev. C.J., (1873), 'The Domesday Survey of Herefordshire', *Transactions of Woolhope Naturalist's Field Club*, 94-99. (1877), *A history of the mansions and manors of Herefordshire*, Longman, London.

Roderick, A.J. Ed., (1959), *Wales Though the Ages*, Vol. 1:

Earliest Times to 1485, Christopher Davies, Swansea.

Seaton, Rev Douglas Prependiary, (1903) *A History of Archenfield: with a description of churches in the old rural deanery*, Jakeman and Carver, Hereford.

Stanford, S.C., (1980), *The Archaeology Of The Welsh Marches*, Collins, London.

Stenton, F.M. (1971), *Anglo-Saxon England*, Oxford.

Thorn, F. and C., Eds., (1983), *Domesday Book: Herefordshire* (No.17), with translation by V. Sankaran, Philimore, Chichester.

Tolkien, J.R.R., (1963), 'English and Welsh', in *Angles and Britons*, O'Donnell Lectures, University of Wales Press, Cardiff, pp.1-41.

Trevelyan, G.M., (1926), *History of England*, Longmans, London.

Victoria *History of the County of Herefordshire*, (1908), Vol. 1, Constable, London.

Williams, D.H., (1969), *The Welsh Cistercians*, Pontypool. (1976), , The Griffin Press, Pontypool.

Trees, Woods and Wildlife

Anonymous, (1853), *English Forests and Forest Trees*, Ingram, Cooke and Co., London, 406pp.

Anonymous, (1870), 'Incidental notes on remarkable trees in Herefordshire – *Moccas Park', Transactions of Woolhope Naturalists Field Club.* 311-321.

Anonymous, (1873), 'The remarkable trees of Herefordshire', *Transactions of Woolhope Naturalists Field Club*, 100, 108, 152, 156.

Bazeley, M.L., (192), 'The Extent of the English Forest in the Thirteenth Century', *Transactions of the Royal Historical Society*, 4th Series, IV, London.

Cambridge Phillips, E., (1891), 'On the Welsh Names of Birds of Prey', *Transactions of Woolhope Naturalist's Field Club*, 254-56.

Cox, J.C., (1905), *The Royal Forests of England,*

Darby, H.C. (1950), 'Domesday Woodland', *The Economic History Review*, 2nd Series, Vol. 3. pp.21-43.

Dimbleby, Geoffrey, (1978), *Plants and Archaeology*, John Baker, London.

Dyson, Mrs. (1890), *The Stories of the Trees*, Thomas Nelson and Son, London.

Edlin, H., (1956), *Trees, Woods and Man*, New Naturalist, Collins, London, 272pp.

Elwes, Henry John, and Henry, Augustine, (1906-13), *The Trees of Great Britain and Ireland*, (7 Vols.), Edinburgh.

Evelyn, John, (1662), *Sylva: or, A Discourse of Forest-Trees, and the Propagation of Timber in His Majesty's Dominions*, Royal Society, London.

Forestry Commission, (1957), *Exotic Forest Trees in Great Britain*, Bulletin No. 30, HMSO, London.

Gerarde, John, (1597), *The Herball*, London, 1633.

Grieg, J., (1982), *'Past and Present Lime-Woods of Europe'*, Symposium of the Association of Environmental Archaeology.

Grieve, M., (1931), *A Modern Herbal*

Hadfield, M., (1961), 'Notes on Limes in Britain' (1), *Quarterly Journal of Forestry*, 55, 303-312. (1969), *'Moccas Park'*, *Quarterly Journal of Forestry*, 63, 254-6.

Hammersley, G. (1957), *'The Crown Woods and their Exploitation in the Sixteenth and Seventeenth Centuries'*, Bulletin of the Institute of Historical Research, Vol. 30, University of London.

Harding, Paul T. and Rose, Francis, (1986), *Pasture Woodlands in Lowland Britain, Institute of Terrestrial Ecology* (Natural Environment Research Council), Huntingdon.

Hart, G.E., (1966), *Royal Forest: A History of Dean's Woods as Producers of Timber*, Clarendon Press, Oxford.

Henry, Augustine, and Elwes, Henry John (1906), *The Trees of Great Britain and Ireland*, Edinburgh.

Hickin, Norman E., (1972), *The Natural History of an English Forest: The Wild Life of Wyre*, Arrow Books, London, 282pp.

Hyde, H.A., (1931), *Welsh Timber Trees: Native and Introduced, 4th edition* (1977), revised by S. G. Harrison, National Museum of Wales, Cardiff, 165pp, illustrated.

Johns, Rev. C.A., (1892), *The Forest Trees of Britain, Society for the Promotion of Christian Knowledge*, London and New York, 431pp.

Linnard, William, (1982), *Welsh Woods and Forests: History and Utilization*, National Museum of Wales, Cardiff, 203pp.

Loudon, J.C. (1835-7), *Arboretum et Fruticetum Britannicum* (Encyclopedia of Trees).

Moore, Peter D., (1977), '*Ancient distribution of lime trees in Britain*', Nature, Vol. 268, July, 13-14.

Mitchell, Alan, (1974), *A Field Guide To The Trees of Britain and Northern Europe*, Collins, London.

Morris, M.G., and Perring, F.H., Eds., *The British Oak: Its History and Natural History*, E.W. Classey, Faringdon (for the Botanical Society of the British Isles) 376pp.

Morris, Rev. F.O., (1850), *British Birds, a selection from the original work*, edited by Tony Soper (1981), Peerage Books, (first published by Webb and Bower).

Nuttall, G. Clarke, (1913), *Trees and How They Grow*, Cassel and Co., London.

Phillipps, Rev. T., (1870), '*The Royal Forest of Haywood*', Transactions of Woolhope Naturalist's Field Club, 54-62.

Prideaux, John Selby, (1842), *A History of British Forest Trees (Indigenous and Introduced)*, John Van Voorst, Paternoster Row London, London, 540pp.

Rackham, Oliver, (1976), *Trees and Woodland in the British Landscape*, (Archaeology in the Field Series), Dent, London, 204pp, illustated. (1981), *Ancient Woodland: its history, vegetation and uses in England*, Edward Arnold, London, illustrated. (1986), *The History of the Countryside*, Dent, London.

Richens, R.H., (1986), '*The History of the Elms of Wales*', Nature in Wales, 5, parts 1 & 2.

Robinson, S., (1921), '*The Forests and Woodland Areas of Herefordshire*', Transactions of Woolhope Naturalist's Field Club, 197-207.

Rose, Francis, and Harding, Paul T., (1978), '*Pasture woodlands in lowland Britain and their importance for the conservation of the epiphytes and invertebrates associated with old trees*', Report for the Nature Conservancy Council.

Step, Edward, (c1910), *Wayside and Woodland Trees: A Pocket Guide To The British Sylva*, Frederick Warne. London.

Turner, J., (1962), '*The Tilia Decline: an anthropogenic interpretation*', New Phytology, 61, 338-41.

Watkins, William, (1753), *Treatise on Forest Trees*, London.

Whitehouse Estate Records, '*Account Book 1791-1813*', and '*Timber Sales* 1797', Hereford Library.

Wilkinson, Gerald, (1981), *A History of Britain's Trees*, Hutchinson, London.

Wood, A.S., (1936), 'Notes on the Sale of Navy Timber situated on the Whitehouse Estate in the Year 1812', *Transactions of Woolhope Naturalist's Field Club*, 33.

Woodward, Marcus, (192?), *The New Book of Trees*, A.M. Philpot, London, 310pp.

Woolhope Club, (1872-3), 'The Remarkable Trees of Herefordshire', *Transactions of Woolhope Naturalists' Field Club*, sketch illustrations of trees.

Woolhope Club Commissioner, (1867), 'A Report on the Trees of Harewood and Pengethley', *Transactions of Woolhope Naturalists' Field Club*, 111-123.

Literature, Poetry and Verse

Anonymous, *Brut Y Tywysogyon Or The Chonicle of the Princes: Red Book of Hergest Version*, translated from the Welsh and edited by Thomas Jones, University of Wales Press, 1955, Cardiff.

Anonymous, (1871), *Relics of Welsh Bardic Literature from the Marches*, Cardiff.

Bronowsky J., (1958), Ed. *William Blake*, The Penguin Poets, reprinted 1968, London.

Clancy, Joseph P. (1965), *Medieval Welsh Lyrics*, Macmillan, London (St Martins Press, New York).

Carnicelli, Thomas A. Ed., (1969), *King Alfred's Version of St Augustine's 'Soliloquies'*, Harvard University Press, Cambridge, Massachusetts.

Cresswell, Ruth Alston, ed. (1947), *Spirit of the Trees: An Anthology of Poetry inspired by Trees, Society of the Men of the Trees*, Abbotsbury, Dorset.

De Selincourt, E., Ed. (1952), *The Poetical Works of William Wordsworth, Vol. 2 (of 5), Second Edition*, Oxford University Press, Oxford.

Fogle, French, Ed. (1964), *Henry Vaughan: The Complete Poems*, Doubleday, New York.

Ford, Patrick, (1974), *The Poetry of Llywarch Hen*, University of California Press, Los Angeles.

Garlick, Raymond, and Mathias, Roland, (1984), *Anglo-Welsh Poetry 1480-1980*, Poetry Wales Press, Bridgend.

Grigson, Geoffrey, ed. (), *The Faber Book of Poems and Places*, Faber and Faber, London.

Grindon, Leo H. (1883), *The Shakespeare Flora*, Palmer and Howe, Manchester.

Gwilym, Dafydd ap, *Fifty Poems* (1942), translated from the Welsh by H. Idris Bell and David Bell, The Honourable Society of Cymmodorion, London, 320pp. *Selected Poems*

(1972), translated, Irish University Press, Dublin. *Selection of Poems in Welsh and English*, Penguin, London.

Henry, P.L., (1966), *Early English and Celtic Lyric*, London.

Hughes, W.J., (1924), *Wales and the Welsh in English Literature: From Shakespeare to Scott*, Hughes Publishers, Wrexham and London.

Jackson, Kenneth Hurlstone (1971), *A Celtic Miscellany: Translations from the Celtic Literature*, Penguin.
Jarman, A.O.H. (1981), *The Cynfeirdd: Early Welsh Poets and Poetry*, University of Wales Press, Cardiff.

Jones, Gwyn, and Thomas Jones, (1949), *The Mabinogion*, translated, Everyman, Dent, London, edition 1974.

Jones, Gwyn, Ed. (1977), *The Oxford Book of Welsh Verse in English*, Oxford University Press, London.

Jones, Thomas, (1955), *The Chronicle of the Princes: Red Book of Hergest Version*, translated from the Welsh with critical text and notes, University of Wales Press, Cardiff.

Mase, G., Ed., (1927), *The Book of the Tree*, Peter Davies, London, 239pp.

Parry, T., (1955), *A History of Welsh Literature*, translated by H.I. Bell, Oxford.

Richards, W. (undated), *Geiriadur Saesoneg a Chymraeg: An English and Welsh Dictionary*, Hughes and Son, Wrexham.

Rees, W.J., (1840), *The Liber Landavensis (The Book of Llandaff 1132)*, edited and translated, Llandovery.

Sassoon, Siegfried, (1968), *Selected Poems*, Faber and Faber, London.

Skene, W., (1868), *The Four Ancient Books of Wales*, 2 Vols. Translated, (*Book of Aneurin, Book of Taliessin, Black Book of Carmarthen, Red Book of Hergest*), Edmonston and Douglas, Edinburgh.

Thomas, Dylan, (1952), *Collected Poems 1934-1952*, Dent, London.

Trahearne, Thomas, (1638?-1674), *Centuries of Meditation, Poems and Thanksgivings*, Ed. H.M. Margoliouth, Vol. 1 Centuries; Vol. 2 *Poems and Thanksgivings*, Clarendon Press, Oxford, 1958.

Vaughan, Henry, (1621-1695), *The Complete Poems of Henry Vaughan*, ed. French Fogle, Doubleday, New York, 1964.

Wordsworth, William, (), *The Poetical Works*, 2nd Edition, Vol. Two (Poems of the Imagination), Ed. E. De Selincourt, Clarendon Press, Oxford, 1952.

Travel Description and Novels
Borrow, George, (1862), *Wild Wales*, Collins, London.

Cambrensis, Giraldus (1188), *The Itinerary Through Wales*, translated by R.C. Hoare, Everyman's Library, Dent, London, (1908), 210pp; and Penguin, London, (1978).

Chatwin, Bruce, (1983), *On the Black Hill*, Picador (Pan Books), London.

Kilvert, Rev. Francis, *Kilvert's Diary 1870-1879*, Selections chosen and edited by William Plomer, Jonathan Cape, London, 350pp, 1964 (first published 1944).

Kilvert's Diary 1870-1879: *Life in the English Countryside in Mid-Victorian Times,* illustrated, edited, and introduced by William Plomer, Century Publishing, London, 1986.

Leyland, John, (1534-1543), *The Itinerary of John Leyland and The Itinerary in Wales of John Leyland*, ed. by L.Toulmin Smith, 1910, 5 vols.

Pennant, Thomas, (1810), *Tours in Wales 1778-81*, London.

Folklore
Frazer, James George, (1957), *The Golden Bough: A Study in Magic and Religion*, Macmillan, London, (first published 1922).

Leather, Ella Mary, (1912), *The Folklore of Herefordshire*, S. R. Publishers, 1970.

Michell, John, (1975), *The Earth Spirit: Its Ways, Shrines and Mysteries*, Thames and Hudson, London.

Philpot, J.H., (1897), *The Sacred Tree or the tree in religion and myth*, London.

Porteous, Alexander, (1928), *Forest Folklore: Mythology, and Romance*, Macmillan, New York, 319pp.

Wilks, J.H., (1972), *Trees of the British Isles in History and in Legend*, Frederick Muller, London, 255pp.